GIVE ME SOME TRUTH

A Novel with Paintings by

ERIC GANSWORTH

ARTHUR A. LEVINE BOOKS
An Imprint of Scholastic Inc.

Library of Congress Cataloging-in-Publication Data available

ISBN 978-1-338-14354-6

10 9 8 7 6 5 4 3 2 1   18 19 20 21 22

Printed in the U.S.A   23

First edition, June 2018

Book design by Christopher Stengel

For the Bumblebee,
always Giving Me Some Truth,

and for the ChameleIndians I've seen,
and the ones I haven't.

CONTENTS

PART ONE
Unfinished Music No. 1. Two Virgins

Memorial Day–Summer Solstice
Strawberry Moon

1

Nowhere Man
Carson Mastick

Your brother doesn't usually show up in your door, smelling all coppery, like blood. Even through booze, I knew that smell. I'd been struggling to study with a month left of my junior year. Did I expect the Sunday of Memorial Day weekend 1980 to be eventful? It hasn't been, any other year. But there my brother, Derek, leaned into my room, looking like he'd gotten into what our mom called the Main Monkey Business. It was not a sight I wanted to see.

Derek had borrowed my Chevelle earlier, a silver '70 SS 454 with two racing stripes and a hood scoop that opened up when you stomped on the gas. A thing of beauty from my dad. Why was I the one given the Chevelle? I wasn't asking. You asked about gifts at our house and they wound up being someone else's, and you might just wind up instead with a Visit from the Belt, for being too curious. Pass, thanks.

"Hey," Derek said, closing my bedroom door quietly, seriously slamming me with his new scent. I put my book down. He was barechested, his hooded sweatshirt around his waist.

"What's up?" I asked. I should have been pissed. The deal with borrowing my car included a No Hard Drinking clause, and his new fumes were definitely Ode to Blood and Booze, Hard Liquor Edition. Normally I would have gone after him, but something was not right.

"You okay?" I asked, instead of *Ass face, why were you drinking in my Chevelle?* "You look kind of, um, pale?" Not really, but he was sensitive about his looks. Among my brother and sister and me, he'd hit the jackpot in the Indian Genes roll of the dice.

Derek responded by making the absolute weirdest request of our lives as brothers. He'd pushed some of those limits in the past, but nothing came close to this wackiness.

"Would you, uh . . ." He twitched his mouth and turned. "Would you . . . look at my ass?"

"Depends," I said, willing to play. "D'you shower today?" The joke stopped sharp when he finished turning, like broken glass in my throat. The left cheek of his jeans was wet and dark maroon, almost black.

"Doused my shirt in JD and stuffed it inside." He slid his jeans down, giving a blast of whiskey vapors. The exploding airship on his Led Zep shirt was soaked, streaked pink.

"What the hell did you do?"

"Questions later? How bad is it?"

"Bad enough." I lifted the upstairs phone extension, pretty rare on the Rez—another Dad Mystery Gift—and called my friend Hubie Doobie. The chances someone from my Rez might become a doctor were slim to begin and Zero for someone like Doobie—he'd flunked kindergarten, after all—but he had those bright-boy dreams, and I knew he'd offer useful information and more important, he wouldn't ask questions. I told him that I'd nicked a butt cheek with yard clippers and asked him what to do. He didn't even ask how.

"Take those jeans off and put these on," I said, handing Derek a pair of briefs.

"They're too tight," he said, sliding out of his boots to get the jeans off. He knew that he could argue all he wanted but that I was right. That was partly why he came to me. The other part was that our dad would have kicked his ass for how bad this looked, bleeding or not.

"That's the idea," I said. "I gotta run downstairs for hydrogen peroxide. It's gonna hurt way more than those tight undershorts."

I unspooled paper towels from the roll I kept under my bed and handed them to him, throwing more on my Guitar Chair. "The Quicker Picker-Upper," I said, stealing a line from a commercial. "Stuff them around the cut and sit down. Cross your legs. Lean on that cheek. Someone stab you?"

"Questions later, you moron!" he blew through clenched teeth. That was bullshit. Clearly, Monkey Business had found Derek, probably somewhere beyond our border signs announcing TUSCARORA INDIAN RESERVATION, and probably? He'd gone looking for it. With my keys. Of course I had questions.

I fast-casual cruised downstairs to the bathroom. Our sister, Sheila, was yacking with our parents in the living room. I was appreciative of her distraction as I snuck by, grabbing peroxide, first-aid tape, and big gauze pads we kept since my dad went on blood thinners.

"Lay there," I said to Derek when I got back, tossing my pillow to the floor. "Bury your face in that. This shit's gonna hurt."

"The floor!" Even excessively bleeding, my brother was trying to call the shots.

"I don't want you staining my bed."

"'Cause *you* don't do that on your own?" Unbelievable, a wiseass even in this condition!

"If you're trying to hide this, whatever *this* is, from Dad, I don't want to need my own lies about why there's blood all over *my* mattress. It's not like that happens a lot." He dropped down clumsily to the floor, and I soaked the gauze pad in peroxide. I started wiping from the outside in, trying to find the wound's borders.

"Uuuuhhhck!" Derek yelled into my pillow when the peroxide hit. Cleaned up, the cut didn't look too bad, a furrow. Not something I'd seek out, but the amount of blood suggested it could have been way worse. It was like a cannibal had run an ice cream scoop along Derek's ass.

If he didn't want it to scar, stitches would have been the way to go, but if he didn't mind a huge new dimple, my first aid should work, according to Doobie. It looked like what they call a flesh wound on hospital shows—the injuries the non-white people came into the ER with. No car accidents or falling down stairs, or wife beating. A flesh wound usually meant one thing.

"Slowing down," I said. "Slide my pillow under your belly and push your hand against your butt cheek."

"Feel like I'm in *Deliverance*," Derek said, bleeding and still cracking jokes. "If you tell me to squeal like a pig, I will kick your ass, bullet wound or not."

"Best way to slow bleeding is elevation and pressure. Better hope you're a good clotter," I said. A bullet wound. That was at least one significant detail confirmed.

"Gotta get rid of these," he said.

"Way ahead of you," I said, showing him the trash bag I snagged. "Say goodbye to Led Zep." I stuffed everything in and tossed the bag out my back window.

"Here." I handed him a stack of folded briefs. "Keep checking to make sure you're not bleeding through. Get a tetanus shot when you stepped on that nail last summer?" He nodded.

"Where you going?" he asked when I stood up.

"Getting clothes from your room." I helped him get them on when I got back. "You can make it to your room, but the more you move, the more it bleeds. Does the Chevelle need cleanup?"

"Sorry," he said, hobbling to the door. "I tried. Amazing how much blood an ass has."

"You mean *you* or your actual ass?" We both laughed, a little. I headed downstairs, as casual as you can with a bottle of Lysol spray in hand.

"Get over here," my dad said, spinning his chair in the living room and grabbing me by the collar before I could even say anything. He'd kicked off his boots and draped his workshirt on the back of his chair. His T-shirt was grubby from work and damp with a couple condensation rings where he'd been resting a beer on his potbelly. "What the fuck are you doing?" he grumbled, yanking my shirt so hard I heard the seam separate a little. "You wanna clean? I got a whole toilet you can do right now. Top to bottom, bathtub included." We were inches away, and I could feel his knuckles on my chest, pressing hard like I was trying to run away. I knew from years of experience that he could twist and ram without breaking a sweat. He was looking to see if my eyes were bloodshot or if I smelled like alcohol or weed, both fortunately a negatory.

"I was just gonna clean bugs off my windshield before they got crusty," I said.

"You don't use Lysol, numbnuts! You'll screw up the windshield. I knew I shoulda given that car to one of the others." Was I gonna mention the real reason I was cleaning up? No way. I'd been here before and it didn't matter what I said, really. I was on his Orneriness Radar right now, and I didn't want this to move into Go Get Me My Belt — You're Not Too Old to Learn a Lesson from Your Old Man territory.

Now that I was being watched, I couldn't leave without a legit reason, so I tossed the bloody bag into my trunk and settled for spraying the seats with the Windex my dad made me get. It was too dark to see, but at least they were black vinyl, and I was just relieved he hadn't decided he needed to *supervise and incentivize*. I went straight to bed when I got back in.

When I woke up at 6:30 the next morning, I cracked Derek's door to check on him, pulling the top sheet back over most of him. Tracks covered, I went downstairs, grabbing my keys.

"Want some coffee?" my mom asked, getting up to grab me a cup. My dad was already gone somewhere and she liked to yack away lazy in the morning, but I had to split. I had some new work, thanks to Derek, and I had other plans too.

"Nah, I promised Lewis him and Albert could ride to the cemetery with me."

"A real promise or a Gas-Money promise?" she asked. "You know they don't have it."

"A real promise. Honest."

"You just remember, you were given that car, and without my help, you might be sitting home most nights anyway."

"I know," I said, heading out before she could drag me back in.

In the morning light, I could see the Chevelle's stitching on the driver's seat was discolored. Probably, no one else would notice, but I wanted it gone. And even though I'd left the windows open last night, JD scent still lingered inside. I'd deal with that later.

I jumped in, and when I got near one of the field car paths cut through the Rez woods, I headed in deep, ditching Derek's jeans, socks, T-shirt, and hooded sweatshirt at different places along the path. I then stuffed the trash bag under my spare, and headed to Lewis's.

Every Memorial Day, Lewis Blake and his Uncle Albert made wooden crosses for family members who'd moved on, painted white with names Magic-Markered on the crosspieces. I'd grabbed tools of my own, to clean up around my own grandparents' graves, but mostly, I was making a deposit in the Lewis Favor Bank that I could withdraw later.

"Hey, Gloomis, Albert," I said, pulling in. Lewis handed me a Styrofoam cup of coffee.

"You ever going to stop calling me that?" Lewis asked, trying to situate the crosses in the trunk. "And what's that weird smell?"

"Are you ever going to smile?"

"I smile, when I have reason to."

I definitely did not have anything to add to that.

I'd hung out with Lewis Blake off and on my whole life, and he always insisted he had nothing to smile about. I wished he'd stand up for himself. Over the years, I'd tested him, seeing if he'd ever grow a pair of balls, but he was still camped out in eunuch territory. He was even the one who taught me the word "eunuch," which I'm sure he regretted. Knowledge is Power.

Why did he put up with all the shit I gave him? The truth? He didn't have a *ton* of friends. I mean, we were about to be seniors in high school, and his Uncle Albert *was* his best friend, and Albert was a little nuts. They even shared a sad bedroom in their ratty house.

It probably started when Lewis had banked all his money on winning the Brainiac Lottery in sixth grade, when we were forced to go to the Central Junior High since the Rez school only went up to fifth.

He was blown away with outrage when all those white smart kids in their Fancy Classes didn't want anything to do with him. And then another guy in particular decided to make his life hell. I still don't know how that one ever even noticed Lewis. The guy was mostly in the Underachiever Classes with me, but somehow he'd sniffed Lewis out.

Like the sucker that he was, Lewis kept trying and put the last of his charisma into making friends with a new kid, one of those guys from the air force housing. I could have told him what was going to happen, that George Haddonfield would up and leave one day, almost without warning. Still, I was pissed that he'd thought he could join the white world that easy. I let him learn his lesson, and when he was ready, I let him come back.

These days, it was in Lewis's best interest that I not fail. He was just another low-achieving Skin now finishing out his time, and he needed someone who'd at least let him sit at their lunchroom table. Plus, okay, yes, I was feeling a little more interested in helping him after Doobie ripped down a flyer from the music wing bulletin board last week. He had plunked this sheet of hot pink paper next to my tray of Fritos and mystery-meat sauce that they called Tacos, and he didn't say a word until I had read the whole thing.

GOT TALENT???? WIN BIG!!!!!
START PRACTICING NOW!!!
BATTLE OF THE BANDS 1980!!!!
FIRST QUALIFIER ROUND, END OF SEPTEMBER
SECOND QUALIFIER ROUND, END OF NOVEMBER
FINAL BATTLE, FRIDAY, JANUARY 16
MARK YOUR CALENDARS NOW!!!!
TOP PRIZE: EXPENSES PAID FOR
SPRING CLASS TRIP TO NYC
PLUS SPECIAL EXCURSION TO
REAL NYC MUSIC CLUBS!
(CHAPERONED BY MR. FAISON)
AAAANNNNNDDDD: $1,000 CASH!!

"Here's your chance," Doobie said. "I'm with you, but only if you get a real band. Even if you get Artie, a trio sounds thin unless you're Rush, and *you're* no Rush."

Doobie had his stethoscope dreams, and he knew that I had even bigger and better dreams of my own that didn't involve all this school bullshit. Even with a year to go, I was ready to be done with school. I'd been thinking about the idea of an all-Indian band for a long time. I already had a band name and T-shirt logo too: the Dog Street Devils. Really, Lewis was the one who lived on Dog Street, but once I came up with that name, I loved the sound. The logo was a drawing I made over and over — that Little Devil cartoon, but with a Mohawk and a breechcloth, riding a Doberman pinscher through a flaming hoop.

That competition was just the kind of opportunity I needed to kick me in the ass. But now Doobie was pushing for Artie, my cousin Tami's boyfriend. Was Artie a decent drummer? Yeah, I guess, but he was also a white guy. I had this funny feeling Doobie was tipping his hand here about a possible fourth member. Had he figured out that Lewis had a guitar? I couldn't see how. To the best of my knowledge, only three people, including me, had ever seen him play.

"Who knows?" Doobie said, pulling me out of my dreams. "If you're good enough, you might even snag the most important bonus of being a rock star." He grinned, so I knew it couldn't be the obvious things like money and fame. I waited. Doobie would deliver his own punch line. "You might finally get laid."

I can't even believe I told him that I was still, technically, a virgin. I mean, I'm no prude. I've gone out with accommodating girls the last couple years and we've done what you might call Everything But. I told him because *he* was more likely to wind up in the same boat so many people we knew were in.

See, getting pregnant young and single is not the same Big Deal on the Rez that it was everywhere else. If I got to that level with some girl and I *wanted* to wear a rubber, word would spread. And *the girl* would be the one telling everyone! She'd think that I didn't consider her hot enough to have kids with. Another subtle way our world is just different.

But I didn't want to be one of those losers knocking a girl up and hitting the road. I knew too many kids born to parents who were kids themselves, and that usually meant grammas raised the kid. If Doobie knocked some girl up, that would be the end of his ambulance dreams. He'd get a job cleaning, or working grounds or maintenance somewhere, and that would be that.

If I got a girl pregnant? I could *never* hit the road for New York City. Never check out Max's Kansas City or CBGB or Club 57, where all the hot new music was. All I'd see in my head was some Rez kid with my blood screaming at a girl who hated me because I was Living Large in Soho or Alphabet City. Someday I'd have kids with someone from the Rez, *after* my rock star years, when I'd gotten too fat for leather pants.

But I was getting ahead of myself. I didn't even have a band to be competitive at Battle of the Bands and win that sweet grand prize. So I could definitely use Doobie, a decent bass player, and yes, I needed Lewis, who'd become a way better rhythm guitarist in the last three years than I'd have ever imagined. Having no friends left a lot of time to practice. He didn't have my skills, mind you, but if I could make him not be such a chickenshit, we'd have a shot. It was May. I had time to get a reasonable band together before Lewis and I started our senior year in September.

To do this right, though, I had to get Lewis to believe *he* wanted to be in my brand-new band. If he thought you were manipulating him, he'd quit in a second, no matter the opportunity.

"Gloomis?" I said at the graveyard, after we'd done the work we'd planned. "How about we sing our dead an Honor Song?"

"I don't know any Traditional songs, and neither do you," he said. True enough.

"Well, what about the kind of Honor Song we both know? I brought my acoustic."

"Like what? I can't think of anything," he replied, but really, he was keeping an eye on the other families scattered throughout the graveyard, doing the same things we were. Playing in front of *anyone* almost made his head explode.

"That's true. Pretty much half of anything you say is meaningless," I said, grinning.

"You serious?" he bleated, narrowing his eyes at me, not quite a righteous snap.

"As a heart attack," I said. Whenever we played together, I restricted Beatles-related songs or that's all he'd choose, but right now I was giving him a limited free pass. I liked the Beatles fine, John Lennon most of all, since he liked jabbing powerful people with a stick. Especially after they broke up.

"I mean, ain't 'Julia' an Honor Song for an Elder who's passed?" I knew full well it was a Beatles song Lennon had written to his mom years after she'd passed. Perfect, plus if you were willing to go all chords and ditch the fancy finger-picking, all it needed to sound decent was an acoustic guitar and two voices that could sound close. He didn't need to harmonize, just fill out my lead.

"Okay," he said. I didn't think it would be that easy, but ten minutes later, with a few stray Indians drifting over to listen to us, we'd gone through "Julia" and a few others that we'd worked up. Lewis kept his eyes closed the whole time. He knew the others there, but he was okay, and he sounded stronger and better as we went along. When I transitioned into "Golden Slumbers," I didn't sing, to see if he'd start. He didn't disappoint, and as "Carry That Weight" followed, a few of the churchier Indians joined him in the chorus. When I skipped over the fast opening of "The End," cutting straight to its last lines, about the balance between the love you take and make, I slowed us to a nice close with the acoustic.

When we finished and some people mumbled Nyah-wheh in appreciation, Lewis opened his eyes, like he was waking from a trance. Over twenty people had joined us. Folks patted our shoulders, gave us hipster handshakes, and drifted to their own memories as we headed out. I let the experience sink in.

Dropping Gloomis and Albert off, trying on the blandest expression I had, I switched gears to make him think this could be a normal part of our lives. I also decided to use up a dash of my good-deed currency. It would relax him a bit to think we were back on even terms.

"You guys clean disgusting crap off the bus seats, right?" I asked. I figured he had access to good stuff, working at the school's bus garage. "You got any industrial cleaner to do that?"

"Yeah, two grades. Pink for light crap, purple for worse. Why?" he said, cautious. I sometimes set him up for some joke about being grubby, so he was a little sensitive.

"In case someone pukes in my car. Can you sneak me out some? The purple stuff?"

"Yeah, I guess," he said, a little smile creeping across his mouth once he realized he was not the subject of a joke. "Probably can't get you one of the squirt bottles, but I can get you some and you can put it in a squirty yourself. You want it tomorrow? Get rid of that weird smell?"

"Yeah, it does smell a little funny, now that you say," Albert said. "What is that?"

"Gloomis's breath," I said, avoiding the obvious: Derek's Jack Daniel's-and-Blood Pants.

"For real, though," Lewis said, laughing to acknowledge the jab. "What is it?"

"I don't know. I'm not the only one who uses the Chevelle," I said. "That purple stuff, if you can get it. You never know when disaster's going to strike."

I had larger plans, of course, involving our future as a band. But there would be time to ease Lewis into that later. It was Memorial Day and I had a little over a month to put my plan into play.

2

Sisters, O Sisters
Magpie Bokoni

"All right, Siren, you worked your magic," my sister, Marie, said as the couple noticed us and wandered into the perimeter of Potential Customer range. She knew nothing about mythology. She was referring to the villain Joan Collins played on *Batman*. "Put that weird shit away before Ma comes back." I tucked my personal beadwork bag under the Table.

I was supposed to work on regular beadwork when we were at the Vendor Table, but I did my own things whenever our mom went on her break. Mine were more like contemporary art, not so Traditional (the stuff we made for sale). Marie tells everyone that if it weren't for my twin brother, Marvin (who looked like a young version of our dad), she'd swear I was an alien. When she says these things, I suggest it's out of insecurity because I'm the cuter sister (and then quickly hold up a threaded beading needle to curb her desire to smack me).

"Are you from an Indian reservation near here?" the new groom asked, while his bride eyed up a pair of beadwork dangle earrings on our display. The Newlyweds had been drawn to our Vendor Table by my drumming and singing (which Marie hates, but tolerates).

Last summer, I started singing Traditional Social songs that men and boys were usually responsible for at gatherings. I accompanied myself on a water drum from the selection our dad made for sale. At first, it had been to amuse myself, but my mom noticed it attracted people and some even clapped a little. Those ones usually felt some obligation to buy something, even if it was just a jitterbug man, or a beadwork key chain. She said I was like the Pied Piper, and when I asked her what that was, she said, "Look it up!" (I haven't.)

"We are from the Rez," Marie said to New Groom. "Technically." Immediately, his ears perked up with worry that he was flirting with fake Indian goods. Marie was all Serious Vendor Girl when our mom was around, but she had a taste for mild sabotage when possible.

"Either you are or you aren't Indian, isn't that right?" he asked. Unbelievable! Like it hadn't been my water drum and singing a Social song that snagged their attention in the first place. Our mom was walking back from the ladies' room (conveniently a million miles away).

"*Definitely* Indian," Marie said. "You heard my sister singing and drumming." New Groom's face was all, *Playing a drum doesn't make you Indian.* But Marie chopped his legs off with her laser eyes and a sensuous run of her bare arm, covered in goose bumps from the chilly river breezes. "Don't my beautiful red skin prove it?"

Today was the Sunday before Memorial Day, our first busy weekend selling handmade Indian souvenirs at the Niagara Falls State Park. Not fun in actuality, but I got to enforce our tribal treaties with the likes of New York State (which gave me some juice in my otherwise wicked-bad powerless Fifteen-Year-Old-Girl Life).

Our mom gave us a few breaks each, but I mostly stayed at the Table for mine. If the tourist shop workers saw you and your dark skin hanging around often enough, they thought you were casing the place to boost Maid of the Mist snowglobes, or a pair of giant Day-Glo sunglasses with NIAGARA FALLS, USA stamped on them.

Normally, Marie might jump all over this fool and accept the losses, but she'd just come back from her own break and was all smiles and good humor. She thought I didn't know what she was up to, but I was two years younger than her, not stupid. I could see the way her Avon Free-Sample Old-Lady Lipstick was smudged. Her Mystery

Man was back. Our mom might have been fooled, but not *this* chick (my eyes worked, thank you very much).

"We just don't live on the reservation, anymore," Marie said to New Groom, having fun laying on her Sad Indian Maiden Voice, thick as raspberry jam on Frybread. New Groom would have called Scotty for the transporter if he could have, but New Bride had already locked her tractor-beam eyes on the earrings. "Our family does and I'm tired of living in the city."

"We long to be among our people," I added, adopting my own Forlorn Indian Face, as our mom cruised in, plastering on her perfect Humble Indian Craftsperson face before she sat.

"So why aren't you among them?" New Groom asked. We'd seen his pushy type before, acting like we were dogs at a kennel, making sure we weren't cockapoos or some mixed breed. As per Parks Department rules, our vendor permit was laminate-fastened to the Pendleton blanket covering our Table (with its appropriately geometric design).

"A sad fact. Indians don't much buy beadwork," I said, a little lie. They *do* buy beadwork, but only a certain kind. Key chains, beaded trucker caps or baseball caps, disposable lighter cases, and eyeglass cases (bingo dabber sheaths were *huge* right now). "So here we are, building bridges to the larger culture with our art." I shifted my look to resemble the Anti-Pollution Crying Indian TV commercial face, but I couldn't squeeze that tear out. "This brooch is designed by my elders to go with those earrings." I slid the little basswood carved pin that my dad designed toward the young couple. New Bride's face said she didn't love Indians *that* much.

"*This* is our specialty," I added, which I did whenever that sour expression popped up. "Each Indian family has a signature." I sprinkled my Mystical Indian Voice in heavy, all clipped consonants and draggy vowels, the Works. "Ours is the Double-Heart Canoe. Very popular among honeymooners." Chopping the "y" in "very" and pronouncing the next word *poplar*, like the tree, I usually closed the deal. (You can spot Honeymooner Hands. New Bride fans fingers, advertising carats and settings. New Groom spins his new ring, like working a burst blister.)

What I'd said—though a sales pitch—was still true. All Indian craft vendors at the Falls had permits (keeping the Porter Agreement alive, though the State Parks official vendors have tried for *years* to break the treaty). We all did signature items. The best sellers were *like* Traditional Indian beadwork that also commemorated something for tourists.

My mom almost *never* went for my ideas, but I kept a sketchbook of new interpretations of our Traditional art. I hoarded cast-off materials to start making real ones soon. Someday, I'd have my own permit and no one could tell me what was worth putting out on the Table.

I had started thinking about my own ideas after my seventh-grade class field trip to the Albright-Knox Art Gallery in Buffalo. A lot of kids said "This is stupid" or "I could do this," in their quest for Naked People Art. But when I saw the Andy Warhol painting of stacked-up Campbell's soup cans, I knew this painting was about its idea, not how close it could resemble a photo. The museum worker told us this was "conceptual art," specifically "Pop Art," because the artist was taking ideas from advertising and movies (like one by the same guy of Marilyn Monroe in another part of the museum). The worker said Warhol was celebrating *and* making fun of the way art surrounds us all the time. By the bus ride home, I knew who I wanted to be.

There was one small issue, from where I stood. I didn't see even *one* Indian artist's work in the museum. Maybe I'd be the first. But I'd have to be bold and new. Traditional crafts didn't get your work in *that* kind of museum. I could imagine making my own painting, or doing it in beadwork, repeating rows of Commodity Food cans, maybe one we liked (Peaches) and one we hated ("Meat"), with their basic pictures on the can in case you didn't know how to read.

For now, I curbed my ideas and helped design our signature piece, the one we were at this moment pitching to New Bride and New Groom. Niagara Falls is honeymoon capital of the world, for some reason, so combining our parents' strengths, we came up with this Killer Idea for Newlywed Tourists. We stuffed my dad's little birch-bark canoes with two of our mom's plump velvet heart pincushions, customizable with the date and initials like a concert T-shirt—*my* idea, no matter what my mom claimed—while Newlyweds watched. I've carved so many initials and hash marks into little hearts that I could be a cardiac surgeon.

"Oh, hon, the cutest!" New Bride said as I dug out the tackle box we kept loaded for customizing (the same box I was skimming from for my own supply of beads and thread). New Groom searched the canoe for a hang tag.

"We could smudge it with some tobacco," Marie said, reaching under the Table for her purse, where she had a pack of Kools. "Get you off on the right foot for a lifetime of happiness."

"Is that extra?" New Groom asked. He had not learned *his* lines yet.

"My daughter jokes," our mom said, kicking Marie under the Table, while she smiled at the tourists. It was just like on a sitcom, except when our mom kicked, she meant it. "We do, though, offer to bead your initials and the date. Usually ten dollars extra, but for you, on this beautiful Memorial Day," she said, opening her arms wide to prove her generosity, "that part, we give you for free." They ignored our dad's carved tiny basswood and soapstone animals, bolo tie slides, insane brooches no Indian woman would wear. (I took after his adventurous streak.) New Bride's eyes slowed a little at the sweet-grass baskets we braided into intricate shapes, but they only came to a full stop at the beaded picture frames among the barrettes, fancy Victorian lady-boot pincushions, ornamented velvet birds, and men's belt buckles.

"Oh, hon," New Bride said, and New Groom got out his wallet.

"My blushing bride here," he said, grabbing her shoulders and squeezing her close to him, "she's a DAR, so her mother wanted us to get married on the Fourth of July."

"Dar?" our mom said, burning her gas tank of charm. "Your name is Darlene? Darla?"

"D-A-R," New Bride said, giggling. "Daughters of the American Revolution. It was important to my mother," she hastened to add. "Both my parents. They wanted us to do it all up, get married on the Fourth of July, invite all their other DAR friends—we're from Concord." Apparently that was supposed to mean something to us. "But *we're* not like that." Then she leaned in, conspiratorially. "We eloped so we wouldn't have to make a big production. It would be nice to have a memento. If they want to throw us a reception on Independence Day, great! But we get to be married the way and the place *we* want to."

"We got these beaded picture frames too," I said to New Groom, knowing New Bride was halfway there. "Make *great* thank-you gifts for new in-laws. Got some with two beaded birds, like lovebirds." (I hate using poor grammar but it made sales smoother.) I pulled an elaborate velvet-and-beadwork picture frame from a bin under the Table. New Bride ran her fingers over the soft, rich velvet, leaving little trails. "I could even bead a couple little bees on it," I said, joining her giggle. "Since this *is* your honeymoon."

"Birds and bees." New Groom grinned. "Not sure your mother would care for that." He nudged his bride. My mom was about to blow a gasket, thinking I'd lost the sale with my little ad-lib off the script I'd been stuck with for a few years. "But it might be a fun secret joke. How long before it could be ready?" I was already breaking out my yellow and black beads to do a couple quick little bumbles.

"Fifteen minutes?" I suggested.

"Half hour," our mom corrected, handing the Double-Heart Canoe to Marie and digging out her receipt book. "My daughters work quick, but it's ver' trick' work," she said, doing a Double-Drop "y." I made big eyes at Marie. We could do this beading in our sleep. Our mom asked for 50 percent down since we couldn't offer it to anyone else with their initials on it.

New Groom, still chuckling about the secret sexy joke he'd be playing on his mother-in-law, said he'd pay in full. When our mom got their initials, she showed him the receipt, with a hundred dollars on the total line. His eyes bugged, but he paid. They said they'd go for ice cream and be right back, not wanting to miss art being created before their eyes.

The Newlyweds were stoked, but I was sick of working on these hearts. The only break we'd had for years was the period my parents couldn't agree on a profit division after our mom left our dad to his Rez Shack when I was eight. She moved us into an apartment in some complex called The Projects, which made it seem like we were living in a classroom science experiment: What happens when you add an Indian woman and her three kids into a set of low-rent apartment buildings jammed with too many people, all colors except white?

Eight years later, our parents still each had the other over a barrel, and with the waterfall so close, they each wished to cast the other one in. But they're Indians. They figured some two-person treaty soon after splitting and we'd been back to work ever since.

"Put this one back," our mom said, eyeing up the canoe we'd been holding. One of the hearts was a little bigger than the other. That had been a Marie job, totally. "They're paying a lot. Find the best one, and get to work. Marie, you do those bees."

"How come I gotta do them?" Marie said, pissed and whiny. "She came up with it, so she should have to do it." Her sense of self-preservation wasn't so good.

"Because you're not talented enough for hearts," our mom said. "And we don't got time," she added, looking into the tote, "and we don't have stock if you screw up. Magpie! Heart Duty!" I was not surprised.

Beading initials and dates on a flat picture frame was easy, but the hearts were 3-D objects, and they had to sit in the canoe right or the personalization didn't show. Also, if your stitching was sloppy, the hearts got lumpy and knotted. No one wants a puckered and dented heart. If you were even a little off, they looked like a Three-Pack-a-Day Smoker's Heart, or a Biscuits-and-Gravy-Loving Heart. Those were Marie's hearts. She just didn't have the knack.

I thought for a second about suggesting we offer Marie's defective ones to Newly Divorced people, hearts with fabric snags, canoes with clumsy finger dents punched in them—Heart Canoe Seconds—but my own sense of self-preservation kicked in. So I just stuck my tongue out at Marie, even though we both knew I'd gotten more work that she was off the hook for. *She* was the smarter sister.

"Don't be making faces at your sister either," our mom said to me. "More important, don't be getting smart with my customers. Your slutty little mouth almost cost us that sale." I had only made the one minor change, about the birds *and* bees, to the sales script she'd written for us years ago. But she refused to take chances on a Memorial Day weekend.

"Slutty, pfft!" Marie said. "Right. You never hear a word we say unless it's one that didn't come from your little scripts." Apparently Marie didn't want to make it to eighteen. You never pushed our mom's limits like that, but lately she'd been acting all bold in unexpected ways. I had a little bit of an idea what was behind it but what she said next shocked even me. "I'm serious. I want to move back home. I want to graduate with all my old friends from the Rez."

"Oh, right," I said, ditching my own sense of self-preservation. "Come on, if you're gonna help here, at least don't come up with nonsense!"

"You stay out this, Slutty Mouth," our mom said, and then, glaring at Marie, all simmer gone from those eyes. "And you! Those friends? Those ones who named you Stinkpot?" Our mom took no prisoners. If she sensed you questioning her authority, she'd remind you of the caliber weapons she had trained on you. "You're almost eighteen. Go ahead. Go join your friends who say you stink. You, on the other hand, Miss Magpie," she said, turning to me. "Think of yourself like Old Man Gray's Magpie. Only repeat what I've taught you. You ain't even close to eighteen."

"But I barely know Old Man Gray! You moved us off the Rez when I was so young, I barely know *any* of those people you talk about." Old Man Gray had a magpie, and he'd taught it to say various vulgar phrases in Tuscarora, and other things he thought would be funny. On New Year's Day to celebrate, the magpie would yell, "New Yah!" back at us when we yelled it at their door. We'd been gone from the Rez for so long, Old Man Gray probably didn't even know who I was or that I shared an ID with the bird he kept in a cage in his living room.

"We're not talking about your name right now. It's your mouth that's the problem. Here!" our mom said, pulling a cheapo pleather-covered book from one of our totes. She bought these crappy diaries at the Dollar Store and used them to keep our records instead of a regular ledger book. "When you feel like going away from my script, write all you want in here. But when you speak, they better be the words I wrote for you."

Oh, please! Few things were sadder than a fifteen-year-old writing in a diary. I might as well bead myself a T-shirt that says LOSER VIRGIN GIRL HERE! Although I guessed I could use the diary to work on my own designs when I hit emancipation age. Our mom tapped the diary cover. "Long's you follow the rules," she added. "White customers don't want some mouthy Indian girl talking about them jigging. You say those cute things *I* thought up for you. That's it."

"But I was eight when you made me learn those things. I sound like a moron now!"

"Fine, I'll give you some new lines," she said (totally ignoring that it's crazy to force your daughter to say *only* words you approve). No wonder Marie was suggesting the most ludicrous thing (giving up twentieth-century luxuries like running water and the accompanying toilet for the three-room shack we'd left our dad to seven years ago). I'd been spoiled living in the First World instead of the Third World (in ninth-grade social studies, I realized that the shacks in the 16mm classroom movies about Poverty in War-Torn Countries were a step up from the one I'd spent my first eight years in).

(Yes, I know I use a lot of parentheses, but that *is* life on the reservation—a parenthetical aside. In this analogy, the larger world is where running water and flush toilets and cable TV and pizza delivery and Chinese food were the norm. The reservation is where "the facilities" were an outhouse, and where a coat hanger was duct-taped to TV rabbit ears like some modern sculpture to negotiate five TV channels in good weather, and where parents tried to claim that a lettuce-and-mayonnaise sandwich was a legitimate meal.)

(Yes, I also know that, even for me, that parenthetical statement was excessive.)

"Stick to the scripts, and if you feel a need to be chatty," our mom said, tapping a finger on the diary's pleather cover. "Write your sassy notes to yourself instead of bothering customers." I flipped through its blank pages, imagining the possibilities, pretending it wasn't totally humiliating. Then she added: "That diary's coming out of your pay."

On Monday night, Marie and I were lying in the dark with the oscillator on, sending out evenly divided breezes back and forth between our beds. Our mom came in and gave us our envelopes from the Vendor Table. We left them on the nightstand, knowing better than to count money in front of her. Mine was probably really going to be a dollar shorter for the stupid diary.

She stood in the doorway of our dark room for a minute, smoking a cigarette, the hallway light silhouetting her. She looked like Freddie Mercury in the "Bohemian Rhapsody" video.

"You girls really want to move back to the Rez?" she asked. She never took us seriously, so I didn't know what to say. Where was the stupid script Dark Deanna made for this scene? (Dark Deanna was what we'd named the vein of evil clouds running through our mom's head that sometimes took her regular brain hostage, and Dark Deanna thought *we* were expendable.) I shrugged.

"I can move back in with Dad," Marie said. "If you wanna stay. I can get another job to—"

"No other job for you," our mom said immediately. "I made some calls and got us steady rides back and forth. Just means we lose a little off the top every week. I moved here for *you* in the first place," she said. "Those boys are still gonna call you what they used to. Things like that don't change on the Rez." Our mom never showed a warm side. In all my life, I couldn't remember even one instance, and I couldn't imagine why Marie was the beneficiary now.

"I know," Marie said, so quiet I could barely hear her over the oscillator. "But it'll be different. I'll make them see a different me. I never wanted to be a City Indian. I miss the Rez."

"Once I give up this unit, no turning back. They have waiting lists for these places."

"Don't I get a say in anything?" I asked. "I don't wanna go back. I barely remember living there, and last I checked, there was no bathroom or shower at the Dad Shack. If I'm stuck at a hot, sweaty Vendor Table all day, I at least want to be able to have a shower at home after."

"No one's tying *you* to the Table," our mom said. "You gotta still keep beading, but your mouth is starting to cause more trouble than you're worth there. If you can find another job, go ahead. But you're not lying around all summer on the Rez with no one keeping an eye on you."

A way out! She was forgetting that my Social songs and drumming attracted customers, but I sure wasn't reminding her. Only problem: seemed like jobs close to our dad's Rez Shack were scarcer than the anthropologist tourists who were guaranteed to drop a couple hundred bucks every Table visit. This felt like a trick.

"If you girls are serious, I gotta make the one-month-notice call on this unit tomorrow. You'll finish out your school year here, and then as usual, we go to full-time Vendor Table in the day, and start packing at night."

"Wait," I said. "Where are we going to fit? This is a stupid idea. What does Marvin think?" Marvin was the *Quiet Twin*. "Marvin? An opinion, please?" I went to the living room and explained what was going on.

"Can't be that different from here," he said, shrugging. "Poor in the city and poor on the Rez gotta be pretty similar, and the Shack is smaller, so cleaning'll be easier." He probably didn't care since he didn't even have his own space here, just the living room pullout couch. While we worked the summer Table, he cleaned, did wash, and took the bus to the grocery store. In between, he made corn-husk dolls and basswood sculptures for the Table, like our dad. He'd recently gotten ahold of some soapstone and his new carvings were beautiful, amazing, and better proportioned than other people's. I hoped he'd someday teach me his secrets.

"I called your dad," our mom said. "He's working on arrange-ments. He's glad we're coming home." I heard something foreign in my mom's voice. Not *romance* exactly, but for a minute, it seemed like she had a heart that wasn't made of velvet and beads and cotton batting, pinched tight with waxed thread. She turned and went to her room, closing the door.

"What the hell, Marvin? What kind of Twin Support was that?"

"Like I said, how much worse could it be? At least there, we got other Skins to hang out with. Maybe I'll have a social life, finally."

"You could have a social life here, if you weren't glued to that stupid TV. *Lost in Space*? *Land of the Giants*? *The Monkees*? Those aren't even shows from this decade. Get out there and live a little. You could have friends at school if you tried." I didn't have a ton myself, but still, a few.

"White guys think I'm too dark, and black guys think I'm too white. I don't fit anywhere in their color chart attitudes about each other, except as None of the Above."

"You could *try*. I have."

"It's easier for girls," he said. "You don't even have to be all that interesting if you're willing to flirt. If you're willing to flirt with homely guys, you could be as popular as you want."

I couldn't believe my own twin was suggesting I had Sluttish Tendencies. Where was this coming from anyway? Marie was the one who was getting busy and no one even noticed. I went back to our room and flopped on my bed.

"Why do you *really* want to go back?" I asked Marie when we'd let a few minutes pass.

"Just do." She didn't even bother with a story. "You'll understand once we get there."

"It's him." She said nothing. "Your Mystery Man. Don't *even* think I haven't noticed."

The guy was maybe in his thirties and had been hanging around lately when we worked, always dressed a little too formal for the park. Touristy guys did not wear sport jackets (not that the tourist guys didn't look like doofuses themselves). I preferred watching the ones who cut the grass and emptied the trash in their Work Blues.

Our mom (too busy rating potential customers) hadn't noticed what I noticed the last few months at the Table. Marie's Mystery Man would show up all tweedy in the distance, catch my sister's eye, and then head to the concessions. A minute later, Marie would go on her break, and an hour later, she would return filled with sudden good cheer and smudged lipstick, like today.

"Look," Marie said. "If you want a different job, I know how to get you one. Then you won't have to bitch at the Table, playing your stupid drum. You can even do your own Weirdo Beadwork monstrosities. Wouldn't it be nice to sing and drum only when you really want to?"

"Are you serious?"

"A real job. With steady pay. Not pay when Mom decides you've earned it. One condition."

"I know, I know. I don't get to ask about the Mystery Man."

"For your own good," she said. (Anytime someone says this to you, it's really for *their* own good.) "You'll understand when you're a little bit older."

"If you wanna live to *be* a little older, you better get stealthier," I said. "Mom's distracted 'cause the season's just started, but she's gonna notice how *every time* a tall, skinny man with a sport jacket and a Man Bag comes sniffing around our territory, *you* take your break time. She's self-absorbed but not *that* self-absorbed. What's the deal?"

"Your own good," she said, blowing the smoke from a Kool through the oscillator and out the window. After she sent her first plume through, I held my hand out, the first two fingers extended like a peace sign. She shook her head, refusing me a drag. I don't know why my sister thought I was a kid when she was the one who couldn't sneak around if her life depended on it. Still, if it got me away from the Vendor Table, I could pretend a while longer.

3

You Are Here
Carson Mastick

Derek had lain low throughout that first day after being shot, but him missing supper was like a dog ignoring pork chop bones on the floor. He hobbled downstairs that night and made a plate while our dad checked his lottery tickets against winners announced on local news. I don't know how my dad did with those, but this was not a super-lucky day for Derek.

The helmet-hair newsman's Top Story: an attempted robbery at a drive-in restaurant in Lockport, fifteen minutes east of the Rez. A ton of Indians worked in Lockport, but no one chowed down at that drive-in, not with a name like Custard's Last Stand. Besides soft-serve ice cream, their menu was mostly Little Bighorn–themed combos, including the Big Bighorn: a triple Angus beef burger and a bacon-wrapped hot dog, surrounded by sweet potato fries.

Did non-Indians even get the references? I only knew a little about General Custer because of a goof my mom made one Christmas, one that Derek never let me live down. She always got us coordinated gifts so that we were forced to play together. The year I was seven, she gave us some twelve-inch plastic Cowboys and Indians from the Best of the West, light on the Indians. Derek won the luck of that draw. He got Geronimo, with all the accessories, including a Tepee.

Sheila got stuck with Jane West, a blond Cowgirl, Johnny West's wife. I got it the worst without even knowing.

That Christmas morning, my shoe-box-sized present revealed a bandanna-wearing, lanky blond plastic Cavalry General: George Armstrong Custer. I was bummed. There were two other Indians in the Best of the West — Chief Cherokee and Fighting Eagle — but living in this house, you didn't want to complain about your presents. So the three of us played for a while, until our mom and dad crashed for a nap. As soon as they were out, Derek charged over to the bookshelf filled mostly with our dad's skin mags.

"You're not supposed to be digging around in there," I said. "Dad'll kick your butt if he finds your drool on his centerfolds." I didn't quite know what that meant, then, but I'd heard grown-ups teasing Derek about our dad's mag stash.

"See this?" Derek said, pulling a paperback book from the shelf. It was *Custer Died for Your Sins*, by someone named Vine Deloria, Jr. The cover showed a cartoon eagle holding a beaded tomahawk in its beak. Derek and Sheila laughed Dirty Rez Laughs at the title. I didn't get the joke right then, but I could tell immediately that Custer and Indians were *not* a good mix. On top of that, Derek quickly let me know there was a real, historical Custer, and that he billed himself as an Ultimate Indian-Killer Cavalry Cowboy.

My mom sure didn't know that either. She'd just gotten us figures that would fight each other. Being a lacrosse-stick-making and bead-working Indian woman, she would have never spent cash on General Custer if she'd been aware, even if he was in the liquidation bin at Twin Fair. I ditched Custer to the toybox graveyard as soon as I could. Even now, I still hadn't read that book Derek showed me, but I knew enough about the original Custer to know this burger-joint-owning ass face on TV was an I-Don't-Care-What-You-Think Indian Hater.

In the news report, Lockport's General Custard didn't look much like the plastic General Custer. He was a stubby, round rascal, with his hair in a freaky long blond pageboy. He had a tiny Brillo-pad chin beard with a big mustache hiding his mouth, like fringed curtains.

A fake Cavalry outfit capped the look, the kind you might find in Theater Club racks. He stomped around in a blue bib shirt with giant white cuffs, and the big brimmed hat with a star on the forehead. Did he look like General George Armstrong Custer? Maybe, if Custer had lived to retire from the Cavalry and develop bad eating habits. Who knew if the guns in this guy's costume holster were real?

Well, *we* all did, now, as he was boasting to the Reporter in the Field on our TV.

"Indian guy with long hair," he said, dragging the "long." "Waltzed in 'round closing time. I was alone, sweeping up. Always send the wife with the night deposit." He nodded like a bobblehead. "Guy was trouble." Asked why, he said the guy wore a trucker cap, a hooded sweatshirt, dark sunglasses, and he'd pulled his T-shirt up over his mouth and nose. The reporter nodded seriously. "Had his hand in the sweatshirt pocket, you know, here." Custard slapped his pumpkin gut. "Said he had a gun, and he wanted — get this — a to-go bag filled with cash and burgers." He waited and then that stupid mustache parted in a giant grin. He was loving this.

" 'Heavy on the cash,' he said. I told him, 'Son, you don't need to go *off the reservation* in my place of business.' " He nudged the news guy and added, "You see what I'm saying here?" The news guy asked why he thought the robber was an Indian. "*Attempted* robber," General Custard said. "His trucker cap, perfectly clear. Had those beads all over it on the brim, like the Indians wear. You've seen 'em at the gas stations buying beer by the case, I know you have. Well, I shot him in the a — "

The news cut back to the studio, saying the suspect was still at large. They showed a police sketch, which looked like half the Rez Men under fifty. They added that the suspect had been wearing a Led Zep shirt. The newsman wished a speedy capture of "the Hamburglar," and the sports and weather guys yukked it up as they went to commercials.

Normally, my dad would rage about how we got the shaft in the news and we'd stay out of his way, but he'd watched Derek limp into the kitchen, knowing when he'd been out the night before, and noting that he hadn't left his room much since he got back. He also knew Derek had a beadwork cap, because he had been its first owner.

And so began a period of sustained harassment like I had never seen before. The Butt Cheek Incident seemed like yesterday, but it was a month ago, and though the story faded from the news, it didn't at our house. First we had hamburgers for five days straight, which our dad cooked, frying up all noisy in the kitchen, like he was doing construction. At the end of the week, I heard him grumbling and slamming pans again and we all sat at the table for the sixth time as he yelled, "Get your asses down here to eat!" He walked in with one serving plate for us, and an additional one, stacked high. He set it in front of Derek and gripped his neck from behind, telling him to "eat up." Derek got through nine before he could leave the table. Our dad let him go only when it was clear my brother was gonna blow chunks all over us. Eventually, he just started calling Derek Hamburglar.

As that month wore on, our house formed a new rhythm. Derek could put up with it or leave, and he wasn't a Moving Out kind. The rhythm was so steady, you could tell when our dad was ready to rumble. He usually started quiet with "Where's that cap I gave you anyway?" Derek would mumble some shit about misplacing it. This was an excuse for our dad to poke at him with a You Gotta Be Careful speech, usually with some unwelcome umph, like a backhand whack or a lacrosse stick jab on Derek's left butt cheek anytime he was in striking distance. He never actually asked about the night in question, and Derek never back-talked, and so it went on.

Our house wasn't the only place the story was kept alive either. The *Buffalo Evening News* had printed enough information for Derek's new nickname to spread across the Rez within a week, though no one would ever say it around any outsiders. Derek's stupid move became a celebration for some and he usually drank free on nights he showed down on Moon Road. He'd been the first Indian to do something about Custard's Last Stand, and I kind of admired my brother for taking a stand of his own. I didn't think I could. Not like that.

I tried to get out of the house as fast as possible when my dad started up. At first I tried to get him to lay off, but then he started giving me lessons on why that was a bad idea. When my dad's monster hand slams you, you didn't forget it. So now if they revved up at night, I split and didn't come home until past two in the morning. I'd check Derek's wound for him, go to bed, and then wait for our dad's bullshit machine to crank again the next day.

Finally, yesterday, the school year ended. I'd set my alarm for 7:00, just in case, but my stupid body still woke up at 6:30 like I was getting ready to go to first period. And I wouldn't have to do that for another two months. For the summer, I was working with my mom repairing lacrosse uniforms as they came in, which kept me in gas money and guitar strings, and didn't require early rising. My mom worked a lot at home in the evening, watching TV, so she usually went in around ten. This morning, I could smell her making coffee downstairs.

"You wanna cup?" she asked.

"Nah, I'm up. Thought I'd give Lewis a ride. His summer hours at the garage start today—I told him ahead of time I'd swing by this morning."

"Nice of you," she said, in a tone that meant: *Why are you being nice?* "Tell him I said to drop by. We haven't seen him in a long time." I guess in her eyes, Lewis was still one of my best friends, even when I blew him off for months.

"Promise." She'd be seeing a lot more of him. Sometimes I was a nicer guy than anyone gave me credit for.

After our Memorial Day surprise gig, I had made plans. By the fall, I'd have Lewis, Doobie, and myself in place as three foundation members of my Kick-Ass Rez Band. And now it was time to let Lewis know about his future, in the usual way. Partway to his house, I spotted him hoofing it to work.

"Get in, Gloomis," I said, pulling over. "Told you I'd give you rides until you could afford to get your bike out of the repair shop."

"Like you haven't stiffed me before," he said. "And quit calling me that."

"You live on a Rez, man. You get the nickname you deserve, not the one you want. You want a different one, quit walking around like someone ran over your dog." He didn't move. He had a backpack over his shoulder and he was still wearing that beat-up leather jacket Albert gave him a few years ago. Except now it fit.

"You gonna get in?" I asked, revving the Chevelle's glasspacks.

"Only if you turn around," he said.

"What's the diff? Your job's five minutes away from any Rez road."

"I wanna see something up that way," he said, pointing the direction he was walking.

"You gonna tell me what it is, or do I have to guess?" I asked, already doing a three-point turn. When I was done, he finally walked around to the other side and got in.

"Still smells funny in here," he said, wedging his backpack between his feet. I thought the odor had faded. Maybe I'd grown used to it? I ignored him and got to the point.

"So how's your playing these days? Been a while since I've needed any pointers from The Bug, but we sounded good at the graveyard. You still doing lessons?" The Bug was our old guitar teacher who I'd stopped going to six months ago, this wooden-legged, Cowboy-song-yodeling Dog Street Skin. He was a chord player who could do finger-picking if he had a good rhythm backer, and his playing got looser the deeper he was into a jug. Dealing with someone else's natural rhythm forced you to work different skills, and even Lewis, keeping time with the two of us, had become a decent player.

"Good to play with someone else," he said. "Besides, The Bug enjoys it."

"Maybe I'll stop by. Always keeps you on your toes." Lewis nodded, trying to stone-face me. I knew The Bug had asked him to play backup for a July Fourth shindig, with pay. My dad had heard about it too and negotiated a deal with both of us playing. Clearly, no one had broken the news to Lewis yet.

"Guess we missed it," he said, shrugging at the crossroads, looking both ways.

"What's the 'it' we missed?" I asked, turning south on Snakeline, heading to his job. "It's early. Wanna grab a coffee at the Shop and Dine?"

"I've only got two bucks. Pay day's tomorrow. What's Tami doing for the summer?" he asked, switching from his broke ass to my cousin who he'd worshipped the last couple of years.

"Washing her hair," I said—her standard response to him. The perfect Rez Joke. One you laugh at *because* you know you're being made fun of in it.

"Asshole," he said. I laughed. He knew I still called the shots.

As we rounded the bend, Gloomis mumbled, "Hmm, there it is," like he'd spotted a pen he dropped. But what we saw as we drove closer was a spectacle I'd never before seen visited upon the Rez—a U-Haul flying out of the driveway of a small shack. The truck had off-loaded a collection of old furniture and boxes with sayings like "Kitchen Shit" Magic-Markered on them.

This might not seem a big deal most places, but it was unheard of here. Nobody moves back to the Rez. Nobody leaves either, but still, a U-Haul leaving fully loaded might have made *slightly* more sense. I'd never even seen that before, but I'd heard the desire, like a fire drill: proceed to the nearest exit.

More shocking? I knew the shack. Maybe this would be the Summer of Surprises.

"Stinkpot's moving back to the Rez?" I asked Gloomis. I took my foot off the gas. She and another girl left the shack and stood by the boxes. "And who's that hot little chick with her?"

"If you're going to call Marie that, I can get out right now," Lewis said. "And I can talk to them myself, and then, as always, walk to work."

"Don't get your panties in a bunch." I tried to remember the last time I saw her, before she and most of her family ditched the Rez for the "big city life" of Niagara Falls seven years ago. She was the girl with greasy hair and dingy Goodwill clothes she was always outgrowing.

But now? Stinkpot's—*Marie's*—hair was long, parted in the middle and curling down a little in front, framing her cleavage. Those boobs, in a white tank top, glowed like a perfect pair of velvet beadwork pillows. Her clothes were still too tight but it was on purpose now, and I couldn't agree more about how nice they fit. "Fine! *Marie's* moving back to the Rez?"

"She told me a few weeks ago," Gloomis said as I stopped. "I assumed it was their U-Haul, but I didn't want to be wrong." News on the reservation spread like a runny nose, and I had a hard time believing I'd missed this bit of Eee-ogg, but I'd been making myself scarce on the Rez since Derek debuted his Hamburglar career. I hadn't even caught on to the obvious clues of change, like the old-fashioned camper trailer now parked right behind the Shack.

"Hey, Carson," Marie said, smiling and leaning into my window as Gloomis got out.

"Hey." I couldn't believe her amazing City Teeth, all gleaming with fluoride beauty. Rez water, thanks to treaties, all came from wells. Without the benefit of forced oral hygiene treatments, our teeth were dotted with dirty gray metal fillings. "Moving back?"

"Such a keen observer! You move up with Lewis to the Brainiac classes?" she said, laughing. "What gave it away?" Her laugh was light, easy, not quite the Broken Glass Joke Delivery most people on the Rez used. A small change in tone really made a difference.

"Listen, I'm giving Gloomis a ride to work, but first we were getting a coffee. Wanna come? Bring your cute friend?"

"Cute friend?" she said as the other girl walked up to join us. "Um, this is my *sister*? *Maggi*?" This amazing girl was Marie's younger sister? Incredible! Made sense, though. I hadn't seen her in seven years and she'd been a kid for real, but it seemed like she had a different name then. An old lady name. Even more old-lady than Maggi. Marie turned to the girl—who was dressed like she was splitting for a nightclub—and poked her collarbone. "And don't you be getting a big head about your looks either. Carson's goofing." I *wasn't* goofing. "Even with all that eye shadow on, anyone taking a good look at you is still gonna know you're only fifteen."

"That's what I'm counting on," Maggi said, looking sideways at me and touching her front teeth with her tongue. Her teeth gleamed like Marie's. She gave a surprising Scandalous Rez Girl laugh, even though she hadn't lived here in so long. "Gimme my gloss," she said to Marie, examining her lips in my mirror. "I need a smooth coat."

"You could always carry your own purse," Stinkpot said, producing a tube that oozed some shiny goo that Maggi worked carefully into the curves of her lips. When she was done shining up her appearance, she pouted her mouth and asked what I thought. I smiled and nodded.

From where I sat, the one major difference between how Rez girls and white girls acted around boys was that Rez girls understood "snagging" was an equal opportunity sport. They never pretended they didn't notice guys. They still made fun of you, but if they were silent about your looks, you knew you were at least in the running. The drawback for guys was that if you weren't interesting, they made *that* clear, no matter who might hear. She handed the tube back to Stinkpot without even acknowledging the favor.

"Your lips are so shiny," Stinkpot said, "crows are gonna carry them away." She pinched a finger and thumb like a beak and swooped over Maggi's face, making crow noises.

"Should try some, yourself," Maggi said in an instant. "Instead of those Old-Lady-Bingo Lipstick samples you steal from Mom." Maggi made eye contact with her sister in the mirror before adjusting it back for me. "What color *you* got on? Fire Hydrant?"

"See how sisters are?" Stinkpot said to Gloomis, putting Maggi's little tube back in her purse and snapping it shut. "They're the worst. You don't *even* want to hear it."

"I got a sister and I like her just fine," I said, grinning at Maggi.

"She means sister to sister," Maggi offered. "And she's right. They *are* the worst. They pretend they don't like that cute top you showed them on sale, and by the time you get some funds from your mom, the top's gone. And what do you know? Two weeks later, there's your sister, picking it up at layaway, and it doesn't even fit her as good as it does you, 'cause she likes the big Family Economy-Size bag of Doritos, washing it down with a Boss of Pepsi."

"Hey, come on," Gloomis said, always trying to make peace. "You just have different styles, that's all. Marie's like the sister on that new show with the hot orange Dodge, wearing these shorty-short cutoffs. And look at me. I've got my steel toes on," he said, impossibly lifting his leg high up into the air to show off his big, clompy work boots.

"And Carson's probably wearing something shiny and narrow," he added, peeking over. "The Indian in Cowboy boots." He leaned back against my car, laughing and smiling at Stinkpot. She grinned, doing an exaggerated lean into him, her bare shoulders resting on his arms.

"No shit kickers for me," I said. No matter what Maggi said, it wasn't going to change his mind about how Stinkpot—*Marie!*—looked. I suddenly understood why he'd backed off on the Tami questions so quickly. In an instant, on this early morning in June, he'd finally moved on. It seemed like the someone else was maybe even kind of interested in him too. If Marie had been a straight-up Rez Girl, I'd know for sure, but her years in the city could have stripped off some of her Snagging Mojo, like bad vinyl upholstery on an old kitchen chair. Marie leaned over to Maggi and whispered something in her ear, and Maggi instantly frowned, getting ready to protest, but the more Marie talked, the more Maggi chilled.

"Listen," Lewis said, looking at his watch. "I actually do have to get to work, and we've pretty much run out of that extra time we were gonna spend on coffee. No offense." I decided not to point out that it was the two bucks in his pocket he was worried about spending, not the time.

"We got things to do too," *Marie* said, pointing to the stuff covering their overgrown lawn. "But I did want to talk to you about that job."

"Tell you what," I said. "You and your sister get in, we'll drop Gloomis off at work, and then we'll go get some coffee and after? I'll help you unpack."

"We need someone to stay here," Marie said, looking at Maggi, who really wanted to punch her sister, or whatever girls did in a fight. "Marvin's packing, and our mom and dad are heading up to get the rest of our stuff. We're supposed to have this in by the time they get here."

"Marvin?" I asked.

"Maggi's twin," Marie said.

"Your mom and dad named a girl Marvin? Cruel even by Rez standards." How did I not remember that Marie had twin sisters and that one of them was given a boy's name?

"Fraternal twins, genius," Maggi said. "You're in the smart-kid classes?" she asked me. Then she grinned and turned to Marie. "Is this why you wanted to come back here?" She pushed Marie's shoulder, harder than a joke warranted. "So you'd seem comparatively smart?"

"You can continue to see what I meant about sisters," Marie said to me. "And *that* sister had better be nicer since I'm the one trying to get her a job." And then she turned to Lewis, smiling, "Which was what I wanted to talk with you about." Lewis tried his best to cover his Gloomis expression. I guess he'd been hoping she wanted to talk with him about something else. "*Are* there any summer jobs in that program you work through?"

"Not sure," Lewis said. "New summer kids don't start for another week. I'm on early because I work during the school year."

"Any applications?"

"Probably at the high school office."

"Special skills needed?"

"You gotta have a physical. I don't think girls get the cough test," Lewis said, grabbing his package and coughing. We all laughed.

"What kind of test is *that*?" Maggi said, fake alarm pasted on her face.

"One you'd fail," I said. "You are definitely All Girl."

"I'm sure you don't have to worry." Lewis added. "Other than that, the only requirement is having a broke-ass family. If your parents make too much, you won't qualify."

"No problems there," Maggi said.

"So you both want job applications?" Lewis asked. "I could probably walk over to the office on my lunch break and get you a couple."

"No, just for me," Maggi said. "Marie's still working the tourists. And who knows what Marvin's doing. Probably our dad will draft him into carving those little animals full-time."

"Just *come* with us," I said, though Marie clearly didn't want her sister to tag along. "We'll dump Gloomis, get you an application, and work on it over coffee. And then we'll drop it off. You'll have a job in no time. I'll even give you the physical myself," I said, giving her my own version of the Scandalous Rez Laugh. "Minus the cough part."

"Not a chance," Marie said, walking toward the Chevelle to join us. "But I'll take you up on that ride." She opened the passenger side door, slid in all the way, bumping me in the middle and patting the seat next to her. "Come on, Lewis. We don't want you to be late." Lewis slid in, close enough that their legs touched too. His cheeks got darker, and he casually crossed his hands over his package to hide the immediate reaction to being this close to a girl he thought was hot. It took all my willpower not to point this out, as I hit the ignition and blackened the road with my Goodyears.

"So how's the guitar playing?" Marie said, leaning a little closer to Lewis as we passed the road sign announcing that we were leaving the Rez. "I see you don't have it with you."

"Yeah, they're not likely to pay me for musical interludes at the garage," he said. "It's going all right, Nyah-wheh. I practice every day and still go to The Bug's. Unlike someone else."

"I don't need to," I said. How did she know Lewis played? Maybe he told her about us?

"I didn't know you played too," Marie said to me. What the hell?

"Since before Gloomis. I'm more advanced, you might say."

"*You* might say," she cracked. I didn't remember her being so quick with a comeback.

"Listen," Lewis said as he got out at the garage, keeping the door open to be close just one more minute. "If you guys are still moving boxes when I get out, I'll stop on my way home."

"Thanks, Lewis," Marie said. "Nyah-wheh. Sweet, but we couldn't bring that much stuff. Look at the size of our dad's place. *Our* place. I'm pretty sure we'll be done before, when you do get out?" She did the quick hour math in her head. "Two thirty?"

"Besides, they got me to help them," I said, throwing the Chevelle into drive as soon as Gloomis shut the door, his lips dropping to the ground from wanting to stay so bad. We left the garage and a minute later pulled into the school's visitors' loop. "Turn right when you walk in," I said to Marie. "The office is second door on the right."

"You still getting sent there on a regular basis?" she said, laughing. I joined—she had me there. In elementary school, I got sent to the office for being a pain in the ass almost once a week, before the teachers and principal realized I enjoyed the challenge.

I sat and spun the dial, catching only obnoxious drive-time DJs, and I half expected Lewis to ditch work and sprint across the school lawn after us. A few minutes later, application in hand, Marie ran out and, hopping in, agreed that she probably did have time for a coffee. I took her down to the not-very-swanky Sanborn Shop and Dine. I got us some stuff and bought Maggi a coffee to go, fixing it to what Marie said were her sister's preferences.

"So why *are* you back?" I asked as Marie bit into the doughnut I'd bought her.

"Well, that was direct."

"Did you want me to ask a bunch of fake questions before getting to the real one?"

"I wanted to graduate with you guys. You know, we're almost adults. I'll be deciding where I'm going to live on my own soon. I wanted to refresh my memory about what it's like living here so I can make a clear choice." She stared at me earnestly as she said this. It was a little too polished. She knew she was going to get this question.

"Bullshit. So what is it? Trouble with white girls? Black girls? Tough being one of the only Indians in that whole high school. Any Skins besides you three?"

"Yeah, there's a few City Indian kids around. It's not that. It's . . . I don't want to talk about it. Not right now anyway."

"Can you tell me if it's about you *or* your sister?"

"You weren't kidding? You really think Maggi's cute?" She was relieved I took the focus off of her, which I was guessing meant Marie was the reason for the move, herself.

"Yeah, why not?" I said. "Look, I know you see her as your kid sister. Trust me, my brother and sister are never going to see me as anything but their punk brother, and they *both* still live at home even though they're supposedly grown-ups! And Gloomis gets the same shit from his. He at least has an uncle who likes to hang around with him, but how sad is that?" Someone had left a newspaper on the Table at our booth. I was tempted to snag it to see if there were any late-resurrection Hamburglar stories. Sometimes, if there were slow news days, they ran No-New-Leads articles about unsolved cases.

"That's not sad. I think it's kind of nice."

"Well, whatever. Guys are going to notice your sister pretty quick. I mean, they're going to notice you too."

"*That's* bullshit. I know how things work out here. The name you gave me when we were kids is going to stick. But that's fine. I don't want any scroungers chasing after me all summer."

"Sorry about that. How did I know that a name like Stinkpot was going to stick?"

"You knew it as much as I did."

"And about not wanting Rez guys chasing after you? Too late. You just left your first Dog Street Puppy Dog at the garage. And it didn't even seem like you were trying."

"I wasn't," she said. "I like Lewis. I don't want to hurt him, but . . ." Here it came. The real reason. It hadn't even taken much prying. "With moving back? I'm just not ready to start thinking about that." I was wrong after all. There was a reason they were back, but I wasn't getting it out of Marie this morning. "Are you really going to help us move boxes and unpack?"

"Treaty's a treaty. I said I'd do it, and so I'll do it. Even if my treaty's with a Stinkpot."

"You're such a jerk," she said, laughing, and then she punched me in the shoulder, knuckles out, almost as hard as any guy who'd done that.

"Okay, new treaty. I promise not to ever call you that again. To make it up to you, I'll let you drive back to the Rez." Her parents had never owned a car, so I had my doubts about letting her take the Chevelle's wheel, but I figured she could maybe scrape by. "Assuming of course that you know how."

"Of course I know how," she said, draining her coffee and holding out her hand for my keys. Marie swung the key ring on her fingers like a pro as we headed out. She hopped in the driver's seat, revved it, and squealed out of the parking lot. Not only could she drive, but she knew how to finesse the specific powers of a sweet muscle car. She glanced at me, read the panic in my face, and laughed, slowing to normal speeds. The Chevelle was my baby. "That's for calling me Stinkpot. Now we're even."

We got back to their shack/camper combo. Maggi sat on the couch on their front lawn, looking at the TV in front of it, even though it wasn't plugged in. Every box had been moved to the shack door, and at a quick glance, it seemed like she'd stacked them logically for the order they needed to go in. Even more amazing, she looked as if she hadn't even broken a sweat.

Marie might not know it, but her sister was a very intriguing girl.

When I pulled into the garage lot that afternoon, Lewis held up a just-a-second finger and yelled inside, thanking someone for the offer of a ride. Weird, how easy a thanks rolled off his tongue. Saying it always felt embarrassing to me.

"So, let me guess," he said, climbing in and wedging his backpack on the floor between his legs. "You gotta pick up some repair stuff from Zach." Still didn't trust me.

"I told you I'd get you," I said, pulling out. "But yeah, I cut out early and told my ma Zach had some jerseys that needed mending."

Lewis didn't say anything. I was just gonna use the ripping-off-the-Band-Aid method for this next part. "And I got something else to tell you."

"All right. What's the scam?" he asked. "I have stuff to do."

"Like practice?" I asked, and he narrowed his eyes. He knew. "We can practice together, later. That's one reason I came. We can talk about what we're gonna play at The Bug's shindig."

I put it out there as casually as I could. The Bug had left it up to me to tell Lewis that he wanted a third guitarist for his Fourth of July bash.

"Are you serious?" Lewis asked. I indeed was. Maybe Albert had put the original spark of an idea in The Bug's buzzing head one afternoon, but my dad could bring in the crowd that was prepared for a BYOB with some extra B to share. We'd have to split the fifty bucks The Bug was offering, but I was the better player anyway. Lewis should consider himself lucky to get paid at all.

"Maybe word got around about our Memorial Day performance," I suggested. "Albert is all about Eee-ogg." Lewis gave a small machine-gun laugh, knowing I was lying. "Come on. We could go cruising too, see if Maggi and Marie are around, maybe hit a drive-in I want to check out." He stared fierce, but his faced sagged, like Frybread dough before you drop it in hot grease.

"Look, I'll even teach you the finger-picking for 'Julia' so you can do something beyond chords in the future. If you're good, I'll throw in the hammering for 'Working Class Hero.'"

"You got your guitar with you?" he asked finally, leaning back in the seat. I had won. An offer of the Beatles always closed the deal, but that was way easier than I thought. He didn't want to give the gig up. I pulled away from the garage, trying not to grin too widely.

"So what the heck?" Lewis said once we got on the road. It was the Rezziest he had ever sounded, his family's fake New York City sophisticated accent knocked right out of him. As crazy vulgar as the Rez was in some ways, in others, it had a straight-up lightning line of the Protestant Church running right through it. Most of the Rez used "hell" instead of "heck" only if they were talking about the place the "unsaved" went.

"I didn't do it. My dad came home and said—"

"What? That I'm not good enough? I'm good enough for those booze hounds."

"I know," I jumped in. "*You* didn't seem to have any problem cutting me out."

"I didn't cut you out. You don't even go to his place anymore for lessons or practice. I do! Albert set it up. I could really use that fifty bucks, so—"

"You think I'd handle your brother's scuzzy uniform if I couldn't use fifty bucks?" I was glad that in his heart, cash trumped fear of performing. It was gonna be easier to introduce the idea of the Battle of the Bands if he thought there was major cash involved. If he could get his shit together for fifty bucks, his head might explode at his cut of a thousand-dollar grand prize.

"I guess not. I sure wouldn't. Even I have higher standards than you this time," he said, laughing. "I won't touch Zach's uniforms." We were good. Not great, but good, and that was good enough . . . for now.

4

Mind Holes
Magpie Bokoni

Just when city life was getting interesting, when I could stay out later, and learn the city on my own, suddenly we were back in a tar-paper Rez Shack. I hadn't loved Science Project life, but this didn't feel like home either. Unlike that time-tripping guy in *Slaughterhouse-Five*, I was instead a girl unstuck in *place*.

Marie would be starting senior year, a homecoming. But Marvin and I were eight when we'd moved to the Science Projects. This place was like a fill-in-the-blank test for a book we hadn't read. Our Rez cousins had friends, but we were City Indian Cousins, Back to the Bush.

Our dad had modified the Rez Shack to the limits of his imagination and wallet. Our "room" was an old Airstream trailer, attached by an enclosed gangplank to a hole cut in the wall. The Airstream had two bunks, a little table, and even a toilet and a shower, which we could use, if *we* took care of it. Small price for a First World bathroom. We had a skylight too—a little plastic dome. From outside, our Airstream looked a bit like the Chariot those Robinsons cruised around in on *Lost in Space* (one of Marvin's TV favorites). But our dad took the wheels off this Chariot when he nailed it to the Shack. If a one-eyed giant showed up, it would be curtains.

Despite Marvin's optimism, he got a shabbier mirror of his old apartment life (hard as that is to believe). This couch's pullout mechanism was busted. And in truth, Marvin missed cable. His TV channels had been curtailed, but lately, he was happy that a local channel had expanded into late-night programming. He'd shaped his whole identity and vocabulary from watching lame reruns of old shows on USA and channels from New York City like PIX or WOR in the middle of the night. He had Times Square Dreams in a Dog Street World.

Unlike him, I at least *had* gotten out of the Shack and met two people from out here, Carson and Lewis. Marie came home that first morning with plans and a job application for me. And by some voo-doo of Marie's, my mom signed, but of course, Dark Deanna had to take the wheel for part of it, latching on one condition.

"I need her beadwork skills," Dark Deanna said to Marie, even though it was my life at play here. "Face it, Marie. Your sister's better with the Double-Heart Canoes. Faster." I could see the hurt in my sister's face, but she didn't deny it. She would never be great with a needle, but mostly because she wasn't truly interested. I got good because I *had* an interest. I'd recently started making more of my own projects, moving beyond my Virgin Girl Diary Sketchbook, even though our mom still dismissed my conceptual art pieces as *too stupid and weird to put out for customers* whenever she caught me working on one.

"You got two weeks," our mom said, finally turning to me. "If this fails, you quit and you come back to the Table. No argument."

"Fine with me," I said, pretending like my sister had not just dispersed the Dark Deanna cloud like she'd had some kind of magic blow-dryer, blasting kindness into our mom's head.

A couple of weeks later, it was weird to be excited about my first day of garage work, but I awoke with lightning under my skin. It felt decent to finally take some control over my life. No more life like Billy's in *Slaughterhouse-Five*, getting slammed through memories and experiences and expected to cope. Trying to find something to grab for lunch, I heard bike tires popping on our driveway's crushed stone. "Lewis?" I yelled out the window.

"You want to ride bikes to work together today?" he asked, wandering in through the kitchen door, leaving it open. I could see his bike behind him. It was pretty decent for a Poor Kid Bike, one of those ten-speeds, with curled handlebars like rams' horns.

"Do you *see* a bike here, anywhere?" I perused the kitchen fruit bowl, but no luck. Just unripe bananas. I was thankful I had dinky jelly packets to help choke down the Commod PB.

"No, I guess not," he said, pretending to look around (as if one might magically appear). "I thought maybe you just locked it up inside," he added. The Shack barely fit *us*, let alone transportation storage. "Or maybe you and Marie shared a bike and it might be your turn or something?" It always came to Marie. I didn't have the heart to tell him about her Mystery Man.

"She up yet?" he asked. I shook my head, and escorted him back out the door. She'd gotten in late again and probably wouldn't get up until my mom dragged her butt out of bed to lug their Vendor Table totes to the driveway end. I grabbed my beadwork bag, and at the last second, slid my favorite water drum inside. I raised it up so Lewis could see, but he just shrugged (still thinking about Marie snoozing, just a few yards away from him, no doubt). I had to speculate as to whether that meant it was okay to take or not.

Our mom called *me* Slutty Mouth, but Marie was the one who seemed to want our mom to catch her sneaking out (dumbest Plan A I've ever heard). Mystery Man didn't seem like the type to move her in with him if they threw her out. (If the crappy little car I'd seen him leave the park in was all he could afford—a weird box with wheels, farting black clouds every couple of feet—there was *no way* he could support my lazy, high-maintenance sister.)

"I don't think it's really advisable for you to ride on my handlebars," Lewis said as we stared at the top bar, its metal gearshifts sticking up at sharp angles. He smiled.

"No, not advisable," I agreed, touching the spiky shift handles. He didn't smile often. You never know what's behind someone else's closed doors, that's for sure, but he was as buttoned-up as they come. His personal life was like those stores that had gone out of business, plate-glass windows all covered in soap. "I don't think I can fit on your crossbar either, but we could walk together? If you don't mind walking a bike."

"Sure," he said, getting off. "Never had a reason to do it before."

"You have a reason now. You get to walk with *me*."

"Color me excited," he said, and laughed when I slapped his arm, another rarity.

"So how come you got here so early if you were planning to ride?"

"Well, you went to orientation with that job counselor, right? Checkered-pants guy?"

"Yeah, Friday. All the other bosses were there in the library with us." It had been my first time inside the school. "But the garage boss wasn't there, so Mr. Checkers brought me over there to meet that woman who works in the office, the one with the big voice."

"Anna. She's nice. Even takes us to the bank so we can cash our checks. She cosigns."

"What's that mean?"

"Um, do you have a bank account?"

"You're kidding, right?"

"I don't either. Anna *has* an account, and she signs our checks with us. So we can get the money right away." We were making steady progress down Clarksville Pass. The garage was starting to come into view.

It's amazing how a building can be there your whole life and you never see it until you have to. The garage was a series of interlocking concrete cubes, with a trailer out front, five thousand buses (an exaggeration) parked three deep, a bunch of utility trucks and vans in the back, all surrounded by barbed wire fence. Seemed like a prison for delinquent transportation.

"What's gotta cross this Anna's palm?" I asked. There's *always* a catch. Like when you live on the Rez with no car and you ask someone for a ride—you always lead with how much "gas money" you have.

"Um, nothing. She's just nice. She does it for free."

"No one's that nice," I said as we reached the massive fence gates. "Catch?"

"I'm telling you, *she* is," he said, weaving a crazy giant chain in the fence and through his bike, locking it there. "But not everyone here is. You're gonna find that out soon enough."

"Well, what's gonna happen?" No one had mentioned that part.

"Don't know. It's like relationships anywhere. We each find our own way, but I thought I could bring you in while they're still drinking coffee so everyone knows you. You're not going to remember all them at first." Sunlight gleamed off the dewy bus roofs as we neared the garage.

Only the one regular door was open. Grimy windows on the giant garage doors reflected the sun coming over the buses, tiny balls of flame all in a row. We walked into the building and he showed me the time clock where we punched in and out (proof of our hours), the table where we'd eat, the office, the ladies' room, and, oddly, the fridge in there where our lunches went. He pointed to a couple lockers, near the fridge, like teeth pulled from a perfect smile, and he told me I could hang my stuff up in one of them. Then we headed deeper inside.

"This is their break room," Lewis whispered before we got close. "But we only get to take ours with them if they invite us. Otherwise, that table I showed you."

"What's the secret?" I stage-whispered back. The little room at the back was crowded with people around a table, reading the paper and drinking coffee.

"I don't want them to think I'm talking shit about them."

"Um, are you?"

"If they think you are, you can be in as much trouble as if they caught you out right," Lewis said. Then he pointed to a floor drain that looked remarkably like the Jackson Pollock painting I saw on that art museum field trip. That painting was called *Convergence*, but I thought of it as *Portrait of My Mother's Brain When Child Protective Services Shows Up*. I wasn't sure what was going on here.

"What about it?" I asked, staring at his pointing finger and then leaning in closer.

"Anywhere you see those, avoid stepping," he said, pulling me back a little.

"What is it?" I asked, right as I noticed a horrible smell coming off the swirl, with a hint of wintergreen on top of the stench.

"Chew," Lewis said, wrinkling his nose. "Kenny, that old guy with the bottom lip bulging out? He chews tobacco." Almost on cue, this short, potbellied man came out and smiled at me, raised his fingers, and contributed a jet of black spit onto his *Floor Drain Abstract Expression*.

"New kid?" he asked, extending a rough hand, like an over-stuffed work glove, to shake mine. "Come on in. We'll introduce you around," the guy said. "As the oldest, I have seniority."

"You wish," one of the younger guys said. "If you had seniority, you'd be retired."

"Kenny," the potbellied man said, ignoring that comment. "Mechanic's helper at your service. It's true, I don't have that seniority, but if I did, I wouldn't retire. I'd have to put up with my wife all day instead of only half." Charming. I wondered if *they* had gone to Niagara Falls for their honeymoon. Most of these garage guys were in their late twenties or early thirties, almost all of them white. Some were cute. One had a nice smile, perfectly framed by a bushy mustache.

"Liz," a woman said. "The only name you need to know." She wasn't wearing the Work Blues I loved, like most everyone else. Her outfit was just beat-up regular clothes, a grungy T-shirt, cutoffs, and sneakers. "I'm the one you answer to." She flipped a wall switch, and an enormous cylindrical machine in the corner roared on, killing any further conversation. Everyone trudged out through us. Lewis stepped out of the way, like the guys would knock him down if he hadn't. But I wasn't putting up with that.

"Maggi," I said loudly to Liz. She'd need to know my name too.

"Save it 'til we get to the wash bay, kid."

"We didn't punch in yet," Lewis said. "I can do them both."

"No, show her what she's gotta do. Meet me at the bay. I'll have buses up." She spun around and peeled out, letting us know she was done.

"Friendly," I said to Lewis as we went back to the time cards. We passed by guys hauling open big bay doors. In the entry, we stuck our cards into the wall-mounted clock and something inside stamped the exact minute and second.

Right as we did, the guy with the bushy mustache came out of the men's room and gave me that nice smile again. "So you're working here, huh?" he said. I nodded. "You hang out with this Loser?" he asked, poking a finger into Lewis's chest.

"He's a nice guy," I said. "He helped me get this job. I wouldn't be here without him."

"He didn't help you get any job," the guy said, stretching his arms above his head, flexing. Where his T-shirt sleeves rode up, his arms were pasty, the tan mismatched from hanging one arm out his truck window when he drove. "Some kid up and quit on them."

"I still wouldn't have known," I said. Lewis was trying to nudge me into the bays, but I pretended not to notice. It was weird and exciting to be working close to actual men in the real world. Most of the men I'd met so far in my life were the New Grooms on their best behavior. I was charged with electricity being here.

"A real gentleman'd give you the ride," the guy said. "But you can see this Loser ain't a real man. Look at these bug feelers." He slapped lightning fast at Lewis's jaw so hard his teeth clicked. Lewis was trying hard to grow a mustache and beard, and now I realized he was probably trying to fit in with the guys here.

You always heard about Indians not being able to grow facial hair, only from white people who didn't know any actual Indians. All they saw were fake TV Indians that cranked out bullshit stereotypes: Our men couldn't grow facial hair; our women had mystical powers; we hung out with our animal friends and whispered to our crops to make them grow; we were soulful (whatever that meant). If we *had* these superpowers, we wouldn't have been nearly genocided off the map.

We knew that a lot of white people thought this way, but you corrected them only if you wanted people to notice you in a bad way. I tried only to be noticed in a good way. Lewis, on the other hand, was on a one-man mission to prove those stereotypes were wrong. And the sad mustache was one particular battle he was losing. It looked like parentheses around his mouth, and his beard did resemble black twist ties stuck on his chin. You noticed it only in bad ways.

"This," the guy said, presenting his own face, "is how a real man keeps a mustache." Agreed! Up close, it was thick and auburn, neatly trimmed and hanging down a little on the ends, bracketing his smile. "My Kiss Tickler."

"Don't you have somewhere to be, Jim?" Lewis said. "We have to check with Liz and get our assignments for the day." Trying again for distraction, he grabbed my arm gently.

"Not that it's any of your business, but yeah, I should get to it," Jim said, subtly stepping between us. He put his big hand on the top of my head and shook it gently, bringing our faces close, looking me in the eye. "You know, I'm a kid short on my team." He gave my head a gentle squeeze. "Wouldn't be hard to transfer. You know how to use a riding mower?"

"Sorry," I said, shaking my head. "I gotta go. I believe in holding up my share."

"Bet you do," he said. "All right." He let me go. "I gotta get my crew their assignments too. Maybe I'll stop here for lunch today. Don't matter where I eat." He stopped and turned around. "Could teach you how to use the rider. Super easy. Just ask for me, Jim Morgan, if you change your mind." He smiled and walked with us through the garage to the far bay, where Liz was pulling a second bus in through a back bay door. She told Lewis to give me a quick lesson in cleaning a bus and then she said she'd be back to check on me later to see how I was doing.

I grabbed the basket of cleaning supplies Lewis said was mine, and slid into the enormous driver's seat. Lewis said front to back was best. The front seemed to be the most finicky, spraying all the surfaces with cleaning solution and wiping away every drop with crappy, budget-grade paper towels. I couldn't quite get over how strange the driver's seat felt. I'd recently watched Carson drive his car, on the few Rez Laps cruises he and Lewis had picked us up for, but by comparison, this looked impossible. The long gearshift jutting out of the floor had a strange geometric design on it that I could swear I'd seen on some *Lost in Space* episode. Too bad Marvin wasn't here to give me the scoop on navigating this ship. Terrifying!

Just before ten, Liz reappeared and got on Lewis's bus for a few minutes. She was carrying a spray bottle of the Purple Soap, heavy-duty stuff, and handed it to him, pointing to the garage entryway, several bays removed from us. We were supposed to go on a scheduled break, and Lewis was heading that way, but Liz came onto my bus.

"Still on the dash, huh?" Liz said, stepping into my bus. I nodded. "Pacing yourself?"

"Getting the feel of things," I said. "I'm a quick learner." (I had, in fact, already learned that Liz was *not* going to be a nice boss, at least to me. Lewis had still been on his dash too, but she was pretending I'd been solo dawdling.)

"We don't get too many girls here," she said, nodding slowly, as if she were, in fact, not a girl herself. "You don't get a pass from the tougher parts 'cause you're a girl."

"Pretty sure I can handle anything," I said.

"Bet you'd like to," she said. "But listen, Magpie—"

"I prefer Maggi."

"When you get to choose, I'll let you know. You just keep to yourself and Lewis. If any of the guys ask you to give 'em a hand, you tell them they go through me." She started to get off and then seemed to remember something. "If someone asks you to get something upstairs? You go up, get it, and come right back on down. Especially if they ask you to help them up there. You're only supposed to be here two months, but sometimes that's two months too long. I'll shit-can you for any funny business. We have an understanding?" (As a matter of fact, we did.) I nodded and slid out of the seat. "Two buses a day. You gotta get better and quicker."

Finally, she left. I decided I couldn't afford a break, even though we were told at orientation that we were legally entitled to two paid fifteen-minute ones a day.

By the time lunch rolled around, I had mostly caught up to Lewis. He nodded, looking over my work, acting like a Little Liz. I started toward the break room, hoping Jim Morgan would join us and that maybe I could sit near him. If not, maybe I could get a chair where I'd at least be able to look at him without being noticed that much.

"This way," Lewis said, putting his arm around my shoulder. "Remember? We only go in there if we get invited." As he steered us toward the time clock vestibule, I shrugged his arm off.

"I don't think that's gonna happen," I said. "I can tell already that Liz doesn't like me for some reason that has nothing to do with me." It sounded lame ass, the kind of thing Trouble Kids always say just after they've been caught putting rubber cement on a teacher's chair. "She was saying shit like I better not head off alone with any of these guys, like that would somehow be *my* fault, like I'm wearing a neon sign that says 'EASY.'"

"I think Dave Three Hawks has somehow got her thinking all Indian girls sleep around."

"That big guy? I wondered if he was from the Rez."

"Yes and yes. We've had a couple Indian girls here, but they don't last. Liz always finds some official thing wrong with them, but after they leave, she claims they were rubbing up on someone. Total bullshit, but just as well you know early," he said. I realized that the table assigned to us was in the sink area of the ladies' room. The stalls were behind two separate closed doors, but still, our table was technically inside. I guess it was sort of a "Lounge."

"Don't you feel weird inside of the ladies'?" I asked, grabbing my lunch from the fridge.

"No pop?" he asked, digging in his front jeans pocket.

"Didn't bring any change," I said, failing to add that I didn't, in fact, have any change.

"I'll get you one." As he went to the machine, I pulled my drum out of my bag and was getting ready to play a little when he put a hand over the skin and shook his head. "If you want to do that," he said quietly, "let's finish eating quick and I'll take you to a better place."

"Why are we whispering this time?" I asked. He cocked his head, gesturing that I should listen to the wall. The Real Workers were talking and laughing on the other side. I couldn't tell if Jim Morgan's voice was among those deep, rumbling murmurs and sudden cackles, all muffled together, but apparently it didn't even matter. I shrugged like, *What about it?*

Lewis didn't seem especially talkative, so we just finished our lunches fast and in silence (since neither of us had much). Then he quietly slid his chair in and gestured for me to follow as he walked to a bus in the parking lot's far end.

"Now you can play if you want," he said. "Those walls in there are too thin."

"Why would they care if I wanted to play my water drum?"

"I used to think being invisible was bad, until I discovered that being noticed can cost you way more, if *you're* not paying attention," he said. This I did understand. Liz wasn't my first bad supervisor — Dark Deanna and her ever-changing mood wasn't exactly fun to deal with.

"Is this where you go when you bring your guitar to work?" Marie had told me Lewis and Carson both played (even together sometimes, though they didn't exactly act like friends).

"I'd never bring it to work. I try never to let them know about anything I love."

I couldn't argue and didn't feel like drumming anymore. So Lewis filled me in on the workers for the rest of our allotted lunch break. I wanted most to know about Jim Morgan, so I waited and listened, but Lewis never mentioned him.

"Guess we better get back in there," he said.

"By my watch, we still got a few more minutes."

"Best if they don't see us coming from the lot. They'll wonder what we were doing."

"Eww!" I said, and his face slipped down a bit. "No offense."

"Yeah, how could I take offense?" he said, leaving briskly enough to put distance between us. For the rest of the afternoon, I stayed on my bus, working. My only company was the endless boring cowboy music that streamed from Kenny's radio in the bay. Finally, someone shouted "Break!" which was immediately followed by a bunch of rustling. That was the fastest they'd moved all day. They pretended it was a break, but it was so close to punch-out time, the workday was pretty much over. Most summer days, according to Lewis, *one* person stayed to punch everyone out. Low supervision. He'd predicted that at the day's end, it would be him, me, and one Real Worker. Everyone else would have left forty-five minutes before.

I watched Lewis follow them, but I stayed to finish my second bus. Liz had already shown herself to be a pain in the ass, so I kept working. When I was almost done, I reached for my water drum and started playing, a little flavor of Indian sound on top of Kenny's cowboy songs. The big bay walls might serve as amplifiers, but no one but Lewis would notice—a Social song backbeat was like an Indian dog whistle. It might get his attention and he'd come back. Then I could apologize.

"Nice," someone said, just outside my bus's open door. It so startled me, I dropped my stick. "Never heard any drum like that before," Jim Morgan went on, bending over to grab my stick from the step well, his T-shirt pulling out the back of his Work Blues. He leaned in, not quite stepping up, his arms on the frame. "No break for you?"

"I got a little behind," I said.

"I noticed that this morning," he said, holding the stick out and grinning, flicking his eyebrows up and down. I stuck out my tongue. "That's not fair to you." Jim looked at Lewis's empty bus. "Was there any Bus Garage Wrestling Federation today or was today a Work All Day deal? I bet they wanted to make you believe it's all hard work."

"Wrestling Federation?" That must be a euphemism for something.

"You'll see. Of course, the Loser would never be man enough to wrestle." Jim untucked more of his T-shirt, reaching under the hem to scratch his side. He caught me peeking at his Happy Trail and scratched higher, revealing more as he went up. I wondered what it looked like at his chest. "Where is he anyway? Out brownnosing Liz?"

"On break. I decided to stay and finish up," I said, keeping my voice low and hoping he would do the same. Maybe Kenny's stupid cowboys would keep Liz's ears out of range.

"You could come on break with me," Jim said.

"Liz'd be all over my ass if she saw that I wasn't where I'm supposed to be. I've only been here six hours, and I already got a lecture. Aren't you supposed to be with your crew?"

"They're good kids," he said, nodding and lighting a cigar. "Know what they're doing. If I'm not there by quarter after, they'll start cleanup on their own."

"Don't count on it," I said. Even at fifteen (maybe especially), I knew people would go to great lengths to get out of work, even if it was harder than the work itself.

"See, that's why things are different here. I *can* trust my kids. You change your mind, just say the word." We heard the compressor come on. Break over. "I'll see you again," he said, and slipped out the bay door. I watched him disappear, his firm silhouette stark against the bright sunlight beyond my bay. When he stepped out, he stayed burnt onto my retinas for a few seconds, and I stared into the void until that afterimage faded. A few seconds later, he passed by in one of the school's big utility dump trucks, waving to me with two fingers, imperceptible to anyone else who might be looking.

5

Strawberry Fields Forever
Carson Mastick

I pulled up to Lewis's, just as a sharp *whack!* issued from the side of their place. "You're hopeless!" someone shouted as I got out of the Chevelle. If this had been my house, that sound would have been my dad prodding Derek, and Derek taking it, biting the insides of his cheek so he didn't yell. Here, it meant Lewis's lacrosse-star brother Zach was practicing. I scoped them through the safety of their front windows and leaned in to listen for any Eee-ogg.

"Can't you at least pretend you're tending goal?" Zach said, cradling with his stick.

"I don't have a cup on," Lewis said. "Your stardom doesn't need my nads as a sacrifice."

"*You* ain't using them," Zach said. "Wear my cup, right there."

"Disgusting," Lewis said. "You haven't even washed it."

"Suit yourself. Small target anyway," Zach said. Lewis pretended to goalie so Zach could practice shooting at a Magic Marker square he'd drawn on the front room wall years ago.

"Was that *ever* funny?" Lewis asked. "First time someone said it to you?" Zach was only five years older than us, but the Rez's All Lacrosse All the Time culture meant MVP Zach was too cool to hang with us. Even as obnoxious as he was, he had a fan club. I reached into the Chevelle and honked. I didn't want to step up and sacrifice *my* nads.

"Saved by the bell," Lewis shouted, ripping the door open. He dropped the goalie pad he'd been holding like Captain America's shield and grabbed his guitar, heading out the door. On the porch, he stopped and turned to me. "You're just here for Zach's uniform stuff, right?"

"I *am* picking up," I said. Zach pointed to a stuffed duffel bag giving off nearly visible stink fumes. "But I thought maybe we'd practice some." I held out my acoustic case. "Maybe we'd call those Bokoni girls to see if they wanna come to that drive-in I wanna check out."

"You still talking about that? Just go!" he said. Indeed, I hadn't yet gone to Custard's Last Stand since I'd last suggested it. It would be safer if I went by myself, since I was way more of a ChameleIndian than Lewis. Standing among Indians, I look like another Indian, but I was also ambiguous enough looking to pass safely for most of the local white variants. "What's the big deal?" Lewis asked, standing still, like he was frozen by the idea of making that phone call. I shrugged.

"Fine!" he grumbled, grabbing the phone while Zach droned on about repairs.

"They're calling me back," Lewis said, lugging his guitar to rescue me. "Let's practice outside. I can hear the phone from the steps. We practicing for The Bug's?" I nodded, a little guilty.

"Well, you know the kind of lame stuff The Bug's gonna want us to play," I said, doing a quick run-through of "Jambalaya," which everyone at The Bug's place called "Goodbye Joe," after its opening lyric. "But let's try something. You know the song by heart, isn't it?"

"What do *you* think?" he said, giving a decent, slightly slower copy of what I'd played.

"Okay, so how good are you at keeping time?"

"Decent," he said, tuning a couple strings by ear. "Be better if we had a drummer, and there's no way I'm wasting money on a metronome. I don't even have a capo yet."

"Here," I said, tossing him mine from the case-candy pocket inside the case. "Keep it."

"What's the catch?" he asked. It was a nice one, brass. It was gonna be hard to shoplift a second one as nice, but worth it. And I kind of liked sometimes using my ChameleIndian qualities to lift from a store. They never watched people they thought were white as close as they watched visible Indians shopping.

"No catch. If you learn to use it, we'll be better prepared." He started to clip it in place at the third fret. "Put that away for now," I said. "Remember? I want to try something."

"All right, what?" He really wanted to use it, but I wanted him to know who was driving.

"Play 'Jambalaya' like you were just playing, maybe a little slower. It's more important to get the timing and notes right than it is to play fast." He gave me that *no shit, Sherlock* look. "But here's where it gets tricky. I'm gonna play some leads on top, not just the same, and not harmony in the same rhythm. We're gonna be playing two totally different parts."

"Yeah, all right," he said, but his face said something different. The old doubting Gloomis was there. Usually, that face disappeared when he played, except for those few times The Bug's juicehead friends barged in during our lessons.

"If you get lost, watch my foot, and I'll watch yours. We might have better luck if we both try to keep time with each other that way." I didn't know if that was really true, but it wasn't like we were going to find a drummer in the next half hour.

"Sometimes I just play along with a record to keep time," he said.

"And you got a copy of The Bug playing 'Jambalaya' lying around here?" He shook his head, like he even had to. "That's what we're gonna have to play. That, and 'Your Cheatin' Heart,' and 'Cold, Cold Heart' and all the other Sad Indians Crying in Their Beer Songs."

"Don't forget 'Kaw-Liga,'" he said, slapping the body of his guitar with the same fake Indian drum rhythm Hank Williams used in his song about a lonely Cigar-Store Indian.

"The only time you see middle-aged Indian men dancing," I said, joining him. "All right, let's try that first. I'm gonna play the fiddle part on top of your rhythm. But . . ."

"What?"

"I'm gonna need the capo for that."

"Indian Giver?"

"Funny. Come on. I'll give it back."

"Honest Injun?" he said, tossing it back. We were getting back to who we were best together, a place we hadn't been in a long, long time. Indians making fun of Indian jokes—especially the kind white people didn't think we knew about, the kind that only happens when you're with someone you really know.

"I promise. Don't I always keep my promises?" He didn't respond and just started the opening chords, keeping good time and waiting for me to jump in. I clipped the capo on and tried a few different places of the fretboard 'til I found a complementary key. Our first run-through was iffy, but mostly because of me. It was hard to play jamming leads and watch his foot at the same time. We both cracked up when I hit a whole bar of sour notes, losing my place. By the second run-through, I had a better sense and we got through most of it before the phone rang. We stopped and I gave him a look like, *Answer it, you idiot!*

There was only one ring. "Okay, they're interested," he said, like I didn't already know the Rez's current version of smoke signals. There were no charges if your party didn't pick up, so a lot of Rez phone calls made were purposefully never answered. One ring: Yes. Two: No. And three: Maybe. It was like a super-primitive Magic 8 Ball. Try Again Later sometimes came up.

"Going out!" Lewis shouted into the screen door to no one in particular. Zach was in the living room, watching TV and practicing cradling, keeping up on his MVP status. "Won't be home 'til late." Good. He thought we were going to the movies. It was possible we might be late, but there was no guarantee. The time would be up to those sisters. Maybe we *would* be late.

At Maggi's shack, the girls piled in the backseat. They both had their hair up and used plain hair clips to do it. They also, by luck, weren't wearing anything signifying *Indians Here!* No feathers on their T-shirts, no beadwork earrings, no big-ass turquoise rings.

Turquoise wasn't even part of Indian life up here, traditionally. But recently, a bunch of people had started wearing turquoise and silver rings or wristbands, or other stuff from Indians around the country. It was almost more common to see turquoise than beadwork barrettes.

As we drove, Lewis and Maggi yacked about these people they worked with, about as uninteresting as someone telling you their dreams. When I'd catch Marie's face in the rearview mirror, she looked blank and dreamy, like she was studying the far ends of the fields. I felt almost like a chauffeur, like I wasn't even a part of this get-together, just hauling these three around. I might have been pissed if it wasn't useful for them to not notice we were heading to Lockport. I'd been counting on Lewis thinking we were going to Lockport's drive-in movies instead of the closer one and I figured these girls would just be glad to get out of their Shack.

"What are we doing here?" Marie asked, suddenly aware that I was driving us somewhere specific. I pulled into the parking lot of Custard's Last Stand, trying to find a spot. Business was booming.

"You don't like ice cream?" I asked, getting out. Lewis and I locked eyes through the open door. He knew now what was up.

"You said we were going to the *drive-in*," Marie said. I looked at Lewis again quickly. He realized, as I did, that these sisters were out of the Eee-ogg loop. They hadn't shed their City-Skin Skins, so they had no way of knowing we were entering a crime scene.

"This *is* a drive-in. A drive-in *restaurant*. You city girls don't know what that is?"

"Marie just had her heart set on the movies," Maggi said. "We haven't ever been."

"You haven't ever been to the movies? Even Broke-Ass Gloomis here gets to the flicks occasionally, particularly if there's a chance for some boob shots across the screen."

"Spare me," Maggi said, ignoring the tease-bait. "Haven't ever been to the *drive-in* movies. A little hard to do when your family hasn't ever owned a car. When our folks borrow a car, the double feature isn't exactly a priority."

"Well, let's get ice cream," I said. "If they got a paper here, we can see what's playing."

"I already know, and it's something I've been dying to see," Marie said.

"All right, whatever," I said. "Ice cream first." If she started campaigning about a specific movie, she was closer to winning the negotiations, so I cut that out immediately.

"Yeah, I could use a Slurpee," Lewis said, finally opening the passenger door, tipping the scales to my preferences, but *only* at the last minute. He'd been letting me know that I might control whether we go to the movies or not, but I wasn't *entirely* driving this car. He was probably still pissed too about the change of plans for the Fourth.

"Those things are so gross," Maggi said, getting out of the car. "They leave your tongue blue."

"Only matters if you're doing something else with it after," I said, joining them as they walked over. They hissed, the least encouraging version of a laugh, and only grudgingly. Noted. They still weren't really among us. Even the prudiest Protestant Rez girls would laugh *a little*, a nervous signal that I'd gotten under their skins like a sliver. If you acted straight-up offended, you were inviting more comments.

Walking through the doors, I scoped out the inside of Custard's Last Stand. What had I expected? I couldn't believe this sad-ass place had brought my brother down. My brother, the unstoppable force of my growing-up life, who slammed anyone from the Rez from bothering me because they'd have him to deal with. All I saw here was an old man with a bad haircut and waxed mustache behind the counter, grinning at customers and all the support of their business.

We hung back inside the restaurant, deciding. An obnoxious group of kids wandered in, streaming past us like we were invisible. Not exactly what you saw in "teen movies," but they strutted enough to suggest they were probably Lockport's football team and cheerleader squad. They sat at a table near the counter and joked while a family gathered their order.

I was here because I'd wanted to see if there was backlash to what the asshole in the Cavalry costume had said on TV. On this night, the place was packed. No loss at all. I'd seen all I needed—we could skip this and still make the first feature of whatever Marie was antsy about. And if we'd turned and left, things might have been different. But then one of the football player–cheerleader couples got up and placed their order.

"Hey, General," the guy said, "how about a chocolate dip vanilla frozen custard?"

"And for the young lady?" General Custard asked, literally lifting his Cavalry hat in a courtesy greeting, twirling a corner of his waxy mustache, like a cartoon bad guy. Maybe Snidely Whiplash, that villain from "Dudley Do-Right." The place had gotten quiet, like the room had been waiting. Even those who didn't seem to know were suddenly aware that the noise level had dropped off.

"She'll have a cherry dip," the guy said, dropping cash on the counter.

"What is she, mute?" Maggi mumbled under her breath. A few people around us heard her, and Lewis nudged her subtly—we were deep out of our territory.

"Now you know we don't serve that right now," the General said, with a wacky new swagger that being out of cherry ice cream dip didn't seem to warrant.

"Oh, and why's that?" the football player said, saying the lines he was supposed to, hitting the beats so obvious like he was one of "the chorus" kids in high school plays. The ones too clumsy to be trusted with real lines. As he said it, grinning, I saw a poster on the wall featuring the real General Custer, outnumbered, but somehow killing *all* the Indians coming up to attack him. Mounted next to it, laminated, was the newspaper article about the General and his brave stand against the "alleged" Indian robber. Did newspapers think the word "alleged" really allowed doubt in anyone's mind, or was it just one of those Cover-Your-Legal-Ass words?

"Well, you know, can't be too careful these days. They ain't caught the guy who tried to rob me of my livelihood, so he's still out there. 'Til they catch 'im, we don't serve *anything* with a red skin. Not . . . even . . . ice cream," the General said, tapping a finger on the counter with each word. A bunch of people laughed, on cue, like this had been staged for our benefit.

"What if Joe Theismann came in here right now?" some family dad shouted, grinning, from a far booth. His wife patted his arm in a Take-It-Easy-Now way, but she was still smiling too. Who the hell was Joe Theismann?

"He could come in," the General said, "long's he took his Washington jacket off first. Then he's just an ordinary football legend, and not a Redskin." Most of the room laughed again. A few puzzled faces dotted the crowd. Maybe tourists on their way to Niagara Falls?

Other than the three friends who'd walked in with me, this was a room packed with people as vanilla as the ice cream being pumped into cones. If there were any more of us, we would have been noticed, since they were more obviously Indian, but we were a small enough group that we could have been mistaken for tan Italian kids. I told myself that, anyway. I was more relieved that we had each, on our own, decided to go ChameleIndians instead of sporting Full Rez gear. I was thankful for every beaded barrette, feather T-shirt, and chunk of turquoise left home, as around us kids smiled and laughed those crazy laughs you get when you can't believe your luck. Somehow, your parents took you out *again* for ice cream. It was probably going to be known for *years* as the Summer of Ice Cream in some families. Just then, I realized why parents, almost in unison, were turning to look every time the bell above the door tinkled.

"You wanna get out of here?" Lewis asked, always himself.

"No," I said, stepping closer to the counter. "I thought you wanted a Slushee, or whatever they're called here. Looks like . . . a Brain Freeze?"

"I don't need it," he said, but followed behind me, not leaving me up at the counter alone behind that group. The football guy ordered something else for the girl and the counter staff was working through the crowd at the three open registers. "Let's just go."

"Help you?" a young woman asked from the second register.

"Lewis?" I said, and cocked my head. I wanted the General to wait on me. I was going to ask for strawberry. There was no way he had cut out one-third of his Neapolitan for his Ass-Face idea of keeping all the redskins out. The brand he sold advertised "real chunks."

"I'm good," Lewis said, turning and leaving, as if he'd come all this way only to decide at the last minute he hadn't wanted anything after all.

"Me too," Maggi said. They had moved up next to us. "Saving my money. I'll spend it somewhere else." Marie didn't even bother to comment as she turned and followed them out.

"Whatever," the counter girl said. "Just you, then? What'll it be?" I heard the bell tinkle behind me. Out of nowhere, "Ten Little Indians" started playing in my head, and not the version most white people know, but the original, the one a lot of Indians know by heart. In the original, the ten little Indians: broke their necks, got Jesus, got drunk, got syphilis, caught fire, or were out-and-out shot. The last one hanged himself. Was that what I was doing here? Offering General Custard and this roomful of supporting customers the rope? No matter what I did, it wasn't going to change the opinions of anyone in the room that moment.

"Nothing, I guess," I said, joining the others. We silently got in the Chevelle. My stomach felt like I'd been shot. Shot by my own inability to do anything when it counted. At the intersection that would take us to the Rez or up to the movie drive-in, Maggi spoke.

"That was sooo screwed up." She didn't lay the blame at my feet for not doing anything, which was just fine, since my own brain was handling that. Maybe *I* could have used a Brain Freeze. "But we don't have to let them ruin our night." When the light turned green, I kept straight.

Eventually we saw the neon of the Transit, announcing its double feature in letters hung over a white backlit sheet of plastic. A weird double bill of something I liked and something I didn't. "I'm fine with this," I said. "But I don't picture you being all that interested in *Fame*."

"Doesn't everyone want to live forever?" Marie said, and then added, "besides, better than sitting home, ain't it?" She was trying hard to sound casual. She might as well have been wearing a perfume called Desperation. I thought of my home, silently agreed with her, and pulled in.

It was still light enough when we got through the gate that only a few cars were in place. In late June, the only time it was warm enough to choose the drive-in movies, the sun refused to go down at a reasonable hour. It was never below the horizon before nine.

"Pull up there," Marie said, pointing to the first row, near the Kiddie-Land playground, where a bunch of kids were dirtying up their pajamas.

"You wanna go on the monkey bars?" I asked, watching a few boys push girls on the merry-go-round, spinning it faster. Their joy was seeing which girl might puke or get thrown off.

"I don't know," Marie said, flicking the lever to get Lewis to move. He opened the door without saying anything. "Maybe. Maybe those boys will behave better if a grown-up steps up."

"Where are you gonna find a grown-up?" I asked. Marie stuck out her tongue. "Very grown-up of you," I added, and all four of us laughed, one of those tension release bursts.

"Any other grown-ups here?" she asked, heading toward the playground.

"Sure," Lewis said. "I'm out here anyway." Always hedging his bets. He couldn't admit that he wanted to go with her, even as he clung like a magnet.

Maggi hopped up front as those two glided past the merry-go-round, where the boys did start to behave. Marie climbed smoothly to the top of the monkey bars, and Lewis followed, occasionally slipping in those no-tread Beatle boots he still wore though they were ten years out of date. Where did he even get them? Some Time-Machine Shop?

"What d'you suppose they're talking about?" I asked Maggi. Lewis was rambling. Marie looked toward the snack bar and bathrooms, in that same dreamy way she'd watched the fields.

Maggi hesitated. She had something she'd wanted to say and changed her mind, before opening her mouth. "Probably going over what they should have said, just brave now that we're away. You know, in the dark, no one can even tell we're darker than most of the people here."

"What makes you think that? You suddenly all Magical Mystical Indian?"

"Hardly. I mean, that's what *I'm* doing." She looked at me, straight on, in ways she usually didn't. "Look, I'm sorry. That was a bad scene. My first instinct? And my sister's? To get out in one piece. You grew up on the reservation. We didn't. There were a few other Indians in the city — "

"But not enough to feel like a group. I get it. I just wanted . . ." I wasn't sure. Had I wanted them to stand with me? My original plan was just to *see* the place, nothing more. I wasn't anticipating seeing that my brother getting shot in the ass would be a *benefit* to business. Lewis always said that, since sixth grade, he felt simultaneously threatened and feared in school. I always insisted that was ridiculous, but I felt it in Custard's dining room.

How could white people *really* be afraid of us? They'd almost wiped us out across this entire frigging country and across Canada too. Wasn't that proof enough that we weren't a danger? Or were they wishing their ancestors had just done the job right in the first place?

"So why'd you want to go there anyway?" Maggi asked. "There's a million places closer to home just as good. It's ice cream. How bad can you screw it up?"

"Previews are starting," I said, flicking lights at Lewis and Marie. I'd have preferred to just stay with Maggi, maybe reach over and hold her hand in the dark. If she'd known about Derek, then maybe we could have talked. No one on the Rez would talk seriously with me. Someone would make a Hamburglar joke, no matter how long we'd been friends, because that was how you survive there. If you're hurting, you're begging someone to tease you, to help you laugh.

But sometimes, I didn't want to laugh. I just wanted to say it was messed up that my brother made a huge mistake, that he'd have a permanent physical scar, and that our dad was working overtime to make sure he'd have mental ones too. I wasn't even looking for answers. Just a safe ear. But I wasn't sure about Maggi just yet. She was *from* the Rez, but not *of* the Rez.

Lewis and Marie came back, and Maggi got out. Lewis climbed in the back, and then Maggi followed him in. He frowned at her as Marie leaned in the door, rather than getting in. "Listen," Marie said. "I'm going to the bathroom and the snack bar. Anybody want anything? Looked like there was a long line, so I might be a while."

"You're the one who wanted to see this," Lewis said. "I was hoping for *Friday the 13th*, but we're here because *you* wanted to be here. We don't need popcorn or—"

"Should do something about that desire to watch people getting killed, Lewis," she said.

"It's only a movie," Lewis said, but I was with Marie on this one. I liked scary movies too, but I maybe didn't like them as much as Lewis did.

"I don't care about *Fame*," Marie said. "Already saw it, but I wanted to see *Little Darlings*." I'd planned on splitting before then. I'd seen *Fame* five times already, a couple alone. It took place in a New York City high school, where they gave grades for music performance, and was pretty great. *Little Darlings* I'd seen too and it was stupid.

Before I could say anything, Marie vanished, which we all pretended was perfectly normal. "Oh, I want to see *that*," Maggi called out at the next preview. She was a *Smokey and the Bandit* type? No, a *Smokey and the Bandit* sequel type? I'd spent my whole life around Rez girls. It was nice to be around someone with a little mystery. Even with Marie, I remembered enough that there were just missing story chunks, pages missing.

Every time I looked in the rearview, Maggi was looking back at me. Lewis was still stewing that Marie had disappeared. I'd figured out pretty quickly that before Marie rang Lewis back on the phone, she'd made arrangements to meet someone here. Maggi's look to me now was: *Please don't ask. Maybe I'll tell you another time, but not right now.* That's a lot for a pair of eyes with too much mascara, but it was clear. I knew the expression of *Please Don't Ask* too well. It was a more desperate version of *Ask Me No Questions, I Tell You No Lies.*

"How come they don't use that David Bowie and Lennon song in this?" Lewis said, pretending he hadn't just been ditched as easy as a used napkin.

"What song?" Maggi and I both asked, simultaneously.

"Um, 'Fame'?" he said, and we laughed.

"I bet they just want songs to be for the kids in the movie," Maggi said. "They don't want you thinking about someone who's already famous. Especially as famous as those two."

"Still, seems like an obvious choice," Lewis mumbled.

"The next movie uses one of your precious Lennon songs, so relax, Gloomis. Jeez," I said, watching the cast of *Fame* singing and dancing on a congested New York City street, jumping on top of cars and everything.

"How do *you* know there's a John Lennon song in *Little Darlings*?" Lewis asked. That one was about two virgins at a high school summer camp, competing to see who could lose their virginity first—not the kind of movie you let everyone know you'd seen all by yourself. So I did what came naturally.

"It's in the commercials," I said, the little lie floating off my tongue like a butterfly.

"No, it isn't," Maggi said. "I wanna see that movie, so I always watch the commercial."

"Oh, are you a Beatles expert now too?" I asked.

"Kind of can't help it, being around Lewis all the time," she said, and he gave her shoulder a gentle push while they both laughed.

"I don't know," I said, using my last card. "Maybe I saw the soundtrack album at Recordland or something. Trust me, there's one in there. Just relax and enjoy the movie. You can listen to all the Beatles you want when you get home, Gloomis."

Lewis grumbled and went back to watching. An hour in, Marie showed, breathless and sweaty, smelling like a man's cologne—even over the popcorn bucket she shoved in before her.

"Long line, I guess," Lewis said, flat. Marie got in, pretending the first movie wasn't half over. By *Fame*'s closing scene, her head slumped and her breathing slowed. Snoring was minutes away, at the longest.

I unhooked the speaker and started the Chevelle. She woke up and didn't have any objection.

Marie hadn't come for *Little Darlings*. She'd seen some feature that the rest of us didn't know about, except maybe Maggi. Her eyes still flashed their pleading signals in the rearview mirror, right up to the moment I dropped them off. I still felt the sting of their bailing on me at Custard's Last Stand, but I kept my mouth shut.

Marie said thanks, jumping out and heading into their shack. "Thanks, Carson," Maggi added. She smiled an apology and leaned in. I leaned too, but at the last second, she made sure her kiss hit my cheek. "Niagara Falls has nothing on New York City, but we already knew that, isn't it?" she said, naturally using this Rez phrase at the end of her sentence. Maybe she wasn't so far away after all. "See you Monday?" she said to Lewis, who nodded, looking at the door that had shut behind Marie. Maggi ran toward their porch light as Lewis got back in.

"How come you left before the second movie?" Lewis asked as we neared his house.

"You have to ask? A movie about camp with that girl from *Family*?" Of all the possible questions, this was maybe the oddest. "You really wanted to see that? For one stupid Lennon song you already own? As I recall, you were voting for the summer camp slasher movie."

"I don't guess I really wanted to see *that* second movie, but I'd like to have some say in what happens to me, even if it's only a courtesy. You left because *you* decided you were done watching." He stayed silent until we got to his driveway, where no one had left a porch light on.

"You wonder why none of us stayed at the counter with you," he said. We hadn't talked but he had known why we'd been there. "If I'd known ahead, I would have stayed." He paused for a minute before shutting the door and leaning into the window. "You didn't trust that I'd go with you if I'd known what you were up to. That's where you failed."

He left, walking up his dark driveway. It was a lonelier drive home than I'd thought it would be. I didn't even bother doing any of the things I usually did, trying to avoid our house until the fireworks between my brother and my dad were over for the night. It was going to be a crappy night no matter where I spent it, so I just went home.

I'd go upstairs and ask my brother how his scars were doing. He'd show me how his were healing, never asking about mine.

6

Men, Men, Men
Magpie Bokoni

Sometimes they gave us a break day from the endless rows of dirty buses, like yesterday. The job usually was so low concentration that while I scrubbed seat cushions, scraped off gum, boogers, and the occasional used-looking rubber (football team and cheerleader away games?), and washed it all out the emergency exit, I could put my mind anywhere.

I started seeing the beautiful art projects I'd make on my own, High-Concept Beadwork, sparked by something Marvin did. I showed him some music magazine Lewis had lent me, flipping to a pullout poster of this scandalous John Lennon and Yoko Ono album, *Two Virgins* (both of them standing face out naked!). Marvin laughed and studied it for so long I asked him if he wanted to be alone with it for a while. He shook his head and handed it back. The next day, when I got home from work, sitting on my bedroom shelf was an amazing near-perfect re-creation, using corn-husk dolls, with commercial doll hair on both, and tiny round glasses on the Lennon one. Next to it, he'd left a baggie with a tiny curled cylinder of husk and two tufts of doll hair, and a note ("in case you want to add on the parts you like best").

Even when his life sucked, he still liked to make me laugh, but the dolls were strangely beautiful and incredibly accurate for such a tricky material. The next time we were alone, I thanked Marvin and suggested we could collaborate, re-creating famous album covers in beadwork, soapstone, corn husk, basswood, and sweetgrass. He seemed open to the idea. It was exactly where we could be Conceptual Artists. I loved picturing myself handing our mom an invitation to our first show (okay, yes, I was getting ahead of myself, but I'd already requested an art class for the fall). Planning them in my head sure made work more tolerable when it was slow, and Lewis regularly hung out with me to break up the day. He was turning out to be okay, I guess, for a boy obsessed with my sister.

But because Liz had maintained her level of fondness for me, even when she shook things up, she'd still given me a bullshit job yesterday (scrubbing the coffee cart with a toothbrush to work the grout between each tiny ceramic tile). Thinking about Jim Morgan had also become a decent distraction when I was sick of beadwork strategies. He'd filled my mind up until I slipped, gouging my cuticle with that raggedy toothbrush. "This is just harassment work," I said to Lewis, bandaging my bleeding thumb.

"Oh, you poor thing," he said as he wiped down the public lockers the Real Workers had in the break room. Even here, they still had centerfolds hung inside of them. Liz had put one of a full-frontal naked guy up in hers so the room had Equal-Opportunity Nakedness.

"I wouldn't be doing stupid shit like this if I worked for Jim Morgan," I said. I'd learned that Jim officially worked for Buildings and Grounds but had to punch in and out at our garage's time clock. If you drove a district vehicle, you came through our doors at the beginning and the end of the day. The more I got to chat him up each day, the more I decided he was pretty cute, even though he was a little older than the youngest mechanics.

"I'd work here any day over being around Jim all the time," Lewis said.

"You're not doing *this* bull job," I said. All he had was a spray bottle and paper towels.

"Look," Lewis said, setting his bottle down. "The Real Workers? They hate being stuck supervising us poor kids. They're always afraid of job security, and our presence doesn't help. We make it look like kids could do a lot of these jobs."

"So?"

"We're getting minimum wage. *They* are not. Consider yourself lucky. Your friend Jim? He has no need to deal with me, but he makes a regular habit of finding me and giving me grief."

"Bull! Like what? I've never seen that. He's only been nice to me so far."

"Well, duh," he said and I didn't like what that "duh" was suggesting. "He's smart enough that the shit he pulls, I couldn't prove it's intentional. It started with him saying his nephew could do my job better than I do, but that he didn't qualify."

"Oh, how terrible for you," I said. Lewis thought *that* was harassment?

"That was the beginning. When I said, 'Oh, gee, sorry your family's too far above the poverty line to get a job here scrubbing toilets—'"

"You never said that!" Lewis was like Marvin, trying to stay as invisible as possible. But when they did end up crossing someone they got out as quick as possible and, later, I'd hear them retell the story, adding Tough Guy things they'd never said.

"I did too, and that's when it got worse. A couple times?" he said, pausing. "When they had me carrying tailpipes to the second floor, he'd come up behind me and pants me, since I couldn't do anything about it, and then he'd snap my nuts through my undershorts while all these others laughed their heads off. You can be sure I'd never come *here* commando."

"Um, thanks? I guess?" I said, trying to force a laugh. That was a jerky thing, but it seemed more like a guy thing. The Reynolds brothers who lived in the Science Projects kept a running tab on which one had pantsed the other the most for every year. "Commando's gross anyway. You should always have something on under your pants. That's just common sense."

"That's just one thing. He always pisses on the floor too, just after I've cleaned the johns, so I have to go back and do that patch a second time. But you're kind of missing the point here," he said. I wasn't, I just wasn't sure what to say to him about the dubious things he claimed Jim had done to him. I didn't want to go there, because his face seemed to say that if I opened that door, he might tell me more things, worse things. So I went back to scrubbing. Mostly, we spent the rest of the day in silence. It made the day seem hours and hours longer.

"I wonder what other kids' summer jobs are like," I said as we punched in the next morning. I decided to try staying on more neutral ground so I at least had someone to talk to.

"Crappier or less crappy?" Lewis said, pretending we hadn't tried to freeze each other out yesterday. We were better. "No kid's summer job is going to be all that fun. Bosses know we're desperate, so we get the jobs they don't want to do. Darwin at his finest."

"Darwin, from over on Bitemark? What's he got to do with this?" I said, showing off how I was getting to know the reservation.

"No, Darwin. You know, Darwinism? Never mind," he said.

"Don't treat me like I'm stupid just because you have a couple of years of high school on me," I said. "What's Darwinism?"

"One of those things," he said. "Hard to describe, but you know it when you see it. I live it. And so do you. It's tied to the idea of evolution and—"

"Oh, that whole Man-from-Monkeys thing? Do you buy that?"

"Just what it means today. For you and me. The more power you have, the more you can make others do stuff you don't want to do. We're at the bottom. Liz could demand we do any job, and we don't have much choice. Or I don't. I need this job to help keep luxuries in our house. You know, like electricity." He laughed.

"Dealing with Liz is just like living with parents," I said. "Control is overrated. We're gonna *have* to be decision makers at some point in our lives. Why rush it?"

Lewis went out and chained his bike to the fence like it was gold.

"It's the way they remind you they're in power," he said, coming back in with his lunch bag. "Like this table. Don't you think there's any other place in this whole garage where we could eat lunch besides a dark corner of the ladies' room?" It *was* gross once he pointed it out.

"Probably," I conceded. "We don't have to stay *here*. We just can't eat with them unless they ask us to." The guys invited us often enough since I started working, but maybe that hadn't been true for Lewis before. I didn't want to speculate out loud that maybe they liked me better than they did Lewis. "But *you* let yourself get bossed around by all kinds of people. Like Carson. I don't even know you guys that well and I can still see that."

"My Uncle Albert taught me that life with Carson is a tally sheet. Most relationships are like this—Carson just makes it clearer. My uncle's had similar go-rounds with Carson's dad. He's a little funny. Gets mad at things you shouldn't get mad about. And we share a room, so . . ."

"Know all about the trickiness of sharing a room," I said. "But if you just take a stand once, they get the message and back off," I said. A frown came over Lewis's face. He was going to give me reasons he couldn't do that (I've been through those arguments with Marie). "Like even here. How come you don't get involved in that stupid wrestling thing the guys do?"

I'd discovered almost immediately that, indeed, twice a week during lunch, the younger garage guys wrestled in the office trailer where the ladies worked. And I don't mean like those TV shows Marvin loved where men shouted at each other and one man waited for the other to climb the ropes and crash-land on him. This was the real deal, none of that showy nonsense.

"Your life would be easier here if you'd do it," I added. "Even once. Be one of the guys."

"That," he said, "would be insane." He was trying not to sound exasperated, but his voice went up in pitch when he felt that way, and it rose now. "These guys? They're giants."

"You could challenge Dave. He's from the Rez, right? He might take it easy on you."

"Pass, thanks," he said, shaking his head like I was a pitiable fool.

"How'd that wrestling get started anyway? Not something you see every day."

"Clearly you've never been in a guys' locker room," he said, laughing. "Not sure, but the trailer is the only place with air-conditioning and carpet in this whole workplace, so it's the only spot in the whole place that's really nice to take a break. I think they feel guilty for being in there with the office ladies, so they put on a show for, um, *everyone's amusement*."

"It had to start somewhere," I said. "Sweaty grown men don't take off their shirts and flop around with each other on their lunch break, generally."

"Locker room. Wrestling is macho bullshit. When you get out of the shower, someone snaps a towel on your ass yelling, 'Slap boxing!' Suddenly, you're on defense. Tons of fun."

"So, like, naked, you're saying? Buck. Ass. Naked?"

"That's usually how you shower. Why am I telling you this?"

"Trying to explain why two adult mechanics sometimes wrestle for our amusement."

"I don't know," he said, shrugging. "You can be sure *I've* never initiated naked slap boxing. Some guys grow up and, maybe, some guys don't."

"Well, maybe one of the reasons *you* get singled out," I said, trying not to be too mean, "is because they know you'll cave. Because you've never started anything."

"Oh, really. Has that worked for you? Do girls slap-box in the locker room?"

"You wish," I said, laughing. "Well, I haven't done *that*, exactly, but my mom didn't want to let me have this job. I stood up to her, and now here I am." After the first week, she'd almost doubled orders, because no one wandered away, thinking they had to stand around waiting for me to bead and trying to say funny one-liners, hoping they weren't risking me screwing up. They could just come back the next day. *And* she didn't have to worry about my "slutty mouth" anymore.

The deal was sealed and I could earn my own paycheck that was nobody else's business. I left out the part that I had to spend a couple hours each evening beading stupid initials, otherwise I would lose this job. Small price.

"Why do you want to know so much about those creepy assholes anyway?" We heard the compressor go off in the break room and knew it was time to get to work.

"Just curious," I said, relieved. "Let's go before they come looking for us. They're always in a worse mood if that happens." Jim Morgan flew around the corner. I felt bad that we hadn't gone into the break room.

"Hey, kiddo," Jim said, putting his big hand on my head and shaking it gently, something he did regularly these days. It was weird not to be able to tell anyone what I thought of Jim, but this was exactly what Liz was "Keeping an Eye On" me about, so I had to play it cool.

Out of nowhere, Liz appeared. Jim headed out.

"Standard day, twerps," she said (that meant cleaning buses). "To shake it up? Each of you do one alone, without the other one's help." Some days, she allowed us to work together and other days, not, even though we worked faster when we were both doing the same bus. "First one done goes on a parts run with me after lunch and the other one does another bus solo."

"Why would I want to go on a parts run?" I asked Lewis as we headed to our buses.

"Well, it *should* take, tops, twenty minutes, but they usually take an hour, maybe more. They go back roads, lower than the speed limit, shoot the shit with the parts dealers, stop for a coffee, whatever." Not exactly exciting, but that did sound way better than breaking down bus tires, dragging exhaust systems to the upstairs storage, or scooping out the disgusting mud traps.

Lewis and I looked at each other across the bay through the giant bus windshields as we Windexed them. At ten o'clock, someone yelled, "Break!" The Real Workers streamed over to the break room as a group, but Lewis wandered over to my bus, assessing my progress.

"I'm way ahead of you," he said, looking at all my untouched surfaces. "If you *want* to go, I can slow down. Be the *gentleman*."

"So generous. Don't worry about me."

"Suit yourself. Listen, I'm totally burnt. I'm just gonna crash in one of your backseats here, all right?" He scrunched in one of the benches before I could protest, disappearing. Almost instantly, tiny snores came from the back. The bay would be empty for a half hour, despite the fact that break was supposed to be fifteen minutes.

"No break for you again?" Jim said, appearing outside the bus door, startling me. I held my hand up to my lips in the shush signal, and glanced in the rearview mirror. No stirring. Jim leaned into my bus, not quite stepping up, his arms on the frames. I stood quietly and came down toward him. At first, it didn't seem like he was going to let me pass, but when I touched his bicep and pushed gently, he dropped it and we went quietly out behind the building where his official truck sat.

"Still getting shorted on your break? You know, they legally gotta give it to you."

"I thought you might come by," I said, and he smiled. It wasn't wholly true, but it wasn't exactly a lie either. I did always look forward to the times he'd catch me alone. We never chatted about big things, but he listened to what I had to say. He even noticed me doing one of my conceptual beadwork pieces one day, when I'd told Lewis I was staying on my bus to work. It was a beadwork version of that drawing on the Beatles album *Revolver*. Marvin was going to make a bunch of tiny soapstone men and corn-husk dolls for the collage part.

"You still working on your *Revolver* art thing?" I nodded. I'd tried to hide it back in my beadwork bag that first time, but he asked to see it. He'd touched it, running his fingers over the beads and the velvet, smiling, telling me it was soft like skin. "Can I see how far you got?"

"I didn't bring it today," I said, a lie, but it was on the bus with a sleeping Lewis.

"Maybe tomorrow?" he asked. "If I come by? Whose head are you working on?"

"Between John and Paul right now." I pretended there wasn't another way to interpret that, but it gave me that little lightning zap I got sometimes when I saw Jim. We heard the compressor come on. Break over. "Listen, these guys are noticing that you're coming over more this summer than usual." It was amazing what you could overhear if you paid even a little attention to others. "That's what they said anyway. Are you?"

"Maybe I got more reason to come over here this summer," he said, his smile widening, splitting that bushy mustache. "I get ya, though. I got an idea. Nice surprise for you," he said, turning his head a little and grinning. "Maybe I'll see you at lunch. You better get back in there," he said, and slipped in the bay door, heading toward the break room like nothing was out of the ordinary. I watched him all the way until he went through the door. When he came back through a couple minutes later, Lewis was up and getting ready to go back to his bus.

"What's Jim doing here again?" Lewis said, behind me. "Doesn't that guy ever work? Even if it's just hassling his own kid workers for the rest of the day."

"Maybe he needed something?" I said, not looking up. Jim passed through without looking my way, his school truck flew back out into the parking lot a little later. He slowed to a stop and waved Kenny over. Kenny jumped up on the boost step and talked with him a minute.

Lewis didn't know Jim had been at my bus, and I decided to keep it that way. "You better get back to your bus." He dragged his feet across the bay and started back on his dash, sweeping paper towels across the giant windshields, and then climbing down to monkey with the hose and soap bucket. Somehow it never occurred to him that stalling only made the day feel even longer.

Just before lunch, Liz inspected our buses and told us she'd let us know after lunch who was going with her. Right after, Kenny invited Lewis and me to the office trailer. Another wrestling day. We were Designated Audience, so we were getting AC and a show — Two Bonuses! There was no way I was turning down AC. The two younger mechanics and Dave Three Hawks, the older helper from the Rez, came leaping in after us, all slapping at each other.

"Ladies and gentlemen," Kenny said, holding a spray bottle as a microphone. He was the perpetual ref/announcer. Dave peeled his shirt off and stomped around the trailer striking Incredible Hulk poses, while people laughed. Anna, who ran the office, sighed, laughed, and grabbed her lunch. "Today's match of Bus Garage Wrestling Federation brings us — "

"Me," Lewis said, standing up and yanking his own T-shirt off. It got caught on his glasses and he had to untangle himself while some of the others chuckled. This was maybe not my best suggestion. Lewis wanted to be like the Real Worker guys who walked around shirtless on hotter days, but he was so scrawny that the few hairs on his chest looked more like two pink spiders stopped halfway across a birdcage from each other.

"*You?*" Dave said, trying not to split his head open with a giant grin.

"This is highly irregular," Kenny said. "I need to consult with our champ." He walked over to Dave, and I was surprised we actually couldn't hear what they were whispering to each other. Dave eventually shrugged and stepped away, going back to Hulk poses.

"Today, we have a special challenger to Bus Garage Wrestling Federation! Weighing in at . . . what d'ya weigh, kid?" Lewis hesitated. "No lyin'. We got eyes."

"A hundred and twenty-three," Lewis finally said.

"Weighing in at the *Sesame Street* weight — "

"What?"

"One. Two. Three. Learning to count, is . . ." Kenny started grinning. "The Count! Ah! Ah! Ah!" Everyone cracked up, since Lewis's sad goatee did make him resemble the Vampire Muppet who counted on *Sesame Street*. I wondered if Kenny watched *Sesame Street* trying to learn how to read as a pre-retirement hobby. "And we all know the Champ. Dave 'The Predator' Three Hawks." Dave's last name was close enough to a good nickname that Kenny had to work extra hard to find him a suitable nickname that Dave would still tolerate.

"All right, fair fight!" Kenny said, hitting the typewriter's carriage return button, dinging its little bell. Lewis crouched, making himself even shorter. Dave did the same, crouching farther. They ran at each other, grappling and chest bumping. Lewis's legs were at an angle just so he could keep his balance. Dave's reach was longer. He headlocked Lewis and reached under his knee and poked. They went down, rolling on the floor. It was clear to everyone in the room — except maybe Lewis — that Dave (who played for keeps) was, in fact, taking it easy on him.

Lewis got a decent footing and put all his energy into one push while Dave was on his knees, and down they went, Dave on his back. Lewis quickly jumped up and sat on Dave's chest, putting all his weight into pinning Dave's shoulders to the floor. People yelled and hooted, counting down from ten, and almost no one noticed Jim Morgan step into the trailer, his T-shirt draped across his shoulders. His Happy Trail, the thick line of hair so neat it looked like he combed it, bloomed into a full-on tree of hair across his chest. It was the first time I'd seen where that trail led up to. He winked at me as Kenny dinged the typewriter carriage return. Lewis war-whooped, jumping up and down. What had I started this morning?

"New round-one champeen!" Kenny said, grinning at Jim. "In a surprising upset, The Count takes The Predator down *for* the count!" Everyone laughed as Dave pretended to need the hand Lewis offered. "And we have a second unprecedented event! What a day for Bus Garage Wrestling Federation! Here to take on the new champ is a guest wrestler!" Others looked around, puzzled. I had a bad feeling, replaying the morning in my head.

"Coming to us all the way from the Buildings and Grounds crew, I give you Jim 'The Bee Gee' Morgan!" Kenny said. Given everyone's expressions, this might have been unprecedented, but I could picture Jim and Kenny talking in the parking lot this morning.

Lewis glared briefly at me and sighed. He could walk away, but he'd never live it down. Jim shook hands and stood straight up, waiting for the bell to ring. He didn't want to give one moment to wrestling theatrics. For a second, Lewis didn't know what to do, but eventually, he charged. Jim held out his arm, stiff, and grabbed the top of Lewis's head. This time, he gripped.

Lewis could make no forward movement. He flailed about, trying to get his arms up high enough to unlock Jim's elbow, but Jim just kept knocking Lewis's arms aside, like Lewis was a particularly large mosquito. Lewis stopped for a few seconds to catch his breath, and Jim immediately let go. Lewis stumbled forward and Jim got him in a headlock, Lewis's head clamped in Jim's armpit. They scrabbled around, turning in choppy circles. Lewis kept trying to get his hands to meet around Jim's back so he could lock his fingers, but he just did not have the reach. He did one lunge into exactly the right position his opponent wanted.

Lewis had a typical Indian ass, which is to say, in the minus territories. (Even older Indian women mostly grew guts instead of butts—people joked that those ladies belong to the Robin Clan.) This was an unfortunate bit of Indian anatomy for Lewis at that moment. Halfway through the match, his Levi's had slid down, even though he was wearing a belt cinched tight.

Jim, almost casually, reached down to the exposed waistband of Lewis's white briefs, grabbed a tight fistful, and yanked so hard that Lewis's feet came off the floor. He grunted and spun slowly, and Jim kept yanking—you could see the sharp detour where the material was wedged deeply into Lewis's butt crack. Lewis tried getting his left hand around to grab some part of Jim's face, but nothing worked. He looked like a drowning man desperately reaching one hand to break the ocean surface, hoping a lifeguard would spot him.

Jim gave one last hard tug and the elastic waistband in his hand loudly ripped away from the cotton around it. He let go and casually got a leg around one of Lewis's. He slammed Lewis on the floor so hard the windows rattled, then leisurely climbed on top, settling fully on Lewis's belly, knocking the wind out of him. Jim leaned forward, one arm on Lewis's chest, an inch from his throat. Kenny, this time alone, counted the pin and rang the bell.

Jim climbed up, victorious, a look of boredom on his face. He had played harder than the guys usually did. When he'd slammed Lewis to the floor, the trailer shook in ways I hadn't ever felt. But I guess there were no rules about how serious or not serious you decided to be.

"Jeez, Jim," Dave said, coming up to him after the count. "If I knew you were gonna go full bore on the kid, I wouldn't've let him win the first round."

"Bull," Jim said. "You should be glad you made that decision. I coulda beat your ass fair and square too. Now where's the prize?" Kenny handed over the pool of prize money, everybody's collected desserts from the lunches and what looked like about fifty bucks.

"Pleasure doing business with you folks. Let's do this again sometime," he said, still keeping his T-shirt hanging over his shoulder.

"No problem," Dave said. "I'll match you anytime."

"Too easy," Jim said. "If that kid could beat you. I need someone to make this interesting." And with that, he left.

"Come on, twerp," Liz said, stepping out and whacking Lewis on the head. "Need you for a parts run." Lewis followed her out, hobbling but trying not to show it. He pretended to clean his glasses on his shirt, refusing to look at me (I was gonna get blamed for this).

The rest of the garage crew stepped into the summer heat, heading back to our bays. When I got to my bus, there was a crinkly lunch bag on the light control box, just out of sight for anyone not in the driver's seat. *FOR U, CASE U GET HUNGRY. ALREADY ATE SUM* was written on it in the kind of grease pencil we all used to mark measurements. Inside, there was a single Twinkie and a half a Hostess cherry pie. No wonder Liz treated me the way she did.

Not that I cared.

"You and Marie still ready for tonight?" Lewis asked. Emphasis on "Marie." It was the end of the day and we were getting the break room ready for tomorrow. We hadn't said a word about the wrestling match yet. I had the spray bottles out cleaning while Lewis set up the two Mr. Coffee machines (regular and decaf) so the Real Workers just had to flip the switches the next morning.

"Six thirty, right?" I asked, knowing seven was more likely. I'd finally grasped the looser schedule of Indian Time, which my mom refused to acknowledge. I now had to juggle her overcompensating sense of time, this uncompromisingly exact time clock at work, and the "we'll get there within a couple hours of the stated time" that Indian Time operated under.

"More or less. You're probably still safe at seven," Lewis said.

"What's tonight?" Jim said with a grin, bursting into the room. He looked at me when he asked, but not before smirking at Lewis. Lewis gave a close examination to the coffee filters, pretending he hadn't heard Jim.

"Some of us are going to some Farmer John shindig tonight," I said. "What's it called again?" I honestly couldn't remember. Our Science Project unit was a ten-minute drive away, and that difference was oddly familiar and disorienting. Like the huge world the crew faced on Marvin's other favorite, *Land of the Giants*. There a safety pin became a harpoon or grappling hook or whatever the tiny crew needed it to be in that episode.

"Sanborn Field Day," Lewis said.

"Always a good time," Jim said. "Why don't we sign you out, Loser, so you can go get ready? Maybe lick your wounds so you can give me a run for my money next week?" He put his arm around Lewis's shoulder and started guiding him toward the entry.

"I'm waiting with Maggi," Lewis said. "We walk together."

"Oh yeah," Jim said. "Now you're the gentleman. No problem, I'll give her a ride."

"It's okay, Lewis," I said, wanting desperately to be out of this situation. "My mom borrowed a car, so we're going shopping a little with my first paycheck. And Jim, that offer? Your crew position?" I didn't want to reveal that, but I also didn't want Jim suggesting he'd made some other offer, as much as I might find that intriguing.

"What about it?" he said to me, instantly softer, nicer. He took his hands off Lewis in the entry and turned to smile at me. Lewis frowned in confusion. Maybe he'd forget to ask for clarification. "Still stands." I smiled and kept wiping off the cigarette machine on the opposite wall, avoiding the curiosity signal Lewis was silently transmitting to me.

Out of the corner of my eye I saw the cogs turning in Lewis's head as he looked between the two of us, like in cartoons of someone thinking too hard. Eventually he just gathered his stuff and walked out the door, glancing back while he slowly unlocked his bike chain.

"Jeez, what is he, a retard?" Jim said, watching him through the open door.

"Don't say that word."

"Awww, been spending too much time being a Short-Bus Kid?" he said.

"You know what? I'm going to go wait out by the gate."

"I won't punch your card," he said, plucking it from its slot. He looked at it, something I had not anticipated. "Magpie? What kind of name is that? That's, like, a noisy bird."

"You're just like the rest," I said, snatching it from him. "You tell me it's better to work for you and then you go and act like Liz." I looked out the door, but Lewis had already gone.

"Look, I'm sorry," Jim said, and put a convincing enough face on. "Truce?" He held out his hand to shake. I took it and he pulled me in for that one-armed Guy Hug. I was surprised, and somehow went with it. "Forgive me, Magpie?" he asked, pressing a little more firmly.

"Don't call me that. I hate it." I pulled away from him.

"Aw, come on. I like it," he said. "How about if only I call you that, when it's just the two of us around. Like a pet name."

"I'm not a pet," I said. "Save it. I've heard every bird joke at least three times on the reservation. And that's when they're being nice. Some people just call me Pie when they want to be mean."

"Why's that mean?"

"Don't act ignorant, Jim. If you didn't think 'pie' could be used as a dirty word, you wouldn't have left me a half-eaten one next to a Twinkie."

"Okay, fair enough. Guilty."

"There's a third reason my name is wicked bad," I said. "You gotta promise to tell no one." I had no idea why I was telling him this, but it was exciting to have a secret with him.

"Who'm I gonna talk to?" he said, getting annoyed. "Okay, I promise. Jeez."

"The Tuscarora word for 'bird' sounds almost identical to, well . . ."

"Well, what? Come on, you can't take me to the edge and leave me hanging."

"It's almost identical sounding as the word for . . ." I gestured to the front of my cutoffs, where I had on a nice, studded belt. (I just could not say any of the variety of words for external female genitalia to this man. Even the scientific ones somehow sounded like scandal.)

"Ooh, you got some mean parents."

"They named me for my dad's mom. He's from a different Rez, so it's kind of like a tribute. And in his language, that's not the case. If you tell anyone—"

"I made a promise. I keep my promises, Magpie."

"Good," I said. I thought about the idea of allowing him to call me by the name I'd always hated. In some weird way, it gave me that electrical shiver I'd recently become aware of.

"So forgive me for earlier?" he said, reaching out in that half embrace again.

"Only if you're nicer from now on," I said, letting him.

"I'm always nice to you," he said, still not pulling away.

"Not really, but I meant Lewis. Nicer to *Lewis*."

"I'm going to need a real hug to try that," he said, and released my hand, embracing me fully. We stayed that way a little too long, and he began to press harder, shifting a little.

"You promise?" I said, pulling away. The front of his Work Blues pants stuck out more than usual, but I only glanced for a second. I didn't want him to catch me noticing. I could do the same things to guys that Marie did. She kept saying I was just a kid, but the evidence in front of me right now was proving her wrong.

"I promise to *try*," he said, laughing. "But come on, enough bullshit about the Loser. I brought a change of street clothes with me. Thought I might hit the shower in there quick," he pointed his thumb to the men's locker room. "See what trouble I can get myself into tonight."

"Okay. I'm gonna wait outside," I said. "It's almost two thirty. Can I have Lewis's card and mine?" He handed me the two I wanted, lifted a small duffel bag, and headed into the men's room. I punched out and headed to the gates, hoped he wasn't going in with the intention of leaving a surprise like Lewis was suggesting he might. After a hot June weekend, that men's room would be rancid.

A couple minutes later, he pulled up to where I was standing at the chain-link gate, in his personal truck (which looked like his district truck, minus the official number on the sides).

"Thought you were showering. And why do you drive a dump truck?" I asked, leaning in.

"Changed my mind. Just swapped out my shirt. And this?" he said, patting the truck's door. "Bought it off the district when they upgraded. Got a great bargain, and I'd been the only person driving it." He stepped out and shut the gate, locking it with a gigantic industrial chain, gleaming in the sun. "You don't like it?"

"It's just kind of an old-man set of wheels," I said.

"Would you like a bicycle better?" he said, laughing. He got back in the truck and patted the passenger's side of the bench seat. "You sure I can't give you a ride?"

"The reservation is, literally, right across the road," I said. "I'll be fine."

"Well, listen . . ." he said, but then didn't have any follow-up. He looked me in the eye, but his eyes flicked down every few seconds. The silence stretched between us, neither of us sure how we should end this day. He shifted in his seat and glanced down at himself.

"Thanks," I said, just to say something. "Um, thanks, for the dessert."

"My pleasure, Magpie." He looked back up and grinned. "Anytime." He dropped his truck into gear and pulled away, shouting,

"Maybe see you tonight." I watched his truck peel out and wondered what accepting that offer would have been like. I could have climbed into the passenger's side, sliding across the bench, and we could have left. I didn't like what had happened today with Lewis, but I also kept picturing Jim scrambling around, sweat glistening on his shoulders, dampening the hair on his chest.

When his truck was out of sight, I admitted the truth to myself that no one from home was coming for me. I began the walk to the border, alone.

7

Cleanup Time
Carson Mastick

Sanborn Field Day, the last weekend in June, kicked off the lame summer things we had to do in our super-dull chunk of wasteland. I was already fifteen minutes late. I tried to creep down the stairs quietly, but then a shout of "Carson!" came from my dad on the back porch. Sneaking out wasn't an option if I didn't want to get roughed up when I got home.

He and my mom sat in rickety lawn chairs there, watching my cousins' dance moves.

"What?" I said to my dad from the mudroom, grabbing a jacket. "I'm almost late."

"I know you're gonna drink," he said, cracking a bottle of Molson.

"Not me," I said. Absolute truth.

"Don't think I'm stupid, buddy boy." He gave me the Serious Chair Lean Forward from his very small collection of Dad Moves. "Now shut up and listen. I found your fake ID a year ago, but I didn't throw it out. You'll just scam another one, even though you're almost legal. So I ain't wasting my time or your money, which is *my* money anyway."

He was wrong about that, since he wasn't my sole income anymore. Every Can-Am tournament Rez lacrosse player was filling my pockets these days. Say what you will about a guy knowing his way around a sewing machine, but I was as free as I wanted to be until I graduated.

"I swear, I'm not drinking. I got other things on my—"

"Will you shut up and let your old man speak?" He paused. "Now, there's a pay phone down near the Fire Hall, out front. You call home and one of us will pick you up. And you be careful. A Field-Day Beer Tent is no place for a youngster with a tendency to get mouthy, such as yourself. And we don't want any other Hamburglar-type incidents, do we?"

"I'm *really* not. And anyway, by the time they shut down, you're not gonna be sober."

"True enough," he said, clinking bottles with my mom, who laughed down a swallow.

"And I am *not* a Hamburglar. I pay my own way," I said. I didn't like throwing Derek to the wolves, but I was telling the truth.

He gave me his *I Know Your Bullshit Look* as I slowly turned away. You never wanted to appear to stomp out unless you wanted your ass dragged back in for a Sit-Down. I was also telling him the truth. A young guy with a muscle car at the Sanborn Field Day was *asking* to get pulled over and I wasn't about to lose my wheels for Driving While Seventeen.

Whoever said "they're gonna have a field day with this" never went to a Field Day in Niagara County. Niagara Falls was a city, but for thirty miles north, this area was Podunk farm villages and the reservation. The Rez was its own Podunk—everyone up in everyone else's business—with a few exceptions. One of them was no cops and no firehouses. Which meant no Field Days.

Around here, the Field Day business was locked down by volunteer fire companies and Catholic churches. You could hit one every two weeks from mid-June to Labor Day. Field Day attractions reminded you of everything you weren't allowed to do, up to the time you didn't want it anymore. First, you couldn't ride the big-kid rides, and you couldn't reach the counter for the Midway-game stuffed animals. When you were allowed on the Salt and Pepper Shaker, you were thinking about the Beer Tent and the Monte Carlo games. As soon as you were old enough to stick around for the bands, you realized they sucked. But six pitchers deep in cheap keg beer, you didn't care all that much. The Beer Tent usually kept a giant pickle jar full of confiscated fake IDs to discourage fourteen-year-olds. Truly, the tent was a field day—for Bargain-Basement Alcoholics looking to get drunk, get in a fight, and get laid, not necessarily in that priority.

Lewis and I rode mostly in silence to Maggi and Marie's, and he smiled that dream smile you have when you knew you were headed to something you were guaranteed to enjoy.

"You two are gonna fit in fine at the Field Day," I said to those Bokoni girls when we pulled up at their hodgepodge house. "You and all the other shit-kicker kids gumming up the Midway games with cotton candy hands." Lewis hopped out and Marie climbed in the back, where he followed. Maggi climbed in next to me.

"So why are we going to this Farmer John Dealie if you guys hate it there so much?" she asked, making a sharp point with a Kleenex to finish touching up her lips in my mirror. No mention of my twenty-minute lateness. Rez Points to her. She expertly put the mirror back.

"You got something better to do?" I asked. She was dressed more like she was going out to a singles bar. She looked hot, but in a weird way, like a thirty-year-old trying to pass for fifteen instead of the other way around. Where did those Bokonis get funds to buy designer jeans when they lived in a shack with a camper attached and an outhouse out back?

"I definitely don't have anything better to do," Maggi said, making minor adjustments to her fancy-ass blouse seams and jeans. In truth, I couldn't throw stones at that glass shack. My parents also bought us clothes they couldn't afford so we didn't look like the Raggedy-Ass Indians the white kids called us. "Not since we moved back to the shack thanks to Stinkpot."

"I told you never to call me that," Marie said, acid in her voice. She gave Maggi three quick whacks to the head, like on Saturday-Afternoon Kung-Fu Cinema, instantly destroying Maggi's perfectly feathered hair. Satisfied, Marie changed into a soft DJ voice to add "and don't even think about asking for my travel can of Aqua Net."

"See what I mean about sisters?" Maggi said, revealing a rat tail. In a minute, she had a part so sharp, a paper airplane would overshoot that runway. "Any cute guys go to this thing?"

"Only one I can think of," I said, grabbing the mirror. We were nearing the Rez border.

"Who's that?" she asked, suddenly interested in what I had to say.

"You're riding in the passenger seat of his car," I said, and put on my Charm Grin that always got me what I wanted—my own secret Indian magic. Maggi laughed her Scandalous Rez Girl Laugh and swiveled her head to study the endless fields of corn dancing in neat rows. As we closed in on "the hamlet of Sanborn," the amplified music and neon lights washed over us. But I didn't feel my usual excitement. Impressing this girl was going to take more than a Midway-game prize or the Tilt-A-Whirl and Octopus.

We parked and headed toward the food stands, tramping on ground that smelled chemically sweet, like those fluorescent hockey pucks floating in men's room urinals. Truth? I'd never noticed that smell before. Who wanted to smell like a urinal cake while trying to eat a funnel cake? But as soon as we hit the Midway, an overwhelming cloud of Fair Food air blasted it out. Hamburgers, hot dogs, corn dogs, and fresh-cut fries showered us with a grease mist.

"There's where I'm going!" Maggi said, veering out ahead of us to a stand with a long line of couples. The wraparound sign shouted FRIED DOUGH $3.00! in bright yellow light bulbs. Women in tight halters showed off their tanned braless backs—the same ones you'd see stretched out on beach towels during the day, bikini strings undone to avoid tan lines.

"So your sister's not a Frybread Queen?" Gloomis asked Marie, nodding toward Maggi, disappearing into the crowd. They both laughed.

"She needs it all sweetened up," Marie said. Frybread, a mainstay at Indian events, was absent here. Fried Dough was its closest Fair Food relative, but we didn't use a deep fryer, and didn't cover it in confectioners' sugar. Not that Frybread was healthy or anything, as a million Indians flirting with diabetes will tell you. But it was survival food through Indian history. Adding sugar was a cheat.

Every local volunteer fire company had Indians among their ranks, but it seemed like the companies never wanted our foods to mingle with theirs, so you never saw it here. Not having Corn soup made perfect sense — that was definitely something you had to grow up with. But Frybread? I could never understand why they didn't even try getting a Rez vendor to set up a stand. Maybe it was because Fire-Hall Indians checked their skins at the door, like heavy coats.

"She's just a kid," Marie added, reading my face. "She was raised in the city. Can't blame her for not knowing. Take that up with my mom and dad."

I examined the Fried Dough stand more closely as Maggi got in line. I could see why so many couples were there together. The counter man would hand the lumpy disc to the woman, she'd tear off the first piece in a cloud of sugar, and then she'd feed it to the guy, like he was a baby bird. That was a sweet deal. The guy would be digging in his pocket to pay while trying not to bite the hand feeding him. Why didn't they just dig money out first?

"Gloomis," I said. "Why don't you two go get us some ride tickets? We can make the rounds and maybe check the bands out later." I held out some cash.

"Rides? Do I look twelve?" Lewis stared at me as if I'd lost my mind. The idea that a guy might want to be in a cramped, fast-moving cage with a hot girl and centrifugal force had never occurred to him. Ten bucks for the Gravity Magic of carnival rides? A bargain, even at rip-off Field Day prices.

"You're the same height as a twelve-year-old, but the chin pubes suggest otherwise," I said. Marie laughed. "C'mon, my treat if you get going!" If you're pushy, people listen. Particularly school-age people. They're used to being bossed around. "And if you see Doobie, ask him what time he's off duty." Hubie was supposed to walk the grounds as a freelance living first-aid kit. He wasn't allowed in the ambulance, but he could lead people to it. He was dying to use the radio strapped to his shoulder, but it had to be justified.

Gloomis took my ten bucks. Did he know that Doobie played the bass? It was possible he had no idea, but either way, he didn't say anything more as he and Marie took off. I was left with three one-dollar bills in my hands and a plan. I flew across the Midway. As Maggi placed her order, I leaned in close, sticking my hand to the counter guy with the bills fanned so he didn't have to count.

"Young lady's already paid," he said. "Gotta do better than that if you wanna impress her," he said, laughing and handing her the shapeless blob of bread blotted with powdered sugar.

"He's right," Maggi said as we walked away. "Nobody likes that guy who reaches for his wallet only after someone else does. Not fooling anyone." She offered me the Fried Dough.

"How would you know?" I asked, shaking my head. "You're fifteen."

"Fifteen in the city is different from fifteen in the sticks," she said back, not a snotty note included. I knew what she was saying. I liked home fine, but I understood that city life gave you something different, sharp. "Marie says everyone out there parties," she added. She still called the Rez "out there," like she didn't quite live there with us. "Aren't there guys who never have the right amount to add to the kitty when people are buying?" She offered again.

"How come you only say guys?" I asked, nodding anyway. "Girls don't contribute?"

"If you think a *girl* buys, then the Rez is more backward than I thought," she said, making a face, sort of an *Am I Really in This Situation?* annoyance face.

"On the Rez, women . . ." I had to be careful. No matter how true it was, Off-Rez people never understood. "They're tough. They don't take crap from anyone, and they also don't expect guys to treat them different. The fiercest I've been yelled at? My mom's friends. They—"

"But *you* were trying to buy this for *me*. You were trying to treat me like—"

"I was being nice. Why'd you climb into my Chevelle, if you didn't care for this?"

"Was either this," she said, spreading her free arm wide, "or the stock car races, and I didn't feel like breathing in car exhaust all night. I'll have plenty of opportunities later. Seems like that's where everyone from out there spends every frigging Friday night." "Out there" again. Truth? I'd spent enough of my Friday nights over the years, watching carved-up cars go 'round and 'round the mud track, hazing the black sky blue with burnt oil and overheating engines, filling the night with a roar like a thousand pissed-off lions. That sounded potentially cool when you haven't done it, but it got old after a gazillion times.

"You hate being back on the Rez that much?" I asked. Silence. Maybe I'd reached her with that jab. But maybe I'd jabbed because she was sort of right. I was treating her the way I'd seen white guys and girls going out. To test. To see if she might be even a little interested.

"A bit of advice?" she said, ignoring my question. "Guys don't really call their cars by the model. Only on TV or movies. Like they don't *name* their cars either. Some of these white girls at Niagara Falls High? When they sat at lunch coming up with names for the cars their parents were buying them for their Sweet Sixteen? I thought I'd vomit up the school turkey and gravy that already looked like vomit before you ate it." I laughed. She mimicked high-pitched girl voices, cocking her head from side to side. "I'm going to name mine Vera! She looks like a Vera. Or maybe Gertie!" And then, back to her own voice, suddenly sharp and bitter. "And they're *always* outdated old-lady names. Always!"

"Like Magpie?" I said, all quiet. She whipped her face toward me. I hoped what she saw was sincere sympathy. I had my weird name because my parents figured out I was conceived after my dad's first raise. They got a TV and a pullout couch on layaway, stayed up late to watch *The Tonight Show Starring Johnny Carson*, and got some quiet time alone while my brother and sister were asleep in the one bedroom. A month later, my mom discovered she was pregnant.

"Yeah, like Magpie," she said, her voice, even quieter. So quiet I barely heard it over the shouting, music, and the laughing of everyone around us having a blast on a beautiful June night. All the chrome and neon lights on the rides and attractions almost vibrated in their brilliance, and her hair gleamed with wild colors. If I touched it, would it send out beams like a prism? It was the perfect moment to reach out.

Suddenly, two guys burst through the crowd and almost plowed into us. One dragged the other by the elbow, grinning so wide I could see the fillings in his molars. Even over the crowd, I heard what the dragger said to the draggee.

"You got to see this drunk wahoo. Guys are coming with all kinds of shit for him to do for another beer. They got a couple pitchers he can see, and as soon as he does something they come up with, they pour him one that's half foam and come up with something even crazier. One guy . . ." I couldn't hear the rest. It blended in with all the other noises, which suddenly all sounded like my mom's knitting needles stabbing into my ears.

Maggi's eyes and mine were in sync. Even with all her years away, she still knew the complications of being who we were. She couldn't think of us as *out there* anymore in this kind of situation. She also knew, but I was glad she didn't say, that I was a ChameleIndian. I could "pass" easily. Even right now in late June, I was no darker than the farmers wandering past us.

When you looked at the Bokonis, though, particularly this close to the Rez, there was no escaping who they were. Lewis too. They couldn't decide to not speak up if they encountered a situation like those assholes were describing. And yet, as we stood there, getting jostled by couples and families, we silently telegraphed two other facts: I probably knew the Indian who was being conned into acting like an ass for piss-warm keg beer, and Maggi probably did not.

"We have to go see," she said.

"If it's inside the Beer Tent, I might not be able to get in," I said. I was glad I wouldn't have to convince her to come with me or leave her behind if she said no. "But agreed, I have to go see if there's anything I can do. Maybe Doobie'll be working there."

"I don't know who Doobie is, but if *you* can't get in, *I* can," she said, dropping the Fried Dough into a trash can. She was no longer a city kid, dodging sticky hands with greasy Fair Food. Suddenly, the Rezzy part of her had been awakened, and she was as tough as any woman I knew that someone had crossed, who'd probably leave you with more scars than you had coming in. "They don't ask pretty girls in summer clothes for ID," Maggi said, grabbing my hand. "Nobody does. Anywhere." She ran to catch up with those two guys before we lost sight of them, dragging me through the crowd even though I was trying to be fast.

Maggi's hand was warm from the Fried Dough, or maybe the June air, or maybe with rage not too far from the surface. Whatever it was, I didn't want to let go. We cut through congestion near the bathrooms and made it to the Beer Tent, where her hand slipped out the second we got a glimpse of what was going on inside. I wished the run had taken us longer—I missed gripping her hand in mine. And I absolutely did not want to see what I was seeing, as we parted the crowd to see how the good citizens of Sanborn had fun on a Friday night in June.

"Do you know him?" Maggi said, gripping my hand again. Even if I didn't know the person on the ground in front us, crawling on his hands and knees, she knew that no one should be in this position. "I'll go get the others."

"Wait. No," I said. I was thankful that Lewis was still in line at the rides. If I could help it, he'd never know what we witnessed here. "Tell Marie to keep Lewis busy and that you'll explain later and then *get back here*. Can you do that?"

"She's gonna think I'm—"

"Can you do that, yes or no?" She let go and disappeared back into the crowd, and I stepped between the sawhorses framing the Beer Tent entrance, pushing my way through witnesses at this end. The people supposedly in charge—checking IDs and breaking up Beer-Muscles episodes before they became fistfights—stood around laughing. They ignored the people surrounding Lewis's Uncle Albert, who was now throwing his arms up and waving them in the air like the *Lost in Space* robot. I almost expected him to shout, "Danger! Danger! Will Robinson! Aliens Approaching!"

Instead, when he opened his mouth, he whinnied. He then blasted air through pursed lips. A middle-aged woman in a too-tight tank top and no bra stepped up and poured a third of a foamy beer into his mouth, spilling the rest down his chin. "Here you go, Juniper!" she said, through a checkerboard mouth of missing teeth.

"You wanna ride on the stallion?" he asked her, breathing hard, sweat drenching the back of his T-shirt and spiking the front of his long black hair, glistening like a mane.

"Settle down, now, Juniper," a man in a summer plaid short-sleeved shirt said, stepping up. "My brother can always find other workers come harvest time. He don't need to be worrying about Wanda and no stallions." Plaid-Shirt Man smiled with his mouth, but even as drunk as Albert was, he must have seen that smile did not reach the man's eyes. Albert shifted away from Wanda. "Get back there," Plaid-Shirt Man grumbled, pinching the woman's flabby upper arm.

"A cow now!" someone else shouted.

"Yeah, that's good," Plaid-Shirt Man agreed, putting his knee gently on Albert's back until he was on all fours again. "A cow. Eat some grass, cow. Chew your cud if you want another beer to wash it down." Albert dipped his head to the ground and pretended to eat some of the grass there, flattened from a couple hundred drunken stumbles tramping across it for the past three hours. "Lots of grass there to graze, Juniper," Plaid-Shirt Man said, stepping back and resting his thick-muscled arm on Wanda's shoulder. "Don't seem like you're doing it justice. Cows who don't clean up get no drinkee to wash it down." Some of the crowd blasted out beer laughs, slapping each other on their backs and shouting, "Do it! Do it! Do it!"

Where the hell was Maggi? She wasn't going to have the muscle help I needed, but doing something alone in this crowd might get my ass kicked. Even drunk, these Farmer Johns weren't likely to hit a girl, and she might be able to reach someone if I got in too deep. Was I really in the position of deciding for someone else how they financed their own pleasure? I kept hearing my dad. I wished he was there, or that I'd thought to call.

I saw a group of City Indians farther down the Beer Tent, all gathered together, paying no attention to what was happening here. Where the hell were all the other Rez Indians? As soon as I thought it, I remembered what Maggi said. The only other option on summer Friday nights was the stock car races down in Ransomville, where most Rez men were. They'd be here tomorrow night. It didn't matter. I was just about eighteen. Starting my senior year of high school in two months. I was a man. It was time to act like one.

I went up to the serving tables. "I'd like a pitcher and two cups," I said to the two guys idly watching Albert do his one-man show: Barnyard Animals I Have Imitated for Beer.

"Hit the road, kid. You ain't eighteen," the clean-shaven one said.

"You're proofing me, but you're not stopping that?" I said, pointing at Albert, who was now raising his face to show green teeth and a streak of grass stains on his chin. I remembered the overwhelming chemical smell of the grass when we'd stepped in and wondered how much he'd gotten into his system, along with the unfortunate amount of beer.

"How a guy affords his beers here? Not my business. A man of *legal age*, that is."

"Look," I said, glancing at his name tag. "I know there are guys from the reservation in your company, Hubie Buckman for one. You suppose those guys'll be happy when I tell them how cooperative you were?" This guy looked familiar, but maybe I'd just been hanging around Beer Tents for too many years already. But Mustache Guy, the other one, I'd never seen before.

"I don't give a shit, kid. They know where they live. Someone out there knows who the Hamburglar is, and they're keeping their mouth shut. Not too neighborly, you ask me. Maybe you're even related? You Mayor McCheese? No, I know! Chief McCheese! That's you." He laughed, which meant he was guessing, making an asshole joke. To him, any young Indian might be related to the Hamburglar—he just happened to be right this time. I had to not make a scene, but I couldn't leave Albert in the middle of this mess.

"Bryce K.?" I said, reading his name tag. "I'm guessing the K stands for Keanich."

"Yeah, that's right. And if you know that, you know how much we pay in taxes on all the property our farms take up." Long stretches of Sanborn were made up of their family farms. They had been here a long time, but he was trying to shove into my face the biggest complaint of white people near the Rez: Indians didn't pay property tax because of treaty agreements. They always conveniently forgot that this entire place had been our territory before those treaties.

"We're *well*-liked." He grinned and decided I should know something else. "We're also one of the only companies with tankers. With no fire hydrants out there, you Indians would be out of luck when a house catches fire. The men of my company know that, even the ones from the Rez. *Especially* the ones from the Rez." I hated when other people called it the Rez.

"Tell 'em whatever you want," he added, leaning forward on meaty sunburned forearms. "Kind of Indian are you anyway?" He grabbed my arm, and held ours side by side. "My arms are tanner than yours."

Maggi finally showed up in my sight lines, and gave me the thumbs-up. Bryce K. was still holding my arm, trying to get Mustache Guy's attention, but that guy seemed distracted by something, or someone behind me, or was maybe just continuing to watch the Albert Animal Charades Show.

"How about an empty pitcher?" I suggested, yanking my arm back. Albert was drunk enough that he wouldn't notice. I just needed to get him clear of this tent.

"How about I call my security here and have you escorted off the property?" he said. "This is technically a private event, on Fire Company property." I had to play my last card.

"How about I tell those guys over there what's going on here?" I said, pointing with my chin to the table of City Indians. I didn't know a single one of them, but maybe Maggi did. Mustache Guy seemed to see something behind me again and whispered into Bryce K.'s ear. They went back and forth a couple times, and Mustache Guy patted Bryce K. on the back.

Just then, I heard several loud growls that sounded like only one thing in the world. The gasps of disgust that followed them confirmed. People spread apart, hoping not to get hit, and Albert, still on his hands and knees, arched his back like a cat trying to be intimidating. But this was not another animal performance. A long jet of vomit gushed from Albert's mouth like that possessed girl in *The Exorcist*.

"Take it," Bryce K. said, shoving a dirty plastic pitcher at me. "Just get him out of here! And make sure he doesn't come back tomorrow night! Friggin' wahoo! Banned!"

Maggi grabbed the pitcher as I hauled Albert up by his armpits. We didn't need the prop after all. Albert seemed to have no more interest in beer, but Maggi kept it, fingers gripping tight in case she needed to clock someone. She was an Indian girl, no doubt. Triple Bonus Rez Points.

"Need a hand?" Mustache Guy asked. Albert was going to be a tough haul on Maggi's side, but I gave him an *Are You for Real?* Look and he backed off, nudging people to clear a path. The crowd parted easily—Albert didn't exactly look like a person you'd want to brush against just then. I got one arm around his shoulders and steadied his hip against mine, and Maggi, a couple steps ahead, took up where Mustache Guy left off, gently tapping people to step aside.

When we were close to the sidewalks, I made a motion toward the men's room. Maggi seemed ready to come help, but that probably wasn't the wisest idea. "Can you drive?" I asked.

"I don't have my license," she said. "I'm only fifteen."

"That's not what I asked," I said. She reluctantly held out her hand and took the keys I passed. She said she'd meet us on the street just the other side of the restroom building.

Inside the john, a line of men three deep waited to use the trough urinal and pretended not to see us as I gave Albert a quick cleanup at one of the disgusting sinks.

"Mastick's kid? That you?" Albert slurred as I washed his chin and Adam's apple off with paper towels that disintegrated into slivers. When he was reasonably clean, I started us out. He was getting heavier, the less he walked of his own power. I was almost as happy to see the Chevelle idling just beyond the Midway as I was the day my dad handed over the keys.

"Take the keys and grab that cardboard from the trunk," I said. Maggi understood her job immediately. She laid them out on the passenger's seat, rolled down that window and got Albert in place on the cardboard, his mouth pointing out through the open window. She came back around, sliding in the front seat, between us.

I drove as fast as I could without breaking the law until I hit the Rez, and then wound the 454 out, the hood scoop popping up, all eight cylinders doing their thing. We glided down near Dead Man's Road at an even sixty-five, about thirty miles an hour more than I should have. The Chevelle heaved and vibrated, scoop leaning and tires skidding on broken asphalt. Clearing the bend, I cranked it back up to eighty-five 'til we hit Lewis's long driveway.

We settled Albert in on a metal lawn chair near the porch, chin down.

"It looks good," Maggi said, inspecting the cardboard. "Still want it?"

"I guess," I said, popping the trunk. She tossed the cardboard and slammed the trunk in one quick move. We flew back through the Rez, both windows down, eighty on the straightaways and down to fifty on the toughest curves, trying to blow out the lingering smell.

"Seems like you've had some practice at that," Maggi said.

"The escort service?" I laughed. "You could say that. You too."

"Could say that. Although 'escort service' means something else. Clearly, *you've* never watched late-night cable TV." She sighed, looking out the window as the Rez rolled by. "Aren't we young to be that coordinated in the transportation of drunk people?"

"Everything's relative," I said.

"All my relations," she said, a formal greeting used at a lot of Indian gatherings. We both laughed a slightly evil laugh. I liked this girl.

"How about we get back to the Field Day, find Lewis and Marie, and maybe ride some rides. Be kids again for a little while."

"Don't you mean Gloomis and Stinkpot?" she said, a little knife in her voice.

"No, not tonight," I said. I couldn't stop seeing Albert, his tongue and teeth green, with all those white people calling him a nickname that I thought was only known on the Rez.

"Maybe tomorrow," she said.

"Yeah, maybe tomorrow, maybe not," I said as we neared the border of our homeland, and headed back to the chrome and neon. She laughed the laugh again that I was already falling for. Hard.

8

Sleepless Night
Magpie Bokoni

The closer we got to the Field Day, the more this boy Carson's mood soured.

"I can't believe it!" he'd say, and punch his steering wheel. The car swerved when he did. "I had it all planned. Why did I have to hear those Farmer Johns talking shit about Indians?"

"Plan?" I asked. I should have figured.

"I need Lewis if I'm gonna win Battle of the Bands," he said, grimacing. "He's shy, but a decent player. Not as good as me," he added, of course.

"Naturally," I exaggerated, but he didn't seem to hear I was teasing his cockiness. "Still not getting how that fits in with tonight, though," I said. His plan had the sophistication of a ten-year-old playing with superhero dolls, I swear!

"I figured, first, you know these bands are gonna play Beatles songs. Guarantee, even if it's just basic ones like 'One After 909.'" I nodded, and I even knew that song. I always recognized the Beatles on the radio, hits anyway, but now anytime they came on, Lewis automatically made a point of noting it. "I figure, if Lewis saw these lame other local bands—playing Beatles songs *and* getting paid!—he'd grow a pair of balls to join when—sorry, didn't mean to say balls."

"I'm familiar with the male anatomy, thank you," I said.

"Not from what I hear," he said, laughing. So my virgin status had gotten around.

"So why would you wanna join a band by watching crappy bands anyway? How does *that* work?" His logic was so flawed; it didn't take anyone else's desires into account. "Seems like he'd *really* never get onstage if he saw other people screwing it up."

"You might understand some male anatomy, but not that part. A guy? If he thinks he can outshine another guy? Will *for sure* try. Or if he thinks people got his back. Like that shithead Plaid-Shirt Man!" he said, suddenly punching the dash enough to rattle the gauges.

"Okay, forget about him. Seriously, I don't know about that plan," I said, but I suddenly pictured Lewis wrestling because I'd teased him. I hadn't really thought he'd do it (but I also hadn't thought Jim would jump in). I'd figured Dave would take it easy and Lewis would feel like he belonged.

"Albert could take that Plaid-Shirt asshole in a second, even if he's a little funny. But that guy was all Beer Muscles. He knew Albert made a big mistake." He hissed disapproval. I looked at him puzzled.

"In the *Book of Responsible Drinking for Indians*," he explained, letting off the gas as we left the Rez. "Lesson Number One? *Never* go into a bar with your ass exposed. If you're alone, you're cooked. Especially when you're the only Rez Indian in a tent full of white guys." Carson rapid-fire punched the dash, as if just thinking about that Beer Tent demanded release. This boy had a rage inside of him that even the best joke couldn't simmer.

"There's even places around here that have No Indians signs up on the door. *Right now!*" I'd seen signs in the city like that. My mom had driven us around when we moved, warning us about neighborhoods. And if we ever saw a No Indians sign, we were not to press the issue.

We got back to the Farmer John Dealie, but of course, we had a worse parking spot. When we finally made it to the Midway, we saw

Lewis and my sister in the distance at the milk can game, watching some fool losing his money.

"Can I ask you something? For real? No bull?" I looked into his eyes, serious. "My sister told me that you and Lewis don't always get along." Marie had in fact said that Carson might blow Lewis off entirely, or that he might abandon us tonight if he felt like pranking Lewis.

"We been friends since kindergarten," he said. I gave him an *oh, please!* look. "Okay. Not the *whole* time, but we're from the same place. You know what that means or you wouldn't have come to the Beer Tent in the first place."

Maybe this was a good learning experience, since I was going to be here for the foreseeable future. I held his gaze.

"And truth?" he added. "Even people I don't speak to on the Rez? I woulda gone in. No one ever has our backs except another one of us. It's why so many Indians join these volunteer fire companies."

We joined Lewis and Marie, migrating to the rides. It felt like days had gone by. Marie insisted that the Trabant was the ride we should go on. The fiberglass cars rocketed us on a giant disk, heaving and tossing us into each other while Top 40 blasted out of mounted speakers, first forward, then backward. Lurching, you felt yourself falling. My head rattled, disoriented. A relieving distraction. We rode a few more rides and made our way to the bandstand, but after three shit bands, we made *Let's Blow This Pop Stand!* Eyes at each other and left. Those "musicians" had clearly spent their preshow time waiting in that awful Beer Tent. They were all sloppy and got worse the longer they played.

"I'll bet you fifty dollars Lewis is not inspired to join your band after that," I said, tugging on Carson's sleeve as Lewis and my sister wandered ahead.

"You're on," he said. "You don't know him." His voice was so cocky that I regretted the level of my bet (though I hadn't shaken on it). "But let's make *this* the bet. If I win, I take you to dinner at John's Flaming Hearth." This was one of two fancy restaurants in all of Niagara Falls.

"How's that a win for you?" I asked, realizing he was suggesting (in a super-clumsy way) that we go out on a date. From what little I knew of Rez culture, this was maybe the whitest White-Boy thing he had ever done. Before I could react, he shook my hand to seal the deal.

"Hey! You guys," he said, letting go and running up. "The Chevelle's this way."

"No, it's not," Lewis said. "You parked by the Fried Dough stand. Remember? Maggi headed there like it was a magnet and she was stuffed with iron filings."

"I, uh," Carson started, but was clearly at a loss. All evening, he had proven not at all to be the slick and smooth guy Marie had prepared me for. Maybe *she* was the one who really didn't know Rez Life.

"I asked Carson to run me back home for something," I said, which wasn't much better (since I was clearly holding exactly zero objects).

"What?" Lewis was all about the Eee-ogg. He just had to know *everything.*

"A Kenny Skoal pad," I said, knowing he'd be embarrassed. Kenny tried to shock me sometimes at work, wiping Skoal drip off his chin with a maxi pad he pulled from a box in the ladies'. It worked, Lewis turned red, got in the car, and Marie followed behind him.

"You remember the school?" Carson whispered in my ear.

"Duh," I said. "They don't wipe your memory when you move off the Rez."

"Meet me there in fifteen minutes, if you really want to know more about the ins and outs of Rez Life. Is that enough time to get from your house?" I found myself nodding to Carson.

After we got dropped off, Marie crept quietly into the Shack, touching up her Old-Lady-Bingo Lipstick and borrowing my eye shadow as quick as she could. She was careful to dodge the creaks in our living room floor.

"Already in bed," Marvin said in his patented bored voice from the living room, carving a little soapstone person. He was watching

Land of the Giants. The stranded little people on this show, for some reason, were helping a giant failed jazz trumpeter fool other giants into believing he had skills. They were always getting stuck in predicaments that played to the strengths of the show's stars, whether or not that kind of story made sense in a show about humans stranded on a planet of paranoid conspiracy-minded giants.

Marie cared less about that story than I did, picking up the phone. Before she could dial Mystery Man's number, though, I stuck my finger on the tongue, disconnecting her. She gave me a *What the Heck?* look, and I motioned her out the kitchen door.

"Listen," I said. "Carson asked me to meet him at the school in fifteen minutes."

"Roof?" she asked, like this was the most ordinary of things.

"He didn't say," I admitted, hating to confirm I wasn't nearly as slick as I pretended.

"Well, I'm going with you. Hang on." She went back in, made her call, this time waiting for her Mystery Man to pick up, making final touches to her makeup in the kitchen mirror. "Corner. Half hour," she mumbled.

"Hey, check this out," she said, holding up a cheapo threadbare T-shirt with the Beatles *Help!* album cover printed on it. "I won it at the milk can booth. Lewis was bummed, but there was no way he was winning." No way he was winning with her either, I thought to myself. I knew what she was doing and I didn't like it, only hanging with him because "an age-appropriate reservation boy" would throw our mom off her trail. Not that it was my business to fix her messes.

"I didn't think anyone won on those scam artist games. I thought they were all rigged."

"They are, but if you show the right amount of cleavage and juice it with a little flirtation, somehow, you can knock those milk cans over with your softballs when no one else can."

"That how you landed your Mystery Man?" I asked, and she immediately gave me the *Shush!* face, still afraid our parents might hear. For someone who claimed to be such an expert in the art of deception, she sure seemed pretty nervous.

I'd gotten to believe that Sneaking Out was as much fun for Marie as whatever happened after her man picked her up. Her plans were unnecessarily elaborate, but she played them like those girls chasing Davy Jones on *The Monkees*. (She'd conveniently forgotten that even the "Arabian Princesses" on that show were played by white girls with tans.) When our parents fell asleep, she'd sneak into the living room and call Mystery Man, let it ring twice, and hang up, beginning a fifteen-minute countdown. She'd finish her makeup, climb the camper table, and go out through the skylight. I always had to hold the table for stability. It would be easier if she snuck out the door, but she didn't want to have to count on even one more person's discretion. Marvin, zoning out on the couch to *The Land of the Giants*, was a liability.

When she'd get back before sunrise, she'd tap on the window, and I'd tap back if our parents were asleep. If they were awake, I tapped twice, and she'd yell for me to help with the chemical toilet. She'd soon need something more convincing, since our mom didn't think of us as the helpful sort.

This time, Marie grabbed a few things from the kitchen and joined me. Marvin waved us out like we were flies, bugging him. "I'll tell him you're in bed if he gets up to piss, but if *Mom* gets up, you're on your own." Our dad would never burst into our room, but Marvin was right. If Dark Deanna checked, we were doomed, and he was not involving himself in that cover-up.

"So why does Carson want to see you?" Marie whispered once we got on the road. "You making promises you shouldn't be keeping?" We stepped softly to avoid nosy dogs. Occasional distant porch lights broke up the dark woods. There were no lines painted on the roads and no streetlights (they apparently went along with the other things we didn't get because we didn't pay property tax, including but not limited to: running water and sewer lines, fire hydrants, trash pickup, regular road maintenance, and police). The trees were a dense canopy. I'd never walked our road at night, and it felt like I was heading into a fairy tale where bad things awaited.

"Nothing like that," I hissed back. "I'm not the one with fewer panties in our dresser than I had in June. We . . . we saw and did something earlier, and he wants to talk about it."

"Oh, *really*?" she said, sarcastic.

"I'm not *you*," I said. "And besides, I didn't ask you to tag along. I can handle myself."

I wondered how Carson would respond if I told him that "Plaid-Shirt Man" worked with me: Skoal-Spewing Bus Garage troll, Kenny. He might really lose it if he knew that the man who got us the pitcher was Jim Morgan. I'd made Please Prayer Hands when I saw Jim behind Carson's back. I had the feeling too that Carson would want to leverage Lewis's uncle to his advantage and he was going to tell me tonight that he needed me quiet. (Not that I was eager to tell Lewis anyway.)

For all the grief I gave her, my sister did understand the world of adults better, and I wished I could count on her now. But we hadn't talked, talked for real, in months.

"How do you know where we're supposed to meet Carson? Or where *I'm* supposed to meet him and *you're* blackmailing me into taking you along?"

"Blackmailing!" she said. "Look, if Carson wants you alone, it's for a reason."

"Sounds like someone else. Mystery Man prefers meeting you alone. Care to explain?"

"Look, I've told you, there's a reason you don't know more. It's for your own good."

"That's what they all say." I walked faster. I was in better shape than her from my job. "How do I know you're not gonna wind up in a Dumpster downtown?" I asked when she caught up. "I couldn't even give the police artist a decent description. All I could say was that he liked corduroy sport jackets, tan pants, those awful blood-clot loafers, and he drives that weird car. If you want to be secretive, maybe driving a car like nobody else's *isn't* the best strategy."

"It's oxblood, not blood clot, Miss High Fashion, and I have to say, I'm regretting letting you see him even that much. And . . . I know what you mean about the car."

"You didn't *let me* see anything! I caught you," I said, then softened. Even though she was just using me tonight, I was still glad she was with me. "We used to share *everything*. Now all we share is a chemical toilet, a shower, and a couple squares of eye shadow."

"Okay, fine. I know where we're going because Carson, Lewis, and Doobie and I used to hang out at the school. Some others too. A guy named Brian Waterson, Carson feuded with him even more than with Lewis. Carson's cousin Tami too. Remember her?" I shook my head. It wasn't fair that Marie had double advantages. She had history here and a new life in that other world, even if it was a secret one. "I answered your question. Now, what'd you see tonight?"

"You know Lewis's uncle?" I figured that was a safe enough entrance.

"Frank or Juniper?" I didn't know either of those names.

"Albert?"

"That's Juniper. They call him that cause when he drinks gin, he is *destroyed*. Kind of the way they make nicknames out here. Be thankful you got an easy one, you're just gonna be MaggiPie. But if you start slinking around, it'll be emphasis on the Pie. Which you don't want Dark Deanna to catch wind of."

"You should talk, but what does Juniper have to do with drinking gin?"

"Gin, my dear girl," she said, putting on a snotty teacher voice, "is made from the juniper berry, which gives the beverage its distinct flavor and faintly blue color." I couldn't tell if this was a put-on or some new identity Marie was developing to ditch her Stinkpot one.

"Damn!" Marie said as we got to the corner the school was on.

"The fence? It's chest-high." It couldn't possibly keep anyone over six years old out.

"No," Marie said. "Not the fence," she added, jumping it. She led us toward a side entrance. I could hear a car in the distance, and she nudged me. We stood near the shrubs flanking the stone steps. She pulled a pocket watch from her shorts. "When did he say he was coming?"

"He just told me to wait here," I said. "Maybe he meant some other part of the school?"

"No, this is it." She snapped the watch lid and slid it back into her pocket.

"If Mom finds out you boosted that, you're gonna have something worse than an old nickname to worry about."

"No, of course I didn't boost it."

"Oh, it belongs to *your man*," I said, dragging the vowels in the Rezziest accent I could manage. "Engraved with 'It's Jigging Time' or something like that?" I asked, laughing.

"The one Rez slang you pick up, naturally," she said. "And, no. I'm not crass like you."

"I'm not the one sneaking out all night to go jigging some stranger."

"Only because I came along," she said. "And that's not why *we* meet late at night."

"Then why? Lie to yourself, but I'm your sister. Even I know that if a man makes you meet him only late at night, his guhn-naeht is involved. Since you gave Mom a bullshit reason for wanting to move back here for your friends, I'm guessing you and Mystery Man are more than friends. You wouldn't make that kind of jump for any regular kind of friend."

"Shut up," she said. "Or I'll leave you here. Besides, you're the one named after a jeet-nuh," she added, laughing at this tired, tired joke.

"Jeet-*neh*," I clarified for millionth time. Naming me for a bird, knowing what the Rez would do with that, was one of Dark Deanna's darkest jokes ever. "I didn't *ask* you to come."

"Yeah, but *you* didn't think to bring what I did," she said. I'd somehow not noticed the two pork chop bones in her hand that she must have dug out of the kitchen garbage.

"No thanks, I ate at the Farmer John Dealie." I laughed. My sister was so weird.

"It's not for you," she said, and stood back up. "It's in case you get stranded and have to walk. You're gonna want something to distract any dogs on the prowl. No leash laws out here."

"Hey, can I have that T-shirt you won tonight?" It would be a perfect pattern for beadworking that cover.

"I guess. I was gonna give it to Lewis for Christmas," she laughed, and then looked directly at me. "Why do *you* need some help?"

"Yes," I said. "Won't you please help me?"

"You're such a freak," she said, laughing again as we watched a car head into the picnic grove with its lights off. It might have been Carson, but you never really knew who might be out on a Friday night, and I was beginning to feel like maybe I shouldn't have come. Marie preparing for Carson stranding me wasn't exactly a plus in his column, and yet, here we were, walking into a world my sister knew better, with only a rasty pork chop bone as protection. People said the city was more dangerous, but so far, I couldn't confirm.

9

In My Life
Carson Mastick

I backed in to the picnic grove, stuffed a few things into a backpack, and headed for the bush line. At the school, Maggi and Marie popped out from shrubs where we always hid bikes.

"Nice bone," I said, eyeing up the pork chop leftovers Marie was hanging on to. "But I can probably offer you a more satisfying one." I laughed.

"You wish, gweess-gweess-Uh. What *are* we doing here?" she asked. "Before you even start, Maggi's too young to sneak out, alone. I, on the other hand . . ." she said, spreading her arms out in front of her like a magician. She'd changed to different clothes and was less sweaty than me. Making an effort always impressed. Still, she'd just called me a piglet in Tuscarora.

"I was going to show Magpie here what we used to do," I said, tapping on her real name, the one she didn't want anyone to know. If she had to learn one thing about life on the Rez, it was that there was almost no such thing as a secret, only the matter of who you heard it from. She'd blame Lewis, but I had watched Marie fill out the working paper forms for her the day they moved back. "Give her a Rez Kid history lesson. You want to go swinging from the flagpole for old time's sake?" I grinned, tugging on the flag's drawstring. "Gonna be too old pretty soon."

"Um, no thanks." Marie laughed. "Think we're already a little too old for doing that anymore." Maggi looked confused, as I'd kind of counted on.

"I wanted to show *you*," I said to Maggi, "the other part of being a nighttime Rez Kid."

"You still have *that stupid hideout*?" Marie asked, standing up on the stone railing to try peeking up at the school's flat roof. I was glad I could surprise her. "The tree's not even here anymore. How do you get up?"

"The roof? Really?" Maggi asked, doubtful. "How's your upper body strength?"

"Car," I cut in, hearing the rumble of a motor and going deeper into the shadows. Both stayed on the steps, Marie leaning on the wall, as a pickup drove past. "Coulda been seen."

"Only if they're expecting to see you," Maggi said, hopping up to join her sister. She jumped, slapping at the awning lip over the door, to see if real effort would make the difference. "*Could* you stirrup me? Think I felt something up there."

"Depends," I replied. The view from where I stood was pleasant, but I'd waited long enough. "Or I could bear-hug your thighs and lift you. How much do you weigh?"

"That is not a question you ask of a young lady, Mr. Mastick," she said.

"It is if she wants you to lift her up. I'd like to pass my next hernia physical, thank you."

"Look, you have a pretty good idea of what I weigh. You've been studying hard enough," she said. Busted. "I can get a foot in the mortar, so you'll mostly be supporting. Marie can maybe do the other foot, and lighten the load. Just do it. We don't have a ton of time." I followed her, though I'd never set a time limit. Maybe she had one?

As soon as I was in place, she lifted herself. She was much lighter than I expected. "Hah!" she yelled. "Knew it." I shushed her. As I'd anticipated, something fell lightly on me and she stepped out of my laced hands. I looked up in time to see her disappear onto the flat roof. A rope ladder dangled before me. Marie and I followed her up.

"Pull it up behind you," Maggi said as I swung my leg over. The rope ladder had been mounted carefully.

"Yours, I'm assuming," Marie said, almost disappointed.

"Of course mine. Why else would I ask you here?" I said as she stepped onto the roof.

"You asked my sister," Marie said, wandering to a secured tarp. "Yours too?"

"What d'ya think?" I said. She pulled a collapsible cane from her bag.

"Wait!" I yelled as she went for the tarp, but she didn't stop. She unsprung the cane and she stuck it in under my tarp, causing a series of loud snaps from inside.

"Mouse traps," she said. "Amateur at keeping your stuff safe." She peeked in. "Oh, rat traps. Slightly impressed."

"Wait, damn it!" I said. When my dad started getting more violent with Derek, I'd made our old rooftop hideout a legit escape. It wouldn't last to November, but it was good for now. Or it would be if these Bokoni girls didn't barge in and ruin it.

"Let's see," she said, pulling a flashlight from her bag. "Lawn chairs, sleeping bag in a zippered plastic bag. Not bad. Cooler." She opened that, and inside was a little bag, which she opened. "Bottle opener, corkscrew? Wine and fine dining, are we?" She laughed and dug back in. "Toothbrush, toothpaste, Speed Stick. Listerine. Ten pack of Trojans? Ambitious." She tossed them all back inside, stopped, unperforated two rubbers, and slid them into her shorts pocket.

"I'm right *here*," I said.

"You pretended you didn't know how to get up there so you could check me out. We can pretend just as easy that these things aren't yours," Maggi said, joining her sister. "Or I could if I didn't know you were intending this little excursion all for me. Thought you wanted to *talk*."

A tiny stab of embarrassment pierced me now that they'd made fun of my Trojans, but seeing the little square outline in Marie's pocket was intriguing. Maggi was cuter, but she was fifteen. Marie and I were both seventeen. *Still, nothing's going to happen, moron,* I told myself.

"Come here," I said. "This is what I wanted to show you. A view of the Rez like you've never seen before." I nodded out toward the way Dog Street stretched before us, porch lights occasionally dotting the tree line. "We used to think we could see the whole Rez from here. Really, you can barely see the Old Gym. The dike? Not even a hint on the horizon." A mile away sat a giant water reservoir carved out of the Rez, built by the US government for hydroelectric power. "That's land we're *never* getting back no matter how much they call it 'a lease.' Invisible, like that thievery had never happened. The world you came home to is very, very small. Everyone's gonna know your business no matter what."

"Okay, so," Maggi stage-whispered, seeming monumentally unimpressed with what I'd shown her. "You're saying I don't have anything to hide." She said it, looking at Marie. I was missing something here, but I wasn't gonna find out what it was tonight. "Now, you come over here. We don't have a lot of time."

She spread my sleeping bag on the roof, and they climbed down there, as if they'd planned this meeting instead of me. They put their arms behind their heads as pillows. I stepped up and Maggi patted the spot between them, so I grinned and sat. She gave me that face, you know the one: *Are you for real?*

"Cool. Just Rez kids hanging out," she said to Marie. "No worries this is going to turn into an after-school special about teen pregnancy?"

"Well, it *might* have been that story if I hadn't decided to come along," Marie said, and then shrugged her head and smiled, a truce.

10

This Is Not Here
Magpie Bokoni

Carson Mastick awkwardly dropped down between us, not at all the graceful rock star he wanted to be. His backpack tinkled with the distinct sound of full beverage bottles. Interesting.

"Forgot these," he said, removing Pepsis and a jacket. "Sorry," he said to Marie. "I thought it was just going to be the two of us."

"We can share," I said, taking one, twisting its cap and passing it to back to him. He took the other, twisted it, and passed it to Marie. Goofy but charming, just the same. We clinked.

"To your return," he said.

"Least you weren't trying to engage her in underage drinking," Marie said, looking at the Pepsi. Nice. Reduced to a pronoun. She nodded. "I'll toast to her not finding Party City."

"Oh, right," I said. "That's me. Party Girl." I wasn't sure which I should hate more, the way she was criticizing Carson (and by proximity, me) or the way she pretended she wasn't heading out for an all-nighter with Mystery Man while we hung on a stupid institutional flat roof (which needed repairs. Pretty soon, the classrooms were going to leak as bad as our Shack when it rained, coffee cans everywhere to catch the drips).

We were lying down, Carson in the middle. Our arms touched. He didn't move away, but I didn't lean in more. If he were more like this, he'd be okay. That Punching-The-Dashboard Nonsense was for white boys in Rebel Outsider movies.

"Maybe we could come back in a few weeks and bring Lewis," Marie said, sounding sad. "Catch those meteors he loves. The night skies out here are always something I missed."

"The city's like ten minutes away. It's the same friggin' sky!" I said.

"No, it's not," she said, not pushing. Translate: *You are a fool, Younger Sister.*

"So listen," Carson said, trying to keep an argument from forming. "Next Friday, there's this party, and I'm working part of it." I already knew about that. Lewis was not a secret keeper.

"Like a waiter?" Marie said, laughing. "This sure ain't a Rez party if there's waiters." She turned to face us and moved her leg closer to him, teasing him about his rubbers. The Taunt was one of her specialties. He was a guy of seventeen, so even a hint of sex as sad as rubbers in a girl's shorts pocket was enough to rile him. He raised his knees to hide the front of his jeans.

"Not a waiter," he said, shifting all nonchalant, as if he hadn't just done the lamest cover-up. "It's at The Bug's house. Starts at four. Just come. Not a date. I'm asking you both." He looked at me to assure me I was included. "Good to catch up, between, um, my work. I was going to invite you anyway, when I asked *you* to meet me here."

"So what's the job? Why all the mystery?" Marie asked. Carson had no idea she was the Queen of Evasions and could tell someone else trying to pull a fast one from a mile away.

"That's my concern. But this'd give you a chance to jump back in the water before the school year starts. You really want the school bus to be your Rez reentry place?"

"Good point," I said. It was going to be tough to join a new school. "But really, why all the secrecy if—what did you say? If everyone on the Rez is gonna know our business anyway?" I played along, even though I knew he was a hired musician. "Are you cooking for this party? Lewis said you've been taking home ec classes. Is that why you're being weird?"

"I signed up for home ec to speed up my lacrosse uniform repairs. Don't even think about laughing! Puts gas money in my car."

"We think that's cool that a guy knows how to sew and cook," Marie said.

"Absolutely," I said, trying to give him an out. Lewis had told me Carson felt funny that his main job was sewing. He said guys mostly took the cooking home ec since the class made its own turkey dinner, so they could Pig Out. Sewing was supposedly for girls and the occasional drama club dork, wanting to learn how to make costumes.

"Definitely cool with cooking. We knew a bunch of city deadbeats," I added. "They come into your unit, see your mom's not home, and *immediately* try to get into your cupboards."

"Magpie's just mad 'cause it's never her *drawers*," Marie said, laughing like the girls out here did.

"Friday's the Fourth, isn't it?" I still hadn't quite gotten the delivery of that Rez phrase down. I'd have to listen closer to others. "We're stuck with Vendor Table duty, but could probably come after."

"What's your job anyway? Maybe we can help?" Marie asked.

"Not unless you're secretly a decent drummer," Carson said. "Or you can talk Lewis into being more confident," he added, looking at Marie. "Seems like *you* got his undivided attention."

"He and Lewis are playing guitar at that party," I said to Marie. "Genius here thinks he's going to pressure Lewis into being a better player," I said.

"*That's* why we stood through those crappy bands tonight?" Marie asked, being fake annoyed. "To give Lewis more confidence? Stupid idea."

"Secrets are hard to keep out here," I said, throwing Carson's own lesson back at him, grinning. I hoped Marie knew I was also talking to her too. "They've been taking lessons from The Bug for a couple years. That party's just Indians."

"Still a little scary—you know," Carson added, attempting to sound impressive. Since I'd given away so much, there was no reason for him to be so mysterious. "Somebody's gonna tease you if you ain't good—but what's one more jab around here going to do?"

"Depends on the jab," Marie said seriously. She was never going to let him forget he'd saddled her with that Stinkpot name, and I couldn't blame her. "If we can swing it," she said casually, before he could launch into a defense, "we might have a drummer for you."

"Marvin? You have a kit in that little house?" That was his question?

"Water drum," Marie said.

"Like, for Socials? Just Traditional?" he asked, raising his eyebrows.

"What do you mean *just* Traditional?" I demanded. "Does it matter?" It took all I had not to whack him in the nuts at that moment. Even if going to Socials wasn't your thing, if you were part of this world, you had to respect it was a big part. (I hadn't even lived here in years, and I knew that.)

"I guess not. But for real. Is it Marvin? I haven't even *seen* this brother you two claim to have. I need a real drummer, not an imaginary one."

"He's real," Marie said, which I couldn't even believe we needed to clarify. "But why do you assume it's him?" Sharpness climbed in her voice. "If you say girls don't drum, I'm going to punch you."

"Social Singers and Drummers *are* pretty much always guys."

"That's not official," I said, assertive. "Chauvinism, plain and simple. I'm back here, so I gotta deal with the rules of this place. But there's *nowhere* it says women can't drum."

"Well, I need a *Rock* drummer. I figured you'd know that, since you knew guitars were involved. I have to play rhythm *and* sing melody because Lewis can't lead, but I need a good backbeat to do it well."

"I *knew* you were talking about a rock drummer," Marie said. "And not that it matters, but I don't even know if they'd let *you* in the door at Socials," she added. Evil. No one was barred from a Social unless they'd been drinking. And beyond that, I had an idea she was wrong about him. I bet if his mom and dad dragged him to a Traditional event and the singers were short a man, Carson *could* step up, but he was the sort who'd insist he just wasn't interested in it. "Anyway, we really do have a drummer in our family, but it ain't Marvin," my sister added.

"Sorry, I'm not inviting your dad. I know he makes drums for your Vendor Table, but this is working toward Battle of the Bands? Remember?"

"Relax. Damn! Do we have to spell it out? Maggi's the drummer."

"You were serious?" he asked, turning directly to me. "Rock or Traditional?"

"A player with a good beat is all that should concern you, desperado," I said, grinning myself. I waited and he raised his eyebrows. Apparently he could wait too. "Fine! Traditional. Our dad taught me how to play his water drums a long time ago."

"No shit!" He sounded genuinely astounded.

"Old Moccasin Dance, Stick Dance, Standing Quiver Dance," I listed.

"That's a man's dance."

"A man's *dance*, not a man's *song*. Those two things are different. *Rabbit* Dance too," I added, for emphasis, a Ladies' Choice Dance. "Drumming drew customers, so that became part of my Table duties. Made me sometimes regret picking up that first drum." I paused and looked at the stars. "Really, our ma thinks she's keeping me out of trouble by having me play."

"She wants to keep you out of trouble and moved you back *here*?" he asked, laughing, almost choking on his Pepsi. "It *is* the Rez." He was intentionally twisting what I said, and you could tell he felt sort of bad saying that, but it didn't stop him. In the few weeks we'd been back, we realized kids here had a ton more freedom than the white city kids I'd known. We could hang out, wander the Rez, do whatever. Marie said when you're a littler kid, you think all the grown-ups are watching you, and probably to a degree that's true. But according to her, once you hit high school, it was more like you had a couple hundred older brothers and sisters to party with, who wouldn't tell your mom and dad as long as you didn't get out of hand.

"It's my fault we're back," Marie said, interrupting my thoughts. "I mean, it's because of me."

"How so?" Carson asked. Just then, three long weird car horn toots came from Torn Rock. The engine would sound strange to Carson, if he registered it, but I knew that rumble.

"Damn," Marie said, jumping to her feet. "Get up, if you want help putting your stuff back." Carson looked at her with a question in his eyes, but he stood up as I did. Marie shook the sleeping bag and rolled it, sliding it perfectly under the tarp and neatly into its plastic.

"Go on," I said. "I got it." I turned to Carson. "I'll help reset the traps. We used to set them up in our apartment, after those city-boy knuckleheads prowled our cupboards." Marie nodded, smiled, and ran to the roof's edge, scrambling up the granite lip before Carson even knew what was happening.

"Where are you going?" he called after her. "What's your hurry?"

"Haven't you ever jumped off a roof before?" she said, teetering. "If anyone asks, we were up here together all night." She held up the ladder. "How you been keeping this hidden?"

"What?" he said, totally confused by how quickly things had changed.

"Relax," she said. "It'll do your reputation some good. Give Maggi a ride?" He nodded. "And nothing funny or I'll knock your teeth in." She squatted, grabbed the little wall, and heaved herself over the edge, disappearing below the granite horizon. By the time we ran to the edge, she was climbing into the weird car.

It was too dark to see well, even the car's color. I only knew that it was Mystery Man's by the boxy shape and the farting exhaust. It was familiar in its weirdness. As soon as she was in, he hit the gas, and in a jet of dirty smoke, they headed west, off the reservation.

"Never seen a car like that before," Carson said, studying it as it disappeared. It definitely was no reservation car—already, I'd begun to know the cars of everyone who lived out here. Marie, herself, would admit this car was too weird if you wanted to be stealthy, *even* for Niagara Falls. People would notice, remember it. "Who was that?"

"Marie and her Mystery Man," I said. "Don't bother. You're not getting an answer."

"What did she mean about this being her fault? *What* was her fault?"

"Our moving back here," I said, working on the tarp. "Your rig's all set. Nice up here. Thanks for asking me to meet you, but why did you? What's this got to do with Lewis's uncle?"

"Here, sit down," he said, patting the wall. A car drove by. We were out in plain sight, but of course, no one looked up here. The roof was like camouflage. "So you guys've been home a month and already she's trying to leave again?"

"Look, forget about trying to figure out my sister. She's not going to be here long enough for your discoveries to matter." I paused to smooth the irritation from my voice.

"You can say things how you want. I know that feeling. There's plenty of times my brother, Derek, drives me crazy. More than my sister, Sheila, and we never had to share a room."

"That Hamburglar business?" He struggled not to react to what I'd just said. No one had told me directly, but like Marvin and Lewis, I knew how to be invisible and listen when I wanted to. "Suit yourself," I said, clearing my throat. "It's not like my siblings are perfect."

I looked up at the sky. The starry night was a gift from the Creator. Marie would laugh at me for saying something like that, but it was true.

"So, Lewis's uncle?" I tried again, bringing us back. This long process was like being shown a map of the Rez, but in the dark, with a flashlight that only worked every so often.

"You haven't been here long. The shit that happened with Albert? It's part of Rez Life, I ain't gonna lie. Some habits are hard to break, particularly those that get handed down." What had happened to Albert? I thought if I knew, I could be a better friend to Lewis. "Albert came back from Vietnam around the time me and Lewis started school. He was always the screwed-up guy. But he was *our* screwed-up guy. Probably on disability. He gets work around the Rez."

"Off the Rez too," I said. I couldn't get that scene out of my head. If I kept my eyes open, I could block it out. But on Monday, Jim

Morgan would ask why I was in the Beer Tent. He'd be wrong in his assumptions, but it was still going to be awkward.

"Yeah, I didn't know about that," Carson said, admitting that I knew something he hadn't. "Bet he won't be working there this harvest season."

"He will," I said. "They give shit pay and only people like Albert will work for it. He doesn't fit in enough for a regular job. All kinds of guys like that in the city. Some women too."

"Really?" he said, then sighed. "No, I guess some tough Rez women work the farms like Albert. But what labor like that is in the city that a woman could do?" He put his hand up as if I were going to hit him. "I'm not even being . . . what was that word? Chauvinist? Just reality. A man's stronger."

"You think hookers do it for perks?" I laughed. Not that it was something to laugh at. In the city, I'd seen women who were clearly prostitutes, and their lives did not look pretty.

"You are twisted." He laughed a little too. "But it's a kind of twisted I like."

"You like my twistedness well enough to offer me that job as drummer?"

"Can you keep a backbeat on a Social drum? Ever tried it on old hillbilly tunes and blues riffs? That's all we're playing."

"Drum's a drum. It's what you do with it that matters," I said. I figured it might sound a little weird with guitars, but I could make it work. "And you know this already but just to be clear. All the drums I use personally? They're Social Drums. Once we've taken one through ceremony, it never sees the light again outside of ceremony."

"Nothing more social than a party at The Bug's," he said, grinning, trying to ease off. "Like I said, it'll be a good Rez decompression for you."

"All right, I'm in, but only if you're straight with me. Why did you bring me out here anyway? I'm guessing you didn't know I was a drummer at all." He nodded, though I had to wonder, considering the way he said there were no secrets out here. "And you clearly didn't have much new to tell me about Lewis's uncle that you couldn't have said before we got back to the Farmer John Dealie." He shrugged.

"I wanted you to come *here*," he said, "because Marie used to do this with us, before you guys left. You're *always* gonna see shit like what happened with Albert. That's our life. You might even be on the receiving end." I pictured Liz, at the garage, who had clearly already arrived at conclusions about me that had nothing to do with me personally. "The most you can do is rise to the occasion for your community."

"I think I get it," I said.

"You probably don't. Not yet, but it's a beginning. I'm not trying to be ignorant here. I mean, I don't know what life *off* the Rez is like, but I'm sure it's different."

"Yup, it is different. That's a word for it." I thought long and hard here for a moment. This was going to get trickier.

I hadn't had any say in our moving back to the Rez, but I was stuck here just the same, and kind of all alone. Even though we were back, our dad was almost as scarce as when we lived in the city (perhaps like us, afraid to say whatever wrong words invoked the emergence of Dark Deanna). Marvin had seamlessly drifted from the city couch to the Rez one, and Marie was plotting her course, launching herself back out of our world one step at a time (using logic that totally eluded me). And I just could not figure out what kept Carson and Lewis hanging out. Not only that—I couldn't even tell which of them would tell me a more accurate version of that story.

"Carson, I don't know you well," I started. "Almost not at all, in fact."

"We can change that situation very easily. You're here now. Back where you belong. Perfect chance for us to—"

"Keep it in your pants." I wanted that to be a joke, but the truth was that he'd planned to bring me here alone tonight (where he kept a handy strip of Trojans and a sleeping bag at the ready). "Your plan about Lewis doesn't make that much sense." He started to protest, but I held up my hand to shush him. "Believe what you want, but I'm telling you. I don't know either of you too well, but it sure seems stupid to me. Has the idea of loyalty ever come into your head?"

"What do you think I've been saying here?"

"You keep saying that, but you don't want to be loyal. You just want others to be loyal to you. Those are different things. What does Lewis get out of this, if it goes forward?"

"A trip to New York City, if we win the Battle of the Bands."

"That's your dream."

"That's what you don't understand. John Lennon lives in New York City," he said, jabbing his left palm with his right hand with each word. "The Beatles are his dream—they're what he still cares about most."

"And you think you and Lewis are just going to walk up to John Lennon's door and say, 'Hi, we dropped by, maybe we could jam?' "

"Ha! Well, no." He started walking back to the tarp. "But it ain't as big a stretch as you might think. Here, check this out." He lifted one part, exactly, sliding out a rubber tote like the ones we used for the Vendor Table. He popped the lid, removed some clothes (an emergency change?), and lifted off a fake bottom, pulling out a sealed waterproof case. He handed me a laminated newspaper article with some photos of (according to the caption) John Lennon, his wife Yoko Ono, and some Indians from the Onondaga Rez, just outside of Syracuse.

"When was this?" I asked. It was too dark to read the small newspaper type.

"Maybe ten years ago? Was a big deal. Yoko Ono's first American art show, or something like that. A bunch of people from here went. A bunch of Eee-ogg that there was gonna be some big secret Beatles reunion concert, 'cause it was John Lennon's birthday. Of course, it didn't happen, but somehow, they ended up hanging out at Onondaga. Here's the thing from her art show." He handed me a newspaper thing titled *This Is Not Here*, printed with a bunch of articles about her work. I didn't know she did the kind of stuff I was interested in.

"Can I borrow this?" I asked. I wanted to be able to read it, to see what someone who really did "conceptual art" had to say about it.

"Sorry," he said, shaking his head. "My dad's. He'd kill me if he knew I had it. He went."

"Did he meet them?"

"Nah, because of the Eee-ogg, there were like ten thousand people standing in the rain, trying to get in *an art show*." He started laughing, taking the materials from my hands and putting them back in the tote. "Probably the most people at one time who tried to get into something like that show." As he lifted the tote's fake bottom, I caught a glimpse of something hidden beneath.

"Is that what I think it is?" He paused and then reached in, pulling out a beaded trucker cap, sealed inside a Ziploc. "The famous hat," I said, taking it. The beadwork design was okay, nothing fancy. Bland. It didn't look like anyone's signature style. That was good. "These used to be okay sellers for us. Local demand died out once that news story broke. No one wants to get pulled over for wearing the wrong cap."

"Yup, the famous cap. Straight from my crazy Hamburglar house." He situated the fake bottom, stacking the clothes on top, and slid the tote back with the hat inside. "Couldn't bear to throw it out, though I should have. My gramma made it for my dad, and he'd been letting Derek wear it."

I stood up and walked back about fifty feet. "So we gonna do this?" I hadn't ever jumped from a roof before.

"I guess," he said, looking glum and maybe scared. I walked to the edge and stood near him. The bold Carson Mastick, scared of a jump my sister had made without a second thought. "I always climbed down the tree. That asshole custodian Billy must have cut it down this week."

I looked over the edge. It was maybe twelve feet, and if I didn't land right, I'd hit the concrete sidewalk, risking my ankle. But we couldn't stay there forever. That was when I saw something that was so totally Marie.

"Truth?" he said, smiling in a shy smile I'd never seen before. Maybe it was an act or maybe it was the real Carson finally showing through. "If I came here by myself tonight, I probably would have climbed down the rope ladder and tossed it back up and hoped no one would spot it. I need somewhere to go that's not my crazy house."

"You ready to jump?" I asked, trying to sound light. "If Marie could do it, and I'm willing to do it, how hard would it be for you?" I smiled, letting him know I appreciated what he'd told me and that I wasn't going to pry. He could tell me more when he felt like it.

"Yeah, how hard?"

"You gonna give me a ride home so I don't have to carry those home with me?" I pointed below. On the ground was the little baggie that Marie had left for me, with the pork chop bone and wet paper towels. She was still looking out for me, even when she was gone.

"Do I get to keep the bone?" he asked.

"Looks like you might need it. Seems like you've lost the one you had there, isn't it?" I said, looking at the crotch of his jeans, unable to resist. We both laughed. That wasn't something I could have said to Jim Morgan without him interpreting it as a green light, but here with Carson, I could joke about the advertising he was doing and he could take it. I left him there, still coughing a little laugh, as I got a good running start. "Coming?"

"Not even close," he said. "Just breathing a little heavy." We both laughed again. I was finally getting this reservation humor. We took a running charge, side by side now. The stone wall grew closer as we ran, but lower, more manageable, becoming just another horizon over the black night sky. We put our hands on the cool granite, launched our legs over the edge and let gravity take its course.

PART TWO
Mind Games

Fourth of July (Independence Day)—
Border Crossing
Blueberry Moon

11

Instant Karma! (We All Shine On)
Carson Mastick

The Bug didn't want Lewis and me thinking we were guests, so we were supposed to show two hours late to the party. I drove up to Lewis and Albert's to pick them up, deciding that I wouldn't mention Maggi unless she showed. In the driveway, Albert was waiting and gave me a *Thanks for Helping Me Out* nod you got when you gave someone a ride in shitty weather. Then he reverted to his old self as we stepped inside, disappearing upstairs. Maybe he didn't want a reminder of his playing Beer-Tent Stallion for warm Budweiser foam.

Lewis was sitting on the couch, practicing some transitions on his acoustic. He wiped it down when he saw me and grabbed his case, glancing at the clock.

"Ready?" Albert asked Lewis, coming downstairs in a new shirt. He stopped at the fridge, grabbing a chill pack of Bud. A gift for The Bug.

"Thought I'd pick you two up," I said, "since we're all carrying stuff to the same place."

"We'll just walk," Albert said. "It's close enough and a little too crowded in your jitney."

"All right, well, I can walk with you guys," I said, a generous offer. "If you don't mind."

"Free road," Albert said. I'd gotten him out of that Beer Tent, but he still didn't trust me. That went way back and applied to my whole family—too many times of my dad paying him after completed work, in cheap beer and venison from our freezer instead of cash.

I passed my guitar case to Lewis, grabbing my backpack and a large cardboard box, and we headed down the road. Caesar, a friendly mutt between Lewis's place and The Bug's, ran up and sniffed Albert's hand, nosed Lewis in the balls, and then licked my boots. He walked with us for a couple houses, then retreated. "All you gotta do," Albert said. "If they don't smell fear, they leave you alone."

"And admit it," I said to Lewis, laughing. "You liked getting a little nudge just now."

"Yeah, I love when a dog's teeth are an inch away from my private business."

"No fear," Albert said. "What you gotta remember, with the maybe dangerous kind."

"The last time I did that," he said, narrowing his eyes, "I lost my academic standing."

"Dropping out of school for a few weeks will do that to you," Albert said. "Four years on, you're still letting that bully get the best of you." I felt like I was entering the middle of a conversation that had started without me. Lewis didn't speak much about the bad way he ended junior high. After that bully craziness ended, he was too far behind to catch up to where he'd been. Now, he was probably below 200, maybe even closer to 250, out of a class of 350. I was way way down, maybe around 330, but we had different goals.

"Good thing you got that job," Albert added. I was surprised *he* was jabbing Lewis. That was *my* role. "You think there's a chance they'll keep you on? Any openings?"

"Not a one," Lewis said. Lazy workers refused to retire from jobs with great benefits.

"Then maybe you should get back to looking into colleges," Albert said when silence had passed. He wasn't letting up. Maybe I'd jabbed something awake in him at the Sanborn Field Day, or maybe

Mr. Plaid-Shirt Man had. "Either that or the military, and you don't want that—"

"Yeah," Lewis said, interrupting his uncle, which almost never happened on the Rez. "Don't want to risk getting a Section 8." No one mentioned Albert's discharge from Vietnam to his face. Most of us didn't even know what that was. My mom said it meant you couldn't cope.

Albert didn't respond to that, so we walked in silence until we neared The Bug's house. I never asked Lewis how he and Albert dealt with each other's privacy with their beds a yard apart. As Lewis got older, that little bedroom must have seemed more cramped for those two, and lately, helping Derek, I was thankful our dad had made sure all of us had our own bedrooms.

From the road, we could finally hear The Bug's crowd and smell the corn-roast fire. Food was an hour away, and I put the conversation between Lewis and Albert out of my mind—we had to work to do. I recognized usuals I partied with on Moon Road streaming in with us. This party would be like those, after dark, and we'd have to be on our game.

If the chemistry was right, The Bug might break out a kerosene lantern, and we'd play into the shadows. I'd practiced like crazy since my dad told me I'd be joining Lewis, and was good enough that The Bug might let me pick songs tonight, even if I had to tell Lewis chords and changes. I wanted him to see he could stay on top of things with pressure on.

When we stepped into the crowd behind the house, people were setting up folding tables and pans of potato salad, hamburgers, and the usual picnic crap. It was a corn roast, but how far were ears of corn going to take us? Albert's and Lewis's hands looked decidedly empty next to everyone else, with just two guitars and twelve cans of warming beer. They both had Basset Hound faces, and that was where my plan came in.

"Lewis, here, tear this tinfoil off," I said, pointing with my lips to the box I carried. He did so at the food tables, while Albert unloaded the chill pack into an ice chest. I revealed my mom's specialty: long rows of Scon-Dogs, always a hit. You fry hot dogs up in a skillet, wrap them in Frybread dough, and dump them into the same skillet with a pool of lard. The dough browned up like a beautiful Frybread. Off the Rez, they looked like lumpy breadsticks, but at a party like this, they were homing beacons.

Though the Fire Hall events ignored Frybread, it was universal Indian food at everything else we went to. It didn't take much: flour, water, baking powder, a cast-iron skillet, and enough oil to pour a half inch in the pan. Some wiseass Rez elders making Frybread for public consumption always claimed that you mixed the ingredients and kneaded the dough until all the dirt under your fingernails had worked its way out—another kind of "dirty joke" on the Rez.

My dad had volunteered to bring the tray of food, but I'd said I wanted to. Which had been smart—everyone was ooing and aahing over my mom's Scon-Dogs and no one noticed that Lewis and Albert hadn't brought a dish. That would buy me some Rez points with Lewis.

"Check this out, Bug," I said, pulling a little amp from my back-pack and jacking it in, motioning for Lewis to pull my guitar out. We had made our way to the porch The Bug was using as a stage and joined him. Someone had dragged out one of his kitchen chairs, and he sat right in the center. He'd put on a button-up shirt but it gapped at the belly, and as always, his work pants were a little short, so you could see the mismatched, pale wooden shin under the white sock. This was some signature look of his. I bet if he ever got a replacement prosthetic that was the right color, people would find that more distracting.

The amp wasn't fancy, a little mesh-front box with a big, round knob at its center. The Bug stretched the strap over his head and frowned, holding my Epiphone Casino. It was a hollow body, with F-holes. He strummed a few chords, but it didn't carry without amplification. As he tuned it by ear, he looked at the snaking bundle of orange extension cords trailing from his sister's house next door, all spoken for with Crock-Pots, coffee makers, that kind of stuff.

"Don't worry about that," I said, flipping a switch on the little amp. "Now try."

The Bug strummed an open G. The crisp, quacky sound rang out from the little amp. It wasn't as dramatic as Dylan going electric at the Newport Folk Festival where all kinds of liars claimed to have been at, but it was startling enough at The Bug's electricity-lacking house. It sounded exactly like an amp should, but in the back, there was no electrical cord trailing out.

"It's a Pignose," I said, " 'cause the only knob is this fat, round one out front. On, off, and volume." I nodded, like I was telling myself. "Battery operated. Genius!" I added, like anyone with half a brain could have guessed. "My dad got it last week. Thought it'd be perfect for today. Speaking of Pignoses," I said, turning to Lewis, "you got a date tonight for your own fireworks?"

"Do you?" Lewis said, up in my face. "Maybe Caesar the Dog can nose *your* nuts for you." My lifelong wish might be coming true, if inconveniently. Lewis was growing some balls.

"Don't like that one," The Bug said, scrunching his face up at the pickup settings. "Sounds like I stepped on a duck with my bad leg." Anyone listening mumbled a laugh at The Bug's joke. You never mentioned his wooden leg in front of him, but if he made a joke, you were supposed to laugh to show you were comfortable.

"Try this one," I said, flipping a toggle. When The Bug strummed that same open G, the sound was soft, like a sonic milk shake drooling down the steps.

"Say, now that's a purty sound." The Bug grinned and played a lazy run up the fret board and back. Every once in a while, he'd throw in a word in a goofy fake southern accent, like he was suddenly on *Hee Haw*. "Leave that," he added, playing a few more riffs.

We were on our way.

12

Midsummer New York
Magpie Bokoni

July was the weirdest month for Indians in our part of the world—particularly if you weren't sure where you fell on the What Kind of Indian Am I? Scale. You could be a Hang-Around-the-Fort Indian, a Gung-Ho-Righteous-Red-Power Indian, or the kind most of us were: a These-Boxes-Are-Too-Rigid-for-My-Real-Life Indian. Every kind played out in July, starting with two of the three stupidest holidays for Indians.

Since our Rez was outside Niagara Falls, the US-Canada border complicated everything. On top of *that*, we were here before this land was considered two separate countries, so most of us had relatives on both sides. *And* we had a treaty with both sides, acknowledging that fact. (Yes, it's a little weird that I'm talking shit about history, national holidays, and international law.)

But if you're Indian, it's your job to know our treaties with the US and Canada. You ask any Indians from here about the Jay Treaty (free crossing between the US to Canada) or the Porter Agreement (granting our Vendor Tables inside the State Park), and they'll give you the details. Our relatives died fighting for them. Not some My-Ancestors-Came-Over-on-the-Mayflower relatives. Real relatives, whose bodies have turned into fertilizer in our cemetery on the Torn

Rock. When those names are connected to *you* in a straight line, *you* remember.

I saw sad immigrants taking citizenship tests on TV every year. All these panicking people with number-2 pencils, coloring in bubble tests, hoping to prove they're up to citizenship. The kids in my class, who've been taking social studies for ten years, writing *Who LUVS Whoever 4EVR* instead of notes, couldn't pass that test. None of them could tell you the Bill of Rights. Most of them only passed ninth-grade social studies (writing out the preamble to the Constitution) by singing the song from *Schoolhouse Rock!* to themselves. We ignored that dumb cartoon (where Indians were largely absent from the cartoon United States mapped out on our weekend TVs). For real, though, we weren't as far removed from the United States or Canada as we'd like to pretend. Which was what made July so weird for us.

Our calendar skews, like the tilted globes in social studies classrooms. We had cousins celebrating Victoria Day the same time we had Memorial Day. They had Canada Day on July 1st while we went to fireworks on the Fourth, pretending to celebrate "Independence Day."

I kept telling my mom that white America's independence wasn't the best day to sell Indian souvenirs, but Dark Deanna wasn't a listening kind of mom on the best days. Her ideas were *always* right, no matter how wrong. During the Bicentennial, she'd made Independence Day–themed beadwork. She backlogged a bunch of 1776–1976 beaded picture frames, but instead of the raised flowers and birds we usually beaded onto them, she had us bead "fireworks" on them. She didn't understand that fireworks, at their core, were *about* the way they vanished. Their lights, blazing across the sky, usually burning out before we even heard the sound.

Our beaded explosions — red, white, and blue beads shaped like fireworks — were epic failures. The red and blue ones were almost invisible against the black velvet, and the white ones looked like wilted daisies. We sold exactly one, to a vacationing anthropologist.

We spent the next week snipping and collecting the beaded dates (each 1776 was red, each dash was blue, and each 1976 was white). And three years later, we were still trying to sell Fourth of July fireworks picture frames and they were moving about the way you'd expect. Every year, Marie and I offered to pull out the fireworks or make a new pattern, anything to avoid dragging that sad tote out every July 1st. But it had become a point of pride with our mom.

With these loser frames, I was going to be hard-pressed to get to Carson's party gig.

I couldn't even hope for rain, since that would torpedo the party before I could get there. I didn't even know how we were getting home, and I couldn't call Carson from a pay phone. He said The Bug had no running water, no electricity, and for sure no phone. Maybe I could show him my drumming skills another time. (Bonus! Water drums were way more portable than even the most basic rock drum kit.)

"Magpie," my mom said as the five-thousandth tourist ignored us. "Get out your drum and sing us a song? Can you do 'Stars and Stripes Forever'? I heard you practicing to the radio."

"My throat's dry?" I said, unable to keep the question mark out of my lie.

"You're not sure?" she said, giving me her Dark Deanna X-Ray Eyes.

"Not sure if it would hold up," I said (I'd recently developed a lead blanket to her X-ray vision, like at the dentist's). "We're out of anything to drink. Cooler's just about empty."

"I filled it this morning!" she said, stunned and outraged. Translation: *I'd be damned if I'm giving up on those frames without an honest try.*

"See for yourself," I said. I'd snuck water, poured the cups into the grass, and refilled.

"I'll take the cooler down to the snack bar fountain," Marie said, the most helpful she'd been in years. I looked around and spotted her Mystery Man on the horizon instantly. Maybe she'd forgotten to let

him know that I recognized him. Lately I'd even seen him boldly reading on a bench in front of us, not fifty yards away. I'd been studying him in the light and realized that he looked almost familiar, but just not enough for me to get it.

"Oh no you're not," our mom said, untrusting. "We can get it together. I might even buy some snack-bar hot dogs. Traditional American food!" she said, laughing. She offered lots of reasons I might wish to be an orphan, but she never played down her evil sense of humor around us, and I almost admired her commitment to her harsh brand of being a parent. "What you want on yours, Magpie?"

"Don't go to any trouble just on my account," I said, and she gave me a look I couldn't quite interpret. Maybe disappointment, like I was supposed to love being her sweatshop worker.

The two of them walked away, the cooler between them. They were definitely going to get annoyed looks from the snack bar workers, though if my mom thought they treated her with less respect than the previous customer, she'd let them know. I always suggested she was inviting Snack-Bar Worker Spit, but she said we had to call attention if we weren't treated with the respect anyone else got.

Mystery Man closed his book and put it in his leather shoulder bag. Even beat up, it still looked like the oversized handbags Bingo Ladies lugged around, and I doubted most Niagara Falls men would use one. He got up fake casually, heading to the snack bar, following my sister.

"Hey," I said when he was within Loud-Voice-This-Side-of-Shouting range. He pretended not to hear me. "Hey!" He looked, acting like he was just noticing me for the first time. "Purse Man. Come here!"

"Can I help you?" he asked, all innocent.

"I doubt it, but I can help you."

"Really?" he said, and he couldn't keep condescension out of his voice. Or maybe I just recognized the tone, since so many of our customers used it as a default to haggle.

"Don't take that tone with me. I know who you are." I was shocked to hear Dark Deanna's voice coming out of my mouth, like storm clouds. She was possessing me—all those years being forced to speak her stupid scripts must have taken their toll.

"Look, I can—" he started to say.

"You're Marie's man. Her Mystery Man," I said, interrupting him. What he would have said could have been useful, but wading through a performance was not a priority for me at the moment.

"Okay, Magpie," he said, smiling easier, clearly understanding I didn't know his name.

"So come on up here and let me show you what you're interested in," I said, digging in the dreaded bicentennial tote. No time for niceties. I was too concerned with getting my butt away from this Vendor Table and, ironically, back to the Rez.

13

Norwegian Wood (This Bird Has Flown)
Carson Mastick

"Let's the three of us do one of those songs you like so much," The Bug said, looking at Lewis. "Them Crickets."

"Beatles," Lewis said automatically. "The Crickets is Buddy Holly."

"Crickets, Beatles. No bedbugs or crabs?" Again, laughs, but fewer people acknowledged they'd heard that joke. Any of them could be The Bug's next target. When it was just us, he was patient—walking us through transitions, lifting one, then another finger. He called that the Slow-Motion Jump, having us move our left-hand positions as slowly as possible, then gradually speeding up—but on days like this, he was more like me, busting Lewis's chops.

"Lewis ain't familiar with crabs," I added. Big mistake, and the grumped-up look on The Bug's face showed it. He did not need a straight man, especially at his own house, where he was always the center of attention. Lewis just stepped back, as I tried a save by doubling down. "You gotta find some girl to actually want to sleep with you for—"

"Here," The Bug said, flicking the amp off. "Put this away. We don't need an electric. Lemme have my gee-tar." Lewis lifted The Bug's acoustic while The Bug passed my Casino back. As I cased it, Lewis gave The Bug his guitar.

"Where's the Crow?" Lewis asked, pulling out his own guitar. I didn't know the story, but like Old Man Gray's Magpie that stayed in his living room, The Crow was tame, and lived in this enormous cage outside The Bug's house. It often flew around on its own, but any time it was out, the cage door was left open for its return.

"Went back to its crow family," The Bug said. There was more to that story than I was probably ever going to hear. "Now what you want to play?" he asked Lewis. "You choose the first song." The more songs we racked up, the more often he asked what we wanted to play when we practiced with him, but neither of us had ever had the choice when we had an audience. "Hurry up, or I change my mind."

"What's this all about, Bugger?" my dad said, coming up to the porch. His eyes were red and watery, even though it was only three in the afternoon. That had been happening more lately. "You and me had a deal. My boy's got a party to play later this summer, and this was gonna be his first run with a crowd. That other one's Crhee-rhu-rhit. Can't have him messing up in front of them."

"Shoulda learned to keep his mouth shut here, then," The Bug said. "Can't jab your own band members and expect them to play decent. This here's *my* band."

Lewis and The Bug, standing together, didn't look like much of a band, but I'd said enough.

"You remember this," my dad hissed at The Bug, heading to the lawn chairs where I'd just sat down. "Get up, Carson," he said, yanking me out of the chair and kicking it closed. I sprang up, pretending that hadn't just happened, and hoping everyone else would do the same. My dad stomped away to his truck, taking my guitar and amp with him.

Were they smart enough to not cross my dad? Most were, with one exception.

"Bug?" Albert said, leaning in. "Don't you think you might should rethink that?" He paused. "There's no way me or Lewis can give you rides." The Bug shook his head and asked Lewis again what song. Albert turned and followed my dad, but I stayed and couldn't hear what they were saying.

The Bug started in on "Norwegian Wood," one of Lewis's favorite Beatles songs. It seemed just too obvious, since it was partly about a fleeing bird, but that was Lewis, all over. The Bug usually pushed him to join in harmony way up the fret board to sound like a sitar, but Lewis considered it a success if he sounded like a decent regular guitar, and he'd never even made it all the way through. Still, The Bug started with the melody today, and Lewis had no choice but to try picking the lines we'd been shown.

Over by the truck, my dad was still packing up the junk he lugged with him to almost any party—his own cooler, a cushion for his lawn chair, anything that set him just a little apart. After Lewis stumbled with the intro, I saw Albert reach into the pickup and grab the Casino and amp. He brought them back to the porch and handed them to me without a word. I flicked the pig's nose, switched the toggle to the quacky sound, and did what I was supposed to. Lewis switched back to the steady rhythm, the part he was smooth as silk on.

We sounded like a stereo and people sang, remembering words, or singing wrong words, and by the end, that tension had passed. Lewis's aunt peeled foil back from tins, and people grabbed plates. When we finished with "Norwegian Wood," The Bug jumped right into "All Together Now," alternating it with "Ten Little Indians," which everyone laughed at, pretending they didn't know the song's origins.

With every new song after that, The Bug went solo, giving no warning on what he was jumping into next. It took me a bit to pick up what he was doing by recognizing chords, so I didn't sound as polished as I wanted in the beginning of each. He was smacking my snout with a newspaper for being a wiseass. Sometimes he did this during lessons too—if I complained in asking about a tough song, he'd sigh and say, "Just like this." Then he'd jam by himself for twenty minutes. When he finished, he'd ask if I had it any better.

Still, I was grateful for the opportunity. A thrown-together band and a bunch of hungry and mildly buzzed cousins and acquaintances weren't what I had in mind, but it was a start. Carrying a show by myself was the goal.

A couple songs later, we moved into some Roy Orbison songs, because The Bug liked to show off his yodeling falsetto. I was glad most of those songs could be played stripped down using the same three or four chords, so I didn't even have to wait for The Bug's nod to switch. A few songs later, Albert started walking toward The Bug with a plate and a cold Bud, and before he was done crossing the lawn with the goods, The Bug had his guitar off and they made a swap. Perfect timing. I was starving and Scon-Dogs were on almost every plate. In a few minutes, an empty tin was all that would be left.

"Okay," The Bug said, stopping me before I could unplug. "I'm eating. You guys are on. Half hour. Hope your calluses are tough enough."

Lewis grinned at me and immediately started strumming and singing "We Can Work It Out," leaving me to catch up. Normally, I'd have been pissed at him grandstanding, but I just jumped in with him. This was one of those Beatles songs that shouldn't have made sense, totally ditching the verse/chorus/verse/chorus structure for something like two choruses jammed together, and yet, you couldn't imagine it any other way. I took over on the Lennon half, and we sounded pretty good.

So far, Maggi and Marie had been no-shows, so right now, Lewis was rhythm, period. But by the time we were closing the first song, Hubie Doobie arrived, minus his bass. When we finished that song, he grinned, holding up a bright orange caution cone someone had stolen. He lifted it to his mouth and nodded. He had a decent baritone and sang a few bars into the rubber megaphone, imitating a bass. It wasn't perfect, but it would work. Some people even gave war whoops.

We kicked into the logical next song, "Day Tripper," the flip side of the "We Can Work It Out" 45. You wouldn't think that an acoustic guitar, a battery-powered electric guitar, and an injection-molded traffic cone could give a big enough sound, but Lewis had always insisted that was the Beatles' magic in the first place—it worked any way you tried it. We were supposed to be background music, but people stopped standing in the food line to watch.

There would probably be nothing but picked-over scraps when those people were done in line, but I didn't care. We were taking off, in ways I could have never imagined. If Maggi made it, we'd have a full rhythm section. I hoped we all knew "Jugband Blues" because we'd have to start taking requests pretty soon. Oddly enough, I wasn't worried. I felt like we'd be up to it. We were becoming a band.

14

Straight Talk
Magpie Bokoni

"Look," I said to my sister's Mystery Man, "*you* want out of here. *I* want out of here and most important to you, *Marie* wants out of here. Following her for a quickie kiss is not the best investment of your resources. Our mom usually sees almost everything. You shouldn't even have been sitting where you were." I didn't have time or inclination for him to treat me like a kid.

"It's a park. Everyone gets the same rights to use it," he said, getting more cocky.

"Not entirely true. *We*, for example, have the right to use it to sell beadwork, and if *you* tried to use it to sell something, you would be slapped with a Cease and Desist."

"You seem to know an awful lot about the law."

"Treaty law. Every Indian's job to remember. Most people would prefer that we didn't."

"And what treaty would that be?" he asked, expecting me not to know.

"Porter Agreement," I said, which was the absolute truth. "Far as you're concerned, quizzing me about treaty knowledge *also* isn't the best use of your resources. You've only got a couple of minutes. Now, you want a history lesson or you want to hear my proposition?"

"I suppose it wouldn't hurt."

"Marie's stuck here, like me, until our mom gives up. Might be an hour. Might be five hours. Daylight lasts a long time on the Fourth of July. One thing would speed up the process."

"I'm listening."

"Will depend on how much money you have on you."

"I have a credit card. Will that do?"

"Do you see a slider machine here?"

"Oh, this money's for you. A bribe?" I gave him an *Oh, please, man* look. "Okay, yes, I have some cash." I figured that when he picked Marie up, they weren't going to his place (his inept stealth here told me he was at least aware their relationship was a little complicated). That meant they were probably headed to one of the thousand rasty tourist motels here. And given the lengths they went to so that no one saw them meeting up, I didn't think he'd use a traceable credit card to pay for those motel rooms.

"These are beaded picture frames Marie's made." It wasn't entirely true, but I suspected he'd be more inclined to buy something Marie made rather than her sketchy family. "Our mom has some totally cracked belief that if she waits long enough, *someone* will buy them."

"Why won't someone buy them?"

"Would *you* buy them?" I asked. He picked up one of the fireworks frames, rubbed the velvet a little, touched some beads, saw the fifty-dollar tag, and set it back down, shaking his head.

"Wrong answer," I continued. "Care to try again? Would *you* buy them?"

When Marie and my mom got back, I was three whole frames lighter. I shot for five, but he was only willing to part with so much. I told my mom that I'd struck it lucky with some German tourists (our most faithful demographic after anthropologists, so she'd believe me). She seemed delighted that her persistence had paid off. As we sat there, eating our hot dogs (with requisite mustard and relish—free bonus condiments, of course), I put Stage Two into play and hoped I'd created more of a Scattered-Showers Deanna instead of full-on Dark.

"Ma?"

"Mm-hmm?"

"While you guys were away, some city friends invited me and Marie to watch fireworks. Maybe since we sold well, you'd let us go? I told them if we could, we'd meet by the Turtle." (A museum where most city Indians worked at some point. If you were a Traditional dancer or singer, you could do okay for tourists all summer. Others worked in service.)

"Who?"

"Markie and Davy Reynolds. They said their ma would drop us off at home after." The Reynolds boys were City Indians from Six Nations, so I knew they were on the other side celebrating Canada Day and wouldn't be back until Monday. I was safe claiming I'd seen them.

Our mom studied our lockbox, maybe calculating the amount of our bail if we got caught illegally on a roof. "Only hundred and twenty new dollars here," she said. "Should be one-fifty."

"I gave the Germans a bulk discount," I said, which was just what our mom did, if business was slow. I'd given the Mystery Man the discount, in exchange for something our mom didn't need to know about.

"All right, get out of here. Marvin's coming with our ride in an hour. He can help me pack up." I thanked my mom, trying not to sound too excited. Marie didn't even have to act subdued. She'd noticed that her man was gone and was clearly not looking forward to the Reynolds brothers. I felt bad that Marvin got stuck with the shit job at the end of the day, but he had all day free at home while we were here, chained to the Table. "No monkey business!" our mom shouted. I waved to acknowledge.

"Turtle's not this way," Marie said, following me, wrapping herself in a big Sad Face.

"Pick up your long lips," I said (freshly learned Rez Slang for "Overt Sadness"). Joy was the only emotion you could express on the Rez without being made fun of. Tears of laughter were the only kind allowed. "We're not going to the Turtle."

As we got to the State Park parking lot, Marie caught sight of her Mystery Man, leaning on his weird car. Maybe he'd parked in this spot right after he'd bought my frames so that he could surprise her in this stupid Romantic-Comedy way. Her Long Lips turned into a Dropped Jaw in two seconds flat. "Unless *he*'s a turtle."

"Benjamin's the German tourists?" she screeched, smacking me and ran to him, all grinning. So the Mystery Man's first name was Benjamin. Another puzzle piece acquired. (He *did* look as stuffy as you'd imagine someone using that full name, but it wasn't going to do for me. Of the variants: Ben, Benji, Benny, only the first one was viable.) Again, this new piece ticked my memory but not enough to clear the haze. Marie almost tripped on those concrete parking barriers as she raced to him.

Marie and Mystery Man (it was seriously going to take a while to think of him as Benjamin) stood stiff near each other, wanting to hug but fearing me as a witness (as if I hadn't just arranged for this meeting myself!). As far as romance goes, this wasn't all that exciting.

"Mom's still at the Table," I said, gently shoving her closer. "And he paid a hundred and twenty bucks to see you. You should at least make it worth his while. Hug him!"

"Shut up," she said, but not mean. You can't sound harsh when you can't stop grinning.

"All right," I said. "Let's get going. I'm already two hours late."

"What?" Marie said, suddenly alarmed, looking between us. She clearly did not like Benfriend and me in the same space. "You're not going anywhere. Not with us anyway."

"Actually, she is," he said. "Part of my discount on your beautiful frames was that I give her a ride to someplace near your house." House. Nice try. I had to give him sincerity points there. He'd definitely never seen our *house* in daylight. Also, points for saying *Marie's* frames were beautiful. Maybe he'd even come to believe it, but a lot of people dismissed our art as "crafts," telling us that they'd done similar things at summer camp when they were kids.

"I got a band to join," I said, raising my bag that held one decent water drum and a rattle.

He unlocked his weird little car with the strange hood emblem, and Marie hopped in. "You should ride in the trunk," she said. We knew people who snuck into the Auto Vue Drive-In Movies that way, but I didn't think Marie wanted her Dress-Shirt Benfriend to know the Indian world of pinching pennies. All the way to the Rez, neither said much. He put his hand on her knee, but she gently slid it back off. I tried to look out the window the whole way so they'd stop being so freaky.

As the sun set, Benfriend pulled off the road near The Bug's, and his little car almost fell into the ditch. I could hear music that might be Carson and Lewis. A lot of cars congested the roadside up to the packed driveway — it looked like they had a crowd. I hoped my little drum and voice would be powerful enough to carry.

"Hey, Ben," I asked, leaning in between their heads. Marie flashed annoyance at my lack of formality. "What kind of car is this anyway? I've never seen one like it, and I sure don't recognize that little lightning bolt in a circle on your hood."

"No reason you would," he said, delighted someone had noticed his Freakmobile. I'd had to *tell* Marie it was a strange one before she noticed. "It's a Trabant. Made in East Germany."

"You went all the way to Germany for a car?" (In addition to looking like it was made of Legos, it was preposterously small and his stork legs barely fit in the driver's side foot well.)

"I went to great lengths! You can only import ones twenty-five years old or older and—"

"You bought a twenty-five-year-old used car? Hope you got a great deal."

"Well, no," Benfriend said, laughing like he had at the Vendor Table. I was no longer useful to him, now that Marie was in his car and I was getting out. "I'm a dedicated Teutophile."

"Toot-o-file?" I asked.

"T-E-U-T-O-P-H-I-L-E. From Teutonic. German."

"Ha!" I laughed. "Our mom is a Toot-o-file too! She loves Germans because they're *crazy* for our beadwork. What are the odds!"

"Imagine that," Benfriend said. "It's my area of—"

"We gotta go," Marie said, suddenly cranking her window up. I waved as the Trabant putted off, and just then remembered that

"Trabant" was the name of the first ride Marie picked at the Farmer John Dealie. Even squeezed into a little two-person carnival ride, thigh to thigh with Lewis, she was daydreaming about Benfriend and his Freakmobile (in truth, his car was almost as tight a squeeze as the ride, and it felt like it was made of the same flimsy fiberglass).

I walked up the crushed-stone driveway and hoped to salvage my Fourth of July, while Marie and Benfriend headed out to make some fireworks of their own. I hoped he had enough cash left over for their motel room. No matter how much he loved German culture, only the Sideshow Contortionist was going to be able to hook up in the backseat of *that* East German car. By the time I rounded the house, the sound of the Trabant was drowned out by Carson's and Lewis's guitars. I felt like my little water drum was gonna get lost, but then I noticed someone who must've been Hubie next to them. Oddly, he was playing what looked like a traffic cone, and I thought: *Well, things could be worse.*

15

One Day (at a Time)
Carson Mastick

Maggi appeared in The Bug's backyard right as we were wrapping up a song, so I announced that we were gonna take a few minutes' break. "Hey," I said to her, trying to be cool but feeling a grin split my face. I'd slid my Casino around to my back, like all the rock stars did. It was pretty impractical—you ran the risk of accidentally kicking it, and you definitely couldn't sit—but it looked totally badass. "You want something to eat?" I asked, walking her to the rickety porch we'd been using as a tiny stage.

"Hey, Lewis," Maggi said. He waved, chugging a Pepsi, sweat running down his face. She introduced herself to Doobie, and being the doofus he was, he said hi through the megaphone traffic cone, then set it down to shake her hand. Surprisingly, he could really blast sound from that stupid cone. "Line's *really* long," Maggi said, giving me the perfect chance.

"The talent doesn't have to wait in the line," I said, stepping aside like a game-show host, maybe Wink Martindale or Monty Hall, ready to make you a deal. I revealed a TV tray with four Chinet plates, the good, heavy-duty ones, all covered in tinfoil. I'd held up a four to my dad while he was in line earlier, and he'd made them. "One for each member of my band. Got here just in time. Lewis was starting to eye up the Scon-Dogs I'd saved for you, since he scarfed his down like a Skee-wheh."

"I was not," he said, pushing me, laughing.

"A Skee-wheh?" she asked, frowning. An obscure word, so I wasn't surprised. "A burnt black what?" Intriguing. Not only did she know the word, but she knew it was just a color and texture. Normally, you'd use it to describe something, like the planks left over after a house had gone up in flames. Where'd she pick that up?

"Skee-wheh was a dog The Bug used to have," Lewis said, narrowing his eyes at me. "He was the greediest thing."

"If you threw scraps down for the dogs," I said, grinning, "Skee-wheh would come flying over and almost choke himself, trying to eat everything before the other dogs could nose in there." I made this weird, disgusting sound, like gulping and inhaling at the same time, making it mushy too. Lewis hated that I could do it so accurate, since it was usually *him* I was calling a Skee-wheh. "That's how he sounded!"

"I wouldn't want to be called a Skee-wheh either," Maggi said to Lewis, folding back the foil to see what we'd saved for her. Some potato salad, baked beans, Jell-O with fruit suspended in it, and, most important, two of my mom's amazing Scon-Dogs, perfectly brown and not even greasy looking after being here a few hours. "But I will share."

"Thanks, that's okay," Lewis said. "I got my own. Apparently an individual Chinet from the trays was in our, um, contract," he said, laughing. "Like insisting on only red M&M's. Our rock star demands. Nice of you, though."

"Well, it was nicer of me to get you the plate, not knowing if you'd even show," I said. I tried on a smile. Shouldn't she acknowledge that I'd been thoughtful?

"I told you I'd try," Maggi said. "Got my drum." She reached into her bag and thumbed the skin. "Brought a horn rattle too, but I don't think the sound's gonna carry out here."

"What do you mean, you brought your drum?" Lewis said. He had a sharp ear for Eee-ogg in general, but if any of those shadowy conversations implied he was on the outside, his radar was even more narrowly tuned. His was like a high-end police scanner, instead of the ones from Radio Shack most people out here had.

"So you really did it," Doobie said, raising his eyebrows in that *I'm impressed* face. "A promise is a promise. I'll be there." He turned to Maggi. "You any good?"

"Are you?" Maggi asked him. "Is there a scale of goodness for playing the traffic cone?"

"Bass," Doobie said. "But I didn't bring it. I don't have a stand-up bass, and an electric one's a waste of time without an amp. I didn't even know these fancy tiny portable jobbies existed," he said, tapping my little Pignose that I'd just unplugged my Casino from to formally welcome her. "And you know," Doobie added, "not all that critical. Most other places we're gonna play are gonna have power. Although it is the Rez. . . ."

"Wait," Lewis said, scrunching his face up. "What the hell's going on here, Carson?" He was trying to be patient, but I could hear irritation starting to creep in. "How did this go from me, to you and me, to now the four of us without me knowing anything about that?"

"Hang on a sec," I said, and walked over to The Bug and told him we needed to organize. He nodded, but looked down at his bare wrist, telling me even without a watch to hurry my ass up or I wasn't getting paid.

"Let's go inside," I said, returning to the uneasy situation I'd created. "The Bug says it's okay that we wanna warm up some. But he saw *that*," I said, pointing at Maggi's bag, "and I had to promise no Traditional songs, so don't even fool around with fills you normally do." I held the door open for them.

We walked in and set up at The Bug's dining room table, which he always kept strangely neat. There was a tray of condiments covered by a dish towel centered on the table, like he was expecting picky guests to drop in, but I almost never saw guests here, picky or otherwise. For our part, Doobie was singing some Elvis Presley–type song into the caution cone, while Lewis simmered like a pot of piss pudding. Maggi was trying to read us, but good luck with that, girl.

"Okay, the bad news?" I said, pulling the center chair up. "We've already blown through most of the Beatles songs Lewis knows how to play. Not sure why The Bug wanted us to lead with that," I added, snapping my eyes at Lewis. He was silent—for now.

"The good news?" I continued. "Most of the other songs they wanna hear are your basic singing cowboy songs." I turned to Maggi. I'd never heard her play. This wasn't ideal but it was what we had. "Mostly 2/4 and 4/4. Look to me for the changes and the count-off once we're out there."

"Is it pretty much those old Hank Williams songs you mentioned before?" she asked, her face open, eager to join. When I nodded, those eyes narrowed down, and her mouth squeezed over to one side. "What is it with these old Indian men and their friggin' singing cowboys?" she hissed like a leaking tire. She was still going back and forth in her Rez Points bank, add a few points, take away a few points. Doobie looked askance at me.

"Anyway, I *know* all those songs," she added, sighing. "If there's an Indian man over fifty in your life, you know them." We all laughed, agreeing. I was amazed at how easy she could raise tension and then bust it back down. It was like she had some secret energy thermostat.

"Let's make a quick dry run-through here anyway," I said, trying super hard not to sound patronizing. "Before we go out to our adoring fans. You three have the easy part, so just keep steady. Doobie, don't sing harmony into that cone. It's too powerful, and there's enough distraction here that it might throw me off. There's only one driver for this bus."

"Unless The Bug decides to jump in," Lewis said.

"Wrong," Maggi said. "Still only one driver, and in that case, it's gonna suddenly be The Bug. Our job's to keep the tires pointing straight on the road so he can clear the driver's seat."

"Guess you *will* have the hardest job, then, Carson," Doobie said.

"How's that?" I said. I knew he was going to bite me in the ass, but the bite might still pull us tighter together.

"You're gonna have to put your ego in check for a little while," Lewis said, doing a one-two with Doobie. "Do you even know how to step out of the spotlight?"

"Come on," I said. "We're wasting time. All right, let's start with 'Kaw-Liga.'"

"In here, we can start that way, but not when we go out there," Lewis said. "That one changes midsong from a minor key to a major. Let's start simple. This might be our only time playing together. Shouldn't we enjoy it?" That was a bit of a surprise, but an interesting one. It held more promise for the Battle of the Bands.

"All right," I said. "Let's see."

"What's The Bug's favorite song?" Maggi asked. Nice. A savvy show person. We'd never done this before, but we recognized her sharpness. None of us had thought of it.

"Yeahhh," I said, dragging the word's tail out into the air. "They all *love* 'Your Cheatin' Heart,' and it's as basic as can be and gets them crying in their beers every time. Maggi, count us off and, remember, no Social song fills!" I couldn't risk even the smallest thing that might derail The Bug's mood. It was gonna be a little touchy already when he saw her actually using a water drum.

"I'm not a moron," she said, and did a simple, steady, boring 2/4. Doobie began singing gentle boom-booms into his cone, and Lewis lightly strummed until he felt their rhythm as his own. I started singing and could see Maggi's eyes bugging to hear the twangiest, scrawny-necked cowboy voice come of my mouth. I grinned, and as we got comfortable, I started adding little lead lines on my guitar. We got through it pretty decently.

"Maybe later," I said when Doobie started getting tricky in singing his bass line. I fought my hardest not to snap my eyes as I said it, keeping my direction softer, and he ironed back out.

"What am I gonna do when we do hit 'Kaw-Liga'?" Maggi said after four more tunes of the Hank Williams variety. "There's no way to play that without mixing in a little bit of Traditional drumming, or a half-assed version of it." True, and we were sounding decent.

"Let's find out," I said, grinning even wider. I grabbed my capo and clamped it at the fret where I'd found a decent complement. "Remember what we did waiting for these girls?" I asked Lewis. Of course, he'd remember, but I was really asking if he was good with our diving into something a little complicated. He nodded, a little wrinkle of concentration developing on his forehead like a set of brackets. "You just remember the big change when we get to the chorus," I said to Maggi. "If you don't make the change at the right time, the rest of us follow you down."

"A pretty fair number of Social Dance songs have time signature switches," she said. "Maybe you'd know that if you went to more of them."

"All right," I said, blowing off that little piece of broken glass her tongue had thrown. "Let's try this and if it goes, we head out there. The Bug's gonna be yelling for us in a minute anyway." We got a decent run-through, just past the chorus start, and I stopped us, smiling wide. "Showtime, kiddies. No matter what, keep on picking and grinning. If one of us screws up, whoever it is, pause, then jump back in. The rest of us are gonna keep playing." They nodded, and we stood up at the same time. It felt kind of dorky, like something out of *Fame*. Did that mean things'd be all right? Man, I hoped so.

" 'Bout time!" The Bug yelled as we came out, but he was laughing, so we still had a safe window. He was Happy Buzzed today. Though it could change lightning-fast, for now, luck was with us. We figured out a way for all of us to fit and then carefully turned to the crowd.

I started us with the quick three bursts of the same picked note, and at the changed note on four, the others all came in. By the second bar, everyone there recognized we were playing "Your Cheatin' Heart" in a pretty traditional arrangement. No one even seemed to notice I was playing the fiddle part adapted to capo'd guitar. The Bug's guitar remained in its case, and I was relieved. If he didn't feel the urge to play on *that* one, we were safe.

For a band playing the first time together, we started out pretty decently. Some of the older couples even got up and danced on a couple of tunes. Not slow dancing since that was not so much of an Indian thing to do. Anyone slow dancing would get made fun of for trying to cop a feel at the party. Our home was more mid-tempo like "Lovesick Blues."

We hit our groove more and more with each tune. Not even people singing badly in the crowd could throw me.

But when we got to "Kaw-Liga," I was shocked. Maggi started in doing the fake-out Indian drumming that starts it, and everyone standing immediately drifted into a natural circle and started dancing. A bunch of other people who'd been sitting suddenly jumped up and met their rhythm too. The rest of us joined her rhythm, and I started singing.

"Kaw-Liga" was a ridiculous song about a Cigar-Store Indian falling in love with an Indian Maiden statue in an antique shop across the street. It was one we should hate, but maybe half the party was up on its feet. They did a wild variation of a Social round dance, like those trick 3-D pictures. Their dance was half-serious and half-goof, and somehow they all made the switch together. I'd never seen anything like it. When we finished, people started shouting "Play that again." I shrugged, and Maggi began once more.

We closed out with repeats of some of the earlier songs, though Maggi chose to sit out "We Can Work It Out" at first. She knew there were changes, but she said she didn't know the song well enough to be confident. I thought Lewis's head was going to explode. By the second round of dueling verses, she had enough confidence to join back in. That felt like a good way to end. We were tired, and it gave The Bug room to jump back in and be the star of his own party if he felt like it. He said he might in a bit, and people largely went back to partying. Someone had been tending the bonfire, and after we put our stuff away, we wandered that way.

"Wow!" Albert yelled, coming up between Lewis and me, putting an arm around each of our shoulders. "All those lessons! Damn!

They worked, isn't it! Even when it didn't seem like it." Lewis pushed him, and the three of us laughed.

For the next hour, people came up and congratulated us, which I had to admit felt pretty sweet. But I also felt a little bit bad for Maggi. Almost three-quarters of them asked her some version of the question: "Now whose girl are you anyways?" She'd tell them, and then immediately, once they could place her with a Rez family and history, they'd get way friendlier. They'd tell her things about her parents that she'd never heard before. Sometimes, she could make an immediate connection right back and the tone would improve even more. I could see the waves of disappointment and delight crashing over her face with each approach of someone.

"We were good, huh?" Doobie said, in a brief lull. We all agreed.

"So you wanna tell me what you were talking about just before we started?" Lewis said to Doobie. He said it friendly, but I could hear all those knotted I've-Been-Left-Out-Again feelings rising to the surface. Could I blame him? No, not if I were being honest with myself. I should have had the conversation with him, but it was harder lately for me to be my cocky self. If I'd told him ahead, he might have bailed, and I wasn't sure I had my old powers of persuasion anymore. That incident at the Sanborn Field Day had screwed me up more than I thought it would.

I felt Derek's absence here too, the whole party. He knew our dad was going to be here, and wasn't super enthusiastic about my playing in general. A lot of people thought of him as a slacker, and he knew that if I seemed dedicated to something, had some ambition, people might notice his lazy ways even more. Was his stupid choice from the pressure of needing to do something with his life suddenly? *No, Carson,* I told myself. *Take Lewis's advice and put your ego in a box for a little while.* Sometimes people just did shit out of their own bad judgment. Still, I missed him here.

"We *were* good, right?" I said to Lewis. "Even with Doobie and Maggi joining us for the first time?"

"A little rocky sometimes," he clarified. He was maybe a bit more unforgiving of himself than I was. "But yeah, for a spontaneous band, pretty damn good." He took a draw from the beer someone had passed him. "But no one just brings a drum randomly to a party."

"I wanted to try something," I said. I had a feasible story, that Maggi had just happened to bring her drum with her, coming from their Vendor Table. And it was true, but it would have also been part lie, even if just a silent lie. "I think we can do this. This is a band. It's not just you and me anymore. The four of us, we sounded good, with only a half hour to even get together. Imagine what we could do if all of us practiced like you and me do. Alone and together. We could be super tight in no time, could branch out beyond the Hank Williams songbook."

"Maybe even some more Beatles," he said, and I knew I was half-way there.

"I don't know so many of their songs," Maggi said. "I mean, I know it's them on the radio, but I don't *know them* know them. I guess I could learn some."

"Some," I said. "I'm asking you to be in *my* band. One bus driver. Remember?"

Just then, Albert swung back around, barging in our conversation. "Check this out!" he yelled, happier looking than I'd seen him in a long time. This would be a tough time for him to influence Lewis, but I'd just have to ride this out too. "Some folks passed the hat for you guys!" He literally held a hat before us, a beaded cap as it turned out, and it was full of dollar bills. "Don't know how much. Didn't want to be rude, but it's all yours. Great band out of nothing, isn't it!"

Lewis took the cap from Albert, neatly folded over to keep the bills from spilling out. He knew, instinctively, that if The Bug found out others had paid us, he might get a case of amnesia before he paid us himself. Lewis was a grinning small businessman.

"So what do you think?" I figured I'd cash some of these new Rez Points while I could. "Starting tomorrow. You and Maggi, after work. I'll come pick you up, we'll round up Doobie from hanging out down at the Fire Hall, and we can get in a good two hours of practice a night."

"What's the hurry?" Lewis said, laughing. "We've got our whole lives to explore this."

"Well, not exactly," I said. At first, he looked stricken. "No, no one's sick! Jeez, Gloomis. There *is* a time limit, but it's good. First! Answer me this, we were better than those bands at the Field Day, isn't it? You can agree to that."

"Oh, hell yeah," he said, and I knew I had him. This had been the right call. Not just for him, but for the whole band. I could see Maggi's meeting people and connecting with them meant something to her. And Doobie seemed always eager to belong to something, though I had an idea we'd have to fight for his free time with the Fire Hall.

But that was a challenge for another day. I started telling Lewis about the Battle of the Bands. Doobie and Maggi filled him in on their parts, and we all agreed that, already, we had a shot if the competition was anything like those shitty bands we'd seen at the Sanborn Field Day. I almost wanted to tell Lewis about what we'd done for Albert, but something about Maggi, the risk that she had better Eye-Snap skills than me, helped me to keep a good secret. Before the end of the night, I had an agreement from the three of them that we'd begin regular practice soon—if not their first day back to work, then at least by the end of the week. That seemed good enough for me.

16

Paper Shoes
Magpie Bokoni

"I'm catching a ride with some friends," I said to my mom. Technically, that was not a lie. Jim Morgan offered the week after Fourth of July break to take me to the Albright-Knox, that awesome art museum my seventh-grade class went to. He'd said it closed at five, so it was best to go on a Saturday. It wasn't a good idea for us to leave the garage together on a workday, and I couldn't hop into a strange car near home (particularly one as strange as a commercial dump truck) without questions. So we had to meet on some neutral ground.

It was tricky for a fifteen-year-old Indian girl and a thirty-year-old white guy to be friends without people getting ideas.

Our last holiday in July, celebrating our right to cross the borders as tribal people existing in both the US and Canada, fell in the middle of the month. The formal programming (speeches, Cute Indian Kid contest, etc.) was held on alternating years there and here. This year's events were at Hyde Park, our side. Border Crossing was an Indian celebration, but enough white people came that Jim wouldn't stand out much. The buying crowd would thin by three, so I could probably get out by two.

Right on the chosen hour, Jim got just close enough to catch my eye. He was wearing what looked like new Levi's, dress boots (weirdly, like Lewis's), and a neat, pale gray polo shirt. It looked like he couldn't decide how to wear the collar—one side was up, while the other drooped. Dark Deanna wasn't in a terrible mood, so I gave him the agreed-upon signal (knocking a drum to the ground and picking it back up). We'd planned to meet in the parking lot of a bar and grill across the street that had a train caboose in its parking lot. I figured there'd be no mistaking the Hitching Post for any other place with that kind of landmark to look for.

"I feel like we're spies," I said, walking up to his truck's driver's side window.

"Get in," he said. I reached up to fix his collar, but he grabbed my hand and put it on my leg. He immediately dropped the truck into gear and peeled out of the parking lot. "Sorry. I forgot. That bar sponsors a team on my bowling league. We don't wanna linger." He put his left blinker on, but I told him to go straight instead. If we'd gone his way, we'd go right by the park and the Science Projects.

"Which way you like it? Up or down?" I asked, and he gave me Side-Eyes, grinning. "Your collar, doofus. You look like you don't know how to dress yourself." He glanced in the mirror, smiled wider, and leaned toward me so I could fold the right side down. I smoothed it against his chest, and he took a deep breath, expanding the collar opening wide. I pulled my hand away (it was having thoughts of its own that I didn't think were good ideas).

We chatted about the Border Crossing, and the history of his bowling league, and a half hour later, we were in Erie County. To him, it probably was nothing, but to me, Buffalo was huge, mysterious. I wanted to think *Exciting* but my brain kept replacing it with *Scary*. What if we got separated (or he left me somewhere)? Who could I call? The only real answer was Carson. (And a part of my brain told me I'd never have those abandonment thoughts if I were in *Carson's* silver muscle car. Jim's world was different, uncertain.)

Jim navigated various thruway exits, onto another thruway, never checking notes or maps, and then we pulled onto a street where I could see the museum directly in front of us. Maybe he really was an art lover! I figured that he'd probably taken an interest in my Freaky

Beadwork objects because he'd (really) taken an interest in me. But it seemed he'd been here enough times that he knew the route by heart. You had to pay to get into the lot, so I started scrambling through my bag. The gas money to get to Buffalo was, I'm sure, a ton, but I could at least pay for the lot.

"What are you doing?" he asked, laughing and paying. "Don't be a weirdo." We walked into the building together, side by side. Neither of us looked over our shoulders, just two people, checking out art. As we got closer to the door, I worried about what I was going to say at the admissions counter. It was cheaper for me to be "Youth," but I wanted to be "Adult." I dug in my bag to have the right amount ready so I could say I was an adult.

"What are you *doing*?" he asked again, this time exaggerated. "*I've* got today. Put your money away." He put his arm around my shoulder and shook me gently, in more of the *Come on!* way I imagined a big brother might. Instead of an admissions desk, there was a donations box, clear Plexiglas on a pedestal, with dollar bills and coins gathering in the bottom, and suggested amounts. Jim put two five-dollar bills in, two "Adults." I smiled and reached my arm around his back, my hand touching his love handle on the other side. I squeezed and let go.

Stepping in, I tried to go left, remembering an Andy Warhol. The only other time I'd been here was with a bunch of other seventh graders and some freaked-out chaperones rushing us the whole time, trying to make sure we didn't see the naked art. Now I'd get to see whatever we wanted, for as long as we wanted.

"This way," Jim said. "I want to show you something." He no longer had his arm on me, but I followed. We were flying by stuff I wanted to check out.

"Can you wait? Jeez, Jim! I wanna see things. No point in being here if I'm not going to be able to look."

"You will. You can take however long you want until they kick us out, *after* I show you this one thing." He clearly had been here before. Jim definitely had sides no one at the garage knew about. I couldn't recall Lewis being interested in art, unless it was on an album cover.

He sure never asked about the beadwork projects I worked on during lunch sometimes, and Carson? Please! He couldn't be any less interested in stuff like that.

"Check this out," Jim said, grinning. It was a big rectangular box, eight feet high by eight feet wide. It was about the size of our old Science Project unit's kitchen (a tight squeeze when my mom insisted one of us help cook). A door cut into both sides of one corner was propped open. The box was wholly covered in neat rows of square mirrors, each about two feet per side.

You couldn't help but look at your reflected self in those mirrors. Even in high-heeled clogs, I only came up to Jim's Adam's apple. People walked by, not noticing us, as if we belonged together. The only person paying attention was a guard in a gray suit (and he was being paid to pay attention).

"Come here," Jim said, tugging his boots off, revealing blinding white tube socks (which suggested better hygiene than a lot of the Garage Guys had). I thought he'd lost his mind until he pointed to a sign. We could enter *Room No. 2* but only if we removed our shoes and we had socks on. "This is the best part," he said. Jim stepped in and seemed to float inside a massive shaft, like the one Luke Skywalker and Princess Leia swung over, escaping stormtroopers. The box's interior was also mirrored, even floor and ceiling, stretching out in infinite directions.

"I can't," I said, lifting one leg and letting my clog slip off, revealing my bare foot inside. I was glad I'd emery-boarded and painted my toenails last night.

"Oh, but you can," he said, reaching into the back pocket of his jeans. Even though I liked how he looked in his Work Blues, these jeans looked much nicer on him. The polo shirt he had on just looked nicer, dressier than those ringer T-shirts he loved.

"What are these?" I said, taking the cellophane package containing two foam oblongs, the color of vanilla pudding.

"Hospital slippers. They gave me a new pair every day I was in. The last day, I was discharged pretty quick. Insurance was already billed, so I just took 'em home. Here." He reached out and tore the cellophane, handing me the two spongy objects. "One size fits all."

"They're men's," I said, holding them in front of me.

"I don't think anyone's gonna care," he said. "Come on, join me." He stepped deeper inside the room. I had no choice if I didn't want to look like an idiot and I didn't want us to draw attention, so I stuck my bare feet into the slits in the foam and entered.

"Wow, this is weird," I said, feeling a little disoriented at first. I reached out to Jim to steady myself and he guided my hand to a table, also covered in mirrors and glass. I hadn't even really perceived the table or its matching chair, but I suspected you weren't supposed to really sit on it. "I'm okay, now," I said after a few seconds. "Incredible!"

"It don't have anything to do with the kind of art *you* make," he said, grinning. "But it's still pretty damn cool." Somehow, I'd missed it on my class trip. Maybe they'd steered us away from it, so an obnoxious gang of seventh graders wouldn't try to barge in? (Not that we were, but I knew how grown-ups thought of us in groups of more than three.)

Inside, infinite yous trailed deep in every direction too. Jim and Maggi, everywhere you looked. Except without shoes on, every Maggi just barely came up to the shoulders of all the Jims. I wondered what their lives were like. Probably, every one of them had to find ways of sneaking out, even just to do something regular together, like going to an art museum.

"See, I knew you'd love it." He pointed at one of the rows of Maggis, smiling at the rows of Jims. We looked into each other's eyes, but only in reflection. "The farther in you go," he said, gently guiding my shoulder, "the stronger the illusion." The real us was no longer visible to the guard, but I'm sure at least a hundred of the other Jims and Maggis were quite visible to anyone looking into the room.

"So why were you in the hospital?" I pointed down to the freaky foam things.

"Appendicitis," he said. "Feels like you're being stabbed, and you don't have a lot of time to get to the hospital from the time you first start feeling bad."

"What do they do for it?"

"Snip it out," he said, holding up fingers and making a scissors motion.

"You got a scar?" This was something I'd learned about guys from all the City Indians I used to hang out with. Those Reynolds boys were excited anytime they could show you a new scar. Sometimes, they peeled their scabs before they healed, to leave bigger scars.

"Yeah, it's not too bad, though. You gotta get your butt to the hospital, and on the table, super fast, but the procedure itself I guess ain't too complicated."

"You gonna show it to me?" I asked, figuring older guys so far didn't seem all that different from younger guys, except they were bigger, hairier, and had more resources.

"Not exactly in a place you show casual friends," he said, patting to the area of his jeans right between the front pocket and the fly, where the denim faded in gentle creases. We were still each looking at the reflection of the other. The only light came in through the open door, but because it was reflected so many times, the room was no darker than the average living room, maybe even better lit than my own.

The reflected Jim was just a shade too removed for me to read his expression, and by the time I turned to face him directly, it had changed a little. I wished I had a camera so I could have captured whatever that expression had been, for later study. Sometimes, I beaded images following the shapes and contours of other images I liked. When you remade them yourself, you understood the lines and shapes differently (less casually). If I made a beaded version of Jim's face just then, maybe I'd understand it better, I thought. Marvin could carve a more accurate one in soapstone, if I'd ever let him meet Jim.

"So what do you say we hit those other pieces you wanted to check out?" he said, putting on a smile. We found the Warhols (weirdly colored repeated pictures of Elvis and of Marilyn Monroe), and I stopped in front of the giant chaos paint splash painting by that guy Pollock. "Do you *really* like this?" Jim asked. "It looks like the drop cloths about the time Rooter gets rid of them 'cause they're too stiff. There's probably a whole pile of . . ." He glanced at the little information card. " 'Convergences' in the painter's storage room behind our break room."

"You can go look at the naked lady statues in the other room if you want," I said. "I'm here. I'm gonna enjoy what I came to see." It felt weird when, at times, Jim seemed to wrestle between being a man and a boy like he was my age.

"I'm sorry," he said. "I really didn't think you liked it. Can you explain it to me?" Just then, an announcement came over the PA that the museum was closing in fifteen minutes. "Maybe over dinner, I guess. Something to eat? Lot of nice restaurants here in Buffalo." What he wasn't saying, of course, was that we weren't likely to run into anyone either of us knew at a restaurant in Buffalo. Not like Niagara Falls.

We left and headed deeper into the city, through busy shop areas, Jim turning down one-way side streets I'd never be able to find again, some that even went at forty-five-degree angles from the rest. I never came here, but it seemed like he wasn't worried for one second.

"Where are we?" I asked as he closely studied the signs around us.

"Here we go," he said. "I forgot to write it down, but figured if I drove around long enough, I'd remember." Now he was having a tough time finding a parking spot wide enough for his giant industrial truck on these strange narrow streets. They had a random mix of houses packed together along with businesses thrown into the mix. "This is a great restaurant. You like Italian?"

I nodded. Most of Niagara Falls was Italian, so it was the most common kind of restaurant you found there. Not that they were like this place — one look as soon as you stepped in and you knew this place was fancier than anywhere I'd ever been. It even had a giant, elaborate gold-colored machine in the lounge that Jim explained made fancy coffee. (Seemed totally like overkill that it took a machine resembling a mini castle on a Vendor Cart, just to make coffee.)

A man in a tux grabbed silverware wrapped in little dish towels and took us to a small table. As we sat, the man plucked Jim's cap off his head, handing it to Jim, explaining that gentlemen did not eat with hats on in their establishment. I thought Jim was going to punch the guy, but he settled down and smiled at me, running his fingers through his hair. Most of the garage guys who wore caps were hiding a thin area, or a spot that had already gone bald. But Jim's hair was full, neatly parted a little old-fashioned to the side, and looked recently trimmed.

A waiter handed us menus, flipped our glasses, poured water, and delivered a tiny loaf of hot bread on a cutting board, asking if we'd like to see the wine list. I didn't want to be proofed, so I said I was good, and Jim asked if he could have a beer. At first I wasn't sure what to do with the dish towel (Jim called it a cloth napkin, so I didn't have to ask). I worried about getting stains on it that would be tough to get out, thinking there was very little I could order at an Italian restaurant that wasn't going to be at least somewhat messy.

"Do you go to the museum a lot?" I asked (the first of an imaginary set of 3×5 cards I had in my head, if we got stuck for conversation).

"Yeah, why not? People think of me one way, but I'm not. I got more going on than just muscle," he said. "Even if I am noticeable in that department." He grinned and flexed the biceps of his crossed arms, their tan almost glowing against the tablecloth.

"Didn't your mother ever tell you no elbows on the table?" I joked, gently prodding one of his firm forearms.

"Another rule like the No Hats one, Miss Manners? Nah, I've always had whatever freedom I want. Does your mom keep you on a short leash like that?"

"Are you comparing me to a dog, Jim Morgan?" I asked.

"Course not," he said, frowning deeply to be sure I knew he was sincere. "If there's one thing you don't have to worry about, it's being a woofer!"

"That's not a nice—"

"I said I didn't mean *you*," he jumped in, cutting me off. I almost said something more, but the truth was, I'd said some things to Marie to make her feel like *a woofer*, myself, when I'd wanted to get to her.

"So back to the museum, do they move things around?" Most of what we'd seen was familiar, but it felt like a few things I'd liked were maybe missing. I'd only had a fleeting memory from the first time, so it was possible I was totally wrong.

"Got me. I ain't studying that close. I brought you here partly to check out that room."

"And partly what else?" I asked.

"Partly so we could go to dinner," he said, at first leaning his head back and then changing directions, ducking it instead, peeking out at me from beneath those thick eyebrows. He went from seeming cocky to shy and vulnerable in a few seconds.

"Goof," I said, smiling, as our dinners came. As we dug into our meal, we loosened up. The waiter came by to clean up our bread crumbs (running a mini version of my mom's rug sweeper across the table), and we laughed at how weird it looked. I had lasagna, and Jim ordered something called gnocchi (tiny footballs made of pasta). My food was like a giant edible brick, bigger and richer and saucier than any I'd ever had. I guess I was used to Bargain Lasagna, the way Dark Deanna made it on the days she pronounced as *Occasions*.

"So why'd you want to know all those things?" Jim asked, shoveling his food in. "Want some?" He pierced a few gnocchi on his fork, the utensil that had just been in his mouth. I returned the offer. We each used the other's fork.

"Do you know if that museum has anything by an artist named Yoko Ono?"

"An artist named Yoko One?" he said, laughing a little. "You trying to get me to believe that you don't know who Yoko Ono is?"

"I really didn't," I said. "I don't know a ton about the Beatles. But I recently found out that she does, um, conceptual art? Like a lot of those artists back there did. Like that mirror room."

"She's known for something other than art," he said, frowning, like he had a much bigger opinion of her than it seemed like he should have.

"No woman breaks up a band if the relationships are strong enough," I said, thinking about my own new band I was sort of in. It felt fragile, like one wrong step could tear it apart.

"Shows what little you know," he said, making a sad but irritated face. "Pretty much every marriage kills off the friendships the guy has. He might have a best man on his wedding day, but that's about the last day he does." I didn't like where this was going, so I decided to use up the last topic I'd saved.

"You don't strike me as a Bee Gees kind of guy," I said, pointing to the cap the host had removed, which had the band's emblem in snazzy gold letters across the front.

"I'm not. It's a joke. My . . . friend, one of the others, gave it to me 'cause I'm on Buildings and Grounds." I remembered Kenny introducing him that way, for his wrestling match. "I shouldn't even wear it. Hate that disco crap." He held it out to me. "You a Bee Gees sort?" I shook my head, a little disappointed. I'd planned to offer adding some beadwork, but if it was just a joke, that was a stupid idea. Beadworking trucker caps was tough to do.

"I wanted to talk to you about Buildings and Grounds. You wanna keep working in the school year? I can request a transfer. Two hours a day, but it keeps cash in your pocket." Lewis had never raised the idea—maybe the garage only needed one kid, him, during the school year. "And I can give you rides. I'll make sure to still be there when you leave. All the time."

That had been a worry, but I was also concerned about band practice. Lewis would be working after school, himself, though, so I said yes, I'd like that.

"Great!" he said, smiling as we left the restaurant. I stopped to look at something. He followed my gaze, and I pointed, raising my eyebrows. "Yup, that's a bullet hole. Someone got shot here about, I don't know, ten years ago? Bullet went straight through the window. I guess they keep it that way because it's kind of, I don't know, exciting?"

"Probably not for the person who got shot," I said.

"Most people who get shot . . ." He paused, lowering his voice. "It's for a reason."

He couldn't know that! I thought suddenly of that little plaque you see at virtually every Indian household, about not judging your neighbor until you'd walked a mile in his moccasins. I still had those funny, papery foam slippers in my backpack. I'd walked in Jim's shoes, sort of. Maybe not a mile, and maybe not any he'd actually ever worn, but they were his, just the same. It didn't seem possible that he could ever walk in mine (if I really thought about it).

I kept thinking of what I knew about Carson's brother. I wondered if he felt like he deserved to get shot. Or if that guy, General Custard, felt like he had the right to do it. He *said* he had the right on TV, but when he was lying in bed, surely, he didn't really believe he was in the right firing a gun at someone a few feet away. I didn't think I'd ever hear the full story of what happened that night in Custard's Last Stand. Only one of the two people there that night was in a talkative mood.

PART THREE
Rock 'n' Roll

DOG STREET
ROCK'N'ROLL

Labor Day
Green Corn Moon

17

Hey Bulldog

Carson Mastick

"What's this?" Lewis asked, getting into the Chevelle, looking at the clothes on the seat.

"Your stage duds," I said, pretending we'd already talked about this. "Gotta look the part, man." Our gig at The Bug's house was two months ago, and our band was gelling. We practiced together maybe not as often as I wanted but more often than I thought I'd get away with. When you're forceful with people, it's amazing how many cave almost immediately.

We were so dedicated that we'd fast pushed into getting through whole sets without breaking down too bad. Other than Lewis's reluctance to stand out, my only real concern was Maggi's drums. They were great and would give us a leg up in "uniqueness factor," but I was worried about the logistics of getting them amplified enough. I was trying out a new plan today. This Labor Day party was our last shot at a test in front of any audience. Next week, school would start, and we'd have to commit to Battle of the Bands or back down. I didn't want an unseasoned band that was going to lose their shit the first time we got on a stage.

"Just put it on," I nudged. If Lewis couldn't commit to stage clothes, we were doomed. Maggi's water drum thing was only gonna take us so far. The white satin shirt with chrome flames was straight out of *Saturday Night Fever*—ridiculous for every day, but stage lights should hit it perfect. I had his back here. "I went to the trouble to arrange for it, in your size."

"Well, where's your stage clothes?" he asked.

"I'm wearing them," I said. I had on black leather pants, a black T-shirt under a huge muscle shirt with a giant Indian chief head on it. My clothes would be at home in *Rolling Stone*, *Circus*, *Creem*, or *Hit Parader*. I could wear this to school, and no one would think a thing of it either. Did I know how? Nope, and I didn't want to mess with my Mojo by thinking too hard.

"Your dad's gonna beat your ass if he finds out you lifted his shirt." We practiced outside at my house sometimes, so he knew what our cozy little home was like.

"I'm not *even* acknowledging your lack of coolness. Hurry up and change—we're already late. We may be stuck going over to this white kid's house on a regular basis, so I want to start off with a good track record."

"Thought this was just a one shot. Some Labor Day party."

"It is, but it isn't *just* that," I said. "Got a surprise for you when we get there."

"What!"

"If I told you—"

"Wouldn't be a surprise, funny. Come on! No farting around. You already pulled this once. I've agreed to the Battle of the Bands! What more do you want!" He dug into the bag I'd handed him. "You can't seriously think I'm going to wear these pants," he said, holding my garage sale purchase up. I thought they were painter pants when I'd bought them, like what you might buy at the Gap. Truth? They were *real* painter pants, like from Sherwin-Williams. I'd added silver piping down each leg. "What is this? I'll look like I'm in band."

"You *are* in a band," I said, then couldn't help myself and grinned.

"I mean *band* band, like marching at the football games."

"Forget that. We're a real band," I said, honking at Tami's trailer as we pulled up.

"Exactly. That's why I shouldn't look like that. What's next? Tassels? Epaulets?"

"What are epaulets?" Tami asked as she and Doobie came out.

"Never mind," Lewis said. "I don't want to give your cousin any ideas. And where's *your* band outfit?" Tami was singing backup today, a safety net. Tami had on pretty much the same kind of clothes she usually wore: short Daisy Dukes, Converse high-tops with socks rolled down at the top, and a strappy T-shirt that seemed like it should have belonged to her little sister.

"This *is* my outfit," she said.

"Not quite finished," I said, popping the glove compartment. "One last addition." I pulled out an assortment of spiked dog collars. "Take your pick." I snatched the black one for myself.

"I was going to grab the black one," Lewis said. Perfect. I'd gotten him to commit to wearing a dog collar, onstage, without hardly trying. "What's next? Muzzle? Poop scoop?"

"Thought you didn't want to give him any ideas," Doobie said, grabbing blue. He put it on. Lewis sighed, going for purple, avoiding lime green or bright red. I hoped the red one would appeal to Maggi.

Lewis passed it to Tami, but she shook her head. "Not officially a member yet," she said.

"Extra one?" Lewis asked.

"Nope, just enough," I said, plucking the red one out of his hand. He wasn't buying it. I guessed it was safe enough to give him the full plan, this deep in. What was he going to do, leave? "As of this afternoon, we have a new band member."

"What? Who? Do the others know?" Lewis asked, and Doobie nodded, smug.

"Her name's Susan," Tami said. "Keyboards. And can she play!" Tami said. She'd been the one to tell me about Susan, saying she could flesh out Maggi's water drum with little pads built into the keyboard, just in case.

"So now wait a minute," Lewis huffed. "*You* get to wear what you want, and *Tami* gets to wear what she wants —" He had a deficit in this not-taking-yourself-too-seriously quality.

"Not in this band," Tami jumped in, pointing at her head. "Hubie? Not complaining either." Tami looped a finger into the ring on Doobie's collar and pulled him forward to pet him. He made whining noises. "It's what you do for your band." She turned to me. "Told you. Susan knows the chords. *She* can provide rhythm." Then she turned to Lewis. "They don't need you."

"Wait, now," I said. Sometimes, Tami went too far. "She can't learn the arpeggios in a—"

"Well, how do you even know she's going to be there?" Lewis said. He was so easy.

"Susan *Critcher*," Tami said, laughing an I-Just-Busted-Your-Ass laugh. "Artie's sister. Just where else do you think she's going to be?"

"Guess I didn't *catch* her last name," Lewis said. I laughed. We were back to good.

As I neared the Bokoni's corner, Lewis suddenly decided to spring some news of his own. "Maggi's already got a ride, by the way. Said she'd meet us there," he said.

"*Now* you tell me?" I said, doing a U-turn.

"Sorry. You distracted me with your, um, wardrobe demands."

"Whatever. All right, you guys. Better get ready," I said. "Almost showtime." Lewis sighed, taking his T-shirt off and pulling the cool satin shirt over his bare chest, buttoning it. "Don't be a dork." Did I have to do everything for this guy? "Leave the top three undone. You're supposed to seem hot."

"I will be hot. This shirt is heavy! I'm going to sweat through before we even get there."

"You'll be fine. It's polyester, not real silk. Doesn't breathe as well." They looked at me like they just discovered I'd been moonlighting as a saleslady at Penney's. "Jerseys are made of the same material! I had to learn about it if I was gonna learn how to do repairs. Jeez. You pinheads act like a guy can't sew!"

"Carson, there's a lot of people here," Doobie said as we got close to Artie's. "What if we suck?" He read my mind. Artie's house wasn't too far off the Rez, and we could have almost parked on our side of the border, the road was so packed.

"Yeah," Lewis pushed. "What if we suck?"

"That's a given *you* will," I said, laughing, trying not to spook us. "Kidding. *Kidding!* Look, we're fine. We killed at The Bug's party. And Doobie's got his real bass instead of a caution cone."

Lewis took in a breath to "yeah, but" so I cut him off.

"Plus, we got a short set list," I continued. "And the people who hired us? Their kid's in our band now. No one's giving us grief. If Artie's folks change their mind, we don't play. And we eat and drink for free. What's the worst that can happen? We suck in front of strangers we'll never see again."

I didn't push it. I knew it was kind of tough for Lewis to come to Artie's house. You could see, just down the way, the group of almost identical houses that made up the Red-Tail Manor compound for air force families. I didn't know which one Lewis's buddy George Haddonfield had lived in, before his dad got transferred and the one white guy Lewis had ever trusted left here without a trace.

The proximity of this party to those houses was one of the details I'd left out when trying to get Lewis to commit. He called my justifications "Jedi mind tricks," but he still fell for them often enough that they were worth a try. Truth? I really was looking out for him. If we were gonna be a band, and have any reasonable shot at winning the Battle, that meant performing in public, with a sense of presentation.

"Put your collar on before you get out." Lewis tucked the shirt into his regular jeans. I passed him my little Pignose while Tami and Doobie got out. "And take the Pignose. I got this," I said, grabbing my Orange amp, which carried way more juice.

"Wait," Lewis said, stopping. "If you two are both amplified, no one's gonna hear me."

"Relax. Would I do something like that?" I asked, continuing to walk. Making him feel like he was missing out was the easiest of my alleged Jedi mind tricks, but it wasn't working. "The Pignose is for you. I'm assuming you don't have an amp."

"Why would I need an amp? My guitar's an acoustic," he said, as if I had not known this.

"There's a pickup inside the Pignose housing. You just slide it up inside the sound hole, tighten the bracket in place, and you're fine."

"And what's Hubie using?"

"Mine's already here," Doobie said. "I left it the last time I was hanging with Susan." Even a year behind us, Doobie was still *Older*, which made him inherently more interesting to sophomores and freshmen. Were he and Susan going out? Who else hangs with someone using the excuse "I want to play my bass for you"?

Artie waved to us as we came up the driveway. I'd never been so relieved to see a white person recognize me. He wrapped his arm around Tami's waist when we reached him. While everyone said hello, I glimpsed us reflected in a house window. We looked like a band.

"See Maggi yet?" I asked the group. We looked awesome but only three members of our band were visible—the three who'd arrived courtesy of my Chevelle.

"There," Doobie said. She was talking with Susan. "Who'd she come with?"

"Dunno," I said. "*You* know, Lewis?" He was the world's shittiest liar. Well, *my* world's worst anyway. You could almost see the nonsense he was gonna tell you forming over his head.

"No," he finally said. All that working up to one stubby "no." "She didn't tell me anything. And I haven't seen Marie." And there was the rest of the story, which of course meant: *I know how she got here, she told me, but I am not sharing that information with you.*

" 'No' would have been fine," I said. "Weirdo."

Some guy in a baseball cap, easily in his thirties, flew toward us. His clothes were too tight, begging anyone to notice. Why did he seem so familiar? He looked like most of the white guys under fifty who lived in Sanborn, but still, there was something. His mustache split in a grin as he reached into the chain loop in Lewis's collar, but there was nothing friendly in this gesture. "Lassie! Welcome to the party. You paper-trained? Or am I gonna have to rub your nose in it if you have an accident?" He let go of Lewis's collar when he was done with his version of a greeting. His breath reeked of keg beer and cigars.

"Hey, you made it," Susan said to Lewis, running over, Maggi trailing her. "Hubie said they'd convince you, but I had my doubts. Come on. You're gonna be near me onstage."

"Lassie here's in your band?" the guy asked, bugging his eyes out like he was onstage in a play, making a "surprised" face so big the back row could see. "What's he play, the skin—"

"Jim!" Maggi said, pushing her shoulder up against him. "Cut it out. You'll scare him away. We both just joined recently. We're the rhythm section."

"I'll bet he's got his rhythm down," the guy named Jim said. Lewis's ears deepened to brick, and Susan's soft pink features turned almost Pepto-Bismol pink.

Susan tugged at Lewis's arm as I made my way to the keg. Tami gave Artie a thanks-for-having-us-crazy-Indians-here kiss. "Have you been using tabs?" Susan asked Lewis. He told her he had. We were doing songs we'd rehearsed, but on the chance he might freak out and lose his place, I'd given him sheets. Playing at The Bug's for a Rez crowd was one thing. This party? Something else. "We set you near my keyboard so you can look on. You need them tonight?"

"If the chords are on top of the bar, I'm good," he said. "As long as I stick to the basics. And I guess that's my job here anyway."

"You'll do fine," she said, and smiled, touching her fingers up and down his arm. "I like the way this feels." Maybe now he'd listen.

"I'm mostly worried about playing with others," he said, getting his tuner out.

" 'Cause usually you're playing with yourself?" that guy Jim said, sitting near the bandstand. He might be a problem. Lewis concentrated on tuning his guitar, trying to ignore that guy. Susan grabbed the pickup from the Pignose case, and attached it for Lewis in a minute.

"Aren't you nervous?" he asked her as she handed the guitar back to him. "I mean, particularly since you're just learning the keyboard chords today? I couldn't be that brave."

"I can sight-read. I've been playing piano since I was six."

"Nice! I love piano, but my fingers are so stubby," he said, holding them up as evidence. Always smooth, Lewis, charming the ladies. "Affects me on the guitar too. I don't bother with some songs I'd love to play. The tabs . . . I swear, you need fingers like that monster in *Alien*."

"You'll be fine. Just look to me for changes if you get lost. Don't trail. Look a bar or two ahead and join in." Good, she was on the same page as us. "I modified my sheet music so you should be able to see from where you're standing." We all headed to the stage.

"You put this all up yesterday?" Lewis asked Susan.

"No big deal," she said. I could almost hear Lewis bitching about the way I could persuade people to help me out, even people who barely knew me. "Only took me a half hour, so saying yes was easy. Say no to everything, people just tune you out." She put on her collar.

"So you already knew about these?" he asked, tugging at his.

"Tami gave me a heads-up last night." She then dropped her voice, but I could still hear her. "Carson thinks they have 'cousin secrets,' but Tami and I have gotten close since she started going out with Artie. I know all kinds of 'Rez-Only Gossip.'" She used "gossip" instead of "Eee-ogg," so she couldn't know as much as she thought.

"Good to know," Lewis said, smiling wide and earnest. He was glomming onto her already, somehow missing the signals Doobie had already sent us. Susan was maybe replacing Marie for Lewis.

From the platform, I looked out. There were easily a hundred *strangers* here. People can ignore a good band, put them in the background, but if you're a bad musician, *everyone* notices. I peeled off my dad's billowy shirt, and pulled a new one out of my guitar case. I put it on, facing the band, to get their reactions. My new shirt had my bright red cartoon devil across the front. It was professionally done, like a concert shirt. I turned to the audience.

"We're the Dog Street Devils," I said into my microphone. Everything seemed to work—Artie and Susan must have sound-checked before we'd gotten there. I closed my eyes and knew I had about thirty seconds to win them over. So I launched into a crazy screeching sound and then repeated it a couple more times, starting to dance fast. I'd been practicing in front of my mirror at home so I could do it and still look like it was intentional.

Maggi heard the first cue and began a decent imitation of bongos on her dual water drums, into her mic, catching her rhythm before my second screech. For basic instruments, they were alive and breathing in her hands. There were only a few minor variations in this song's chords. Lewis shouldn't need the tabs. It was one of the few rock songs The Bug actually liked.

I wasn't sure how the crowd was going to take to a group of high school kids playing the Stones' "Sympathy for the Devil," but my job was to sell it. They didn't need to believe we were as good as the Stones. They just needed to enjoy it enough to fill in the gaps with their memories. The crowd started moving, kids coming closer to the stage, adults nodding and smiling to music they'd grown up with. Even the grandpa types seemed familiar with it.

Doobie shared Maggi's microphone, and Lewis leaned into Susan's. They began their "Woo-Hoo" chorus right on time. At my lead guitar solo, we all locked eyes for a couple seconds each, grinning like we'd been performing together a thousand years. For this first song, we were on fire! I'd been playing this alone for two years. The set was going to get tough, but it was a great moment to be alive. I was leading a band, in public!

When we made a hard cut at the end, people clapped and whistled. The only stone face I saw was that guy Jim. He was leaning against a tree, lighting a fresh cigar off the butt of his old one, eventually grinding embers out under his heel as he stared at me. I didn't even know this guy. What the hell was his problem?

We moved into "We Can Work It Out" after the opener, which Lewis had wormed into becoming one of our signatures despite my best efforts. We smoked on this song too. The longer we played, though, and the more everyone else dug our set, that guy seemed to focus more on me, and not in a good way. Were Lewis's troubles going to follow me around all the time? First that thing with Albert, which I couldn't stop thinking about, and now this. Lewis might be more liability than asset. This was a familiar feeling, but the stakes were higher these days. Our band was for real, convincingly coming together. After all my hard work getting him to this point, was I gonna have to unleash my rhythm player and find someone else to wear that collar before the Battle of the Bands?

18

I Felt Like Smashing My Face in a Clear Glass Window

Magpie Bokoni

When most of your audience was a little drunk, I wondered how good you had to be. Still, their clapping transformed my terror into excitement, and, in the end, satisfaction. I'd played for strangers at our Vendor Table, but those were Traditional Social songs. And at The Bug's party, I was kind of a semi-stranger. These people, though, were mostly strangers, and they believed we were a band.

I still didn't even really feel like a part of this band. I'd even snagged a ride today from some Rez guy, not wanting to ride with Carson. Any favor from him seemed to come with something you owed. I was the only one with an "I AM FROM THE REZ!" type instrument, even though I'd lived there the least (with the exception of Susan, but you couldn't count her).

The crowd was dense for a family Get-a-Day-Off-From-Work party, but I was watching two unhappy people ignore me—the only two guests I knew. At a Vendor Table, tourists know you're trying to sell them something and refuse to look at you, even sideways, for fear of you making eye contact. This avoidance felt different. Jim Morgan, who usually smiled widely at me, didn't even look my way once. Instead, he moved his eyes between Lewis and Carson. Benfriend was here all by himself, his Trabant parked along the road.

Marie and our mom were down at the Falls, entrenched with the Vendor Table right until school started. Before the rest of the band arrived, I hung out with Susan and Jim. I noticed people come up to Benfriend, and he'd be friendly, in that fake friendly way he used on me (you recognize an obligation smile), and then he'd shake hands or pat the other person on the back to let them know their conversation was over. Once we started, *he* didn't look my way, even once.

"You did great," Susan said as we closed our set. She hugged me and Lewis, stage-whispering as the crowd cheered. "I'm really glad. We sound so much fuller this way." I'd thought *she* was a last-minute addition. Lewis seemed as puzzled as I felt. We silently wondered if Susan's "filling out our sound" was another in Carson's endless supply of lies. We didn't sound *fuller* because of my water drums. Her synth pads had that concern covered. *I* was the Doubted Extra, not her. And Lewis knew he was doing rhythm parts Carson normally had covered between solos.

"Careful. Kind of sweaty," Lewis said with an embarrassed smile when she hugged him, making sure no one contacted his skin. He grabbed a shirt from his guitar case and headed behind the garage.

"Say, who is that?" I asked Susan (fake casually), nodding at Benfriend.

"Ben Gaward," Susan said immediately. "Kind of cute, huh? Very smart. I can introduce you, but be sure you don't call him Ben. He likes—"

"Benjamin," I said.

"Worse," she laughed. "He likes the *German* pronunciation, might even correct you."

"The German pronunciation?"

"Ben. Yaw. Mean. Can you even believe it?" she said, conspiratorially whispering. (I instantly loved this more than Benfriend and vowed to use it on Marie as soon as I saw her.)

"Whatever," I laughed. "Okay, so who is Ben-Yaw-Mean Gaward?"

"Dad's some official for the city schools. Ben-Yaw-Mean teaches German and eleventh-grade English at the city high school. Didn't Lewis tell me you used to go there?"

"We moved back to the Rez when I finished ninth," I said (suddenly remembering Marie's excellent eleventh-grade English grade, even though she hated books, and finally realizing why Ben-Yaw-Mean seemed so familiar. I'd seen him in the school hallways my whole freshman year).

"I overheard Dad telling Mom Ben-Yaw-Mean's going through a messy separation. High school and college girlfriend. He says she's a different person; she says he refuses to grow up." Susan shivered. "God, I hope I never say such things. Which is worse?" She laughed.

"Couldn't really say." A lie. We'd faced questions like those, twice. People asked if we were Rez Indians that City Indians didn't like, or City Indians deciding to try out Rez Life. Apparently there was a right answer, but I didn't know which girls we were. Even Marvin was stuck in between. He'd adapted to the fifty channels on city TV and now he was stuck with rabbit ears and a dozen channels (three of which were public TV and one in French, beaming in across Lake Ontario).

"Mom thought it was a good idea to invite him. Mom and Dad know almost everyone in all the schools around here, including all the single ladies. They thought he might find someone." I had a hard time thinking of my sister as a "Single Lady," since I was the only one who knew she still loved the stuffed armadillo (plush, not taxidermy) permanently staked out on her bed.

"Adults. Kind of creepy," Susan finished, shivering. "Soon-to-be ex or not. At least wait until you're really hanging your clothes in a different closet, before you start scouting for new girls."

The sun had gone down, and I really wanted to wash the heavy air from my face. But the Critchers had tents up and their garage strung with party lights. All food and drink was in the garage, and they had rented a sani john at the far end. These arrangements were a polite border barrier saying, *We like you but we don't like you that much. Please stay outside of our home.*

I wished that I'd thought to bring a towel. I had an idea and asked Susan for a discreet favor. If we were going to be bandmates—and she did seem pretty cool—this could be a good loyalty test. But as I'd suspected, when I started to follow, she stopped me at the plate-glass door and told me she'd be right out.

I suddenly felt like I was in Marvin's *Lost in Space* universe, and I was an alien monster. Susan had flipped the switch on the force field, keeping me outside of the spaceship where her family lived. I'd have to tell him this when I got home. He'd be amused (maybe, or just more aware that these days, I had a social life he didn't). The landing a few inches away was done in indoor/outdoor carpeting. We weren't even trusted to stand in the mudroom. We were Less Than Mud, even to our bandmate.

"Here you go," she said a few minutes later. She'd changed into a fresh outfit, dropping a paper-towel-wrapped package into my opened bag. "The porta potty's okay," she said, squeezing out a wan *sorry, you understand* smile. We both knew she hadn't been in the portapotty herself, but it was what *I* could use. Fortunately, I didn't need the item for its intended purpose.

I headed to where Lewis had gone, unwrapping the package. Susan had been generous. I'd be able to wipe my face down, and help Lewis. Our summer together had given us a new appreciation for the maxi pad, aside from Kenny's gross joke habit of catching Skoal spit with them. We used them to clean hard-to-reach areas and to wax the superintendent's car. You peeled the adhesive, slapped them across your palm, and—boom!—instant buffing cloth. You could even use these as disposable towels, as long as no one saw you.

Though it was dark behind the garage, I could see Lewis's silhouette. He stood with his shirt off, turning, like a living weather vane in the faint breeze. Each rib cast its own shadow on his torso in the rising moonlight. Susan left with a towel she'd offered him, and he checked her out, maybe memorizing the curve of her bare back with its dotted line of delicate bones.

"Don't be getting any funny ideas about that girl," a new voice said in the dark, Jim's. "Her old man wouldn't take kindly to you sniffing around his little girl."

"Sniffing around?" Lewis said. "You're so tacky." It seemed like they had been talking already before Susan showed up. Lewis slipped his shirt on. "We're just in a band together, and this was the first—"

"Don't tell me lies," Jim said, holding his hand up. He tapped his temple, shiny with grease and sweat. "I know lots of things." He poked Lewis on the breastbone, like he did at work sometimes, then turned and faced the garage and unzipped his cutoffs. "Now, if you'll excuse me, I gotta water some flowers."

"Least the garage's big enough that you'll hit your target this time," Lewis said. "Think your buddy'd appreciate you pissing on his property?"

"You man enough to find out?" Jim said, not moving. He seemed to change his mind and zipped his cutoffs back up. "Critcher Senior's a buddy of mine. He won't mind. Good to have friends," he added, facing Lewis. Lewis did not back down.

"Mind your own business anyway, Loser," Jim continued. "Why don't you go check out your microphone wire? I don't lie." I had no idea what Jim was talking about, but proximity was the real message here. He stepped up into Lewis's space, a few inches away, daring him to swing. Lewis might have been stupid enough to think he wouldn't be blamed for any questionable activity—he didn't feel Jim's natural charisma.

I hated to admit it, but after Jim had hugged me in the garage entryway in June, I hadn't stopped thinking about it. Even after our museum trip, and the fancy restaurant I'd never find again, I kept thinking about that embrace. Jim pressed against me, his slightest move giving me a shiver, his breath making my hair dance a little. Ever since, I've wondered what would have happened if I hadn't punched out and left that day. I had to remind myself that when he hugged me, he promised to be nicer to Lewis and that had clearly been a lie.

Promised to try *being nicer,* a surprising voice inside my head whispered. *He didn't say he'd succeed.* Whose voice was that?

I wanted to step out, do something. But then Lewis stepped back a few inches.

"Good dog, Lassie," Jim said. "Good you know your place."

"Already used that joke once today," Lewis said. "It wasn't funny the first time."

"Who's counting?" Jim said, stepping close again, inches from Lewis.

"We're not at work," Lewis said. "You can't get me fired from this party if I respond to your bullshit." Lewis was sober, but even buzzed and a little unsteady, Jim was a groundsman who worked all of his muscles every day. He had a hundred pounds on Lewis.

"Funny boy," Jim said, reaching up to pat Lewis's cheeks. At the last slap, he used more juice. It sounded like kindling cracking. "Oops," he said. "You know why they asked you to be in that band, Lassie?" he asked. (I wondered what that meant, and if I should even ask either.)

"Gloomis!" Carson shouted, suddenly appearing. Like that, it was over. Jim casually took one step back, and to Carson, this would have looked like a normal conversation. "We're down to the last couple nights of summer. Don't want to waste—" He studied Jim. "Do I know you?"

"Don't think so," Jim said. "Nice show." He headed back out into the party.

"What was going on there?" Carson asked Lewis as soon as Jim was out of earshot.

"Don't worry about it," Lewis said, tucking his T-shirt in as they wandered back to the party. If I showed up from where I was, Lewis would know I'd seen that exchange. The party was breaking up.

"You seen Maggi?" Carson asked. Lewis shook his head.

"I think she's . . ." Susan said, discreetly gesturing to the sani john (had to give her credit for doing that with discretion!).

"All right," Carson said. Just then, Jim stepped into the sani john, showing them all I was not in there (apparently Lewis's criticism had made some impression).

"She got here before we did," Lewis suggested. "Maybe she got the same ride?"

"Maybe she went for a walk," Artie said, walking up with his arm around Tami. "You know, to *clear her head*." (Code for vomiting.) "She can ride home with Tami," he said, kissing her lightly, then adding, "later." She slapped his arm and laughed, kissing him back.

There was no easy way for me to merge back into the party unnoticed, so I just decided to head out and try my luck getting a ride home. I left the sounds of my bandmates and the party behind and squeezed into a neighbor's yard to add distance. A few minutes later, I emerged down the road just in time to watch Carson's car leaving.

It was going to be a long, dark walk home.

Behind me, a roaring car revved through the night and raced toward me. I screamed a tiny bit. It wasn't Ben-Yaw-Mean's dumb farting car. This was a black T-top Trans Am, something even Carson would ditch his Chevelle for. It rumbled around the corner, showing off gold striping, like the *Smokey and the Bandit* car (including the giant bird decal and the air scoop tags). That Pontiac's sleek beauty did not change my dread as it slowed, though. This wasteland wasn't like when trouble found you in the city. There was nowhere to run in these acres of fields.

The Trans Am's windows were tinted deep. The driver revved hard again. Suddenly, an orange glow inside allowed me to see the occupant. I could feel my face bloom into a wide smile I couldn't help. Jim Morgan's grin grew bright in his cigar ember, his mustache framing it in harsh contrast. He rolled down the window and let out a plume of pungent smoke.

"Scare ya?" he said, laughing the dirty-old-man laugh he used about half the time.

"Jerk!" I said, slapping his forearm, giving a giggle in return. I walked around to the other side. "So whose car is this?" I asked, climbing in.

"Who d'ya think?" he said, laughing, driving away. "Nobody lends someone else a Trans Am, no matter how good friends you might be." He patted the dashboard, like it was a dog.

"What happened to your red truck? The official vehicle of the Bee Gees."

"Maybe I don't want to be like all the Bee Gees in the district anymore. Particularly after you called it, what was it? Old-Man Wheels?" I'd said something like that over the summer, but no one finances a new car just because some girl said your car was lame.

"How long you had it?"

"Just a week. You're my first passenger. Feel special?"

"Special?" I thought for a minute. "No, I don't feel special. Now, if you were *giving* me this car," I said, laughing myself, "then I'd feel special."

"Fat chance, kiddo. Do you even have your license?"

"Not yet," I said. I left out that I wasn't quite old enough to get my permit. He didn't need to know that I was fifteen. *Why don't you want him to know that?* the voice in my head said. I recognized it this time: Marvin, when he mimicked Dark Deanna. I didn't know when that started happening, but I wished it would quit. *Because fifteen is a problem, Marvin. Go away!* I said back. *Only a problem if you're thinking about one thing,* he said back, before leaving me to my own decisions.

"Could teach you how to drive this baby," Jim said. "Would you like that? Just me and you, cruising around. Me showing you what to do." Marie told me kids as young as ten drove cars on the Rez, even by themselves. You just couldn't go near the borders. But if I was driving Jim's car, it would not be on the Rez. Getting caught would be deadly. *Getting caught driving? Is that what you're worried about getting caught at?* Ghost Marvin said, one last shot.

"I'm in no hurry," I said.

"So, um . . . listen. You in a hurry to get *home*?" Carson hadn't gone back to the Rez, and I was supposedly with the band. I had time. Particularly since Marie couldn't report when the party broke up. I wondered why she hadn't shown toward the end at least, particularly with Ben-Yaw-Mean there.

"I probably have a little while. Why?"

"You'll see," he said as we drove past the Rez, eventually turning by the Sanborn Field Day grounds, overgrown. He parked in front of a closed diner. "Sit tight," he said, and ran to a door next to the diner entrance. A light went on upstairs, and shortly off again. He came out with a backpack. He still had on his shorty-shorts but a different T-shirt draped over his bare shoulder.

"Check this out," he said, tossing the bag to me. We headed farther away from the Rez. I dug in and saw a Polaroid OneStep. "You can borrow it on open-ended loan. I'll only ask for it back when I need it." I'd seen commercials for these. You pressed the button and the picture kicked out the front like a tongue, developing before your eyes. The bag also held a few cartridges of film and several boxes of flashcube bars, and a magazine called *Avant Garde*.

"What's this magazine?" I asked, starting to pull it out. So much more to say. Like: *Open-ended loan of an expensive camera?*

"That mag's for you to check out later. When you get home. But the camera, it could be good for your art. That guy you like so much? The one painting soup cans? He takes Polaroids all the time. Mostly movie stars. Maybe you'll be like him. And maybe you'll make something I'd buy," he said. He'd remembered that I liked Andy Warhol. And he must have looked that Polaroid info up himself. (Jim hadn't *really* struck me as someone with *that* level of an interest in contemporary art, but maybe I was wrong about him. Going to museums, a lot of people did, but studying Andy Warhol took effort, and the magazine here looked pricey and like it might actually be about art.)

"I know your family doesn't get what you do," he said, suddenly looking directly into my eyes. "But I do. Not all art is made for tourists to like. I get that."

"You got a lot of art in your apartment above the Sunrise Skillet?"

"You could come and find out for yourself," he said, turning his head shyly, grinning.

"Yeah, we'll see." I said. "So how do you use this?"

"It's a OneStep! Look in the viewfinder and press the button. I thought you could take pictures of your stuff and your sister could put them out at the trinket table." *(Trinket table?)*

"Someone might be interested enough to buy it," he added. "But they won't know if they never get to see it. Liz at the garage buys all kinds of turquoise shit on vacation in New Mexico. Comes back with a little suitcase full and charges people double."

Liz, figured. I knew the type. Wear down the Indian jewelry maker, argue you're buying in quantity, then go sell it at jacked-up prices to people the silversmith would never have the chance to meet.

"You can practice now," he added, pulling into a closed fruit stand parking lot. "Take a picture of me and my Bandit." He tossed his shirt on his seat and went to the car's front end, leaning against the hood. He rested his hands behind him and crossed one ankle over the other, a total pose, trying to look casual. All he had on were those corduroy cutoffs, short white tube socks with the stripes at the top, and sneakers. He stretched back so his belly didn't hang over his belt, making himself look more fit than he really was (not that he was super paunchy). "How's 'at?"

"You might want to either tug your shorts up, or stuff your undershorts down," I said. "Waistband's showing."

"Good catch," he said. He undid the belt, the button, and slid the fly down, cramming the elastic waistband down all the way around. "Better?" he said, spreading his arms.

"Probably should buckle back up before I take the picture," I said.

"You and me are the only ones who're gonna see it. Nice thing about Polaroids. No lab. No one else has to see it except the person taking the picture and the person in the picture." I lowered the camera until he made himself more presentable. He caved and leaned back again when he was ready. I looked into the viewfinder and took the picture. The flash popped, and the camera made a grinding sound, spitting out the photo down front, which was a hazy, milky color.

"I don't think it worked," I said.

"Got to give it time," he said. "Come here, lean on the hood with me. It's still warm, and the air's getting a little sharper." The hood did feel good on the backs of my bare thighs as we watched Jim emerge in the developing film, like he was walking out of a fog. When it finally finished, it wasn't as clear as a regular photo, but it was an okay picture of him. The flash really picked up how fair his skin was. It made his bushy chest hair stand out even more than normal. I handed the photo to him, but he held up his hands, as if he could stop me.

"For you. If you ever want to be reminded of me when we're not in the same place. And," he said, digging back in the Trans Am's glove compartment and coming back with a pen, "here's my number. If you ever need a ride or *anything*, you call me. I don't care what time, I'll come." He'd written it and *JM* next to it in the white surface below the image. "I'm serious. You never know."

"Okay," I said. I slid the photo, the camera, and all the accessories into my own backpack. I couldn't stop thinking about the possibilities. Since I rarely worked the Vendor Table, I'd gotten to love beadworking fully again, especially since I kept getting all kinds of new ideas for album cover variations. I'd started to work on a sweet-grass braided matt, to be the background for a corn-husk version of John Lennon's *Rock 'n' Roll*. I wondered if I might be able to incorporate the Polaroids into what I do, if there might be some way of combining photos with my other recent projects: sassy versions of our family canoes (that I'd started calling Broken-Heart Canoes). It was exciting to wander into new areas with a totally new tool.

"You gonna return the favor?" he asked, lifting the camera from my hands.

"Really?" I said, sarcastic.

"No, *no*," he said, pausing just long enough to confirm his secret hope. "I just meant, you know, leaning against the hood. Not, you know, not—"

"I believe 'topless' is the word you're looking for, Uncle Pervy," I said, laughing, to let him off the hook. I didn't like what he was suggesting, but it *had* been nice of him to give me a ride, and unbelievably nice with the camera.

I wanted to ask him why he was always such a jerk to Lewis, but I felt like somehow that would screw this up, whatever *this* was. He was the first person to really see me. Even Lewis, for all his sensitivity, never wanted to talk about *me* with me. It was always Marie Marie

Marie and/or Beatles Beatles Beatles. Even earlier at the party, one of the first things he said to me was asking if my sister was coming. I'd mentioned my art ideas to him a few times when we first started working together, but he *never* asked me more about them. Not once. And his mom *did* beadwork. He knew how important it was to us. And here was Jim, totally on the outside, trying to help me. Even though he was calling beadwork "trinkets," he was still trying.

"I wasn't suggesting that at all. You're pretty enough you don't need to resort to those gimmicks. Guys'd line up if you opened a Kissing Booth at the Sanborn Field Day." *Kissing Booth?* What a Bizarro! "Do me the honors?" he asked, raising the camera.

"Sure," I said. What harm could a photo do? Everybody had pictures of their friends.

I leaned on the hood like the calendar cheesecake girls our mechanics had up in the break room, but I had no tools to sell. The flashbulb blinded me while Jim watched the picture develop. "Okay?" He held it out, a decent photo. I looked like me. I nodded, and he held out the pen.

"Jim. It's my mom and dad's house. Their phone. If I get a call—"

"Does that loser Lewis have your number?"

"Don't call him that." I couldn't turn away from it now. "What's your problem with him anyway? Why are you always hassling him? He's totally not big enough to have ever caused you trouble. And besides, it's different when he calls, because—"

"'Cause he's another Indian?" he asked, cutting me off. Jim was now acting like a jealous boy, not the man I was beginning to know better. Out here, miles from home, I didn't like where this was headed.

"If you're treating him this way because he's Indian, how am I supposed—"

"It's *not* 'cause he's Indian. I just don't like the kid, for my own reasons. He knows why."

"I can assure you, he doesn't. And if you really like me, *really* want to be nice to me, you'll leave him alone."

"Okay, I'll leave him alone," Jim said. "But you know, not everything happens to someone because of their race. Some people are just assholes."

"Yeah, well, *you* know that some people do things to other people *solely* because of their race. You helped me at the Sanborn Field Day Beer Tent. You knew what was going on." He nodded and looked down. "I'm not sure I ever thanked you for helping me."

"What a gentleman does, when he sees a young lady in trouble."

"Just the same," I said. "Thank you." *A lady,* he'd said. I leaned over and kissed his cheek, rough, stubbly, and smelling of aftershave. He must have spruced up in his apartment.

"Look, me and Lewis, it's more like . . . shared history. My parents know his. My grandparents knew his. And now we've got our band. We're signing up for Battle of the Bands. Ever work those things?"

"I could," he said. "Never had a reason to before. Other than the overtime."

"Maybe I could be a reason?" I said. His face transformed, as he smiled the warmest smile I'd ever seen. When it appeared, that other Jim vanished, as if he lived in a different dimension and just occasionally broke through to ours, only to hassle Lewis. This smile made me want to hug him, like when I saw those crappy stained shades on his apartment windows. I'd felt something catch beneath my breastbone that moment, and I felt it again now. I bet that place was very lonely sometimes.

"What time is it anyway?" I asked. I turned his wrist to read his watch. His arm shivered a little, like he was chilled. "I gotta get home, Jim. Sorry. Where did you want to go out here?"

"Was gonna take you to a drive-in out this way. Figured you might want something to eat. Didn't seem like you got anything at the party."

"Sweet of you," I said. I didn't ask if it was *that* drive-in. "This too." I tapped the camera. "Can't tell you how much I appreciate your trust. This is one of the nicest things anyone's done for me."

"Just a camera," he said, but smiled anyway. "And, uh, go ahead and use that film in there and, uh, if you need it, I got more. Just let me know."

"I don't mean the camera. I mean, that's great, but I mean . . . that you believe in me, and you don't hardly know me at all."

"I know you're talented, and sweet, and good-hearted and . . ." We both knew the word he wanted to say. I wanted him to say it too, but it was a scary word. Once someone said it, you knew what that meant. No one had ever said it about me, but guys in our old school said it about Marie. They thought grabbing the crotches of their jeans when they said it would convince her they'd be a good match. Maybe that was how she ended up with Ben-Yaw-Mean. I'm almost positive he never groped himself and told her she was *sexy*. He was too Toot-o-file for that.

"Anyway, you're welcome," he said. He gave a gentle smile and another nod. "Guess we should get you home. Drive-in rain check?" I nodded, though I wasn't taking him up on it. I wanted to keep good thoughts about Jim Morgan. "Got a leftover plate in my trunk. Want some?"

"I'm good," I said, looking at his watch. "Thanks, though. Sweet."

We got back in the Trans Am and listened to a cassette. It was the Beatles, but not a sequence I recognized. I was coming around to them more now. And after that booklet Carson showed me, I was way more interested in Yoko Ono too. Everyone said she broke up the Beatles, blah blah blah, but it turned out she was an artist on her own before she met any of them. She even met Paul first! She was Yoko Ono, a badass conceptual artist, not Mrs. John Lennon.

"You make this, yourself?" I asked.

"No, new album," he said.

"Oh, right, the Beatles put out a new album and I didn't hear about it."

"A new collection. Not even all that new now. It's, I think, a couple years old. Called *Love Songs*. Can make you a copy if you want. Or you can have this one."

"They take songs people already have, put them in a different order, and call it a new album?" He nodded. "I didn't even know you liked the Beatles."

"Honey, I was buying Beatles records when they were putting them out," he said, laughing. "I'll have you know I saw maybe the one and only performance of the Plastic Ono Band. So *there*."

"You lie!"

"No lie. It wasn't on purpose, though. It was a rock-and-roll revival show. Mostly, I was there to see the Doors, but it was a lot of old Rock and Rollers, Chuck Berry, Jerry Lee Lewis, Little Richard, and—real weird—Alice Cooper.

"Are you making this up?"

"Swear to God. Some college stadium in Toronto. They kept saying some secret special guest was coming. There were rumors it was gonna be Lennon, I guess the other reason I made the trek up there. And sure enough, the secret guests were John and Yoko, Clapton, a drummer I didn't know, and that guy Klaus something."

"Voormann," I said, stunned. "What was the show like?"

"How do you know Klaus Voormann?"

"Um, artist who made the cover of *Revolver*?"

"Oh yeah, that's right. How'd your *Revolver* art thing come out anyway? You never showed it to me. Anyway, show was good, but John played mostly old songs, 'cause they'd never played together before. Only one Beatles song. That crowd wasn't feeling Yoko's experimental stuff—mostly her laying on the stage in a bag making screaming noises while John and Clapton made feedback guitar noise."

"My *experimental* beadwork's almost done," I said. "I'll show it to you. Promise." Jim grinned.

"You want these love songs?" he said, turning on Snakeline. We were almost home. "Never know when they'll come in handy. You could find yourself falling for someone."

"You think they'll ever get back together?"

"They kept saying all that you need's love. Maybe they don't have that for each other anymore. Maybe all they got is a gaping hole. That's one I know." He held the tape out to me, pulling over by the wooded, houseless strip before the Shack.

"All I have's a record player," I said, opening the door.

"Could lend you the album, if you want."

"No thanks. New sequences always sound weird to me. I keep expecting the familiar and something new comes up instead."

"Something new can be good, you know," he said, and gave me the sad smile he'd had earlier. I almost couldn't bear to look at it. I might get back in.

"Good night, Jim, and thanks again."

"Thank *you*," he said, lifting the photo of me from his console catchall. He'd put his shirt on when we'd gotten back in the Trans Am and now slid my picture in his T-shirt pocket, just a line of muscle, ribs, skin, and hair between it and his heart.

Heading up the driveway, I wondered if those Beatles songs were the magic my dad used to get my mom to come home. Maybe Marie had nothing to do with it after all. Maybe our dad had sent out radio requests, telling the DJ to say, *This next song's from Mel to Deanna, "All You Need Is Love,"* knowing it would work. My mom used to say my dad was so handsome, she knew in elementary school she was going to marry him. I couldn't imagine who he was back then, what she saw. Even their senior pictures on our living room wall (her in a feather boa and him in a white tuxedo) looked like the sample photos in place when you bought a frame. Or I should say, it *would* look like that if there were non-white people on Picture Frame Planet. Even people with brunette hair had a hard time in that world.

In the Shack, Marvin gave me a disinterested look as I scrounged in the fridge. I decided he probably wouldn't be amused by my force-field story after all.

"Where were you?" I asked Marie once I got to our room.

"Vendor Table, duh," she said. Maybe she didn't know Ben-Yaw-Mean was at the party. "Bigger question, where were *you*? Party ended hours ago."

"And where'd you get your Eee-ogg? Ben-Yaw-Mean Gaward?"

She whipped her head at me. I'd planned to save my info for when I'd need her silence, but I needed it now. I just wanted to lie in bed, picturing Jim's smiling face, the warmth of his touch, the scent of his aftershave, and way I was beginning to like the surprisingly rough feel of his cheek, when I pressed my lips against it.

"You going out with him tonight?" I asked. Silence, but I knew. She had her Going Out lipstick on. "It *is* a school night," I added, and turned to stare right at her. "For *both* of you." For the first time in years, my sister was speechless. I enjoyed the moment. Like all good things, it was sure not to last.

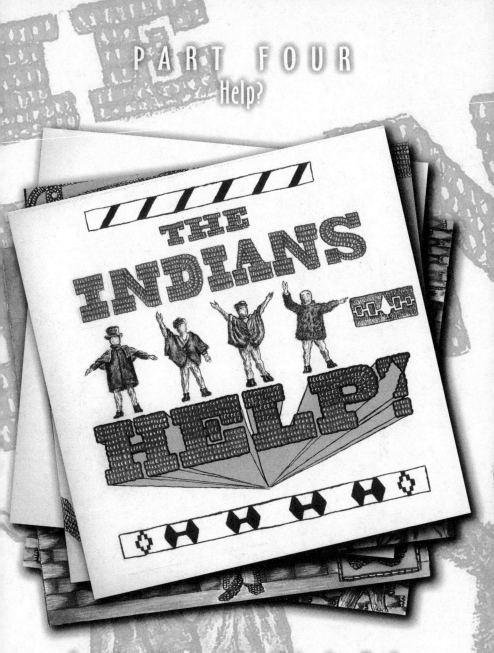

Canadian Thanksgiving (Columbus Day)–
Thanksgiving
Harvest Moon

19

Cold Turkey
Carson Mastick

Things were shaping up. The band was continuing to evolve with new and solid arrangements. Maggi's water drum had turned out to be a bigger success than I'd anticipated. It gave us a sound like no one else, and it was awesome marketing. With our newest members, and the chronic tension between Rez kids and white kids at school, we found ourselves as Poster Children for Finding a Cultural Bridge. If we won, the prize money would be smaller for each of us, but we'd all still be awarded the New York City trip part of the prize.

To keep us on top, I developed Money Punishment—the one place you'd always feel it. If you missed practice, you had to pay five bucks to each band member for wasting their time. It was rare, but everyone paid with no complaining. And when we had free time, it wasn't free. It went to the band. We'd had today off. It was Canadian Thanksgiving, or National Genocide Awareness Day, or, as we refused to call it, Columbus Day.

"What about Moondogs?" Lewis said as we broke our gear down.

"Gloomis, we are *not* a Beatles cover band," I said as I cased my Casino. Lewis thought he could sneak this obscure one in, but I researched all the names the Beatles had before they'd settled on the right one. This one was a decent attempt, but not decent enough. "And we're already in the schedule under the name we agreed on."

I still loved the ring of Dog Street Devils, so that's what we were going with. We'd been assigned the second Battle of the Bands elimination round, the Wednesday before Thanksgiving. The final Battle wasn't until January, just before third-quarter marking period ended. If I won Battle of the Bands and made my rock-and-roll life connections in New York City, I wouldn't have to worry about marking periods or the fact that I'd blown off school for the last three years.

"We'll play *some* songs," I added. "Some! I get it! They're classics! People love them even though they split ten years ago. If that's who *you* want to be, start your own damned band."

"You're opening with that Stones song all the time!" he said, scrunching his face up. "I just figured, you know, Dog Street and the moon, like in the Traditional calendar."

"Like many moons ago?" Susan asked, giggling a little.

"Well, where'd you think that phrase came from?" Lewis asked.

"Cut the bull, Lewis!" I said, shutting down that intraband arguing nonsense quick. "No Moondogs, no Quarrymen, no Silver Beatles, no Eggmen. We are the Dog Street Devils," I said. Lewis, as the only other senior in the band, apparently thought he could give me some shit. "Told you before. No room for two leaders in this band."

"Fine," he said. "So, hey, was Mrs. Marchese afraid to be alone in the home ec room with the Devil on Friday?" He hunched, prancing on tippy toes, pretending he held a pitchfork.

"Why would I be in home ec on Friday? I don't need extra credit."

"Funny." He scrunched his mouth. "Can't you be serious? If we blow this project . . ."

"Artie, these two are in your cooking class?" Susan asked. Artie and Tami had driven Susan and had both stuck around to listen. They were competing too, so were probably spying, but an audience kept me on my toes.

"Artie's got it the period after us," Lewis said. "You guys doing the same thing we are?"

"Canadian Thanksgiving?" Artie said. "Heck yeah! I'm not Canadian, eh? But it's turkey!" Artie stacked Susan's keyboard rig near the door. "I'm doing some sweet potato thing," he added. "Our mom just mashes, but we have to do *a recipe*. It *is* cooking class. Plus, mini marshmallows! I'm all over—wait!" Artie stopped himself, his grin widening. "*You* guys are doing the turkey?" he asked. Lewis nodded but looked worried. "Indians bringing the turkey to Thanksgiving? Marchese is so twisted."

Mrs. Marchese, our home ec teacher, said it would be good for us to know different cultures, so our holiday dinner project coincided with the Canadian one. She was a weirdo, but at least we weren't having Columbus Day dinner. Each student pair had to cook one part of the big feast, and Lewis and I had wound up with the turkey.

"Who do you think brought the main courses to the first Thanksgiving?" Lewis said. Every once in a while, he would go all Indian Patriotic. "It wasn't your sorry-ass ancestors."

No matter how long we all hung out, things would never be easy between Lewis and Artie. George Haddonfield had been friends with Artie too. Nothing specifically bad there—we're used to sharing. But when George and his family up and moved away in eighth grade, it was like they vanished from Earth. As far as I knew, Lewis had never heard one word from him. Always, I could see, right on the edge of his nerve, he wanted to ask Artie if George had ever reached out to him. Either answer would have killed Lewis, so he just kept himself in the dark, but sometimes it bled over into the shit he said to Artie.

"No offense," Artie was quick to say. "Seems like Marchese is putting you in a box."

"Who's doing your class turkey?" Lewis asked, before the Artie chatterbox train could start again.

"Two guys on varsity football. Twenty-five pounds of turkey is nothing to mess with. Almost dropped it a couple times." He was about to launch into a story and paused. "Um, Carson? How come you *weren't* there? For real. I hung out to give our turkey guys a ride home."

"What are you doofuses talking about?" I said.

"Tell me," Lewis started saying slowly, looking directly at me, "that you remembered to go in Friday after activities bell and move our turkey from the freezer to the fridge."

"That's tomorrow," I said. "We're not eating until Wednesday. How long could it take? Ice in a cooler doesn't stay ice, even over-night. How hard could it be for a turkey to thaw?"

"Shit," Lewis said.

"Lighting Can," Maggi said, and peeled open the coffee can we kept, our other costly way of shaping our public image. Tami had decorated it with *$$#!%@$$*. Any time one of us swore when we practiced at someone's house, that person had to toss five bucks in the can. It was a rule. Susan and Artie's dad didn't seem thrilled on those nights he was stuck having a bunch of Indians in his base-ment, so we tried not to give him any more reason to be annoyed. When we had a decent amount in the can, we'd get something to help with our stage-lighting rig.

"Gloomis, you said we'd wash it in class on Monday," I added. "Remember? You were all 'save the giblets,' doing Dan Aykroyd's doing Julia Child on *Saturday Night Live*!"

"How'd you think we were going to get those giblets out?" Lewis said. "It has to be *thawed* enough! Weren't you listening in class? You had *one job* to do!" Artie looked down. He could have called, or just taken mine out. Still, this was my fault. All on me.

"Sorry, guys. Wish I knew how to help you," Artie said. "But I'm empty. Zero ideas." He ran Susan's keyboard out to his truck. They knew I was in trouble, in a particularly Rez Kid way. Did white kids forget the primary step in their major quarter grade? I'd barely passed first quarter.

I'd been cooking since I was seven, though. Sheila and Derek had taught me how to take care of myself early, but I didn't know Marchese's fancy way. I got a D+ on our first project, so Marchese assigned me and Lewis the turkey to get my grade up by the end of the quarter. I told Lewis it was the Indians-and-Thanksgiving thing and he'd been naive enough to buy it.

"Can I use your phone?" Maggi asked me.

"You don't need to ask," Tami said, sharper than she needed. "It's the Rez," she added, just to be annoying. Artie and Susan passed each other that *Wild Kingdom* look, like they were observing a foreign species. Maggi stretched the phone cord to the back porch. I wondered if I'd be able to sneak in a ride offer to her when we were done tonight.

"Freezing out there," Maggi said, rubbing her arms, as she came back in. "First frost is gonna come early this year. How do you guys yack on the phone without getting frostbite?"

"Usually use the upstairs extension," I said, laughing. She stuck out her tongue.

"Swear," she abruptly said to Artie.

"Swear to what?" he said. I hated when Maggi did these cutesy things. It was the only thing about her that was a turnoff. In the moment, I was kind of glad, for real. I didn't need the distraction.

"Just swear."

"Okay, crap."

"A real swear," she said, peeling the lid on the coffee can. I had an idea where this was going. We each said a round of swears and chipped into the can, adding up to thirty-three bucks.

"Am I done in my part of saving your ass?" Artie said, and everyone laughed. He dropped another five. "I'm not even *in* this band. I got to get Susan home. Still a school night."

"Dad's paranoid sometimes," Susan said, leaving out: *When we're on the Rez with you.*

"Yeah, you're fine," Maggi said. "The fewer people who know details, the better." Artie narrowed his eyes. "No offense," she clarified. "And settle down. We're doing something . . . not exactly aboveboard, and I don't want you having to lie if we get caught. Better for *you*," she said. I was intrigued.

"Tami?" Artie said. He knew he was asking her to divide her loyalties.

"She's fine. She can go with you," Maggi said. Tami looked relieved and disappointed. Then Maggi looked directly at me. "Be better if it was just Lewis and me, but you're not likely to hand us the keys to *the Chevelle*."

"Not a chance," I said, laughing even in this screwed-up moment.

"I didn't think so. Anyway, we better get going," she said, getting her coat on and handing me and Lewis ours. "You might want to leave your guitar here," she said to him. "I don't know how long we're going to be."

"Just leave it next to mine," I said. "No one's gonna touch it."

"Call me when you're done," Tami said to me. "Even past midnight. My folks are bowling, so they're out to one o'clock, easily."

"Too bad you guys are stuck with me," Susan said, giggling. Artie shared Susan's sentiment, minus giggles. They'd already benefited from the bowling schedule of Tami's parents. They all piled out of the room and into the night.

"All right!" Maggi said as soon as they were gone. "Tops has fresh turkeys. They stock them now for all the Canadian shoppers. Thank your Bush cousins next time you see 'em."

"What are you talking about?" I asked, zipping my jacket.

"Tops is open until midnight. It's now past ten o'clock. We're getting you a fresh turkey. Do you know how big the one is in the school freezer?"

"Exactly twenty-seven pounds," Lewis said. "One and a half pounds per kid in the class."

"That's a lot of turkey to eat in one meal," she said. We headed out and climbed into the Chevelle.

"Thursday's leftovers, and Friday's variations in leftovers." Lewis made a face. We'd be eating so much recycled turkey for a week, I'd have a wattle by the time Thanksgiving came.

"We get a turkey. Then what?" I said. I couldn't get in there before teachers tomorrow, and two Indian kids wandering the halls with a giant turkey before classes wouldn't be ignored.

"You just gotta trust me," she said. "The less you know, the better. I'd do it alone, but I can't lug something that heavy myself." As we drove, I snuck glances. Her eyes, reflecting green dashboard lights, sparked with an edge. Our thighs touched. For the first time, I didn't mind my stupid heater being so pokey, and I wished the grocery store were farther away. Lewis's eyes just looked worried. No surprise there. Worry was his default setting.

We ran immediately to the butcher shop section, which was dark. They only stayed active until nine. "Shit! I was afraid of this," Maggi said.

"Lighting Can," Lewis and I said in unison.

"I'm out. Will have to IOU," she said. "Doesn't matter now."

"What about them?" I said, pointing. A row of neatly wrapped birds sat in a cooler case with SALE! FRESH! cardboard signs over in the back. The Canadian holiday was over, and this was what was left. We headed over to check them out.

It was weird to be here late, examining fresh turkeys of all things. For our occasional beer runs, we always hit convenience stores. It was Old-Man Behavior to buy grocery-store Labatts. I felt like one of those old men, as I fondled plump birds, trying to help Maggi find what it was she was missing.

"A twenty-seven pound turkey's probably an Order-Ahead thing. Especially right after Canadian Thanksgiving." She made weirdly mature examinations as she worked her way through the turkeys. Like a well-preserved, smoking-hot, little middle-aged woman.

"Got one!" she yelled, and other late-night shoppers frowned. They saw wiseass Rez Kids that our No-Good Parents weren't keeping an eye on. We were *running amok.* "Someone always hides the primo stuff at the cooler bottom, hoping no one else discovers it before they scrounge up the cash." She struggled, staring at me. Eventually I tumbled and yanked it out.

"Hello Mr. . . ." She scanned his sticker. "Mr. Twenty-Four and Three-Quarters. You're not quite the man we were hoping for, but you'll have to do." She slapped a Social song rhythm on the turkey's breast. That bird sang out the sweet, wet sound of gloriously non-frozen meat.

At the checkout, Maggi pulled our Lighting Can fund from her purse, wanting me to see My Personal Screwup. The checkout woman studied us and decided she didn't need to know why three teenagers were buying a turkey with small bills at half past ten on a Monday night.

"Frozen ones are a little cheaper," she said, quietly, "if money's an issue."

"No, no," Maggi said. "Money's *not* an issue. But thanks, you did remind me I have this coupon." She handed over a twenty-five-cents-off-per-pound coupon, and the woman applied it.

"Where'd you get a coupon for fresh turkeys when we needed one?" Lewis asked.

"Stuck on that kitchen bulletin board at Carson's. I spotted it when I made my call. Still good 'til New Year's Day." *Shit!* I thought. That meant my mom was counting on using it. "You still got any of yesterday's papers?" she asked the cashier. The cashier silently slipped the paper into our cart. "I'm sure this is where that coupon came from. I'll go through it in the car."

"Cool," I said. "So now what?"

"Now is where your trust comes in. Do you trust me?" We nodded. "To the high school, then. I'll tell you where," she said plainly, like I was dropping her home.

"Then what?" Lewis said, suspicion leaking like gas.

"You *don't* get to ask!" she said, razor-voiced. "I'm saving your asses and not because you deserve it. I want this band to win, and we aren't going to, if *any* of us is distracted. Got it?"

We got it, for sure. I pulled out of the Tops parking lot and flew down to the school, slowing only when we hit the employee parking lot, as instructed.

"Okay, here. Stop here," she said. I'd never been to this part of the school.

"Now what?"

"Now," she said, impatient. "You let me and the bird out, and you drive away and go home. Don't wait. Don't stop and don't turn around. I promise, I'll be home tonight. Drop Lewis off so he can get his beauty sleep." Lewis chuckled, but I was not in a laughing mood.

"But—"

"No buts," she said, sharp. "You don't get to ask. I *might* tell you, someday, but don't count on it. Just consider me your Fairy God-Drummer."

"This is crazy," Lewis said. "You're not dressed to be outside."

"Look," she said to him. "I appreciate your concern. But I've got this covered. If I don't do this, you're as screwed as he is. You want Carson's lazy-ass mistake to lower your grades?"

"Of course not," he said, snapping his eyes at me. "But I can stay, help you. I promise. Whatever it is, I won't say a word."

"Lewis," I said. "I don't like it any more than you, but we don't have a choice right now."

"That's right," she said. "You don't." That weird feeling I'd had in the grocery store—that I was talking to a very petite, youthful-looking middle-aged woman—was back. How long had she been stuck living in the adult world? Did she like it? She seemed to be there so naturally. My dad just about levitated with joy if I made panny-cakes once in a while. She was so grown up, she didn't even seem to notice it.

"Where do you want this?" Lewis asked, struggling with the bird. Maggi couldn't lift it. At first, he'd just sat in the car, not letting her out. We were having the same second thoughts.

"Just set it there, on the sidewalk," she said, holding herself close in this fierce wind tunnel. I wished I'd worn a hat, and I didn't even own one. "Now, please go. No hanging around. Go up Bitemark Road so I can see your taillights heading into the Rez. And before I forget. One last thing, here, I found the coupon."

She handed over the newspaper but jerked it back when I reached for it.

"One condition, don't look at the paper's front page."

Of course, now I absolutely *had* to look at the front page. But I also wanted that coupon up before my mom noticed. "Fine," I said, reaching out and grabbing the paper from her hand and climbing into the Chevelle. Lewis got back in and we did a U-ey so I could roll down the window and give it one last try. "You sure?"

"Go!" she yelled, her hair whipping around so crazy I could barely see her face. "The sooner you're gone, the sooner I can take care of what I need to!"

Watching her grow smaller in my rearview mirror was one of the hardest things I've had to do. She shook in those tight designer jeans and that Kmart puffy ski jacket. Lewis wrenched himself around and we watched her get smaller, a colorful speck against the gray walls. I wanted to take her, and hold her, warm her up with my body, like the hypothermia lesson from Health.

"What if I pulled into that jitney path on Bitemark, and I run back," I said. "You can drive, right? I mean, I gave you your first lesson back in junior high." We both tried to laugh, but neither of us could, really. We were both too scared.

"No," Lewis said. "You can't."

"Look, you gotta overcome this fear you have of always getting caught. Live a little."

"It's not that. I trust her. She's up to something. She has some plan we don't know about. By the time you ran back there from here, she'd be long gone."

"I guess. I just hate when people lie," I said. "We're a band. Supposed to stick together."

"She's *being* a good band member," he said. "She's saving your ass so we can all concentrate on being good. You're just mad you can't control her like everyone else." I wasn't *even* going to give him any satisfaction over that burn, but it stung. Before I took Lewis home, I swung past her place. The light in the little camper they shared was on. Marie was home.

"Turn around," Lewis said as we got near the border. "She's not where we left her."

"But what if she is? What if she's hitchhiking home right now? She's maybe gotten the turkey in place and is making her way home. We could pick her up. Least we could do for—"

"You might be okay lying to yourself, but I don't want you lying to me right now," Lewis said. "I don't want to walk home from here, but I can. I've—"

"I know. You've done it before and you'll do it again. Give it a rest? It's just . . ."

"The feeling you're experiencing is *care*," he said. "Unfamiliar. I know. And I hate to break it to you, but once you start, it's almost impossible to stop." Lewis felt those things, but he didn't usually share them with me, because I'd hassle him. I was surprised to find him right. I was used to the jazzed feeling around her because she was hot. And she dressed *purposely* to be hot. Even more effective. But lately? On top of those feelings? Or maybe below? There was this *caring* thing. What was she up to on those nights we weren't practicing? What was life like, dealing with her freakazoid parents and living in that wacky camper?

It was like I'd suddenly been saddled with someone else's feelings. Was this maturity? Was I going to start running through freezing late-night fields to impress a girl who didn't even like me? Wouldn't life be way easier if I just hooked up with someone? Both have a good time, no strings attached, and maybe do it again sometime or maybe not. This worrying and wondering late on sleepless nights was super weird. *So why couldn't I stop worrying and wondering?* I didn't like this feeling at all.

"You mean like you cared for, what's his name? Haddonfield?" I said, refusing to say George's name fully. "That white boy could just walk away, not even a second look back. Like you never even existed in his life. Where'd that caring get you?"

"Well, I guess you'll never know, will you." He said it like a statement, not looking for an answer. But we both knew I could ask Artie and potentially force information onto Lewis that he didn't want to hear.

Neither of us said anything more, even as I dropped Lewis off, and headed to the school. No Maggi, no turkey. I fought the urge to go in but the one thing she asked was that we trust her, so I fought it. In the parking lot, I grabbed the newspaper. Its front page was missing. When I got home, I immediately called Lewis. "Am I gonna have to come there and rip it out of your hands?"

"You're not gonna want to see it," he said.

I waited.

"Fine! Human interest. 'Custard's Last Stand Throws Fundraiser.' Photo was stand-up comedians, some in Spaniard hats and some in braids and feathered. Guess who wore the fake plastic nose and glasses, so the audience would know who was supposed to look even dumber."

"Shit," I said, breathing the word out in one long burn.

"Lighting Can," Lewis said quietly. "All proceeds to Knights of Columbus." I told him I'd get the paper from him tomorrow. He protested 'til I reminded him that I still had his guitar.

Lying in bed, I thought about Maggi. Knowing what she was facing, getting out of the Chevelle, pulling off whatever risky thing she was doing to save my ass, she *still* tried to protect me from seeing that newspaper. Would I ever stop feeling this strange ache behind my ribs? I wanted to take her away from her weird, adult choices, and bring her back among us. If I held my hand out, to invite her back to Midway rides and ice-cream stands, would she come? Would she feel that she belonged with us or was it already too late to help her find her way back home?

I had no way of knowing, but whenever I closed my eyes, all I could see was her tiny figure, shivering in my rearview mirror, with a fresh, cold turkey, and it was all my fault.

20

Nobody Sees Me Like You Do
Magpie Bokoni

I felt like an idiot, standing on the sidewalk outside the boys' locker room corridor, watching those guys head back to the Rez. The parking lot was weirder and scarier at night. It was surprisingly darker. Circular pools of light stretched out the parking lot lamps, like in movies where airplanes are landing (bringing someone home for BS kiss-kiss-kiss reunion with violins and tears and hugs).

I didn't even know why I was doing this. I didn't like Carson *that* much. I mean, yeah, he laughed at my jokes, even when everyone else on the Rez pretended they weren't funny. Lately, that was even enough to crack the grim mouths on some of these Easter Island Heads. But every time I thought Carson might be a contender for spending more time with, he did something to prove he was still a kid. Like this stupid turkey.

Eventually, the Bandit Trans Am arrived. "Need some help stuffing a bird?" Jim said, smoking a cigar and leaning out the window. He'd obviously practiced his line. Again.

"Jeez, about time. It's freezing!" I said, swatting his arm through the open window.

"Easy, don't damage the merchandise." Instead of his usual Carhartt, he had on a thick suede jacket (which I thought should have been way above his budget). Not practical for here.

"What took you so long? I was beginning to think you'd changed your mind."

"Had to wait for your boyfriends to leave," he said, still doing his dirty-old-man laugh.

"They aren't my boyfriends," I said. I felt funny that Jim had waited in the dark, watching us get that turkey out of Carson's car, and that he then sat there while I froze, watching the taillights.

"You gonna let me in the building? It's freezing out here," I said, shivering, but pretending not to.

"Warm in here. Get in." He patted the seat. "That bird ain't going anywhere." He covered my hands in his enormous calloused ones. "Jeez, you *are* freezing," he said. "No gloves?"

"Didn't think I'd need them," I said. "Cold for October, and who knew I'd be smuggling an illicit turkey? Time is it?" I didn't want my parents calling Carson's. They were glad I used our art in my everyday life. But they weren't going to let me be out all hours just with the excuse of drumming. Their Water Drum Allegiance only went so far.

"Won't be long," Jim said. "Just get your hands somewhere warm. No frostbite."

"I can't go home smelling like a stogie." He flicked the entire cigar out the car window.

"That was a ten-dollar smoke I tossed away for you," he said (impressive sacrifice!). He let go of my hand and leaned over, flicking up the passenger side lock. The heat felt like our kerosene heater's delicious warm air vents.

"Okay, close your eyes," he said. He rummaged through some things, and I enjoyed the warm air and the car's humming rumble. "Now hold out your hands. Keep 'em closed. And close your fingers together but still pointed straight." It was getting harder to keep my eyes shut. On the Rez, someone might give you something nice, but someone else might let a goober drop into your open palm. Just then, incredible warm softness surrounded my right hand.

"Worth the wait?" he asked. I nodded. Jim had slid gloves on me, rabbit-fur lined and warmed from the vents. I hadn't realized how cold I'd gotten. I wanted to stay in that warm car cocoon forever.

"Heater works nice. I guess it doesn't have a big space to . . ." I couldn't really finish, because the temperature wasn't the only thing distracting me. Jim was wearing those designer jeans he'd sported at the museum, the nice suede jacket, and a pair of cowboy boots, looking even better than he had on our Buffalo trip.

"Even the backseat gets warm," he said. "I can show you if you've got time."

"School night and my parents are going to wonder where I am."

"Parents," he said, and let out a little cluck. "When I was in high school, my parents didn't care where I was. I could be out all hours. They're just trying to keep you like a kid."

You are a kid, Ghost Marvin said in my head. *No, I'm a young woman,* I pushed back. These two voices wrestled inside my skull. When I wanted to watch *Five Deadly Venoms* on Kung-Fu Theatre and eat Cap'n Crunch with Marvin, then I was a kid. When I wanted Jim to smile at me, I was a young woman, like Marie with Ben-Yaw-Mean. There, that made sense.

"If I'm out late, they'll ground me like a kid," I said. (Totally not true. Rez parents never punished themselves by being stuck at home with us. We had more creative punishments, and I wasn't up for chopping wood or shoveling the driveway all winter if I was caught out late.)

"I only got one master. I'll let you in here, park, and let myself in near the loading docks."

"Why don't I just come with you?"

"I already got a dolly for the bird on the other side of that door. You're standing guard. Let's go, if you're in such a hurry." He grabbed a different set of keys and ran to the door, unlocking it and lifting the turkey as if it were nothing heavier than a rubber chicken.

He held the door for me, close, making me squeeze through. He pressed his hands on my shoulders. "Stay right here." He locked the door from the other side, went back to the car, then dropped the Trans Am into gear and headed away. Lewis would think this was a prank, that Jim had locked me in and left.

A shiver washed over me. This dark hallway felt wrong. Like I was the last girl on earth. *The last young woman,* my mind corrected.

I didn't want to move, in case those *Dawn of the Dead* zombies flew out of the gym (a crazy thought I couldn't shake).

The door behind me burst open a couple minutes later, and I let out a scream. Jim chuckled. He carried a big canister flashlight. "Was beginning to think you'd ditched me," I said.

"Just making myself presentable," he said, smiling. He'd left his jacket somewhere, and underneath he'd worn a button-up shirt, a regular one without a name patch. It was unbuttoned three down, and though I'd already seen him shirtless, that sweep of hair peeking out the collar was still sexy. Almost like a mystery all over again. He'd also combed his hair into a clean and casual part tonight. "Would I ditch you?" he asked.

"I don't know. Would you?"

"I'd never leave you anywhere alone." He looked directly into my eyes, a warm smile softening his features. "Take this." He handed me the flashlight. "I'll wheel the bird and you walk behind, shining the light, so we can see where we're going." He pushed, and I shone the light, hitting his jeans back pockets. They were *Jordaches*. Jim Morgan never struck me as a sixty-dollar-a-pair-of-jeans kind of guy, but the evidence on his butt was plain.

"So how come you're dressed so nice? Did I steal you away from a date?"

"A guy can dress nice if he wants. You don't know what I'm like when I'm not driving a damn riding lawn mower or pouring gravel for that friggin' track. I'm a snappy dresser."

"No guy who *is* a snappy dresser uses phrases like 'snappy dresser,'" I said. He seemed disappointed. "And I did see you in your shorty-shorts at Susan and Artie's."

"Like what you saw?" He grinned. I laughed, though I *had* liked what I'd seen. He worked hard and his legs showed it. "You'll see," he said. "What young people say changes fast. Another year? You'll say something *you* think is hip and some kid's gonna laugh at you."

"Hip? You mean 'groovy'?" I said, but he ignored my comment this time.

"So you're in eleventh?"

"Why?" I asked. I'd been able to dodge his questions without actively lying so far.

"Just wondering. Only eleventh and twelfth graders get to take Cooking. Least that's how it was when I came here. How come I haven't seen you before you started at the garage?"

"You went here?" This would be easy to get him off topic. "How'd you like it?" Working with older people, I discovered they thought about their younger selves more than about who they'd become as adults. If you could get them thinking about the past, they drifted (made me wonder if I'd look back on Rez Life with more fondness than I had, living it).

"Loved it," he said with a grin. "Played football—all-state, even. I'm in that case down by Calderone's office. Big as life." Calderone was a vice principal. Football players hung out at his office.

"Show me?" I asked, using my Impressed Girl Voice.

"We're going right by there," Jim said, unaware he was grinning. The case was full of trophies and framed photos. Each photo contained out-of-shape men wearing whistle necklaces, their arms around young guys in pads and uniforms. Aside from the hairstyles, the young guys looked almost identical: sad high school mustaches and a pose combining Tough, Humble, Casual, and Cocky (which I had to admit would be difficult).

"Find me," Jim said. He had to be in his thirties. The recent notables were on top shelves. I spotted him, in 1967–68. Fifty pounds lighter, with the requisite mustache and long hair.

"Look how young you are!" I said, squatting down to get a closer look. "Did you go to college after? Or did you have a job like mine?"

"The welfare jobs?" he said, laughing. I didn't join him.

"I'm not on welfare. We're just poor. We get by."

"I just meant . . ." He thought for a minute about how he might want to answer. "First of all . . . you going to college? Like art school?"

"College? I haven't thought that far ahead." I laughed, myself, relaxing a little.

"If you're in eleventh, you better get thinking. It ain't that far ahead. Anyway, when I was in high school, a lot of guys went to college, to get out of the draft. I didn't, but whatever."

"Why didn't you? If you were all-state, wouldn't that get you a scholarship or something?" His story wasn't adding up. (Mine too, since I was truly only in tenth grade — it was getting harder to remember my multiplying stories. All because of Carson's stupid turkey error!)

"I *hated* school. I only did homework so I wouldn't be disqualified from playing ball. Why would I sign up for more once I got out of this shit hole? I wasn't a Joe College."

"Weren't you worried about the draft?"

"Not with one uncle working for county government, and another on the board of trustees here. One made my number disappear from the draft lottery, and the other got me this job. It wasn't even ever posted. My uncle asked me if I wanted a job. I said yeah, and bingo! There was a new Grounds job, Tier II. I collected my diploma on Saturday, and on Monday I was reporting for work. Never looked back."

"What's Tier II?"

"If layoffs come, other people get let go before me. A *lot* of other people."

"That doesn't seem fair," I said. "What do the other grounds-people think of that?"

"Who cares? My last name's Morgan, but they know that my mom's maiden name is Reiniger, and in this rinky-dink county, that name means something."

"Reiniger Field," I said. I'd seen the giant electronic sign at the football field and wondered who that was, but had no idea who you would ask. It wasn't a name I otherwise knew.

"More than Reiniger Field, but yeah. Thought you were in a hurry to do this," he said.

"I am," I said. I was a little worried. We were close to the room, and when we got there, I was going to have a harder time pulling off my Turkey Dilemma Lie. I'd never been in the home ec classroom, and I didn't even know where the friggin' fridge was that I was supposed to swap out the turkeys from.

"Wish I still looked like I did back then," he said, glancing away. "Once you hit your mid-twenties, though, your pants start fitting a little tighter. I used to like that my shoulders got bigger, but no one thinks you look better with a spare tire."

"You look better now," I said.

"Bullshit," he said, laughing, but then he put his arm around my shoulder and drew me closer to him. "But you're all right, kiddo. Thanks for saying that. Let's get your turkey home." He expertly tilted the dolly with one hand, keeping his other hand cupped around me, sliding it to my hip. It was a little awkward, his stride so much longer than mine, but we each made the effort to match. I was letting him guide, hoping I seemed like I knew where I was going.

"I have to stop here," I said, with relief, as we reached the B Wing. The home ec lab was clearly labeled and it was right across the hall from the girls' room.

"All right," he said, pulling out his enormous key ring. "I'll swap them out. I'm assuming it's the only turkey I'm going to find in the freezer."

"How do you keep track of the keys?" I said, heading to the girls' room.

"Master key. Can get into almost anything here." A grin crept over his face. "Almost." He flicked his eyebrows. "Some things, you need to wait to get into. 'Til you have permission."

"Pig," I said, laughing.

"What are you talking about? Dirty mind? Guilty conscience?" Jim badly pretended we weren't talking about the same thing. He wanted to be sure we both knew we *were* talking about the same thing. It was exciting to have a man notice me. Marie wouldn't leave me in her dust.

"Just swap the turkeys," I said. "And put the new one in the fridge, not the freezer," I added, laughing as I stepped into the girls' room. He gave me a look like, *Well, duh!* It had never occurred to me before, but there was no lock on the lav door, except the kind you needed a key for. That felt a little unnerving with just the two of us here. I touched up my gloss and eye shadow, and stepped back out. Jim was locking the home ec lab, Carson and Lewis's frozen turkey on the dolly. I looked down the dark halls and a shiver came over me. The near total darkness really was freaky.

"Seems funny to be here when no one else is, don't it?" Jim said, shining his flashlight down the darkened hall. "I like walking around like I own the place. I go places these fancy-pants morons think are private." He waited for me to ask who, but I didn't want to know. "Anything you wanna see before we leave? Teachers' lounge? Principal's suite? My keys go everywhere."

"Yeah, teachers' lounge. I always wondered." We walked down the back of the building, him jangling his key ring like a cowboy's spurs in one of Marvin's stupid Westerns. We stopped at the door and Jim unlocked it, holding it open for me.

"What you waiting for?" he asked.

"It's so dark," I said. You could see almost nothing a couple feet in.

"No windows," he said. "They like it that way. They also took out the overhead fluorescents, messing with the ballast lock."

"Why?"

"They like their *special lighting.* Stupid garage-sale floor lamps and rugs, old end tables, junk. A couple nice couches. Even a comfortable recliner. Just go in and grope around 'til you feel a pole."

The first thing I noticed was the overwhelming odor of stale cigarettes. It smelled like a bingo hall. I slid my hand along the wall, felt the switch, and kept going. Just as the door was closing behind us, I heard footsteps from the back cafeteria hall.

"What is that?" I asked, mad that I could hear my breath catch in fear. The door was totally closed, and the room was black. The only light was a faint glowing sliver under the door.

"Just Vern," he said. Vern was one of the other groundsmen. He seemed close to Jim's age, but he was bigger, bulkier, his arms knotted in veins as thick as electrical cords. "He's working tonight. I had to let him know I was coming. Keep quiet and he'll be by in a minute."

"But you didn't—" I started to say. Jim leaned into me, covering my mouth with his hand. It smelled of soap, cigars, and some cologne that was vaguely familiar.

"Morgan! Oooh, Mooorgaaan!" Vern said, in a singsong voice, like you might use trying to coax a strange cat to come up to you. When Jim didn't respond, Vern's yells got sharper, more demanding. "Morgan! I know you're down here. Saw your light. Trixie's coming on for the next shift, and she usually gets here early. I don't want to be in trouble for unauthorized visitors."

Jim let a series of hushed curses. He opened the door. "Here, Vern," he said, irritated.

"What the hell?" Vern said, coming our way, with his own flashlight. "What you doing anyway? You only enter the building if you're on the clock. If you want to switch—" he said, stopping when he noticed me behind Jim. "Who's that?" he said, grinning and looking worried at the same time. "Hey, Maggi. What's doing here? You come with this chump?" He laughed, trying to sound casual, but shone the light into Jim's eyes. "He knows the No Guests rule."

"She's no guest. She works here." Jim held his hand up. "Get that light out of my face."

"He was doing me a favor," I said. "I needed to get something here."

"I bet he wants to swap favors," Vern said, and laughed, pointing the light now at me. "You needed something from the teachers' lounge, did you?"

"No, we already got what I came for," I said. "I was just curious."

"Curious," Vern said, exaggerating his vowels. "Know what they say about curiosity."

"Killing the cat?"

"Just being a nice guy," Jim said. "No return favors necessary."

"Okay, Nice Guy. Get your butts out of here." Jim shut the door, and we started to walk, Vern beside us. He stopped and shone his light back on the turkey. "Forgetting something?"

"Shit, almost," Jim said. "Thanks. I owe you."

"Present for me? For letting you in when you're not supposed to be here?" Vern said.

"Um, no." Jim tilted the dolly, and the bird reclined.

"That wasn't really a question, Morgan," Vern said.

"It's mine," Jim said, suddenly irritated. This was news to me. I didn't have any plans for it myself, but the band and I were out serious cash for the one Jim had just deposited for me.

"Not anymore, Jimbo. I agreed to let you in here, for a six of Labatts. Not you and this little chickie. Price went up."

"I'm not a chickie," I said. "And that's my turkey, if you want to know."

"I don't," Vern said, reaching for the dolly. Jim let go, easier than I would have thought. For all his supposed family connection, he let Vern walk all over him. "And no," he added. "It's not your turkey. Now get going." He walked us out through the Bee Gees break room.

"Don't forget your fancy duds, super stud," he said, tossing Jim his suede jacket off a coatrack. Jim shrugged it on as we walked out. Vern lifted the turkey into the trunk of a Ford Maverick and turned to us with the same stupid grin. "Drive around behind the junior high," he said. "You'll be able to see Trixie pull in, and she won't see you. Give her five minutes. I'll keep her busy, and then you can head out, clear. You wouldn't want to get caught now, would you?"

Jim shook his head and we got into the Trans Am. "Thanks for the giving!" Vern yelled as Jim followed the dirt path to the junior high's far side.

"Sorry you lost the turkey," I said. I felt kind of stupid, apologizing to Jim for not being able to steal my turkey away for me, but it seemed like I should say something. He just looked forward.

"My mom still cooks a big dinner, on the hopes that some of us might show up," he said, finally. "My brothers usually go, 'cause they're single and lazy. My ex-wife and my mom didn't get along too well, so I haven't gone in a few years. This year, though . . ."

"You're married?"

"Some part of the word 'ex' that you don't get?" he grumbled. My parents referred to each other as the Ex the whole time we lived in the city, but when we moved back, they stopped. "Here comes Trixie," he said. The dashboard clock read ten to eleven. "You'll be home before the hour."

"Yeah," I said. "When the late news says, 'It's eleven o'clock. Do you know where your children are?' they'll be able to say yes." As soon as those words were out of my mouth, I knew they were the wrong things to say. "Wish I could offer you something to make up for the turkey," was what came out next.

"It's late," he said, letting out a sigh that rattled in his chest, and then he dropped the Trans Am into drive. We pulled out and headed to Bitemark.

"I live the other way," I said, then remembered that he already knew that.

"Going this way so Trixie don't see." He took us down Bitemark, and headed toward Snakeline. As we got close, he slowed down, killing the headlights and putting it in park in a strip of road that was mostly woods. This was a little dangerous on the Rez. There were no sidewalks, no curbs, almost nothing. It went road, a strip of cinders and gravel, and then the drainage ditch. If someone came flying up on us and wasn't paying attention, we could be seriously rear-ended.

"Thanks, Jim," I said, pulling off the gloves he'd given me to wear. "For everything."

"What friends are for, am I right?" he said, and we smiled. He could hear *Young Woman* in my voice, not *Rez Kid*. As I handed over the gloves, he stopped my hand. "Keep 'em. You seem to like them. And you got a little bit of a walk ahead. I don't want to stop the car in front of your house."

"But, Jim, these are expensive."

"Don't worry about it. Gift from my ex when she wasn't my ex. Just as well I get rid of them. Too many memories." He let go of my hand, and I put them back on.

"Thanks for picking up the phone." I was babbling a bit, but I didn't want this to end, this . . . *Encounter*? He'd claimed all program employees got his number in case we had to call in. I didn't think others had it on a Polaroid of shirtless Jim in tiny cutoffs.

"Why I gave you the number. Wouldn't have, if I didn't want you to call if you felt like it." He swallowed hard and tried to smile at me with sad eyes. "A lot of the guys hate being called at home," he said, looking down. "But I'd never mind." I felt like crying, picturing that empty apartment. I got out and walked to his side of the Trans Am. He also got out.

"To make this the real movie car, you gotta pinstripe 'Bandit' here, under the widow," I said, tapping the door. We both heard the hitch in my voice.

"Bandit, yeah, that's me. Not even a good Turkey Bandit." He laughed, but it wasn't a real one. He just wanted me to feel like I'd told him a good joke.

"You know, when you called, I thought maybe you wanted to talk about that magazine I gave you." I had wondered when this was going to come up. The magazine, *Avant Garde*, had indeed been an art magazine, about exactly the kinds of things I was interested in. The cover feature, though, was "Wedded Bliss: A Portfolio of Erotic Lithographs by John Lennon." Some were cartoons, but not like what you'd see in a comic book.

"It was pretty intense," I said, not knowing what else I should add. They were only drawings, not like naked photos, but they didn't leave a lot to the imagination. Marie flipped through it with me, and she thought they were explicit enough that we should keep them hidden—who knows what would happen if Dark Deanna came upon a magazine with drawings showing John and Yoko having sex. I was really glad I hadn't shown Marie the Polaroid.

"Did you like it?" he asked, hopeful.

"I did. Lots of interesting things in that whole magazine."

"They're kind of in-your-face, and they're John's and not Yoko's, but I thought you'd be mature enough to enjoy them for what they were. If you want to be an artist now . . ."

"I get it. I'm no prude. It's just . . ." They gave me that freaky electric-blue feeling I'd started having more and more around Jim. I felt like I wouldn't be able to look at them in front of him. That made no sense, considering the centerfolds at the garage. But those were just photos of naked people trying to act sexy for the camera.

These drawings were—I don't know. Somehow more intimate.

And the drawings of Yoko were vague, loose enough, that they could almost be of me, and I'd never struck any of those kinds of poses, in my whole life. Not even alone, in the mirror, where I sometimes tried out what I thought were sexy faces and gestures. Even though they were drawings, somehow they *were* erotic. But the thought of saying that to anyone, especially to Jim, here, alone together, gave me those sharp blue shocks again.

"Thanks, Jim, for everything," I said, hoping that would encompass the magazine without needing to say anything more, outright. I leaned in to kiss his cheek. As my lips touched his skin, he turned. I didn't move away, and our lips found each other's.

I was surprised, at so many things. That he did it. That his lips were coarse like his cheek. That his mustache was bristly. It looked like it'd be soft to touch.

But I was most surprised that when he opened his mouth, I opened mine too. I'd been so sure he'd taste like a cigar that I braced myself to pull back. But he didn't, so I didn't. He tasted like toothpaste, or something sharply minty. He reached his hand to my head and pulled me closer. At first, I thought he was going to mash my teeth against my lips, but he didn't. He just turned me a little, and his tongue entered my mouth softly but steadily. I felt my breath come in sharply through my nose. The air was so cold, it hurt, but I was being kissed by a man who knew what he was doing. It wasn't like those clumsy Goodbye Embraces Carson gave every now and then. Those had been intriguing; this was different. I didn't want to stop.

A car squealed through the distant intersection, and I pulled away. I was standing in the middle of the road. "You got some gloss on your mustache," I said, reaching up to wipe it off.

"It's okay. Leave it," he said.

"It's Bonne Bell Strawberry Lip Smackers!"

"I like the taste," he said, and laughed. He ran his tongue along his mustache.

"Goof," I said, laughing too. "I'll get you some if you want." He smiled a heart-melting smile I could stare at for hours. It gave me a shiver. "Listen, I gotta—"

"I know. I hear it. See you tomorrow." I stepped back and was about to hide in the bush line, when I saw that captivating look in his eyes. I got close again and raised my arms around his neck. They barely reached, and my face rubbed against the chest hair poking out though his open collar as he pulled me in and hugged me just as tight. I felt his whole body pressing up against me, and a growing firmness at my belly. No one had ever hugged me like that before, not even that time in the garage entry. I wasn't sure I liked it, but maybe I just didn't like it standing in the middle of Snakeline Road with a car barreling down on us in the distance.

"Thanks, Jim," I said, and he leaned down so we could kiss again. It would have gone on longer, but the oncoming car lights were beginning to spot the trees. I gently pulled away. He breathed out heavily and climbed into his Trans Am, and cruised off into the night.

The noisy car in the distance got closer, so I jumped into the woods to hide, until I recognized the farty exhaust, and then the weirdo head-lights. I ran out and crossed the road, my shadow on the road like a giant spider. The Trabant stopped, my sister climbed out of the passenger's side, and Ben-Yaw-Mean peeled out.

"What the hell are you doing on the road?" she asked, running over to me. "Weren't you supposed to be home an hour ago? Did that bastard make you walk? If he did, I'll kill him."

"No, nothing like that," I said, putting my arm around my sister's shoulder. "Relax. But thanks for caring." I leaned into her. "You smell kind of funny. What is that?"

"Binaca," she said, sliding a little cylinder out of her back jean's pocket. "Want some?"

"What is it?"

"Just open your mouth," Marie said, popping the cap and pointing a little sprayer at me.

"And why do you need that?"

"You're getting to the age where you're going to find it useful," she said. "Open up." She blasted the atomizer into my open mouth. At first it stung, like my mouth had been splashed with a million little ice cubes, but then came the flavor. It was excruciatingly familiar.

I felt that sudden lightning shiver again I got when Jim surprise-kissed me.

"Where do you get that?" I asked, grinning.

"Take this one. A gift," she said, handing it over. "Let's say it's, um, a present for your entry to adult—hey, where'd you get those gloves? Nice leather." She rubbed the soft palms of the gloves Jim had given me. "Did you boost them? Be careful. Kids, excuse me, *young ladies* as dark as we are *always* get followed around by store security."

" 'Kay, thanks. I won't do anything like that again." Easy enough. Way easier than telling her I'd called the home of a man in his thirties that I knew sort of secretly, a man who'd come and helped me without question. And definitely easier than telling her that I might have come close to losing my virginity that night. Or at least that I could have, if I'd wanted to. We were silent the rest of the walk to the Shack.

I didn't want to trip up, so if she was quiet, I was cool with that. Inside, Marvin was watching *The Monkees* and our parents were already in bed.

"How was band practice?" she asked in our room, which she usually didn't.

"Okay," I said. I could handle this. "I kind of feel unnecessary, now that Susan's a part of it. You know, her synthesizer can play drums. It's almost like I don't bring anything."

"Hey, don't kid yourself. You bring vocables, in addition to a drum that doesn't sound like anything on a little electronic rinky-dink piano." She put an unfamiliar record on our turntable and lit our Listening to Music candle. This was nice of her, but truthfully, I didn't think using either of those did much.

I didn't like calling them vocables, but that was the accurate term. Some older Social singers taught me those songs. They made sure I knew that after the US government tried to wipe us out, they tried to vacuum our culture right out of us, so we only remembered the sounds. Whenever I'd add a variation sound, the elder would correct me and say that we remember the sounds and keep them, to honor the dead. To honor the memory. Heavy stuff for a twelve-year-old girl,

I told them, but they said if I wanted to be a part of this memory, then I had to be more than just that alone.

Now I *was* more than a girl, and I remembered the vocables, but I had new sounds to make, new experiences to feel, new words to learn.

"Carson's looking for something to make his band unique," Marie said. "Something to get noticed. You're that thing. You're the thing that gives the band its unique flavor."

"Like Binaca," I said in the dark. "What a funny word. Do you know what it means?"

"What it means?" she asked, laughing. "You're so weird. It's just a name. Like McDonald's or Coke."

"Words *always* mean something," I said. "McDonald's was the name of the family that invented the fast-food burger place, before some shark named Kroc bought out their name and their recipes and 'trade secrets,' and Coke used to have cocaine in it." I had taken a Social Studies class with an old hippie teacher who taught a very different version of American history.

"Whatever, Brainiac girl. Try getting a good job with that knowledge." I looked at the cylinder in the candlelight.

"Binaca," I said slowly, luxuriously bleeding the syllables, reading the label.

"Binaca means 'Binaca,'" Marie said, softer. Sometimes, she just became nicer like this and I could never predict it. She leaned over and cupped the candle flame, blowing it out. "Maybe it means 'Cover Up Your Breath Secrets.'" We glowed green in the stereo tuner light.

She was wrong, but I was going to keep silent. Binaca means "The Taste of Jim Morgan," I thought, and sprayed some more into my mouth, drifting off to sleep with my tongue tingling.

21

All You Need Is Love
Carson Mastick

Canadian Thanksgiving came and went, and my ass was saved. Our bird was so juicy and tender. I owed the band huge for saving me from my screwup, though of course, I was still the one responsible for carrying us. But they'd been great. I started adding new songs to give everyone a fair shake at showing off what they could do. Well, almost everyone.

That thing Maggi brought to the band? I still didn't know exactly what to do with it. At first, I couldn't even remember the word for the Traditional singing she'd started sprinkling in. "It's like revocable," she said after one practice, "just with the beginning chopped off. Like if you screw up again, your leadership is revocable." Vocables. The remembered sounds of forgotten songs. Memory is revocable. Easy to remember when she put it that way.

So yeah, things were decent with the band, but some ideas outside of that world had itched themselves into my brain, starting with that article Lewis and Maggi didn't want me to see.

"Was it all worth it?" I asked Derek when I came home to find him with a new Dad Brand black eye. My family brawls sustained, and Custard's business was booming. I'd given intervening a shot again recently, which prompted my dad to clench the fingers of my left hand, asking me if I still loved playing the guitar, because it didn't seem like I did from his vantage point. I was out, on that front.

"Remember this?" Derek asked, dragging his butt-shot body to the bookshelf housing our dad's porn stash and some dirty comics. That old Deloria paperback again, *Custer Died for Your Sins: An Indian Manifesto*. "But you didn't read it the first time I showed it to you, isn't it?"

"I was, what? Seven?"

"You're seventeen now. You read it sometime in the last ten years?" I shook my head, and he tossed it to me. "Read it, and ask me again if I think it was worth it. Deloria says we shouldn't let anthropologists onto Rez land, because they only come for their own benefit."

"Those the guys who get chased around in *Curse of the Mummy's Tomb*–type movies?"

"Just read it. For real this time." I owed it to Derek to try. "Look, I ain't asking a lot of you. You're the golden boy, and no matter what, that's all Dad's gonna think. That's fine. I get to be my own person."

I'd never really thought of Derek having these kinds of ideas. Until the butt shot, I thought he'd mostly skated through life, paying it almost no attention.

"And Carson? Our world is changing. *Our* world," he stressed, which I guess meant the World of Indians. "I missed the Longest Walk, and Wounded Knee, but this? Showing how screwed up it was that a restaurant named Custard's Last Stand is doing fine? That's something I could do. You and me, we're different, but if you think you're gonna coast through life because you don't look as Indian? You're wrong. Someone's always gonna find out, and if it's the wrong person who finds out, you're gonna be screwed and not even know it."

"Then why'd you have to tie it to a stupid attempted robbery!" I said, something I'd never come right out with before. "That totally screwed up any believability you had."

"How do you think we lost this land? Now *that* was a robbery," he said. "I was just making the point a little more obvious." I had to admit, I had *not* gotten that, because all I could see was my brother's bad behavior. Some of what he was saying now, though? I got immediately.

Other parts, I just didn't understand at all, still! Why would people do bad things to us? I know that sounded ridiculously naive, almost Lewis-level denial. But I'd heard white people talking about their Indian Princess grammas on a pretty regular basis.

Whenever I demonstrated How to Make a Lacrosse Stick with my mom at public events? You heard fake-out, made-up connections every friggin' time. It was usually women with giant turquoise earrings or pasty guys with big, flashy triple-row bone chokers around their necks and maybe a quahog shell facing out at the Adam's apple, to show off the swirly purple underside we used to make wampum beads. You might see those chokers on Powwow-competing dancers, but no Rez guys would wear one as an everyday thing. How could some people be so delighted about their alleged dead gramma as proof of their connection, and then other people who interacted with us daily have such a different take?

For sure, no one at school was claiming they had secret Indian relatives. Maybe that's what Derek was warning about, the kinds of shit the more Indian-looking kids got sometimes, if they were alone. I suddenly wondered about the way all the Indians hung out together in school. I just thought it was because we'd grown up together, but now I had to wonder if there was more to it, if it was more a matter of survival.

I started reading the book that night, and from the section called "Indian Humor," I began to grasp Derek's choices a little better. Was I planning to bust back in to Custard's Last Stand to pick up where he left off? No, of course not. The major thing I understood clearer from Deloria was something I knew all along, but I'd never seen it written down. We make fun of ourselves and each other, trying to get someone to change the way they act without yelling. When I jabbed Lewis, I wanted him to grow a set of balls. I wanted better for him. When Derek decided to try intimidating someone dressed up as Custer, he partly thought other Indians would find that funny. When everyone from the Rez called Derek the Hamburglar, even our dad, they understood his reasons, but they thought the risks he took were too high. They wanted him to smarten up.

I read that book cover to cover. Then Derek gave me some more stuff, including a newspaper called *Akwesasne Notes*. He said it was a real Indian newspaper, put out by one of the Mohawk Rezzes. From there, I found other books on Indian history and what was being called our new awakening. I even found some books dealing with Custer in our school library.

I'd saved that newspaper story too, and every time I read it, I burned all over again. At first, I didn't know what to do, but I made sure to get it laminated. If it pissed me off, it should be easy to piss others off too, with it. I didn't have a plan at first, but the more I read *The Notes*, as Derek called it, the more ideas started itching against the back of my brain. Almost every issue covered protests at different Rezzes and the ideas behind them, the people who were organizing. Before I did anything, though, I wanted to talk with Albert.

On Halloween, I headed to Lewis's after school, when he and his mom would still be working. Albert was stuck giving candy to early trick-or-treaters.

"Trick or treat!" I yelled, walking in the door.

"Where's your costume?" he said, gripping the bowl close. "You're the Devil, isn't it?"

"Wearing it on the inside," I said, slapping my chest. They had lame bargain-store candy like those nasty Mary Janes. Whoever thought a wad of peanut butter and molasses was a candy anyway?

Lewis and Albert's house was like those Historic-White-Settler-Type People attractions. Last year, we'd taken a sad field trip to a dump called Genesee Country Village. It was supposed to show "Settler" life on "the Niagara Frontier." Tired-looking women were stuck in long dresses and bonnets that stuck way out in front, hiding their faces in shadow. They sewed quilts and sat at spinning wheels in old wood-framed houses. Outside, men in britches, long socks, and buckle shoes cut wood or chased sheep around. No Indians. No black people. Super-accurate reflection of Settler Life. But no Rez kid needed this particular Immersion Experience. We were already deeply familiar with what our teachers called Authentic Rustic Homes. Our families and friends, like Lewis, lived in them. Minus bonnets and britches.

"Lewis ain't here yet. You know that, isn't it?" Albert said, lifting the Beatles' *White Album* to his face. What was he studying? It was a blank white square, with raised letters spelling out "THE BEATLES" in the lower right, with a number printed in the low leading edge. An original copy. They don't make them like that anymore. Now the letters were printed in dull silver on a flat cover cardboard, with no more numbers.

"I want you to come with me to Moon Road tonight. I have a plan for dealing with that asshole who runs Custard's Last Stand."

"That's *your* business, not mine, isn't it? What's it got to do with me? Wasn't any relative of mine who tried robbing him," he said, never lowering the album.

"It's important to me," I said. He set the cover down flat on his chest and pinched his lips together, pulling in a drag on the cigarette perched there.

"I don't care what's important to you," he said, exhaling a coughing cloud. "I know what you're thinking. You boys ain't been around that long, but you think you been, isn't it?"

"Yeah, but—"

"Yeah, but you thought pulling my ass out of that Beer Tent made me owe you one. I knew what I was doing. Eating a little grass never hurt anyone. What they call roughage."

"It isn't like that."

"Ain't it? What's it like, then?"

"Well, it's about Veterans Day. I think we should honor—"

"Nope, tell me the truth, right now, or I'm going back to my music and the costume kids. I just finished being happy with a warm gun," he said, standing. "And now I'm gonna flip that album over and get friendly with my dear Martha. Unless you got something real to say—"

"Okay. What were you fighting for? In Vietnam?"

"Me? Nothing, man. I didn't sign up. I was drafted. Wasn't smart enough to get a diploma, but I guess I was smart enough to hold an

M-16. When your life depends on it, you can get smart pretty fast."
I was beginning to understand this, myself. "I was fighting to
survive."

"Exactly. That's what I'm doing, and what Lewis is doing. Our
band."

"Your *cover* band, you mean?"

"All bands start off as cover bands. And we're different. We got a
water drum player."

"Who's that now? The one from The Bug's party?" Suddenly,
Albert was interested, which struck me as weird. He never seemed all
that Traditional to me. I was just trying to show him we weren't like
everyone else.

"Maggi Bokoni. Her family just moved back from the city this
summer."

"That girl they call Stinkpot? The one Lewis moons over? I told
him he can borrow *my* girlfriends," he said, laughing. Albert and my
dad shared taste in recreational magazines. "They're a lot easier to
deal with."

"No, that's her sister. Maggi's younger. The one with the twin
brother."

"Oh yeah. That's the one works with him, right? The garage
girl?"

"Yeah, she's working at the school now, but her. Lewis likes the
other one. Marie."

"Mr. Underdog, my nephew. This band one's cuter, I bet. If you
compare, side by side."

"Yeah," I said, all poker face. "Guess you could say that."

"And does he *really* like the other one, or is it 'cause *you* like
this one? This another one of your *Stay Out of My Territory, Lewis*
moves?"

"No," I said, looking down. Was this that weird mind-reading
thing Albert did to Lewis?

" 'No' means 'yeah,' isn't it? This the one that was with you in the
car that night? That Sanborn Field Day night?" I nodded. "She gonna
be part of your plans?"

"Supposed to be," I said. "But I gotta get a lot of things together, and you're Part One. If you're not there, the rest falls apart."

"Is your thing gonna be outside? Veterans Day's late in the year. Always cold and gray. No one ever comes out to those Honor the Vets things. Is that what this thing is?"

"Something like that, but important for you, specifically. And there's other people I wanna ask, but I need *your* help. You still got any of your army clothes?" He nodded. "I'd like you to wear—I don't know. You got a shirt with your name patched on it? To remind—"

"Me that I used to belong? You think I need symbols? That I'm that messed up?"

"No, to remind . . . to show *others* you belong. That you served. Like the way Lewis still wears that jacket you gave him. He still wears it to show you how important *you* are to him. To be connected to you." The album cover in his hands gave me an idea, even all split-edged and stained with a ghost of the vinyl inside. "Like that there. I know the numbering thing was kind of a joke. A limited edition of a few million—how limited is that? But you know what? They don't make them like that anymore. The photos inside? Now they're on flimsy paper."

"I know," he said, pointing to a new copy on the shelf. "Anything limited disappears. Makes me worry about the future of Indians. What happens if young people forget to learn our stories? If they count on someone else? On older people, like me. Like old albums, we wear out."

"I'm not getting to what I mean," I said, but I had to get going if I was going to pull this off right. "Trust that it's important? I'll come back tonight. I want us to go down to Moon Road, with a proposal. A couple hours down there, you'll be back here, looking at your girl-friends and I'll be out of your hair. You'll have all the private time you need with them."

"I got all the time in the world for my gals," he said. "I plan to be around long enough for the Beatles to smarten up and get back together."

"Wouldn't hold my breath about that one." I lifted my shirt and pulled out a 45 record, with a glossy sleeve. A brand-new single that had been getting a little airplay, but somehow, Lewis hadn't mentioned it. Maybe he didn't know it existed yet?

"Keeping a 45 in your undershorts waistband. Like your Hamburglar brother, isn't it?"

"Funny," I said. He wouldn't have given me the jab if he weren't on my side. He was trying to find the joke in our heartbreak, just like Deloria said. "Just make sure Lewis sees this when I drop you guys off, tonight, okay?"

I handed the 45 over, and Albert studied the picture sleeve closely. He squinted hard, trying to make sure his eyes weren't telling him lies. I grinned, trying for casual and cocky, but failing. "Yup! Can you believe it? New John Lennon. Coming out of his five-year retirement. But, um, it doesn't look like he has any reunion on his mind."

"'(Just Like) Starting Over,'" Albert said, studying the sleeve. "Kind of funny, isn't it. Maybe he's secretly an Indian. Lewis didn't think that Stinkpot girl—jeez, what's her real name? I can't be thinking of her that way. Marie." I nodded. Decent recall for Albert. "Anyways, Lewis didn't think . . . *Marie* would come back, but here she is. Big as life. Starting over."

"But this is the Rez. Everyone always comes back," I said. "Eventually."

"Don't I know it," he said, sitting down. I thought I was going to have to argue some more, but just as I took a deep breath in, he flicked the stereo switch off and reached for his boots. "What time we going to Moon Road?"

I picked up Lewis for a ride home and told him of my plan. When I went to their place that night, he was waiting, with Albert, carrying his guitar case. I had two cold chill packs of beer in the trunk, which would buy me maybe twenty minutes to make my case when we got there.

As soon as we turned down Moon Road, a ton of chrome winked in the dark. There was no electricity down there, so it had been the

Default Party Road since before Lewis and I had been born. It looked like people were getting into it deep. I pulled slowly among the twenty or so cars there, some running, all tuned to the same station with their windows down. At a quick glance, it didn't seem like Derek was there.

We got out and set the chill packs on the Chevelle's hood, opening a couple. We saw people from school and some older folks we knew, and Albert started making slow rounds to key people. Eventually he stood in the middle of the road and gave a giant war whoop that carried into the woods. "All right, then!" he said when he figured he had everyone's attention. "Everyone here knows about what happened with the Hamburglar. You all been chasing that Eee-ogg for months now. But you don't know everything, isn't it? These boys want to say something, and if it matters to anyone . . . if it makes your heart lean one way or the other, I'm in with them. I'm gonna do it." People stirred, some reaching in car windows to shut off radios.

"I guess that's where I come in," I said.

"You need an invitation?" someone said, everyone cackled, and I knew we'd be fine.

"So you all know what happened. What you maybe don't know is that he had reasons."

"He wasn't just hungry?" someone in the dark said, making that weird mumble sound that the real Hamburglar did in TV commercials. Some of the crowd laughed.

"All right, then," Albert said, sharp. "Let these boys talk."

"Custard's Last Stand," I said. "You know by the name that place ain't gonna be friendly to Indians. I mean, General Custer himself, the *real* one. The dead one from the Battle of the Greasy Grass. Supposedly the greatest Indian Killer of all time, because he knew how to work publicity. And still a hero to white people."

"I'm already out of school," someone shouted. "What's your brother's dumb-ass move got to do with me?"

"If you leave the Rez at all, it's got everything to do with you," I said. "That place? It's got a big poster up inside, some fancy art that shows Custer as a champion, like he's won, surrounded by dead Indians

247

he's killed and a whole bunch more he's in the process of killing. I went to the library and looked it up. Was given out by Budweiser, the company you all love so much. And they say it's one of the most popular pieces of art in the country. It's a poster that celebrates the *idea* of massacring Indians."

"Well, what about it?" someone else yelled, cracking a Bud, as if that meant nothing.

"There's all kinds of places like Custard's," I said. "You know, like I know. Mostly, we just don't go. *We* don't . . . but other people do. Some of you probably saw this in the *Cascade*," I said, passing out Xeroxes of the Columbus Day fund-raiser from the Chevelle's trunk. "Listen, I'm not asking for a lot, and if you don't want to help me for *me*, at least help me for your kids. You want them wandering into a place that has a No Indians sign at the counter?"

Albert stepped up, making eye contact with the men he'd talked to when we arrived. "I came down here with these boys to let you all know I'm in. Like I said before. I'm going."

I'd been smart to bring Albert. In all the ways people knew my dad screwed people over, they knew Albert would go the extra mile. He'd helped most of these guys chop and stack cordwood when they couldn't afford to pay him; he'd moved furniture with them, painted barns, stacked hay bales, braided corn, you name it. He was finally asking for something in return.

"Okay, look," I started again. "You should be as pissed as I am."

"Hamburglar's not *my* brother," someone said from the dark, where it was easy to be invisible. Lewis leaned in and flicked on my headlights, putting me in the spotlight.

"I know," I said. "His Ass Toothache and our dad's contributions to it are our problem." A few more people laughed. This time, with me. Lewis helping me be visible was working. "But if any of you've seen the TV, you know that guy dresses up like Custer, every damned day. Even now they're trying to rewrite history."

"School's over for us," another guy mumbled from the dark, less bold.

"My report card says I'm not a big fan either," I said, to another surge of laughs. "But for this? You should care." I paused, waiting to see if another smart-ass rose from the shadows. "Because? Custard just sponsored a Knights of Columbus fund-raiser. I don't need to tell you that guy in the warbonnet on the *Cascade*'s front page isn't from the Rez. Think about this! What's the only thing Custer and Columbus have in common? It ain't a sense of fashion."

"Oh, just like you, isn't it?" Albert said, putting his arm around my shoulder. "Come on, now, let's tell these folks what you want to say and let them get back to their thing."

"Got it," I said. "Okay, listen, just for a minute. You know who the real Custer was?"

"Indian killer," came through as a grumbly chorus.

"A not very successful Indian killer, as it turns out," I said. "There's that big Bud poster, and history class. Even the little you know seals that reputation." I stomped around in my highbeam spotlight. "Custer! The Greatest Indian Killer!" I boomed, and then I switched back, pausing.

"But it's bullshit. The real Custer, staking out his place in history, botched up his last try and got himself and his men killed. The whole Cavalry group, all six hundred, felt the burn of the last Indians they were pushing onto Rezzes. *Other* dumb-ass Indians guided him. They thought they were gonna be treated right in the end."

"Assholes got what they deserved!" someone yelled.

"Maybe, or maybe they saw what was coming. I know a lot of you didn't pay attention to this shit in school, or dropped out, like my brother. But it doesn't end there. All of this! I mean, Jesus! The country just celebrated Columbus Day, for his 'discovering' this place, like we didn't exist at all! Add to *that* the 'Founding Great White Fathers,' and every other lie and the silence about our almost being wiped off the face of this planet. Some of you have grandparents who were forced to go to the Boarding Schools." The crowd noises were changing. A few people war-whooped in a way I'd never quite mastered, their voices carrying out across the fields.

"No one even bothers to pretend it was an accident. We live on a reservation, where the government still tries to find ways to make us disappear." I got quieter. "And sometimes . . . we help, by closing our eyes. We let them dismiss us. Erase us. Our lives don't even seem to matter if this asshole can brand his business to celebrate a history that didn't exist.

"But now, when I close my eyes," I said, wrapping up, "I don't just see darkness. I see the people at that drive-in, that idiot in his fake Cavalry outfit with his real guns, keeping alive one of the country's most celebrated Indian killers. I see his ghost still doing it a hundred years after he finally pushed us too far. No, I ain't Sioux. A couple families out here claim they got some Sioux ancestors, from the boarding-schools years, but not mine. Just the same, I understand now why my brother couldn't let it go, even one more day. And I almost never understand." A good laugh came through. They were still listening. "I understand why he tried to do something for all of us, as dumb-ass and half-cocked as it was."

The murmur swelled, starting with guys Albert had helped, but catching among others.

"Let's get there, right now. Smash those giant windows," one of Derek's friends said.

"No," I said. "Not like that. He'll be expecting us tonight. He'll be expecting tricks, and we sure don't want the treats he has to offer. And besides, I don't want you guys getting in any trouble. You got too many mouths to feed. Even those of you who don't admit you belong on the Old-Men's Fireball Team." They laughed again, as a group, my tiny joke breaking the tension. Only guys who'd gotten someone pregnant were considered "Old Men," for competition games, so a lot of young guys got teased about that. Their laughing made me realize I was never teased in that way. Somehow everyone knew I was still a damned virgin!

"He thinks he can do this because he thinks we all look alike. You saw the news when it happened. He said he knew it was an Indian, because the guy had long hair and a hooded sweatshirt and a beaded cap. Now," I said, pausing, "it turned out he was right, *that* time. And now he thinks he can put up his No Indians sign and feel like a badass to his friends because he thinks he can see us all coming, and then he can swipe it off the counter before any of us sees it."

"How do *you know* there's a sign?" Lewis asked.

"I've seen it. I've been back inside." Everyone knew what I was saying. Some were ChameleIndians, like me.

I told them I wanted to make a peaceful protest, in the town park across the road from Custard's Last Stand. Our band would play, and I'd provide food and cook on a few grills. I asked them to join us, but I also asked them if they could go a little further.

Custard was heavily promoting his Veterans Day Celebration. In honor of General George Armstrong Custer, impossibly brave US Cavalry Veteran and West Point Graduate, he was picking up the tab of any veteran who came in for food on that day. It was less than two weeks away, so I was hoping that was quick enough that these guys wouldn't forget.

It was going to be a simple protest. I asked them to spread the word across the Rez and to any City Indians they knew, and for anyone with room to give a ride to someone without a car. I wanted them to wear hooded sweatshirts and trucker caps, and to wait in their cars in Custard's parking lot until I got there, with Lewis, Albert, and, toughest of all, my dad. I told them I'd have a surprise for them when we got there, a gift to acknowledge their help. It would be worth their while.

My plan was to have the ChameleIndian veterans enter first, have a seat, order their food, and wait. The more obvious-looking Indians would hang back, until Lewis, my dad, Albert, and I entered. I wanted as many witnesses there as possible to see what happened when Albert, at the super-Indian end of the Indian-looking spectrum, stepped up to order his Free Veterans Day dinner. And no matter what happened next, they would know we had not gone anywhere, that Indians were still here, and more important, we were here to stay.

When I dropped Albert and Lewis off, I headed back to the school, alone. I had to get my dad to see that, as stupid as Derek's plan had been, there was real thought behind it. Was I afraid to ask

Derek if he'd known there would be bullets in Custard's gun? No matter what, I had to conquer the fear of being at our house, if I was going to do anything about changing the world beyond its walls.

I suddenly knew how to show off Maggi's talents too. It had been four months since she'd revealed she was a drummer, and already, we were a tight, almost magical band. As if it was meant to be. At the protest, I'd ask her to sing the Standing Quiver Dance song in front of everyone. It wasn't exactly a War Dance Song. We didn't have something formally designated that way. Not a War Dance, but a Letting You Know We're Ready If We Have to Go to War Dance. It was a song of people standing together, identifying as a group and maybe even sacrificing as a group. A love song.

At the school, I dismantled my hideout, reclaimed all my belongings, and lowered them to the ground. I detached the rope ladder and let it drop into the mulch around the hedges. Maybe some other desperate kid would find it when he needed a place to go to. I walked back and looked at the ghost image left where my tarp had been protecting the brittle, flat tar roof. That was all I left behind as I took a running shot, thinking about Maggi's and Marie's boldness. My hands hit the stone half wall as I launched myself out into the air for the last time, seeing how far I could go, letting physics do its thing.

22

What a Mess
Magpie Bokoni

Marie, Ben-Yaw-Mean, and I leaned on the Trabant in Custard's parking lot. The place was draped in red, white, and blue bunting. Poster boards with Magic-Markered WELCOME, VETERANS! YOUR MEAL IS ON US! sat on top, flanked by a couple of cardboard eagles.

"So what's the story, now?" Marie asked. "How's this supposed to play out?" Older Indians were gathering in the lot. They recognized us as Indians (even with Ben-Yaw-Mean).

"Carson says there's a No Indians sign sitting right out on the counter. I didn't see it when we came here. Not saying it *wasn't* there, just . . . it was kind of an intense experience."

"One way to find out if it's still there," Ben-Yaw-Mean said. "Back in a minute, ladies."

"Couldn't you get him to wear something less, um, teachery?" I said, looking at his trench coat and duck boots as he walked away. "I mean, it didn't have to be a Carhartt, but jeez."

"*You* could be a little nicer," Marie said, shrugging. "At least less bratty anyway."

"Not bratty. The idea was to be inconspicuous. You see another tan trench coat here?" Knowing I was right, she didn't scan the crowd, instead laughing to end this Meow Mix between us. She *did* follow my eyes to the front of Custard's Last Stand. Through the glass front, you could see that the place was full. Older men wore trucker caps with MIA/POW, NEVER FORGET with military bars, AIR-BORNE, GREEN BERET, and that kind of thing. Most had on Carhartts, or hunting jackets, or leather jackets, a few shearlings, and some olive green.

"Inconspicuous?" She snapped her eyes back at me *and* at my bag. "Your giant purse screams Powwow bag, since you added all that beadwork. Thought you hate carrying a purse."

"Your man's coming," I said. "And he looks pissed."

"It's there," Ben-Yaw-Mean said, kicking up gravel. " 'No Indians.' Damn! In this age?"

"Clearly *you* don't teach social studies," I said, and felt immediately bad. I'd hoped it wasn't *really* there. It maybe confirmed all of the things I didn't want to be true.

"Should have brought my camera," he said. "That sign'll be gone once the reporter shows." Marie and I both bugged our eyes at him. "I did some homework and called in a favor," he said, smiling. He *so* wanted to be Marie's White Knight. "Be right back."

Once he was talking to some guy in the distance, I shoved Marie's arm. "So! He's okay," I said. "Nice, even. How long did you wait before you, you know? Did the Moon Road thing."

"Who says we have? A lady doesn't say," she said, ducking her head. "And Rez girls even less." She peeked, sly. "You know what Ma says about the Indian word for 'love.'"

"We don't *even* have one!" we said, dragging it out all Rezzy, imitating Dark Deanna. We pushed each other, laughing. Our parents loved each other, but like our allegedly nonexistent word, they never showed it. You wouldn't hear *anyone* say that someone else was hot or that they were even interested. That silence was how you were supposed to know. If there was one person you never made dirty jokes about, *that* was the one. Sometimes I felt like I was in a foreign country without a handy Traveler's *Translations of Helpful Phrases for Reservation Love*. It didn't seem like shyness, exactly—more just the way our people were.

"Well, *there's* the guy who wants you to go to Moon Road," I said as Carson's car pulled up near us. "If Ben-Yaw-Mean, you know, isn't up to the job application."

"Carson?" Marie laughed. "The guy who named me Stinkpot? Get real."

"Not Carson," I said as Lewis and his Uncle Juniper stepped out.

"Well, spot's been filled," Marie said. "Lewis is cute, cute enough, probably. But like I told you, he's just a boy." Her saying that made me realize how much she was shaping my ideas. She'd discovered actual men, first, of course, but now I better understood the difference between boys and men.

I knew how I felt around Jim Morgan, especially when we were alone, and I also knew that I was recognizing (from the inside) Marie's dreamy looks whenever she came back from an encounter. It was a different kind of connection than hanging with the guys. Whenever I'd show Jim a new Polaroid, he'd study it (grinning, because the Polaroid was his) and ask about details I didn't think he could see in such a tiny picture. And then lately, he'd hold me close and we'd do that deep kissing we'd started that night in the road. Sometimes, we didn't even look at my art.

"What's up?" Carson said, strolling to us, like he hadn't orchestrated this whole thing.

"You tell me," I said.

"Got your drum?"

I patted my bag and nodded.

"Okay, we're going to get kicked out before we can do much, but that's a public park across the road. They can't do a damn thing about our being there. We'll play a few songs, just me, you, and Lewis. Doobie doesn't have a portable amp." Carson had left Susan out because she was not fitting into his scenario, but it was shitty to not figure something out for Hubie.

"Got your shirts on?" he asked, and we nodded, flashing a peek. Carson delivered them around the Rez as he'd got confirmation from people that they'd come.

"You got another one?" Marie asked as Ben-Yaw-Mean came back toward us, with a guy carrying a satchel. "For . . . my friend. He's on our side." She glanced at Lewis, who was totally unaware of his approaching nemesis. (He didn't even know Ben-Yaw-Mean existed.)

"Carson Mastick, I enjoyed your band's performance at the Critchers' Labor Day get-together," Ben-Yaw-Mean said, sticking his hand out. "Benjamin Gaward." (Weird, he pronounced it normally.) Carson waited a second, deciding, before he took the hand and shook it. "And this is my friend Steven Paulson, from the *Cascade*. I told him of the peaceful protest you're planning." Carson snapped his eyes at both Marie and me. Funny, I noted that he did it better than either Marie or me. "No, he can be trusted. I'd stake my name on it."

"How do I know *you* can be trusted?" Carson said. "We don't know each other."

"Well, you know *me*!" Marie said, snapping her eyes right back.

"I know that name," he added, to Paulson. "You're the guy who did that article on Custard's Columbus Day thing. Didn't mention the fucked-up wigs and headbands and feathers."

"True," Paulson said, handing over a card. "I thought the photos'd speak for themselves."

"Pictures never speak for themselves," Carson said. "Know who Edward Curtis was?"

"I do, as a matter of fact. I had college elective. History of American Photography."

"Is this really the moment for a pop quiz in the history of photography?" Lewis asked.

"You look around. Some of us look like Curtis's Vanishing Indians, but we aren't all the same, and now's the day to stand up for ourselves and be recognized." I was surprised Carson himself knew who Curtis was, but all kinds of people thought wrong things about me, so I guess I shouldn't be surprised by anyone's secrets. "Anyone look? Sign still there?"

"Still there," Ben-Yaw-Mean said.

"If you can get a picture, I'll run it," Paulson said. "To go with the ones I take. I can report on it, but a story's different if readers see the sign. Like when northerners saw civil rights coverage of Whites Only drinking fountains. Made them understand that segregation wasn't, you know, all lynchings and lunatics in white sheets. It was everywhere."

"So take a picture," Lewis said. We weren't easily convinced.

"If I walk in with my camera out, that sign's gonna disappear before I can get a shot."

"Lend us your camera," Lewis added. Bold for him. "We won't steal it."

"*Cascade* employees only." He scanned the lot, to see if anyone had brought cameras. "And I'd become part of your plans, which I can't. My job's reporting on action, not becoming a part of it." All four of us *pfft'd* simultaneously, and Ben-Yaw-Mean looked crushed. "It's true. If I don't do objective journalism, my editor could kill the story."

A few ChameleIndian guys came up, laughing. Through their open sweatshirts, Carson's Dog Street Devils T-shirts peeked out, the little devil with a Mohawk and breechcloth.

"Got your caps?" Carson asked. Each revealed one stuffed into a jacket. Most were old, grease- and sweat-stained caps, John Deere giveaways or from "Cap Night" at the stock car races.

"All right, you guys go in, and tell those other Skinjuns to wait until I stand at that front window. Then *they* should come. I told them already, but remind them. It'll be better this way."

"Wait," Marie said, and the guys turned to her. "Yeah, you guys. Come here." Ben-Yaw-Mean unlocked the Trabant's trunk. Inside, she had grocery bags filled with trucker caps. Each had PROPERTY OF THE INDIANS on the front. It had become a Rez fad to buy *anything* printed with PROPERTY OF THE INDIANS on it, even though the actual "Indians" was a baseball team from Cleveland with a ridiculous exaggerated Indian face as a mascot. Marie passed her caps out, a few each to deliver to others, and told them to keep the hats hidden until the right moment. They smiled, admiring the caps.

Each cap had beautiful beadwork around the brim, lovely waves of purple to lavender to white—the colors of our treaty wampum belts. As the beads neared the facing, they grew like vines, framing the silk-screen logo, connecting at the top, a beaded version of our Sky World image. The simple deep dome had a little plant sprout coming out of the center, each with a flourish I'd never seen before. It was only right. Those curls represented the tree of knowledge in the world we'd come from, tumbling into this less perfect place. (I totally thought I might steal that idea for when I did the finishing touches on matching Conceptual Pieces I was making for Jim as a Christmas present, featuring the back covers of Lennon's *Mind Games* and *Imagine*.)

"These are gorgeous! Amazing!" I said, reaching into one of the bags. "Who did these?"

"*I* did, you little bitchlette," Marie said, snapping her eyes at *me* this time.

"I didn't mean it that way," I said softly. "I meant . . . well, you always hated beadwork."

"No, *you and Ma* always hated *my* beadwork. Once *you* ditched us, I could show what I was doing. Without Ma second-guessing my color and pattern choices." Our mom *had* always praised my beadwork by slamming Marie's. Hers wasn't bad, just less adventurous.

"I'm sorry," I said. "I really didn't mean that. I was just . . . shocked. I didn't know you could do this. That's all." If we were on a TV show, we might hug here, but that was definitely not the Indian sister way of doing things. "I wanna put one of these on." I looked into the bags, and they were all amazing. "Whose patterns are these? Yours?" I rubbed my fingers along the beaded brims, the work tight and even. It would hold up for years, never snagging or sagging.

"Mm-hmm. My own," she said, a shy smile opening across her face, like the brides in TV movies. "Developed whenever Ma took breaks, at least in the beginning. If she said Dark Deanna things, I'd have a hard time coming up with the perfect designs."

"Wait, have you taken pictures? Before these guys walk off with them?"

"I made sure of that," Ben-Yaw-Mean said. "I have a pretty nice camera."

"Who are you again?" Carson asked, admiring Marie's work too. "You were at Artie's?"

"He's my friend," Marie said. "And don't even give me that look, Carson. You have older friends." She was passing Ben-Yaw-Mean off as an *older friend*. Interesting. Maybe one day I'd be able to do the same with Jim. *Yeah,* Ghost Marvin said inside my skull.

"How'd you make so many?" I asked.

"I had a little help," she said, smiling at Ben-Yaw-Mean, the least likely beadworker on earth. I was afraid to look, to see if I could tell the difference. My sister had made what all beadworkers hope for: her Signature Item. The guys taking the caps tucked them carefully into the hooded sweatshirts Carson had asked them to wear, clearly loving the Honor Gift.

"Carson?" She held one especially for him. She'd used tiny seed beads to make his Mohawk-wearing devil on the front, and she'd clipped little horns on the sides.

"Thanks. Nyah-wheh. I'm gonna put it in the Chevelle, okay?" He handed the cap to Lewis, who slid it gently into his jacket. "I feel like I have to wear this one." He reached into his own hooded sweatshirt and pulled out the original cap, the one that was the reason we were here.

"Is that such a good idea?" I asked.

"Look at those people in the park, on that picnic bench?" Carson pointed with his lips, a Rez gesture I had yet to master. "See that blond guy with the bad haircut? That's my brother. He chopped his hair off and bleached it to be here. He's not going in. He's done some seriously stupid things in the last six months, but he's not an idiot. He said he wanted to see how I might try to finish what he'd started."

"What he *started*?" Ben-Yaw-Mean said, straining his scrawny chicken neck. My eyes almost smacked Marie's head, they popped so hard in disbelief, for just a second. She hadn't told him, and somehow he hadn't figured that we'd know the guy who tried to hold up Custard's Last Stand. Everyone else was Cigar-Store Indian Faces all around.

"He's the reason there's a No Indians sign," Carson said.

"Nope, that there's bad intel," Lewis's uncle said. I'd forgotten he was even here. He had some strange ability to almost make himself invisible. "That owner there, he pretends that he just put up his No Indians sign after that numbnuts stunt. But it's been there all along." I'd never heard him speak so many words. "I knew about it. Long time ago. I just stayed away. Sometimes it's better to just not go where you ain't wanted. He said it's 'cause he had trouble with drunk Indians before. Like white customers don't come in drunk." Juniper looked to me and to Carson. "He's open late. It ain't *families* coming in for a burger at two in the morning."

In my head, I could still see Juniper (Albert, remember that, Magpie!) on the ground, bucking up like a horse at the Sanborn Field Day. Not exactly a graceful drunk person, but neither was that white woman rubbing up against him that night.

"You all ready?" Carson asked, and people stood up.

"Wait," I said. "I have a camera." I dug in my purse/beadwork bag and handed it over to Ben-Yaw-Mean. "That sign'll disappear if *I* go in with it, but *you* can." Marie eyed up Jim's camera. *Now you gotta tell her something about that, isn't it?* Ghost Marvin said. *Where's your head at?* For not even being here, my twin sure was making his presence known. *And why is it that I'm not there?* he butted in. *Because you didn't bother to ask me?*

"That'll do," Ben-Yaw-Mean said, taking it from me, as if any fifteen-year-old might be carrying around a hundred-dollar camera. He slid the strap on his shoulder under his giant trench coat, and strolled up to the building with Paulson, just two white guys out to get a burger.

"Remember," Carson said, trailing them. "Wait until I stand up in the window, then come in. Not too fast, just like you're here for lunch." As he walked past ChameleIndians, they casually got out of their cars, right on cue. It looked like a normal lunch rush.

"Juniper! Lewis!" Carson's dad came flying across the parking lot, alone. "What's going on with this?" He held the newspaper article I'd unsuccessfully tried to hide from Lewis the night of the Turkey Swap. Carson was going to be pissed because of the subject, but if Lewis had studied it (really studied it), he'd have seen Jim in the crowd shots, sitting in a booth and yukking it up. I never asked Jim if he knew Custard, or just happened to be there. I didn't want to know.

"Your boy's got more balls than I thought," Albert said, stepping up, effectively slowing him. "You can find out now, or in the papers tomorrow." He wandered toward the building, though Carson hadn't yet given us the signal. Others took Albert as a signal, leaving their cars.

Inside, Carson and the ChameleIndians were scattered at tables, or at the counter, waiting for their numbers to be called. They'd already ordered. The No Indians sign was still visible.

Just as we entered, the Polaroid's flashbulb went off. Custard had been reaching for something under the counter, and suddenly jerked up in surprise. His stupid costume Cavalry hat popped off his head, its strap tightening against his Adam's apple. Albert and Carson's dad went to the counter together. Ben-Yaw-Mean watched to see if he'd gotten the picture.

"I'm a veteran," Albert said, taking the beaded cap from his jacket and putting it on. He looked down at the No Indians sign. Custard knew something was going on but hadn't figured out what. He hadn't slid the sign off. All the Indians put their beaded caps on. "My friend here's another veteran," he said, gesturing to Carson's dad. He also didn't know what was going on, but Carson, suddenly, from behind him, slid the original beaded cap onto his dad's head. Lewis passed the custom cap to Carson. "We appreciate your honoring us. I'd like a Big Bighorn."

"That, um, offer," Custard stuttered, "it was only good" — he glanced quickly at the clock above the exit — "until two. It was for *lunch*. Sorry about that." He swiped the counter with a cleaning rag, knocking the sign from visibility.

"I don't see that anywhere, General Custard," Albert said calmly. Some guys who'd been eating and watching this unfold came up and stood close behind Albert.

"There some problem, sir?" one of them asked, looking at Custard.

"Just trying to accept the invitation of recognizing my service," Albert said. The puffy olive-green jacket over his sweatshirt had his name on the chest, block letters, not the cursive on Jim's shirt name patches. "Like *you*." The veteran customers were silent, unsure if they should side with another actual veteran or the man in the ridiculous Cavalry costume.

"We're done serving," Custard said, emphatically, then shouted to his employees. "Shut the fryers and grill down! We're closing early today in honor of our veterans!" He then turned back to Albert. "Sorry. See this sign?" he said, pointing to one permanently mounted on the wall. "I'll read it, in case you can't. We reserve the right to refuse service to *anyone*," he said, pressing his finger hard on the counter. "This is a private business establishment. I have the right—"

Two younger workers came to the counter with trays full of food (several people's orders?), and shouted a number. A couple ChameleIndian men got up from a table and came to the counter, but they hadn't put their caps on yet. They took the trays and lip-pointed to a couple women, who came and took them back to the tables. The men stayed at the counter.

"What the hell, Juniper?" Carson's dad nudged Albert. "Do something! Anything!" Albert stood firm. "Never mind, goddammit, I will!" He got close to Custard. "You're taking my order! A . . . a . . ." He looked up at the menu board. "A Big Bighorn, hold the onions. Fill it." I'd never heard a food order placed as a realistic threat before.

"Harvey, we came here for respect," Albert said. "To accept the meal that this guy's offered us, isn't it? Isn't it what we do? What you're doing, that's not the way we do things."

"Damn straight, it ain't," Custard said, not backing down. Other men who'd already eaten gathered at the counter. "You fucking illiterate Indian. Read my goddamn joined the others and sign. If you can."

"Think you fellas better leave," one man in an Airborne jacket said. Albert looked at Carson, who'd joined the others and put his new custom cap on. Carson had convinced thirty to forty grown-up Indians to join his cause.

"I knew about your other sign," Albert said, calmly, turning back to Custard, not a whisper but not a shout either. "And your poster full of dead Indians." He cocked his head to the left. I hadn't seen it before now, but it was exactly as Carson had described. "Most of us do. Grown-ups anyway. It's why we don't come here. Not to obey your cracker ass, but because we don't need to put ourselves in that place." He turned to the Airborne guy who'd come up to him. "You know that feeling?" The guy had looked like he was going to challenge Albert, but something now passed between them. He stayed silent.

"These kids. Sometimes they make mistakes, walk into places they maybe shouldn't go and they see the poster and that sign. That one," he said to Custard, pointing over the counter. "The one you slid down there, once you saw brown people with long hair. Me, turns out. Imagine if that was your kids seeing that about themselves? Imagine going into a restaurant that had a poster on the wall of a bunch of white guys being slaughtered by Indians."

"Juniper, get the hell out the way. Let me handle this," Carson's dad said, pushing Albert.

"Jesus, Dad!" Carson suddenly yelled. "Sit your ass down and listen for once!" Carson's dad whirled, raising his arm like he was going to take out his son. He stopped, seeing what was behind him. The whole spectrum of our Rez, wearing Carson's red shirts and Marie's amazing caps. Light, dark, long hair, short hair, straight hair, curly hair, even red and blond hair, pale skin, pink skin, ruddy skin, and brown skin. All glowing on these round-cheeked faces, not those stupid high mythical cheekbones every white person claims to have when they tell you they're "part Indian."

A rumble went through the crowd. Some people calculated if they could get out quick. Others held their breaths. Some women held on to kids, like they might have to make a break for it. What did they think was going to happen? What did *I* think was going to happen?

"Now, black people?" Albert said, continuing on as if nothing had happened, like he was trying to explain to a kid why Clean-Up

Time was a part of playing with toys. "They know you use *that* word when they're not in hearing distance. They know you probably say it the second they're out of earshot. They know how visible they are. But you see, here," he said, sweeping his arm again, "we don't all look like the Indian of your imagination. We're around you all the time. Might even say you're surrounded, General Custard."

"That sounds like a threat," Custard growled.

"A fact is not a threat," Albert said. "And really, you can't refuse service to a group of people. You see, my nephew here," he said, and Lewis joined him. "He taught me some things about civil disobedience and the civil rights movement a few years ago."

"As groups, we're not looking for civil rights," Lewis said. "We have treaties in place, from when you took our lands in the first place. We're Onkwehowe."

"What the hell's that mean?" Custard asked.

"The original people," Lewis clarified. "But either way, you can't refuse service to an identified group of people. No matter what kind of bullshit sign you put up."

"Oh, can it, you little turd," Custard said.

"You can shut down," Lewis said, looking directly at Custard. "But we're going to stay here, outside. And if you open up again today, we'll be back. I want my uncle to get the meal you promised for his risking his life for your sorry ass. Are you even a veteran, General?"

"You can't stay in my lot," Custard said, ignoring Lewis's question. "It's private property. And in America, *I* get to say who's on my private property."

"I guess that's a no to the veteran question," Carson said. "That park over there isn't private." He turned to the room. "We got food and we're gonna play music for as long as it takes." He turned to Custard again. "If you open up before midnight, we'll be back." He turned back to the crowd. "You're all welcome."

"Fuck you, wahoo," Custard said. That was the spark that did it. In a blur, Carson's dad flash-punched Custard in the temple. Custard slipped in his boots, arms flailing. He hit the french fry warming racks, and fries flew like greasy confetti as he and the racks clattered to the floor. It was like a sign had lighted up. People started running, swinging, jumping up on booths, holding trays in front of them like shields, and heading for the doors. I guess the guys who'd already gotten their free meal felt like they had to defend Custard, or maybe they just wanted to.

A series of tinkling noises started filling my ears. Glass was smashing all around me, but it wasn't noisy enough to have been the plate windows. Then I remembered the other poster on the wall: "Real Root Beer Served in Frosted Mugs." This had suddenly gotten serious.

"No!" Carson yelled. "This was *not* how it was supposed to go!" He tried to drag his dad from the brawl's center. "Peaceful! Damn it, Dad! Why couldn't you listen to me?" His dad threw him off like he was a Construction Paper Cut-Out Guy from the posters.

Out of nowhere, someone yanked me from behind, pushing me through the crowd. I tried fighting but, though I hadn't seen him when we entered, I knew I was no match for a full-grown man. "Are you crazy?" Jim Morgan asked as we neared the door. Jim was no veteran. He'd told me himself how he'd gotten out of it. I guess he and Custard did indeed know each other.

"Jim, let me go. I have to be here with my friends!" I said, almost free of his grip until he lunged forward one more time, wrapping an arm around my waist.

"Sorry. I can't let a girl I love risk getting hurt for this bullshit," he said. Even over the shouting and war whooping, and approaching police sirens, I'd heard him. "Cops are coming. I'm getting you out of here. Once you're visible to law enforcement, you're never invisible again. Come on!" I didn't have much choice, with his forearm in the small of my back, and his hand latched solid on my hip. He hit the door with his back, and we fell in the gravel, me on top.

An explosion rocked the inside, then another, and another. The screaming crowd flew at us to the doors. "Oh, shit!" Jim said, rolling on top of me and trying to get us out of the crowd's path. He pulled me aside him as we crawled along the foundation. We made our way to his Trans Am a couple rows back where cars were peeling out. "Get in!" he yelled, opening the door and lowering his hand to my butt, guiding it to the passenger's seat. He released the lever, and the seat dropped to full recline. "And stay down."

Maggi, what are you doing? Ghost Marvin said. *Ditching people from the Rez to run off with some random old white guy?* Even as I ignored the voice, I realized it had become Marvin's regular voice, not the one he used to mock Dark Deanna. *But, Marv,* I said back to it, *he's not random. He just told me he loved me! Doesn't that count for something? And I've already been in this car before so just settle your ass down!*

Jim ran around back as I unlocked his door. "I said stay down!" he said, jumping in. He dropped the Bandit into reverse. For a few brief seconds, I could see Custard kneeling on his counter, arms up in the air, fists gripping pistols. He was shouting something that looked like "Thanks! Thanks!" Some of the men who'd been there when we walked in stood in front of him, arms outstretched with hands spread wide, apparently not afraid.

"I can't leave!" I said. "My sister's in there. I gotta make sure she's safe."

"I'm sure she's fine," Jim said, driving as fast as he could without drawing attention (to the degree that was possible in a Bandit Trans Am). "Look, you can call from my place. Or we'll stop at a pay phone." Eventually, he put the brakes on at a stop sign, looking in the mirrors and ahead of us. He dropped it into park, and I could see he was breathing heavily.

"Jesus, I was so scared you'd get hurt," he said, leaning over, taking my jaws into his hands and covering my mouth with his. I breathed in, sharply, accepted the kiss, opening my mouth to meet his parting lips, but then I pulled back.

"I know. That crazy asshole was shooting? What if someone got killed? Jim, I need to get home, to know what happened."

"No, no, no," he said, brushing his mustache against my neck for a second. "Those were blanks. He's not an idiot. You can't have a real loaded gun on you in that kind of job."

"That's not true," I said, pulling back farther. "He shot someone, this spring. I don't even know how he's still around."

"He's still around 'cause," he said, still holding my jaw, and gently turning my head to lock eyes with him, "they . . . were . . . blanks. Maybe Giorgio was closer to that idiot robber than he thought. But no one came in to any hospital around here with a gunshot wound. A blank *can* seriously mess you up if you're close enough." He let go of my face and sighed. "A mess. A serious friggin' mess."

"How do you know they were blanks?"

" 'Cause he told me. I've known Giorgio for years."

"Giorgio?"

"He says George, so he can do all that stupid General George Custard bullshit. Up until now, it's been a gold mine." Jim somehow couldn't grasp that such a place would be screwed up to any Indian.

"What were you afraid of me getting hurt by then?"

"That fucking mob! What do you think?" He leaned in, squeezing me close, then let go.

"It wasn't a *mob*!" I insisted. "It was a peaceful protest." He dropped into drive.

"Peaceful protest, my ass. I saw that guy sucker punch Giorgio right in the face and drop him to the floor. That was no love tap." We drove silently, passing both pay phones in Sanborn and the road his apartment was on. As we neared the Rez, I finally spoke.

"Jim? Thank you for, you know, looking out for me." I did what he'd done, reaching up and touching his chin. It was rough with stubble. "And for what you said back there. I feel it too." I felt so drawn to him, such longing to be with him, that the selfish part of me put all my other nagging questions in a tote like my mom used, and slid it to the bottom shelf of my brain.

"You do?" he said, pulling me close, even as he drove, my face against his chest. I nodded, and the chest hairs tickled my cheek. I was facing down and could see that, even in all this commotion, he was growing excited. I was too. I reached out and touched his thigh.

"Oh yeah," he said, and shifted in his seat, raising his butt off the cushion so my hand slid closer to where he wanted it. He swallowed hard. "Assuming your friends aren't in jail," he said, breathing funny, "you still doing that Battle of the Bands thing in a couple weeks?"

"Jail," I said, laughing, trying not to sound nervous. "Yes, we're still doing it." I tried to sit back up straight. "Why?"

"I signed up to be the only facilities guy," he said. At first, he kept his arm around my shoulders, leveraging me in place against him. I tensed my mucles, pushing a little harder, and he let go. "I get there a couple hours early, unlock everything, make sure the lights are on, and I lock up at the end."

"I've seen teachers there, at the last one."

"Yeah, chaperones. They don't go into the facilities area. Mostly when I do these, I crash in the break room. Our couch is pretty comfortable," he said. "Ever try it?"

"Yes, goof," I said. "I've sat on the break room couch. Nothing exactly remarkable."

"I wasn't talking about sitting. I could bring a couple bottles of wine. Some candles."

"Jim, I need to tell you something," I said, and he eased his foot off the gas.

"That the Polaroid camera that started the shit-show back there was mine?"

"No, not that," I mumbled. "But . . . yeah, it was yours. I can get it back . . . tomorrow?"

"You can still hang on to it," he said, sailing through the Rez. After a few heavy and silent minutes, he continued.

"So is it that you're not seventeen?" My tiny gasp betrayed me. He looked over, with that typical Jim Grin. "I'm your boss. I have access to application records. Let's see," he said, and recited my full birthday. "Correct?"

"Correct. So I'm not legal. Yet?" I smiled, hoping that might be good enough. *Like he didn't know already,* Ghost Marvin said, back to mocking our mom's voice.

"It's like smoking weed," he said. "Only illegal if you get caught. I'm not gonna tell anyone if two people who love each other want to share that love all the way. You?"

"No," I said, my voice shaky. "I don't want to cause trouble?" Even I didn't believe myself. There *were* issues with what we were considering. A voice louder than Ghost Marvin's, though, told me to forget about the idea of what was legal or not. It was, maybe, the Maggi in Love Voice. But I didn't want to do this wrapped in a lie. If this was the man I was planning to lose my virginity with, he should have at least considered these real complications.

"Well, there you go," he said. "I mean, today? When you were in danger, I realized that I love you. That I want to share that love the way people do when they know. I hoped it was maybe mutual."

I nodded, my throat suddenly dry.

"You weren't just saying that because I did?" he asked. The pleading voice killed me.

I shook my head, trying to swallow, and took a deep breath. I put my hand back, a couple inches from that place he wanted it. He did the same thing to me, and that now familiar lightning bolt feeling came over me again. I couldn't decide if it was awesome or terrifying. If we stayed much longer, I'd move my hand and begin that final path. I didn't even know what that really would feel like. Was there a wrong way to touch it? Could you accidentally break it?

Just then, we turned onto Snakeline and we each brought our hands back into our own laps. I wondered if two weeks was enough time for Marie to tell me everything I needed to know about losing my virginity. Or if she'd even be willing.

You know why you're not asking me anything? Ghost Marvin said.

Because you're an even bigger virgin than I am? I said. Maybe that would shut the window in my head that my twin had somehow pried open. This was one of the weirdnesses of being a twin. I was close with Marie, but we were just regular sisters. Marvin and I were something else.

Wrong, Ghost Marvin said. *You're not asking me because I'll tell you the truth instead of what you want to hear, what you think will make this seem like a good idea. The truth you're afraid of, isn't it?*

Shut up, Marvin. And could you get out of my head when I'm with a guy? My guy? It's seriously creepy. (I knew he wouldn't, but I could hope. I wondered if it was worse for identical twins. Man, I shivered, thinking about what that would be like.) Ghost Marvin continued to tell me all the ways this was seriously wrong, and he didn't shut up until I climbed out of Jim's Bandit and watched him leave. Silence! Finally!

When I came in the house, Real Marvin was watching one of his dumb shows. I almost expected him to tell me I was making a big mistake, but he didn't say anything. I guessed that meant Marie hadn't wound up in jail. A plus.

My stomach fluttered, but I couldn't tell fully what the cause was. It had been a long day. Was this fear, excitement, or a little bit of both? Maybe Marie could tell me the truth about that too.

Yeah, right, Ghost Marvin said.

23

(Just Like) Starting Over
Carson Mastick

"You wanted to see me, Mrs. Marchese?" I stepped into the empty home ec cooking lab for a command performance, delivered on a pink piece of paper at the end of class: *SEE ME!*

"Carson Mastick," she said. "Have a seat." She pulled two stools out.

"I'm running kinda late, Mrs. Marchese. My band only has practice space for an hour and a half, and we're still working on last-minute arrangements for Battle of the Bands tomorrow."

"You don't need to worry, Mr. Mastick," she said, still smiling. Was it ever good when a teacher called you *Mr.?* It was almost always fake respect that meant the slap was going to be way harder when it came. She pulled clippings from last week's papers out of a manila folder. "You've had quite a couple weeks, it seems."

"Didn't go exactly as I'd planned," I said. I didn't bother picking up the clippings she'd just let fan out onto the counter. I already knew what they said. My planned protest concert had turned into a psycho brawl inside a dive. We never played a single note and hauled ass out of there when Custard pulled out his guns and the cops showed.

The coverage had turned into mostly a wash. It started out supportive—the paper reported that Custard's No Indians sign had been up for years, not just after he had his own "personal excuse" to discriminate. They gave Albert a few quotes, and when the reporter followed up, Custard admitted it was true. Then there was a side article about the long history of Indians serving in the military, even before the US had forcefully insisted we were citizens, and another about the "shadow of Southern segregation policies," including side-by-side photos of Custard's No Indians sign next to Whites Only signs from the civil rights news archives. They even wrote about the success of the Longest Walk from a couple years ago, a countrywide Indian protest march, going from San Francisco to DC, when activists discovered the federal government was developing bills to get rid of our status again.

But then, per usual for what happened when people get busted doing asshole things, the tide changed. That reporter had given us a fair shake, but then Custard's supporters claiming to be "witnesses" quickly jumped in, taking over the paper with their onslaught of This Country Was Founded on Free Expression articles and editorials. Guess they didn't see how stupid it was to use the "Founding Fathers" bullshit when dealing with Indians. They weren't *our* Founding Fathers. We were already here, so we didn't need to be found. "What *had* you planned?" Mrs. Marchese asked, interrupting the place I'd wandered off to. She had a weird patience that said she was asking questions in a friendly-*seeming* manner when there was something else on her mind.

"Well, it's kind of screwed up that that guy Custard—I guess that's probably not his real name—that he even *thought* he'd made up a good name for a restaurant. Don't you think it sends a message? Particularly in a town between two reservations? I'm guessing up in New England, they probably don't have Lee Harvey Oswald Omelets kind of restaurants."

"That's a bit of hyperbole, isn't it, Mr. Mastick? Isn't it possibly just a clever pun?"

"Hyperbole?" I hated when teachers used hard words when easy ones were around.

"An exaggeration to make a point," she said, her Understanding Smile in place.

"Okay, maybe. But why *would* you?" She raised her eyebrows. "Why name your burger dive after a doofus US military guy who got VD at West Point and was the last-ranked, whatever, West Pointer in his class? And *then* add his stupidest decision to your restaurant's name? The decision that *killed* him, and killed most of the men following his orders."

"You must be getting an A in history," Marchese said, with her Seriously Off Smile.

"That ain't exactly the way history's taught here, Mrs. Marchese. I got that history from a book called *Custer Died for Your Sins*."

"Vulgar title."

"It's hyperbole, Mrs. Marchese. A pun. A lot of Indians love puns, including Vine Deloria, Jr., the person who wrote that book. Truth? I *don't* read a lot of books I don't have to. But I read that one. Maybe that jerk-off General Custard should read it. Then he'd get why we think his burger dive has . . ." What had she said a minute ago? "A vulgar title."

"Perhaps he should. Someone should recommend it to him."

"Listen, Mrs. Marchese? I really do want to get to my practice." We'd agreed to do the songs we'd worked on the longest, but that didn't mean there wasn't always stuff that could use a polish. Our set list included my Stones songs, a little Beatles for Lewis, and even a bone for him Susan had advocated for. She wanted Lennon's "Imagine" as the song that showed off her keyboard skills. "Look, I'm sure you didn't want to see me to talk about my history grades, so why *did* you want to see me?"

"I told you. There's no hurry."

"Battle of the Bands is *tomorrow*," I stressed. She really wasn't getting it. "You never ignore one last chance to tighten up." I still wanted to do a couple run-throughs of the closer I'd thought up last week. We began with Maggi setting it up, doing "Amazing Grace" translated into Tuscarora. Maggi'd been raised saying words that began in the back of your throat with abrupt changes, so those syllables come naturally to her, and we arranged for her voice and water drums with regular harmonies. Susan couldn't wrestle those sound shapes, so we had her doing soft harmony vowels, and the rest of us played light. Finally, we'd end with "Radar Love," a barn-burning showstopper spotlighting Doobie and allowing the mixing of Maggi's water drums with the drum pads on Susan's keyboard. It was going to be awesome.

"But you won't *be* in the Battle of the Bands, this year. Maybe next?" Marchese said, a tight grin splitting only the lower half of her face.

"Mrs. Marchese, I won't be here next year. I'm graduating next June."

"Another incorrect assumption, Carson. I'm happy to shed a little light. Shall I? Yes? Did you look at the papers when you enrolled in the Battle of the Bands?" That was when I knew I was in some serious trouble.

"They just explained the rules," I said, which was all that I remembered seeing.

"The rules state that you cannot participate if you have a deficiency report. It's like all the other extracurriculars. If it's on school property, your grades must be at least passing."

"But all my grades are passing. I don't have any deficiency warnings. I did last year, but I got caught up on my work. That stuff doesn't carry over from year to year, does it?"

"Deficiency warnings went home yesterday. Yours is probably on your kitchen table now. It won't be addressed to you, of course." Marchese pulled a white-and-red plastic plunger thing from her apron pocket. "Do you know what this is?" She set it between us. I had an idea of what it was and had a worse idea of where it had come from.

"It looks like . . ." I could not think of a single thing it looked like other than what it was.

"I'll help you. This is a doneness indicator, a very simple device. Many commercially sold turkeys now come with them embedded in their breasts. Personally," she said, examining it like it was her first time, "I've never found them very accurate. Sometimes, they don't pop, or when they do, the turkey's so dry it crumbles like pencil shavings. This is why I have students use a probe meat thermometer when we do our turkeys."

"I remember," I said.

"Do you? And where do we put the meat thermometer probe?"

"You stick the probe into the area between the breast and thigh and it should read one hundred and sixty, and then you take it out to let it . . . rest? That's a funny word for a cooked turkey, but that's what you said, and it continues cooking for a little while longer. It should be one hundred and sixty-five before serving."

"Correct. Excellent. You will make an excellent cook if you decide to be."

"So why are giving me a deficiency? I'm guessing it's you, or I wouldn't be here."

"Assertive," she said, again, sounding impressed, but her forehead crease assured me she was not. "But I shouldn't be surprised, given your splashy presentation for the newspaper. That couldn't have just been happenstance that a reporter from the *Cascade* was there. Clever."

"Dumb luck," I said. "I had no idea until I got there. But I wasn't gonna turn him away. Only a fool says no to coverage with Battle of the Bands coming right up."

"Do you know they sell food at the Battle of the Bands and other school events?"

"I guess," I said. Weird switcheroo on the topics, but she was proving herself to be kind of a freak anyway.

"Do you know how that food is arranged for? How that works?"

"Vendors, I imagine?" I said. "I'm from a reservation, Mrs. Marchese. Vendor Tables are a way of life."

"I see," she said, picking the turkey popper up again, spinning it casually, wanting me to continue being aware of it. "Do you know Custard's Last Stand has been one of the most popular vendors for events at this school for years?" I shook my head. "He, like *you*, will not be at the Battle this year. The Music Boosters thought his presence would reflect badly on the program."

I looked down at the big front-page picture on the top newspaper. Flipping out on top of his counter, Custard gave the perfect image of what he and his customers were really about. Right under the title "LAST STAND?" was him wearing that ridiculous Cavalry costume, both arms up, each holding a handgun in firing position. The caption insisted he'd used blanks, totally safe, and that he'd fired them to restore order in a dangerous blah blah.

"If you're waiting for a crying Indian, Mrs. Marchese, you should watch for that Anti-Pollution commercial. Though that guy ain't really an Indian anyway."

"Still a smart aleck, even having just been told you're being held back a year."

"I went from deficiency warning to flunking? What is it you think I've done, Mrs. Marchese? Holding a protest at a shitty drive-in twenty miles away from here has *nothing* to do with my grades. Free speech and all?"

"You failed your turkey project. I don't have to tell you, that *is* your major project for this course. I'll leave it as a failing grade, but if you contest it, I'll file the reason as cheating and that will wind up on your transcript. No college application is going to be competitive with that on your transcript." *College application??? Was she kidding?*

"How do you cheat on a turkey? You saw us wash it out, save the giblets, and prepare it, and you *saw* the done turkey! You even ate some and didn't throw up! So, no food poisoning."

"That's why I haven't already filed it as a cheat. I can't quite figure out *why* or *how* you swapped out my turkey for another. I only know that you *did*." She held up the plunger. "Mr. Mastick, I dislike these so much, and I believe so firmly that my students should know the proper safety techniques, that I special-order my turkeys. Mine don't come with these doneness gimmicks." She dropped it like it was leaking radiation. "And yet, *yours* had one."

"Maybe it was a mistake," I said. I was busted, but her evidence was seriously flimsy.

"It wasn't. We invoice with a single supplier. Specializing in culinary class requests."

"I don't know what you're talking about, Mrs. Marchese."

"Well, I encourage you to take the F. I looked at your transcript. I see you won't be able to add a class for your final two quarters. Perhaps summer school?"

"I still don't know what you're talking about. If you're done, I'm gonna leave now."

"Aren't you curious?" she asked as I grabbed my guitar. Apparently she wanted me to be curious, so I set it down and stared at her. "You don't strike me *really* as the political activist sort. Perhaps I'm wrong. Perhaps I'll check out this book you mentioned from our library."

"It's not *in* our library," I said. "But be sure to check some . . . most Rez houses."

"I see. Still, to go to the lengths you went to at Custard's Last Stand, I assumed you must have a vested interest. In the library's yearbook archive, I saw only two other Mastick alums, Sheila and Derek. No extracurriculars in their Senior Profiles beyond Indian Culture Society. Other than that? No distinguishing characteristics, except one, on their transcripts. They happen to share *your address*. Brother and sister? The yearbook years would suggest Derek might be a little older than twenty. Isn't that the age of the suspect in the failed robbery?"

"I wouldn't know," I said, trying to steady my voice. It would do me no good to flip out on Marchese. I'd been enough of a wiseass in my time that this could move me from Prankster to Troublemaker in the school records, and I couldn't afford that now. I might be able to figure something out once this cooled down, to get out of summer school and graduate on time, but only if I kept my mouth shut.

"Oh, but you must be a faithful follower of the newspapers, or you wouldn't have known about this incident at all."

"I saw that gasbag Custard on TV. He said he could recognize Indians just by looking at us. He doesn't know we're everywhere." The long, silent avoidance between us and Custard had ended that night. I kept thinking of the weird way Lewis's Uncle Albert, who sometimes made very little sense, was able to knock Custard's dick in the dirt, just with words. And Albert would have totally smoked him without even one swing, if my dumb-ass dad hadn't jumped in.

"Some of us could walk in, and he'd never know. I got to thinking, there's only two reasons you'd name your restaurant that. One, if you were stupid, unaware of what a shitty name that would be to Indians, or two, if you *wanted* Indians to stay away. You couldn't *really* ban Indians, without risking legal shit, but you could make it a place Indians wouldn't wanna go. I had a look-see. I blend in easy, when I'm not wearing a beadwork cap." I pulled the cap Marie had beaded for me from my bookbag, held it up to Marchese, and then dropped it back in.

"You know what I saw on the counter there? I bet you do, since it seems like *you* have a, what? A vested interest. This?" I slid the article back to her, with the photos of Custard's No Indians sign and the Whites Only one from the South. She had a good poker face, but like most teachers, she didn't like kids arguing back. If I'd thrown a tantrum, thrown a desk, yelled "Fuck!" or something, she'd know what to do. My calm, it seemed, bothered her.

"Now he's been exposed," I continued. "And anyone who goes there is telling people something about themselves." What I didn't say was, *would it matter?* Would they keep coming back because of their choices? My gut suggested that: Yes, Yes, they would.

"If I were to submit your brother's name," she said, stone face recovered. "To the police? To bring him in for questioning? Might they find a scar on his backside that shouldn't be there?"

"I don't check out my brother's ass. I don't know what scars he might have." *Thank you, Marchese, for the tip.* "He's been in a couple accidents. Got some stitches from scrap roofing materials a couple years ago. Tetanus shot. He's played lacrosse. It's a big thing in my family."

"Not for this school, he hasn't."

"No, he always thought playing against white kids wasn't challenging enough."

"I see. It didn't look like you played here either. Same challenge concerns?"

"I play the guitar, Mrs. Marchese," I said, lifting my case. "Can't risk messing up my hands. Lacrosse—particularly the way Indians play—is too tough for me." *Thanks again, Marchese. I wouldn't have thought of this.* "I work on sticks. And I repair players' uniforms. Ask Mrs. Gronka, about my work in her sewing class. I got an A. It's gonna look weird if I get an F here. *Is* there some vested interest *I* don't know about, Mrs. Marchese?"

Stone face.

"Whatever," I continued. "I'm gonna go tell my band the bad news. Probably see Mr. Groffini, tell him too. Our guidance counselor was rooting for us. I think he even volunteered to be a chaperone." Her face never changed as I swung my guitar case around and stomped out the door. I considered slamming it, but that would have been a Kid Tantrum move.

I found Doobie and Susan in the practice room we'd signed out, playing "Come Sail Away," one of our Just-in-Case Songs. We'd only been given a half hour to play, but it could change, depending on other things. Like an encore, if we'd won. I'd wanted us prepared, but I hadn't prepared the band for this kind of information.

"Maggi and Lewis already went to work," Doobie said, not stopping the run he was doing on his bass. "They got tired of waiting on you." He'd been kind of cool to me since I hadn't asked him to join us at the protest. He didn't understand that I'd done it for him, knowing there was no way to plug in his amp, and the idea was too serious to drag out that stupid orange caution cone. If things had gone right, he would have just had to sit there while we played.

"I'll deal with Lewis later," I said. "Either of you happen to know where Maggi might be in the building?" They shook their heads. If she were cleaning hallways or classrooms, I'd be able to find her, but since September, she said her new boss mostly assigned her places that were for Facilities Employees Only. None of us were allowed back there while she was on the clock.

"Okay," I said, and let out a sigh I hadn't even expected. "Listen. Bad news. I've been disqualified from Battle of the Bands. I don't want to talk about it right now. I'm hoping I can get it straightened out, for me, later, but there's no way that's gonna happen in time for tomorrow. I'm sorry. I just found out. Like ten minutes ago. It's why I was late."

Doobie didn't say anything, his face doing the same stone-faced statue imitation Marchese had been giving me. He started playing the bass line from "Silly Love Songs," the McCartney song I'd rejected on principle, then put his bass away and started packing up.

"That's it?" I said. "No questions?"

"I've known you for thirteen years, Carson," Doobie said, looking at his amp. "I don't know what they're saying you did, but I know you probably did it. Whatever it is, it ain't the first bridge you burned and probably ain't gonna be the last. I'll be here next year, you know, Hubie Doobie the Flunked-Out Booby. Maybe I'll try with a different band then."

"Really?" Susan whispered to me. "That's it? You're not even giving us an explanation?"

"It's a long story," I said. "And one I'm still trying to sort out."

"You know, Artie asked me to be in his band, but I didn't want my brother bossing me around. And . . . and I know guys form bands 'cause they think it's going to get them laid." I took a quick narrow glance at Doobie. He didn't look up, but his ears glowed red. "And you're all just Maggi Maggi Maggi. Know what? She's not even into you. She likes someone else."

"What?" Who could that be? I ran through the possible suspects. Couldn't think of a one.

"If you'd ever listen to someone besides yourself, you'd know that." Susan grabbed her keyboard, slid its cover on, and locked it.

"You want a ride?" Doobie asked her, and just like that, they left. It was almost four. Lewis would be at work for another hour and a half, so I headed there.

I'd never been inside the garage gates before. I was amazed to see that the back row of spaces looked like a Used Muscle-Car Lot. There was a Mustang, a Charger, a Maverick, a Camaro, a Trans Am trimmed like that *Smokey and the Bandit* car, an Omega, and a Cutlass ragtop, all wicked well kept. Lewis had told me that the security door near the Dumpster was never locked when the place was open and that it led to the areas he mostly worked, so I headed in through there.

Inside, the only sound was a squawky radio pumping Hicks-in-the-Sticks Music, but I could hear voices from another bay. In the distance, three guys in blue work chinos stood around, one holding out a light so another could spark a cigar. "So where's the Loser?" the cigar guy asked. "You guys finally fire him for spoojing in your locker room shower?"

All three of them laughed low, dirty chuckles. Cigar guy looked familiar. Maybe like so many guys around here, he just *seemed* famil-iar. Trucker cap, work boots, a big loop of keys, and a pale blue shirt with a name patch was a pretty common sight. *Jim.* That name wasn't going to narrow anything down for me, but I swore I'd met him somewhere.

"We just don't let him use it anymore," one of them said, grinning.

"He banked some hours the last couple weeks," the last man said. "Told us he wouldn't be in today and tomorrow. Had some things to do, for his band? Some school thing?"

"Tried to get us to buy tickets," the first one said, and they both laughed.

"Like I'd pay to come back here after I punched out," the other one said.

"Guys'd be better off if you just got rid of him. Little fucker can make people disappear."

"I ain't worried," the guy with the lighter said.

"Telling ya," Cigar man said. "My nephew was just messing with him a couple years ago, boom! Suddenly, my sister had to do all kinds of shit 'cause that Loser had convinced those assholes in the princi-pal's office that he was *getting harassed.*" On this last, he raised his voice, like a little kid's, the same way I'd made fun of Lewis in the past. "Fucking candy ass. Little bit of advice, you guys? Always watch out for a *smart* Indian. There aren't too many, but boy . . ." He trailed off and puffed on the cigar a bit to get the ember hot again.

Was he talking about Evan Reiniger? I looked closer at this guy's face. Behind the bushy mustache, I could see a resemblance. They had the same intense eyes, like someone on the hunt. Evan was the guy who'd tortured Lewis in junior high, torpedoing his Brainiac status. I hated to admit it, but Evan had given me the first window in what it meant to be a ChameleIndian.

For some reason I never found out, Evan hated Indians. I never mentioned anything about where I was from when we first met, so his eyes ran right past me, and once he found Lewis as his everyday target, I just decided to keep my invisibility. Some people you knew were dangerous, even after one conversation, and Evan had that craziness in his eyes at all times. I knew Evan had gotten thrown out of school at some point, but I never knew the details and I sure wasn't asking Lewis.

"I like my Indians young, dumb, and looking for fun," he added, streaming nasty stogie clouds. He opened his mouth a little and flicked his tongue quickly. I'd seen guys do this to girls at bars and some drinking parties. Did that ever work? What the hell was wrong with them?

"Careful where you're sliding your dipstick," Lighter Man said. "Don't forget the 'wild' in 'Wild Child.'"

"I ain't worried. When they say 'she went off the reservation,' you know what they mean?" he started. He shaped his hands like a pair of parentheses, and lowered them to belt level. "She went *off* the reservation!" He humped his hips forward a couple quick thrusts, jangling his keys, like the first guy. "It means she's willing to go all batshit crazy with you." *Off the reservation?* I'd never heard this phrase before in my life.

"Still, pushing your luck, Jim. At least be less obvious. Pinstriping? Jeez, like mounting a twelve point rack on your car to announce how good a hunter you are."

What were they talking about? They laughed the Dirty-Joke Laugh middle-aged Rez men used at parties to tease guys like me. It was strange to enter this world that Lewis and Maggi knew all the ins and outs of. For all my New York City dreams, and thinking I was all smooth, they knew the white world way better than I did, the world "Off the Reservation."

One of the guys headed to an industrial sink, scrubbing his hands, and spotted me. "Help you?" he asked, coming toward me. He wasn't running, but there was a sense of urgency. This world was more rigidly controlled than I'd thought.

"I'm looking for Lewis?" I said, uncertainty in my voice.

"Ain't here. But, kid? See that sign? Authorized personnel only."

"Thanks," I said, and turned to leave.

"Kid? Not that way." He pointed me to the main door. "That way."

"Sorry." I altered my course. I definitely didn't belong there. What had Lewis learned that I didn't know? Was I getting a deficiency warning in Growing Up?

A few minutes later, I was on my way down Snakeline. I needed to tell Maggi about the band news *in person*. She should have been off of work by then, but there was no sign of life at her house, so I just kept going. Just below the school, I saw a familiar figure walking toward Torn Rock, and pulled over. He got in. Typical.

"Good," Albert said, settling heavy. "Now I don't have to go all the way to your house."

"For what? My dad want you to work on something?"

"Something. I hear you got problems with that Attack of the Bands, isn't it?"

"Battle of the Bands," I corrected. "Word travels fast."

"It's the Rez, man," he said. I didn't think this was exactly major Eee-ogg.

"We were disqualified," I explained, and he nodded like he indeed already knew. "I can give you a ride home, if you want. I went looking for Lewis at the garage, but he wasn't there. They said he'd planned to miss today."

"Yeah, he ain't home. Hubie Doobie called the house. Why you disqualified anyway?"

"My home ec teacher. She failed me today. Said she'd figured out I was cheating and then hinted that she was just gonna let it go until

I'd hassled Custard's Last Stand. That's the bullshit reason I'm not practicing right now. She disqualified me."

"Were you cheating?" He lit a cigarette, even though I didn't let people smoke in here.

"I'm not sure," I said.

"If you ain't sure, then you probably cheated and you just ain't telling yourself, isn't it? Or maybe it's just me you ain't willing to tell." Technically, I *had* done everything by the book. My turkey was awesome because we cooked it right. The only thing I'd done was swapped out the frozen turkey because I'd screwed up. Did that really count?

"Did Lewis maybe cheat too?" he asked.

"No," I said. The only things he'd done was come with me to the store, and then keep his mouth shut after, when we walked into class. Was that cheating? I didn't think so.

"So then he's not disqualified. Just you?"

"I guess, but there's no band without me."

"Lots of people want to think stuff like that, isn't it? Even if it ain't true?"

"But it *is* true," I said as I pulled into my driveway. We got out, and I could hear my dad shouting at Derek, as usual. "Not sure you wanna go in there."

"Don't get to choose duty. Ain't always a matter of wanting," he said, and stepped up to my porch. I joined him and rattled the knob so that my dad might quit before we entered and became witnesses.

24

I Have a Woman Inside My Soul
Magpie Bokoni

Maybe because we'd spent most of our younger lives together, Marvin had recently started commenting that I wasn't around much (in real life too, beyond the naggy Ghost Marvin taking up residence inside my head). Even he, who spent most of his time not moving from the couch and his goofy sixties shows, had finally sensed disturbances in our environment. I didn't *want* to leave him completely behind, but I didn't know what was going to happen after tonight. So two weeks ago, after Jim shared his plans for the Battle of the Bands night, I'd made myself promise that whenever Marvin asked me to do something, I'd do it. Even watching his dumb shows. It gave me an excuse to work on my projects, and he didn't mind that my lapboard crowded the couch.

"Here, watch this one," Marvin said today. It was the Wednesday before Thanksgiving, Battle of the Bands day. The night Jim and I would explore who we were going to be. Marvin's favorite, *Lost in Space*, was on: the Robinsons who'd screwed up their voyage. They were permanently in uncharted territory, in a tiny, two-deck flying saucer. They were accompanied by "Debbie," their pet Bloop (a chimp in a fur hat with giant "alien" ears and a sound-effects voice that went "Bloop! Bloop!"). She was a constant for two seasons and then—*bloop!*—she vanished. You just knew the trained chimp had grown uncooperative so they wrote it out. That's what happened sometimes when you didn't fit into others' plans.

"Where are they?" I asked. Two characters, Will (Brainiac fourteen-year-old) and Dr. Smith (sneaky, lazy, conniving older-man asshole), squeezed through girders and shifting electronics. I was mildly embarrassed that *I* recognized they weren't in the *Jupiter 2*.

"Inside the robot," Marvin said, with complete sincerity. "He wandered through this mysterious gas, and now he's a giant and it's messed up his timer diode."

"His timer di —"

"Robot Heart," he said, cutting me off. "It made him into a giant. That's the timer diode, there." He pointed to a giant inflated pulsing vinyl cylinder with a tapered tip. It raised, then drooped, raised, then drooped, stretching the blue and red veins painted on its surface.

"That doesn't look so much like a *heart*," I said, and started laughing.

"Shut up!" he said, throwing a pillow at me, but he was laughing. Even he could see that it looked like a *Robot Hard*, particularly when it deflated a bit. "Thanks for ruining my show."

"Wasn't me who put a giant inflatable guhn-naeht throbbing inside the robot." He pushed my shoulder. "Is this why you made me sit down? To get a peek at the robot's, um, unit?"

"The robot dies for a few minutes," he said, exasperated.

"Dies?"

"The, um, diode timer," he said, screwing up the name. I *had* ruined it for him. "They bring him back. And he starts shrinking while they're trapped inside. The walls close in. Things get more cramped. Don and John and Dr. Smith —"

"Don? The cute pilot? How does *he* wind up inside?"

"*Cute?*" Marvin scrunched up his nose. "You got guhn-naeht on the brain!"

"Nothing wrong with saying someone's cute." I'd never told Marvin that Don the space pilot was the real reason I'd watch *this* show. I wished an alien would just eat Dr. Smith.

"Dude's like *thirty*!" Marvin said. Isn't it, though? Now that he said it, Don the space cowboy and Jim Morgan *did* share features. Was I contemplating my first step into adult life because of *Lost in Space*? "He's gotta be, what? In his forties now?"

"Who knows what he looks like now," I acknowledged. "But he sure *is* cute here."

"Just shut up and watch!" he laughed. The characters ran through *the shrinking robot*. Will would somehow save the day, almost get killed, and his dad would pull off a last-minute rescue. Maybe Marvin needed to see himself as Will (Misunderstood Boy Genius), trapped, silently saving us. Maybe that's how he got through being stuck on the couch each night.

"Marvin, I gotta go," I said as Sexy Don leapt out of the shrinking robot escape hatch. You didn't see how lame the special effects were, when you're a kid. In my memory, the escape hatch really shrank as Will worked toward it, not these shoddy swapping-out prop effects. I hoped I'd remember this night of my own accurately, the night to come, when I was older.

"How you getting to your thing?" our dad yelled. He hadn't yet retreated to the bedroom. I couldn't blame him for doing so—our Shack felt like that robot, shrinking around us. Maybe Marvin wanted to let me know he understood. I opened my mouth, but our dad barged in, already shaking his head. "Marvin! Walk your sister. I don't want her alone on the road anymore." Marvin shut off the TV and grabbed his coat. "I already heard some Eee-ogg about it."

"Sorry," I said to Marvin as we left. Apparently it took Rez gossip to kick our dad into the Concerned-Parent role. "I know you'd prefer your couch, and see what's 'To Be Continued: Next Week!'" I said, imitating the *Lost in Space* announcer voice.

"You kidding?" My twin looked at me, then into the darkening trees. "I was planning on coming. Just not this early." We walked in silence for a bit, and then he went on. "Why *are* we going so early? Last practice or something?"

"I hate racing around ahead, any time I have to be good at something," I said. Of course, that wasn't the full story. I hadn't shared everything with Marvin in our fifteen years together. *Like I couldn't have figured that out,* Ghost Marvin said. But I usually told him the truth, and assumed he told me it in return. Tonight, though, was something entirely different.

"How come you guys didn't ask me to come to that Veterans Day thing?" Marvin asked. "Or Dad? He's a vet." Partly (I speculated), he was asking why he hadn't been involved in that art. The newspaper covered Marie's beaded trucker caps and Dark Deanna (lover of free advertising) had laminated it for our Vendor Table. Marie's caps were now a hot item all over the Rez, and Marvin was missing out on the revenue.

I felt double bad because lately Marvin was also losing out on revenue from the little basswood and soapstone people he carved too. He'd begun making them strictly for my own experiments, the projects our mom would never allow at her Table. His items now consisted of terrified little people trying to hang on to a little canoe, screaming in their new loss (scary shit you could never sell to tourists, particularly not honeymooners at the brink of Niagara Falls). I was so busy helping with Marie's caps, though, that I hadn't made anything new for his latest crew of figures. His people were like their own lost little family, lying in a sweetgrass basket until I had time to be inspired by my brother's twisted imagination. And he was doing a beautiful soapstone Lennon profile for the beadwork back cover of *Imagine* I was making for Jim. The beaded one I'd done wasn't a good enough resemblance, but Marvin had a great eye for the details of people's faces. He promised to guide me in doing one of Yoko's face for the *Mind Games* one.

"I didn't know how things would be," I said. "Marie never told *me* about the caps. I was as shocked as anyone else. Don't know how she was able to hide them."

"Seems like people can get good at hiding all kinds of things when they really want to. You know, I'm not going to cover your asses full-time anymore. I got a life too."

"Oh yeah? Looking forward to a *Lost in Space* and *Land of the Giants* marathon?"

"Not anymore. Now that I know you're just scoping out Major West's tight sixties pants. Is there someone on *Land of the Giants* too?" There was, actually. Irwin Allen's shows were all about people trapped in a hostile environment, and they were pretty similar, right down to actors. He loved survivors. Maybe he'd scoped out Rez Life and wrote these shows about getting used to that tension. "Your silence sounds like a yes."

"Like you're not checking out the girls in all their sixties mini outfits."

"You think I need the TV for that? If you were ever home anymore, you'd notice I go out too. I just don't make a big production out of it. I joined the Rez Social singers. They're always looking for people, and you're not the only drummer in this family."

"Are you serious? That's great!" I screamed, which felt weird in the middle of the road. A couple dogs barked, but I was relieved they were behind us and not ahead, potentially waiting. Since I'd been home so little lately, I hadn't even noticed that Marvin had started to come and go. "But Mom and Dad . . ."

"They want as much breathing room as we do," he said, shaking his head at me. "At first, I joined the Social singers to give them some. I wanted somewhere to go, and since you and Marie were out doing your own thing, I figured I better find my own way. Davy Reynolds taught me some songs in the city, and we had plenty of drums at the house . . . I found my way." What he'd left off, the *without any help from you*, was clear enough.

Before I could say anything more, Jim's car pulled up behind us. Our shadows blossomed and stretched out in front of us. As Jim passed by, his Bandit slowed, and he rolled down the passenger's side window. "Maggi? That you? Need a ride somewhere?"

So that was his plan (????). The old standby, Incredible Coincidence.

"Jim?" I said, trying to sound astounded. "Jim Morgan?" I turned to Marvin and raised my eyebrows with what I hoped was a *Lucky Break!* Face.

"I can read," Marvin said, pointing to the *Jim* pinstriped on the driver's side door, just below the elbow now leaning out.

"A guy I work with!" Marvin raised his eyebrows as we ran around to the other side. On the passenger door, I glimpsed that he'd added his personal version of my name, *MaggiPie*, with a little pin-stripe bird, next to it. I got my electric-blue shock wave, a sharp charge from my toes on up, but this time, it held another color — a little red. A touch of fear.

I opened the door, blocking Marvin's view as I flipped the bucket seat so he could get in. I did my best impression of shocked thanks, smelling a hint of Binaca below Jim's cologne. He wasn't wearing Old Spice or Hai Karate or anything lame.

We made bullshit small talk on the ride, and Jim pulled over to the shoulder at the first school driveway. "Thanks, Jim!" I said, getting out. "Would have been a long, cold walk. Hope we didn't hold you up from wherever you're going." He winked and flicked his eyebrows at me as Marvin climbed out. We were already anticipating each other's thoughts, like a real couple.

"Nice car," my brother said, grinning. "What's that air freshener? I don't see any little hanging Christmas tree." I kept the door wide, though the wind was blasting in.

"Called Eau Sauvage," Jim said. "Aftershave. Doesn't look like you'll be needing it for a few years," he added, laughing. Marvin let it slide. Jim drove off.

"Oh Savage?" Marvin said as we walked toward the school, twisting his mouth to the side. "Was that guy kidding?"

"He's fine," I said, trying to sound dismissive. We wandered through the lunch atrium (littered with bored teacher chaperones) to get to the gym, where Booster Parents collected money. "I'm in one of the bands, but I'm paying for my brother here," I said. We got our hands stamped and were told that if we left the building, we couldn't reenter without a wristband that the door chaperones would give us, which you could only use once.

The Wednesday before Thanksgiving was supposedly a big bar night, so the school held the second elimination round on this night to reduce high school drinking. Really, they were just giving kids a cover excuse to be out of the house and sneak to whatever bars didn't check ID closely. Maybe I thought that way because Battle of the Bands was *my* cover excuse.

I hadn't told my family that Carson had been disqualified, which more or less disqualified us. I didn't know how I'd explain to my brother afterward why we'd never stepped onstage. But that was a problem for another time. I'd grabbed my drums and bag anyway, and had planned ahead to spend my evening with Jim, locked in the privacy of the maintenance break room. I'd even lifted a few rubbers from Marie's private stash, just in case. I used up one, practicing on one of our dad's unripe bananas, so I'd seem like I knew what I was doing.

The decoration committee had lit the gym to sort of resemble a music club. They'd set up banks of colored lights, balloons, giant cardboard stars, and streamers. The stage was halfway down, the back part walled off with curtains. Teacher chaperones guarded the divide so only band members would be allowed back. They didn't even allow crew. Amps, drums, microphones, and keyboards were all "house," so we didn't have to bring any. Guitarists could bring plug-and-play effects pedals or pickup mics but that was about it. I had a pickup mic for my water drum, since I hadn't been planning to use the house drum set.

Awkward-looking parents and siblings filled the bleachers. You were partly judged on how loud the audience cheered for you, but I had no idea if anyone from the Rez was here.

"Hey, man," some guy said to Marvin, doing a complicated handshake. Marvin seemed happy to see a friend (*Thank you, Pseudo-Cool Guy!*). I slipped away, heading to a sleepy-looking teacher with a clipboard. I showed him my school ID, and he let me through after a cursory look into my bag. (I always kept a tampon box for things I didn't want messed with — in this case, the rubbers I'd lifted from Marie.)

Behind the curtain, the bands practiced without amplification, members watching each other to stay in time as they played. To do so onstage, though, was the mark of an amateur. Timekeeper was the drummer's job to hold everyone in sync. For back here, each drummer tapped a small tom or a snare with a dampener pad on its skin.

Big posterboard signs instructed us that we could use the near locker rooms and that our lockers were subject to random chaperone inspection. The far locker rooms, the ones closest to the pool, were locked and off-limits. The signs also noted that those exits were set for fire-alarm mode. If any were opened, alarms would go off. I was supposed to watch for Jim to stick his head in through the back gym doors. That meant the fire-alarm locks were off for ten minutes. I tried to look busy, but it was going to be clear soon that no other member of my band was there.

Jim's head popped in. He nodded slightly and disappeared. Trying for a casual saunter, I wandered to the girls' locker room. My fingers and toes were ice cold, trembling. My tongue and lips felt tingly, like that feeling when your arm has been asleep. My mouth was super dry, and I wished I'd gotten a pop. Once inside, I transferred one rubber to the little horse-head pocket of my Jordaches so I wouldn't have to dig if the right time came.

"Maggi?" a girl's voice called as I reached the door to one of the stalls. Startled, I dropped my bag, spilling its contents, including the tampon box. I quickly stuffed the shiny red Trojan square back in. "Sorry," Susan Critcher said. "Didn't mean to startle you. It's just . . . didn't anyone tell you? The band's not going on." She sighed. "It's a mess. Something about Carson—"

"What are *you* doing here?" I said. Harsh, but she was really messing up my plans.

"When Carson canceled, I agreed to play in Artie's band. I figured you guys might not even show. Did something happen?" I heard Jim give a quiet cough out in the hall, to let me know he was there and waiting.

"No, no," I said. "I just . . . I guess I just wanted to have that backstage feeling. Even if I wasn't going on. Anyway, I want to splash a little water on my face and check my makeup." I headed to a stall first, hoping she'd take the hint.

Sitting down, I carefully undid my top's buttons. I'd lifted a matching set of frilly sexy red bra and panties (tags still on) from Marie. *Without asking*, Ghost Marvin said. *Typical Maggi*. I did plan on returning them. Maybe. (Like Carson's tote, her lowest dresser drawer had a fake bottom where she hid her specialty Ben-Yaw-Mean foundation garments.) They felt so delicate, I was afraid that they might tear before I'd get a chance to reveal them to Jim. I sat and breathed quietly, but I hadn't heard Susan leave.

"Maggi?" she said finally, just a few yards away. I knew she'd been lurking!

"Could I have some privacy, please?"

"I just wanted to make sure—"

"I'm *fine*, Susan. Don't you have a band to get ready with?" Damn it! I was trying to keep annoyance out of my voice.

She still hadn't gone. "Look, I'm sorry," I said, trying to soften. "You're going to go up there. Enjoy. Maybe after, you'll tell me everything over some fries."

"No fries. Some pizza place is at the table Custard's Last Stand usually has."

"Pizza, whatever. Please? I want to be alone."

"Okay, but when you're done? Come hang with us backstage? Tami's supposed to be there. Artie put her on the list and gave her a tambourine and maracas to get her past the chaperones. The guys are calling her Davy Jones, like the Monkees?"

"Got it. Okay, maybe, but please? Privacy?" As soon as the door back to the gym shut, I flew out and stepped to the far-side doors that opened into the hall. Jim waited, grinning, his shirt unbuttoned and his Jordaches straining in front.

"Jeez, I didn't think that girl was ever gonna shut up," he whispered, laughing. "I wanted to barge in and tell her to get the hell out. Who *was* that?" He reset the locks and went to hug me.

"Not here?" I asked. I walked us to the break room, at the terminal end of the brightly lit plate-glass hallway.

"Don't worry, baby," he said, touching my collarbone and gently turning me around. My lips tingled again, and my tongue felt thick. He'd never called me that before. It felt thrilling *and* terrifying. My fingers trembled. It was hard to swallow. "Told you. I'm the only maintenance tonight. Only one with keys." He patted the jangling ring at his hip.

Outside the windows, it was full dark. Meadows and woods stretched out unseen behind the school, sports fields, and bleachers. Anyone out there could see us, our bodies inches from touching. One thrust forward and we'd connect.

Jim leaned a little, to release his keys, and his hip touched mine. That scent, O *Savage*? was coming off of him, and the skin on his chest and his ears was getting red. He licked his lips, and his hands shook a little as he unlocked the door. I didn't know whether to shift away or shift closer. I wanted this to be perfect and, as long as we were out in the hall, it wouldn't be.

"Close your eyes," he said, grabbing my hand. I did, and he led me into the break room.

Once inside, I immediately noticed a new scent in the room, something sweet. "Stand here. Keep 'em closed," he said, touching my eyebrows. He let go and I heard him strike a lighter, and I got the tiniest zap of lighter fluid scent in my nose. "I got some of those scented candles," he said, taking my hand again. "Okay, open them."

Though I cleaned it every day, I didn't recognize the room in front of me. He must have worked for hours as soon as day crew had punched out. All the work orders were stacked neatly on the desk, pens in a little cup. At the table, the chairs were pushed in. The table itself was covered in a cloth. It was otherwise bare except for a dozen roses, two cans of nuts, one "Fancy Mixed" and one "Party Peanuts," a box of assorted chocolates, long-stemmed candles, a bucket with several short bottles of wine coolers, and two glasses.

"I put the candles out when I left, just in case. Don't want to burn the house down . . . except with you." He grinned. The couch had a soft cover over it, and a couple new pillows. The cover was plush and suddenly all I could think of was Major West and his velour space cowboy outfit.

"What's so funny?" Jim asked, a slight gruffness creeping in suddenly.

"Nothing. Nothing," I assured him. "I was just thinking of something my brother said earlier. This is amazing. I would have never believed our crappy break room could be gorgeous."

"You like?" he asked. He rubbed my shoulders from behind, resting his chin on my collarbone and pressing against me. I could feel everything, the room, the lighting, the way he smelled and felt, the sheer presence of him so close and private. I was startled to discover that, after all this time of wondering what this particular set of events would feel like, I itched with anticipation and something weirder, some uncertainty I didn't recognize (maybe premonition regret). Those feelings were all puckered tight together, like one of Marie's clumsy velvet hearts. He stepped to the table and twisted the caps off the wine coolers, filling the glasses. The only wine I'd ever had was some nasty stuff that Carson called Mad Dog, which tasted like grape juice mixed with nail polish remover. I'd enjoyed the buzz, but I was sick to my stomach the whole next day.

This fizzy wine Jim gave me didn't taste like either of those things. It was sweet and tart and made my tongue want to curl up at first. It was weirdly warm and tingly going down, even though it had been chilled in my mouth. "Oooh, that feels . . . like someone just gently slid an electric blanket down my throat," I said, and felt a slight change already. Jim's eyes bugged out. "No, in a good way," I said, then laughed, realizing how stupid that sounded.

"Just take a few more sips. That weird feeling'll go away," he said, filling my glass back up. It fizzed and settled, and my brain did the same thing. He resumed his position, pressing a little harder for a few seconds. "I got this too," he said, pulling away again, lifting an album from the desk. He quickly adjusted the front of his pants. I felt a little shiver. I'd seen pictures of a naked man in a magazine before (in Liz's locker, of all places). It wasn't like I didn't know what to expect, but I didn't know how (what word should I use here? They all sound dumb and obvious) *determined and insistent* this would feel when he leaned against me. It was like there was Jim and then there was this pushy friend he'd brought along who was dying for some attention. (Was this the wine cooler talking? Or Jim's assertive thing?)

I wasn't sure I wanted to, um, meet Jim's "friend" for the first time, here. *Then what are you doing here, alone, with this man in a locked room?* Ghost Marvin chimed in helpfully. I wanted this memory to be special, to last a lifetime. And now that I was here, velour covering or not, I couldn't see losing my virginity on my school's maintenance crew break room couch. Who wants a lame memory?

"Probably not gonna be able to hear once the bands start, but we could put it on now." He held an album cover in his hand. "Came out last week. I wanted to surprise you. That's mine, but there's one in the Bandit for you, sealed. Every time you hear it, you can think of our first time."

"*Double Fantasy*," I read. He handed it over. It was a new album by John Lennon and Yoko Ono, with a front cover close-up of them kissing. Her face was clearer than his, taking up more of the cover, but they were unmistakable. His hair looked like it had around *Rubber Soul* and *Revolver*.

"They take turns," Jim said. "The first song's Lennon's; then the second one is hers. Then his, then hers. Kind of weird. Their styles aren't even close. He's sounding like, I don't know, a little like the oldies he played on that last album, and she's sounding like . . . did you see that punk band with the big beehive hairdos on *Saturday Night Live* last winter?"

"The B-52's? Yeah, they were awesome!" That was a show Marvin and I both loved.

"If you say so. You'll probably like her songs, then. They sound kind of like that."

"She *has* a name, you know. Right here." I pointed to the album cover. "Yoko," I said, dragging out each syllable, like someone trying to teach kids a new word.

"Very funny. Clearly *you* weren't listening to the Beatles when they broke up." Ugh, that tired old oo(t)-gweh-rheh again. He took the album from me and put it on a portable record player with a built-in speaker from the AV room. The magic of Jim's big key ring.

He blew dust from the vinyl and put it on. I'd been expecting the single I'd been hearing on the radio a lot, but I didn't recognize the first song.

"Side Two," he said. "This is called 'Watching the Wheels.'" The gorgeous melody was soft, the piano warm, and the vocals, even double-tracked, so unmistakable. Maybe *because* they were double-tracked. I'd read that John Lennon was uneasy in his vocals and insisted that producers "treat them" in some way. One of the most amazing vocalists ever, and he almost always refused to allow listeners to hear his voice stripped away, naked down to its essence.

"Maybe you'd dance with me," Jim said, taking both of my hands in his and drawing me close to him. We didn't go into the formal positions I'd learned in that stupid Ballroom Dancing class I'd taken to get out of regular gym. Instead, he spread his legs so my feet were framed by his. His hands met, somewhere around the small of my back, and mine reached up from his sides to touch his shoulder blades. With my ear against his chest, I could hear how fast his heart was beating, even though we weren't dancing hard.

We rocked slowly on the small break room floor, and when the song ended, we continued rocking in the silence before the next one began. It was a Yoko song, arranged to sound like old cabaret music, with audience noise and musicians tuning up mixed in. Jim slid his hands into my back pockets, squeezed gently and pulled me closer so our bodies met. He pressed himself firmly to me, eased off for a second, and then pushed forward again. He stepped away, his breath uneven. "Whew. Don't want to rush things."

"We don't *have* to rush things," I said. "Whenever the right time comes, we'll know."

"What?" He looked straight at me, like his question was pounding on my forehead. "I just meant that I didn't want to . . . well, if a guy's too excited . . . things can happen, things you don't *want to happen* can . . . too fast." With an arm around my shoulder, he led me to sit on the couch with him. My head rested on his chest, my arm on the cushion between his spread thighs.

"I want our first time to be . . ." He looked at the ceiling, like you do when you can't remember a pop quiz answer. "Special." He smiled, relieved that he'd found the right word.

Jeez, that was a big challenge! Ghost Marvin said.

Go join your real self in the gym and get out of my skull, I scolded.

"That's why I wanted you," Jim said, pressing against me again, "to hear this next song the first time we do something real. It's called 'Woman.' It's about how special a woman is to a man." He shifted so that, suddenly, we were eye to eye, my legs somehow now on top of his right leg. I didn't even know how that had happened. "The way *you* see me, Magpie. No one sees me that way. To everyone else, I'm just the ripped guy who does all the tough jobs around here."

"Jim, I have to tell you something," I said softly. "And I don't want you to get mad." Yoko was still singing about being John's angel. When we hit that song Jim was waiting for, I felt like he was going to expect something I wasn't maybe prepared to give him after all. "I'm still a virgin. I've never done this before. Or anything, really."

"Are you serious?" he said, swallowing hard. "Are you just saying that to get me going even *hotter*? I haven't been with a virgin in, like . . . well probably forever."

"Not even in high school?"

"Football players had certain perks," he said, grinning, as if I hadn't shared some incredibly personal information. "These cheerleaders we called the Stress Relief Squad helped you anytime you needed to let off steam. They weren't virgins." He wanted me to meet his grin. Excitement and upheaval fought each other inside of me. What had those girls felt like after helping a teenaged Jim *let off steam*?

"Are you really? Like, really one? These girls around here sure ain't virgins, getting felt up at their lockers." I almost pointed out that it was *guys* doing the feeling, but I kept silent. He laughed. "Except the dogs, maybe. Those woofers are virgins 'cause they don't have any choice. What's a hot, beautiful girl like you doing, being a virgin? You saving it for the right guy and it's turned out to be me?"

Jim reached down and arranged himself again, looking at me, then at my hand, trying to silently suggest that he'd love it if I helped him. I wanted both to look and look away. He let out a deep sigh and leaned back on the couch, closing his eyes. His hips raised for a couple seconds, and he made a funny little grunt. A minute later, he opened his eyes and leaned in hard to kiss me. The song he wanted me to hear played, and he gently worked his tongue into my mouth. I let him. He rubbed my thighs, stopping an inch from the place where Marie's fancy panties ran a ribbon of lace. As his hands jumped to my ribs, he buried his mouth in the curve of my neck.

"You sure you still want to do this?" I asked, sliding my legs off his lap and sitting up.

"You kidding? Of course."

What answer were you expecting? Ghost Marvin asked, laughing a long series of *pffft!*

"Even if it is . . ." I said, knowing I sounded like a total narc. "You know, illegal."

"Like I said. Only illegal if you tell someone. I'm not telling anyone. You don't? Problem solved." He smiled, gently touching the area of my ring finger where nothing lay.

"Look," he said finally. "I ain't ignoring what you're saying. I love you. I'm taking *you* seriously." He looked directly at me. "I'm okay with the secret if you are. But it's gotta *be* a secret. Just between me and you. Not me and you and whoever your current best friend is. Especially not if it's that loser you've been forcing me to leave alone." Lewis. Maybe Jim thought I'd been promising this night as a payoff, when I asked him to quit hassling Lewis. Like this was somehow a reward, a contract.

I realized then, I didn't *have* a best friend. It wasn't Lewis, though he was a friend. And it wasn't Marie now that her life was all Ben-Yaw-Mean, and it wasn't Marvin anymore because we'd somehow lost each other when we weren't looking. (I'd been spending more time with his fake voice in my head than in conversation with my real brother.) It *sure* wasn't Carson.

As I thought that, I looked around. I was in the crappy break room, where the main decoration was a cheesecake calendar featuring a bikini woman bending over a cultivating machine. Every day, I had to make coffee here for a bunch of guys who never said thank you.

"Wish you'd told me you were fifteen before I had your name pinstriped on the Bandit," he said, interrupting my thoughts.

"I did! I told you two weeks ago, when you grabbed me at Custard's Last Stand." (*The same day you let me know you knew my age,* my Ghost Voice said.) "If it's any consolation, it was really . . . sweet?" I said, hoping to ease the conversation forward.

"It was on the Bandit that day. You just didn't see it, I guess." He started to smile and then abruptly didn't. "You saw it tonight? In the dark?" I nodded. "Think your brother saw?"

"Dunno. As soon as I saw it, I tried to block it."

"You *are* a smart girl," he said, rubbing my thigh. Girl. Not Young Lady. Not Woman.

Out in the gym, the MC came on. I could hear everything, clearly, but Jim stood up to shut the record player off. "I patched the PA to the mixing board," he said, pointing to the ceiling speaker I heard afternoon announcements on every day as I mopped this floor after the final dismissal bell. "Technically, I *am* still working."

"Jim," I said. "I know you really want to do this. I do too. I want *you* to be the man. I want to do this with someone I love," I said, kissing him. Immediately, he pressed against me.

"You know it. It'll be super special," he said, reaching to unbutton the top of my blouse. "Is that a red bra strap I see? You wanna show me what a bad girl you are?" His breathing had become rough again, and when he swallowed, his throat clicked a little.

"But I don't *want* to lose my virginity in our crew break room," I said, buttoning my top.

"Jesus!" he grumbled, suddenly red. His teeth clenched, like he was doing some sad ventriloquist act (which I guess maybe made me the dummy). "You're the one who wanted this to be special, aren't you? Look at all I did and now you're just giving me friggin' blue balls here!" His face scrunched in a way I'd never seen. I'd heard guys mention blue balls in the lunchroom, telling exaggerated versions of their weekends. Right now, I had a pretty good guess what it meant.

"Can't you understand?" I asked, hating the desperation in my voice. "I want it to be *special*. Is there something else we can do?" He was breathing heavy, but not the same way as when we'd held each other. Then he smiled. He tried to make it look like a nice smile, but there was something else underneath.

"Sure," he said. "Sorry, babe. It's just, when you spend two weeks thinking all day and night about that *one thing* you're sure is gonna happen . . . it takes a little adjustment. All I've been thinking about for two weeks is The Thing." I said nothing. His smile softened. "But I get it. I get it." He glanced at the table. "We can be like these two," he said, holding up the album.

"That sounds great, Jim." They were kissing passionately, clearly in love. I was relieved.

"They take turns. Each one relaxes, enjoying while the other works," he said. "All right?"

"Yes," I said, though I wasn't really sure what I had just said yes to.

"Okay, first," he said, leaning back, "you unbutton my shirt and take it off me." That was nice, familiar. I'd seen him that way before. That cologne (O *Savage?*) changed the longer he wore it, and I smiled at the Binaca when I kissed him. He held his arms out, so I undid the cuffs.

"Get your hands inside and slide them over my shoulders," he said, leaning forward. He raised his arms and told me to lift the shirt over his head. His breath, inches away, warmed my belly, and I stepped aside. Standing, he kicked off his fancy boots. "So you can do the pants next," he said.

I unbuckled his belt, and as I undid the button, he sucked his gut in. I liked feeling that hair against my hands, and his warm belly inside the waistband. I did this slowly. The next step was the point of no return. "Go ahead," he said. "It ain't gonna bite." I unzipped the fly opposite the bulge, but he made it surge, even without his hands.

It pushed against my fingers. (I didn't know guys could do this. I hated having been too chicken to ask Marie for details!) He laughed as I tugged his jeans down. He rested his hands on my shoulders (which pulled my hair some), and yanked his feet out of the cuffs, grinning wide. I quickly stood, handing the jeans to him. "Go ahead, give me a gentle squeeze." His voice hitched. "A preview."

Somehow, this is not what you expected. Yes, there's your handsome man, the man you've been imagining as your forever love. He stands in front of you, shoulders back proud, wearing just white briefs and short tube socks with racing stripes up top, a couple of scabs on his shins from some job scrape. He clearly thinks this is what you've been waiting to see. And by every indication he gives you, you've made the right choice in borrowing your sister's lingerie.

You don't know what you thought he'd look like with his pants off. Maybe you'd never gotten that far in your Single Fantasy version of this night. You definitely didn't count on his choice of underwear reminding you of your brother rolling off the couch, grumpily folding his blankets before getting dressed every morning. Or worse, your dad grabbing a coffee before going back to your parents' room to get ready for the day. How did you ever imagine this moment as the greatest thing you'd ever dreamed of and *not* picture a boring pair of white briefs with the front pitching forward (a detail you'd somehow never arrived at on your own)?

I had the hardest time not laughing at how ridiculous he looked, standing in those briefs and socks, designer jeans with the giant key ring in his hands. I did what he'd asked, which caused a reaction in him. It still felt strange to me. I didn't want to ruin this for him, after he'd laid out roses and chocolate and wine and mixed nuts and the velour couch cover. I didn't want to say *Take those off.* That would lead us in one specific direction I wasn't quite ready for, and yet, I didn't want to say *Put your clothes back on* either. That, I knew, would stop the kissing, the hugging, the holding, the ways *only he* recognized who I was becoming. I tried concentrating on him from the waist up, the way he'd looked shirtless, wrestling at the garage, the day I'd become aware of him as A Man (instead of a guy at work).

"Could we blow some of these candles out, Jim?" I asked as he set his jeans on the table I wiped down every day. That stupid key ring jingled like chimes in a budget percussion array.

"I guess," he said, his eyebrows raising, making him look sad, disappointed, and worried. "I thought you'd like them." He blew out the two on the table. "Least I can still see you in these hot red lacy things. You did that just for me, right? I want to be able to see." He came closer, tugging my blouse until it hung loose. His fingers trembled against the buttons. "Good thing girls' shirts button the opposite side of men's. Feels the same and I'm still having trouble."

I put my hands up and tilted his jaw so he'd be looking at my face, where I wanted him to be looking. Even shoeless, he was still a lot taller than me. He smiled, moved his hands up, pushing his fingers through my hair. He hunched his shoulders and leaned forward to kiss me.

"Next up, we have . . ." the MC boomed over the PA. There was a weird pause and then: "We have . . . the Dog Street . . ." I broke the kiss. "Devil? Devils?"

"Wait, Jim," I said. "Listen." We could hear rustling and mumbling over the speaker.

"What? There's nobody out there. I'm the only one with the keys."

"No, it isn't that." The MC then introduced someone calling himself the Quarry Man, and I knew whose voice I'd hear, though I couldn't quite believe it.

"Thank you, Nyah-wheh, Mrs. Thatcher," Lewis's voice announced. "Good evening. I'm at a little bit of a disadvantage tonight," he said, making a slight hiccup. "Some of my band couldn't make it . . . well, all of my band, I guess. Please bear with me."

"Lewis," I said. Jim listened, his hands bunching up my top's bottom hem.

"Sounds like the Loser. Didn't you say he got shit-canned from this thing?" Jim stepped back to look at the lacy bra, a tiny red bridge between the sides of my blouse. Someone in the audience said something. Jim puckered his mouth, like he was going to whistle, but just a breath came out. I fought the urge to close my blouse. This was the sight Jim expected.

"Yes," Lewis echoed on the PA. "Of course." I felt like he could somehow see me. And then I heard him sigh and start the strumming pattern for "Working Class Hero." When he began singing, he sounded clear but vulnerable, but as he went on, he grew stronger with each line.

25

You've Got to Hide Your Love Away
Carson Mastick

The Wednesday night before Thanksgiving, Derek and Sheila were out. My deficiency sat in the kitchen, which was thick with aromas from tomorrow's dinner. And in all my privacy, what was I doing? Just playing "I'm So Tired," on my acoustic. I cursed Lewis for infecting my head with the Beatles, but they somehow always captured what life really felt like. How was that possible? That a Rez Rat like me could be touched by songs by these tight-ass British guys?

Lewis. What a case. When I finally found him and told him what happened with Marchese, he didn't even seem pissed. His tone was all *I Knew You Would Fuck This Up for Us.* But we hadn't spoken much since—he hadn't even mentioned the Lennon 45 I'd left for him. When I called him earlier, he said he had things to do.

I heard someone come in the house. Maybe my mom lugging groceries? I decided to help her. Downstairs I found Albert instead, studying our kitchen pegboard. He nodded and grabbed the Chevelle's keys.

"What the hell are you doing?" I asked.

"I'm taking these out to your car, isn't it?" he said. "And then you're gonna get your coat on and follow me, and then you're gonna drive." He headed toward the front door, keys in hand.

"I'm not going anywhere, and you sure ain't taking my keys."

"Wrong on both counts, there, Junior."

"I'm not a Junior. There's only one of me." Albert must have popped a big rivet in his already screw-loose head. I grabbed my boots and jacket to at least snag my keys.

"Lucky for us," he said, holding the door for me. "Listen, we can argue and I can try to teach myself how to drive after I throw you in the backseat, or you can listen while you drive."

"Bullshit."

"I had hand-to-hand combat training. You?" He opened the driver's side door, keeping the keys. "Good boy," he said, grinning. I wished I could say it was warm, but I didn't see Albert smile much, so I had no idea. Was this as close as it got to natural? "High school gym, Jeeves. Drive on."

"You kidding me?" He shook his finger like, *Get going!* "Why are you doing this?" He refused to say anything more. When we got to the school, I considered parking and running for it, but what Albert had said was true. He'd been drafted and shipped off to Vietnam, and these days, worked his ass off as a laborer. He was a man, all wiry muscle. I still didn't really know what level or kind of nuts he was either. But I could at least know what we were doing.

"Well?" I asked as we settled in a parking spot.

"Payback," he said. "Gimme those keys."

"You crazy?" I said, like I had a million other times to a million other people.

"Little bit," he said. "Not much to worry about . . . most days. Keys?" I shook my head. "Look, I know you way better than you think. I know that if I get out of this car, you're gonna slam the door, lock it, and peel out, isn't it? I can't let that happen. You're gonna give me those keys, and we're gonna go in there. I'm gonna buy your ticket, and when I'm ready, I'll give you the keys back."

I didn't see a way out, so I held my hands up and he took the keys out of the ignition.

We entered the building, Albert with his arm around my shoulders. No one gave us a second look. Of course, they wouldn't. There'd be tons of family here, fathers, mothers, brothers, and sisters. Even aunts, uncles, and cousins. Bands were encouraged to bring their own hype. The music boosters wanted to move tickets, and that only happened with family member coercion.

"You know," I said. "I might not be able to kick your ass, but my dad still can." Pathetic. I squeaked like a kid, and he laughed a tiny laugh. We passed through the lunchroom atrium, where each food vendor stand was several people deep, workers on their toes, just to keep up.

"Well, maybe you can ask him to do that a little skinny bit later," Albert said, guiding me to one of the lines. "For now, let's get us some pizza, maybe some of that secret marinade chicken, and then when we're done, we should grab a seat in the bleachers before they fill."

"Pizza," I said. "And chicken." I smiled wide. Each food vendor had a banner taped behind them. Custard's Last Stand was not here. "She wasn't lying, but why did she care?"

"Why did who care?" Albert asked, holding up two fingers when we got to the counter.

"Not important. You ever gonna tell me why you're doing this?"

"Got me. Your dad called today, said there was a hundred bucks in it for me, to make sure you got here. And another fifty if I got your keys. So a Nyah-wheh is in order, isn't it?" He dangled my keys in front of my face and then pocketed them. I held out my hand, and he shook his head. "Your dad said I'd know when to give them back to you. He's maybe giving me too much credit. All I know is we're supposed to meet your dad and the Hamburglar in the bleachers. I'm going." He stopped, looking at his belly. His hands were in his jacket pocket. Taking my keys out, he looked me in the eye, something Albert never did. "You do what you feel you should." He handed me the keys and walked in. I did the only thing that made sense.

"What are we waiting for?" I asked Albert after the second band had played. We sat in the bleachers with my dad and Derek. "Is Lewis coming?"

"He'll be here," Albert said. "Bet on it. Just wait and enjoy the show."

"Enjoy," I said. "Right! I'm supposed to be up there!" The third band started. Each had been decent. Artie's hadn't gone on yet, but Tami claimed they were good. If they were so good, how come his parents hired *my* band for their party? We would have had this locked, I told myself, but as I looked around, I wasn't all that sure. I'd been cocky. I hadn't sold a ton of tickets, or even pressured the rest of the band to. I'd thought, after what we did at Custard's Last Stand, a bunch of Rez folks would be here. "Where is everyone?" I finally asked my dad.

"Right here," my dad said, spreading his arms to indicate the large crowd.

"You know what I mean. Like from the Rez?"

"Skins?" he said, laughing. "High school bands and no bar? Gotta do better than that."

"But after the *Cascade* articles? The protests? I mean, look out there. No Custard's Last Stand! *I* did that!" I said, sticking my pointer finger into my own chest. "Me!"

"That was a success," he said. "Right, Hamburglar?" My dad whacked Derek's shoulder. He looked at us, eyebrows raised. "Never mind." Derek hadn't been out much in months, except for night trips to Moon Road parties. He seemed glad to be anywhere, but maybe a little worried. His roots were growing out, and he didn't want to wear a cap for obvious reasons.

The bleachers were filled with bored dads and moms. You could tell band families easy. They'd whoop and cheer for a band's set, and then settle in and yawn. On the gym floor, where the people we knew stood, they crowded and moved and sweated, like they were at a club show.

"All right," the MC said, running out. "Another hand for Springheel Jack!" She spread her arms, clapping like she was a robot. The MC was one of the music teachers, but not the guy we called Mr. Tromboner, with the tiny, pointy jazz beard and the mustache with the stupid gap down the middle. This MC wasn't even a guy. It was Mrs. Thatcher, our seventh-grade chorus teacher, who had single-handedly flicked a switch inside Lewis, making him a Beatlemaniac.

"Next up, we have," she glanced down at her sheet, and then back at the black curtain behind the amps and drum set. It ruffled a little. "We have . . . the Dog Street . . ."

What? Both my dad and Albert grinned. These bastards had set me up.

"Devil? Devils?" The curtain opened and Mrs. Thatcher went back to consult with whoever was there, then ran back to the microphone. "Sorry. A last-minute change. I didn't see the note," she said, showing her clipboard. "Please welcome the Quarry Man!" she shouted. She'd gone from hyped to uncertain, to scared, to befuddled, and back to hyped in thirty seconds.

Lewis Blake stepped out, wearing a beaded trucker cap and one of my silk-screen T-shirts. On top of it, he had the satiny shirt I'd made him wear at that Labor Day party. As the spotlight came up, I saw the painter pants I'd sewn piping onto, the ones he'd refused to wear. Quarry Man. Lewis had decided, with that name, to be a one-man Beatles cover band. He was using a twist on the Quarrymen, the first name John Lennon had ever come up with for his band, a name I'd already banned for our group. Sly bastard.

"Thank you, Nyah-wheh, Mrs. Thatcher," Lewis said, stepping to the main microphone. A pickup mic cord trailed out of his guitar, and he plugged it in to the patch cord. "Good evening," he said, sounding surprisingly calm. "I'm at a little bit of a disadvantage tonight," he said, and cleared his throat. "Some of my band couldn't make it . . . well, all of my band, I guess. Please bear with me." A quiet laugh washed through the audience, like low tide.

"Play if you're gonna play or get off the stage!" someone deep in the floor crowd yelled. Another murmur, but one whose flavor I couldn't tell. Was it in support of Lewis or the shouter? I stood up, but Albert and my dad grabbed my shoulders and firmly sat my ass back down.

"Yes," Lewis said. "Of course." He closed his eyes and strummed a familiar pattern. Ballsy move, one that'd disqualify him, and maybe even get him suspended. We were required to submit all songs we'd wanted to play, and needed to get the Extracurricular Activities Committee stamp of approval to do them—literally a stamp with "Approved" carved into its surface. I was sure it was to keep inappropriate songs out of the event. Songs like this one.

You *could* play "Working Class Hero" without its controversial phrases, but *So freaking crazy* or *Still friggin' peasants* didn't have the sting of John Lennon's original. When we were in third grade, some congressman tried to ban the song because he'd heard it on the radio. Our fifth-grade teacher told us, thinking she was a badass, telling fifth graders about the dirty word "fuck" and, in her mind, the dirtier phrase "Federal Communications Commission."

Lewis went with the original lyrics all the way. The spotlight was so isolating. Just him and his guitar, but still, he got through it. His progressions weren't fancy, just jumps from G to A-minor without transitions—but he did get the hammering note right, even with its odd intervals.

"Thank you, Nyah-wheh," he said, insisting on adding the Tuscarora. It was a trick I'd taught him. If your song ends softly, you want to give the audience a clue about when to clap. There was some polite clapping, a couple of war whoops. Maybe there were a few Skins on the floor? The judges scored partly on audience response, though, and there was no way that audience noise was going to be enough. Lewis was toast.

26

Now or Never
Magpie Bokoni

As Jim pulled off his socks, Lewis launched into a second song. I swore he knew where I was: "You've Got to Hide Your Love Away." His confidence grew and so did my guilt for not checking about this. I'd assumed we wouldn't go on, and I'd had other things on my mind.

Every time Lewis yelled "Hey!" I felt like he was talking to me. First it felt like he was yelling at me for not being up there. But especially as Jim slid my blouse off and smiled, staring, I felt the lyrics stinging me a little. "Nyah-wheh, thank you," Lewis said, ending.

"So what's next?" Jim asked. "Your jeans or my skivvies? Seems like it's you, but I'll drop the skivs first if you want." He slid his thumbs into his waistband. "If it's you, gotta ditch those boots. Don't want you tripping." I sat, and Jim crouched, sliding my boots off. He rubbed my socky feet. I should have worn nylons. *Clueless!* I kept hearing myself inside my head.

"I've got time allotted for three more songs, but I'm only going to do two," Lewis said. "I want to use up a couple minutes here." The crowd came through again, kind of grumbling.

"Jim," I said. He had both my socks in his hands. "Wait."

"Oh, for fuck's sake," he said, standing. I didn't like that I'd annoyed him, but I was relieved to see that his briefs weren't pointing out so much in front anymore.

"My band isn't up here tonight because of our lead singer and guitarist," Lewis said over the PA. "Our leader, I suppose, made a mistake. People make mistakes. I've made my share. I once crossed the wrong person, here at school, a couple of years ago. And it cost me. Man, did it cost me. I used to be in those smart-kid sections. I crossed a bully, who was given a free pass to beat the shit out of me whenever he felt like it."

Someone shouted something from the audience, but I couldn't hear what it was.

"Hah! That Loser's talking shit about my nephew. Lot of balls," Jim said, listening. "He's the one who's still in school, while my sister's kid Evan is stuck in the working world. I'll give him something more to bitch about. Remind him what it's really like."

"Your nephew?" I said. "I thought you'd been *teasing* him when I asked you to stop."

"You said it, yourself," Jim said. "Family's family." I put my socks back on. Jim's face scrunched up, and he let out a growly sigh. "You can't just fuck with someone and not expect costs. I didn't do anything that I couldn't *claim* was just teasing." I pictured the harsher things Lewis had hinted at, violent things he wouldn't give me full details on.

Those detailed things you chose not to ask about? Ghost Marvin asked.

I didn't ask because I figured even what Lewis hinted at couldn't be true.

Is it true that this guy said sex with you isn't illegal if you both keep your mouths shut?

What's your point, Ghost Marvin?

My point is that you know I'm really you. And Jim let you know who he was a while ago. You don't need all the details of Lewis's shitty treatment to know this guy's just fine doing those kinds of things.

"Easy to say stuff like that when you're hiding in the dark, isn't it?" Lewis's voice cut back into the room across the crackling PA. "It's a little trickier up here, when you're visible. I thought I could walk away from my bully. Every teacher I spoke to said he'd get tired of me, if I just had patience." Lewis paused. "He didn't. I thought civil disobedience was the way to go, peaceful protest. I did it until I finally got people to really listen. When I came back, the bully was gone, but a place's memory is a long and tough thing. I failed a couple classes. Some teachers, who thought I'd given a white kid a raw deal by claiming he was a racist, decided I didn't qualify for making up missed work."

Not just the teachers, I thought. Now I had to add Lewis to the list of people I wanted out of my head. I wanted to just be here with Jim, take the steps we'd been planning to, but the Jim standing before me wasn't the one I was seeing. I'd doubted Lewis because I'd never seen anything that extreme firsthand. I couldn't bring myself to ask Jim, at first, but his expression told me it was at least *possible* Lewis had been giving me truth I didn't want to hear.

"But you weren't just teasing," I said. "You *were* doing it, weren't you?" Jim shrugged. He'd been the first person to make me feel special, ever. That feeling was beginning to crumble.

"Look," Jim said, his face softening. Lewis was still talking, but Jim was looking into my eyes. "Don't put those back on your cute little feet." He gently massaged my foot once more and just touching me was stirring him up again. "I'm *not* hassling him anymore. And really? I guess my nephew could have come back, but he's like me. He likes the cash coming in, from the internship they set up to get him out of here. He took the GED." I remembered Jim telling me how he had avoided Vietnam. He and his family lived in a different world from me and mine.

"None of that matters now," he said. "I stopped! For *you*. Not for that Loser. For *you*, because *I* love *you*." He touched my shoulder, standing directly in front of me, gradually moving his hand to my collarbone, slipping one finger under the red satiny bra strap. If he slid his hand just a few inches lower, he'd be at the place he was planning to get to. "*You* come even before family now." His belly was inches away. "That's how special." I heard a synthesizer chord behind Lewis. Susan? I could picture her backstage. Maybe she'd gone looking for me once Lewis went up there, but of course, she couldn't find me. Because I was here, almost exposed.

"Jim, I'm . . . I don't know." I quickly put my blouse back on. "Listen, I love you," I said as I slid into my boots. "I think? I don't know. I'm new to this. I've never loved anyone before but this feels like what I think it's supposed to feel like."

"You can't just go," he said, looking sad in his pair of saggy, stretched-out briefs.

"I don't even know what to think about what you just told me."

"I was being honest! You keep saying you wanna be with a guy who's honest. So I *was*! You want me to lie?" He looked pleadingly at me. "C'mon, let's start over. I'll even take these skivs off myself," he said, snapping the waistband of his briefs, "so you don't have to. We can—aww, don't cover those up."

"I'm going out," I said, buttoning my blouse. "Lewis is like family. And . . . I need time. My sister and I, we have a Vendor Table set up at the Holiday Bazaar on the Rez. The Old Gym. You know where that is?" He nodded, irritated, grabbing his socks and jeans. "It's this Saturday. White people come, so you don't have to worry. No one will notice you. Just come in. I get off at five. Then we can, I don't know. Go somewhere and talk this out? Okay?"

"How about if I get us a room somewhere? Would that be better than this? A real room?"

"Let's make that decision on Saturday," I said, grabbing my bag and running out. My water drums bounced against my hip, and I flew down the hall. At the locker room door, I remembered that it was set for fire-alarm mode. Just as I was about to run, Jim stuck the key in, but before turning it, he leaned in and kissed me hard. I didn't allow a gap to form and he didn't try. He reached up and cupped my boobs, first softly, and then with a firmer grip. He groaned and leaned firmly into me. "I didn't even get to see these," he whispered, stepping back. He sighed hard and unlocked the door, letting me go.

27

Gimme Some Truth
Carson Mastick

"Yeah, yeah, everyone's a racist," someone else shouted as Lewis tried to tell a years-old story of his run-in with Evan Reiniger. "Play your songs or get off the stage, you fucking pansy!" People were getting aggravated that he was hijacking their night. You didn't even need to read lips to know the kinds of things they were saying. *Lewis! People don't want to hear your bullshit.* If only I could send him the telepathy Albert could.

"I never claimed he was a racist," Lewis said calmly. "I said he was an asshole bully who'd singled me out. To this day, I have no idea why me. But he was successful, because others helped him be invisible when it was useful to him." *Like me,* I thought. I could blend in when it was convenient. There was no way Lewis or Maggi or Doobie were ever going to be confused for white, but for me, it was as easy as making sure my Rez accent didn't leak. I'd gotten good enough to fool Evan.

"Whenever he was punching my face," Lewis said, rage beginning to color his voice, "a ton of other skinny kids were saying to themselves, 'Well, at least it isn't me.' My shop teachers failed me, because I'd figured a way around a bully. Maybe they wanted me to punch him back and get my face pounded some more. They didn't think I had the balls to be a man. Do you suppose they ever give grades based on something other than the work you did in their classes? If not to you, then to someone you know?"

The murmur came again, but this time, it was different. They were listening to Lewis. It was like he'd gotten them to forget they were at a Battle of the Bands, missing out on one of the biggest drinking nights of the year for a bunch of crappy wannabe kid musicians.

"I found out we weren't going on tonight just . . ." He looked at his watch. "Twenty-five hours ago. I told you, my bandmate screwed up. He was notified *yesterday* that he's gonna fail and *that* was gonna disqualify him. And that he was going to have to either go to summer school, or stick around another year. I'm not saying what he did was right. . . ." *Thanks, Lewis. What the hell?* Now my chances of straightening this out with Groffini's help were totally out the window.

"But he was just trying to fix an accident. And he did it partly to help *us*, as a group. The thing he's *really* being flunked for, something some of you probably saw in the newspapers, he did to help *me* out." Maybe partly true. He would have failed too if we'd had to face a frozen turkey, but it had been *my* fuckup. I was getting zapped for the Custard protest and the turkey was just a concrete excuse Marchese was using to do the zapping.

Lewis probably knew I could have gotten Evan Reiniger to quit pounding him. He knew I'd been friendly with him. Maybe he didn't want to believe Evan hated Indians, even though it wasn't a secret. But he could guess that I'd saved my own ass by throwing him to the wolves.

"But I screwed up in class too," he said, bleeding into the time he had left. "My bandmate and I were partners, but *I* didn't get a failure warning. So how come two guys mess up and only one gets punished?" Lewis was losing his audience again. I understood what he was saying, but now he was dragging in unnecessary stuff.

The curtain behind him shifted. Hubie walked out and sat at the drums. Did he play? Susan Critcher also stepped out from behind the curtain, heading to the house keyboard, adjusting a few settings.

"All you people with your proud immigrant stories, your Ellis Island stories? Imagine a restaurant that waves your flag upside down and has a poster of the Statue of Liberty flipping *your* flags the middle finger." A white sheet unfurled against the black curtain, and a projected image suddenly shone, of what Lewis had just described. "Could *you* ignore?" He was pissing some people off. Italian dads next to us started grumbling, which was kind of funny. The Italian flag looked the same either way—they only believed it was upside down because Lewis *said* it was upside down. The Statue of Liberty flipping the flag the bird? Well, that was something else.

"You'd feel compelled to do something, wouldn't you?" Lewis asked, in his irritating Explanation Voice. "There's a local restaurant named after General Custer. If you've eaten a burger or fries at a school event, you've eaten food from there. Maybe General Custer doesn't mean anything to you. Particularly if you didn't pay attention in American history. The *real* General Custer was a Cavalryman who tried to make his reputation as an 'Indian Killer.' This restaurant owner likes dressing up in a costume to look like that Indian Killer. What do you think *we* see?"

"Freedom of speech?" another heckler yelled.

"Yeah," Lewis said, smiling. "Freedom of speech. My bandmate planned a peaceful protest. It didn't end that way. Sometimes, protests wake something up inside of us that we can't get back to sleep. But all of you would do something, by the looks of things, if there were a restaurant celebrating a man who tried to wipe out your whole race. Freedom of speech and all." Susan hit a chord, which must have meant something to Lewis. He looked back as the curtain moved once again, and Maggi appeared onstage, water drum in hand.

28

Don't Count the Waves
Magpie Bokoni

It was a short run from the locker room to the back of the stage. The curtain girl saw me and pulled it back as Lewis was still speaking. The spotlights blinded me as I stepped out. I looked down so I didn't trip, avoiding Hubie's eyes, staring at me from the house drum set. I probably looked a little disheveled (and could only hope I'd gotten my blouse buttoned back right and reasonably tucked in). I was going to be drowned out if Hubie played.

"I promise. I won't go over my allotted time," Lewis said to the crowd, as I found an acoustic setup onstage. They'd strapped a regular mic at chest level on one of the vocal mic stands. It was meant for a guitar, but it would carry my water drum and voice. "I've got a couple more things to say and then," he continued, glancing back at us and grinning. "It looks like some of my band has joined me. *They* didn't piss off the wrong person." He waited until I nodded that I was ready.

"The man who owns Custard's Last Stand is the husband of our home ec teacher, Mrs. Marchese," Lewis said. Their home ec teacher—it was that simple. But maybe hard to believe that she'd risk screwing up her job over his stupid vendor license (*"Except a vendor license is valuable,"* Dark Deanna whispered in my head). "After her husband's bad news coverage, Mrs. Marchese decided that Carson

Mastick needed to fail for an assignment we'd done over a month ago. Something she'd already given a passing grade to. We'd performed the steps right. We'd done what was asked. And if you think that sort of thing can't happen to you, you're getting a useless diploma, because you didn't learn how the world works, when you ask for . . ."

He glanced at his left hand to make sure he was fretting right. He then glanced at each of us. It was dorky to pause like this, and I still found myself tearing up. I hoped I'd anticipated his plans or that I could figure them out after a couple bars.

". . . the truth."

I waited a beat, to confirm. I was right! We jumped into "Gimme Some Truth," a John Lennon song we'd practice whenever Carson was late. The others added intro filler bars so I could catch up, but otherwise, we were on.

And I have to say . . . WE WERE SIZZLING HOT! We had no lead guitar, so I started singing in vocables that I hoped sounded like the lead. Susan and Hubie covered the rest. But it didn't matter. Most eyes were on Lewis as he stepped to the mic and blasted his way through, demanding the truth instead of the lies he was sick and tired of, offered up by politicians and hypocrites that were pigheaded, neurotic and narrow-minded. Anyone who knew Lewis knew which people he was calling "politicians" and "hypocrites" in his demands for the truth.

He sang with a confidence I'd never heard before. I'd listened to some music know-it-alls around school talking about singers *shredding their vocal cords*, but I'd never known what it meant until that moment. Lewis was lost in the song, immersed in all the things it meant to us in the moment. I knew about some of its real meaning. That hippie history teacher Marvin and I had told us all about Richard Nixon and his Watergate spying scandal (a favorite topic). Lewis, even, in his endless campaign to win me over to the Beatles, told me President Nixon had spied on Lennon, fearing he could sway younger voters, pushing hard to have him deported as undesirable.

In this room, though, at this moment, no one cared about any of that. Lewis's blistering delivery gave us all the sense, the tiredness, the desire and pleading, the demand that people stop stabbing you in the back or trying to trick you, as only a rocking tune could, and we worked in perfect sync with him.

Hubie used the kick drum and sang baritone notes into a microphone, since he didn't have his bass or his traffic cone. Susan carried a lot of weight, like her keyboard was somehow several instruments at once. I kept my water drum doing a major tom and snare sound, and tried my hardest to shape my vocables like a hot electric arpeggio with a fuzz pedal. It was a secret I'd been practicing mostly by myself with a little help from Marvin listening to me sing with the record. The band grinned at my invention. Together, we did what a band does. We drove it home with the right sound—fun, easy, and ass-kicking all at the same time.

Real cheers swelled at the end of the song, but some people left the auditorium, probably pissed that Lewis had left up his Statue of Liberty flipping the bird. We smiled, taking it all in. I felt weird. Susan looked at her watch and spoke into her mic.

"Thank you, for sticking with us." Another cheer. "Maybe some of you are wondering what I'm doing up here. Well, I got a little first-hand knowledge in what it means to be the minority in the room, to not get the jokes, not know how the table is set. But my friends showed me the way. I'm never going to know what my friends' lives are really like, and I wouldn't ever speak for them. You can ignore what Lewis said tonight, but I can't." She stopped and came forward, to the main mic, and Lewis stepped aside.

"Still, I can tell you, I walked around the mall with them one Saturday, and a security guard came up and asked me if I was being bothered by 'these boys.'" I remembered that, distinctly. "We joked, but I was back in the mall a couple days later," Susan continued. "And not one person noticed me. I even shoplifted something, just to test how I wasn't being watched. That one small window shook up my world." She looked at her watch again and whispered to Lewis. He nodded, then she nodded at me and Hubie, and we came forward.

"I can't believe it," I said, stepping to the mic. "We still have a couple minutes from *our* allotted time." I didn't know if we really did, but I was going forward. I elbowed Lewis, gently, smiling. "We haven't rehearsed this next song with Lewis yet. We were going to surprise him and Carson Mastick, our absent leader. We figured they'd both know it even though it just came out last week, and Lewis says he does, so we're going to go for it." I stepped back to my own mic.

"After five years," Lewis said, "John Lennon's finally come out with a new album. He and his wife, Yoko Ono, shared the credits. They called it a *Heart Play*. I don't know what that is, and . . . I don't have it yet. David Bowie also recently released a new album, so I, um, already spent my music money for the month. But my friend Carson left me the new single, a gift, no strings attached. Like friends do." Lewis looked up to the stands and waved. Maybe he thought Carson was here, but I doubted it. Not like him to go somewhere that denied him the spotlight.

"The single is called 'Starting Over,'" Lewis said, "and that seems like a good enough way for us to go out on, tonight. Nyah-wheh for listening with a Good Mind." He started alone, as we'd anticipated. We had it covered, just in case, but he took it on, singing about people and precious connections, and the ways they grow. He closed the first verse, still solo, him and his acoustic, singing about the ways we find each other again.

It was my turn, so I hit four machine-gun notes on my water drum, sharp and high near the skin's edge, and the others joined in, as if they'd been playing this song for years. The song was about two people who love each other, but as he sang it, I realized Lewis was changing the lyrics a little. He was singing a song about us, our group, and the ways that we could find ourselves again, just like we were starting over.

29

I'm a Loser
Carson Mastick

The band finished, and the crowd cheered. Nothing spectacular. Not enthusiastic enough to acknowledge what they'd pulled off. But no one else knew how good we should have sounded, and how they, just them, together, shouldn't have sounded as smooth as they did. I didn't know how to feel about that. Had I wanted Lewis to be weak alone? Had I wanted all of them to be bad once I saw them walk on to help? To be good? To be decent but not as good as they would have with me?

They lingered for a few seconds too long, and the cheering died down before they unplugged and disappeared. A rookie mistake that wouldn't have happened with me. But I *wasn't* there, because I was more gullible than Lewis. I'd always believed bad things had come to him by his own fault. I guess bad things had come to me of my own fault too, but not entirely.

What if I'd just told Marchese that I'd forgotten to thaw the turkey? Would she have made an accommodation? What if I hadn't taken on Custard? Would I have taken him on, if I'd known he was her husband? I'd like to believe so, but I couldn't tell myself a lie, to make this easier. I'd always believed that I'd always gotten by on my charm. I didn't like to admit that I used it, but maybe it wasn't even true.

Some people feared my dad as much as I did, with good reason. Maybe I'd been given a pass for stunts I pulled, out of that fear.

Or maybe my real gift had been the one I used regularly but hated to acknowledge: my ability to blend in. Even in budget rock-star clothes at school, I still looked like a flashy white kid. I could take the easier path with someone like Evan Reiniger because of my ChameleIndian powers. I'd known what I was even before I'd come up with a word to describe it.

Mrs. Thatcher stepped up to introduce Artie's band. Was Susan going to get back up there with them? Was that allowable, or had she disqualified herself by performing with Lewis? Was Tami going on even though she knew I got kicked out?

The bands were allowed to clean up in the locker rooms and encouraged to go out front and be good sports for our competitors. Would they let me back through to see Lewis and Doobie, or was I banished from that too? Artie's band came on, with Tami on her sad tambourine. They sounded decent, but I could hear the places he'd been maybe counting on Susan to fill out their sound the way she had for Lewis's band.

Lewis's band. Weird! Even in my head, it wasn't pleasant. What should they be called in that lineup? Hard to be Quarry Men when two of the four people onstage were girls. And they couldn't be the Dog Street Devils without me. Without *me*. It was *for* me, but not a part *of* me. If anything, it was apart *from* me. None of those songs were ones I'd ever practiced. I couldn't have jumped up, even if I'd been allowed to at the last minute. Together, they'd found some extra practice time. Someone had come up with arrangements.

I made my way near the backstage entry area, and the chaperone there, the jazz-beard Mr. Tromboner himself, was shaking his head at me before I could even get in hearing range over Artie's band. They finished an intense version of Queen's "We Will Rock You" and kicked up Sweet's "Ballroom Blitz" without even a breather. It made sense that Artie, a drummer, would want to lead with songs that high-lighted him.

Just as Mr. Tromboner was about to turn me out, Groffini showed up out of nowhere and put his arm around my shoulders, nodding. Tromboner reluctantly let us through. We didn't say anything because there was no way to be heard until we got to the locker room, where we found Lewis and Hubie both drying off after hitting the showers. Each of them had a change of clothes laid out on the benches. Groffini, such a Bizarro, shook hands with them and gave congratulations, even while they stood there buck-ass naked.

"Come on in here when you got your clothes on, guys," he said, pointing to the coach's office with the big plate-glass windows that looked out onto the lockers.

"Why do you have keys to this?" I asked as he ushered me through and offered me one of the less comfortable chairs. He flopped down in the nice desk chair.

"You really need to ask that?" he asked, bemused. Somehow, I'd forgotten that, in addition to being the Rez guidance counselor, he was also the head lacrosse coach. The other guidance counselors seemed to be divided up randomly, but Groffini was the only one who worked with us, and he didn't work with anyone else. I wondered if he was paid by the treaty funding that supported our education—as with so many other things, we were sort of *within* the school district, but not quite fully *of* the district.

Lewis came in, mostly dressed. "Who knew you could get up there and pull it off!" I said. "Pretty damn good!" I gave him sort of a one-armed, slap-on-the-back guy hug. This was the Rez equivalent of letting off fireworks to celebrate, and he grinned a bit, sitting to yank on his stupid Beatle boots.

Doobie joined us a minute later, stuffing his T-shirt bottom into his jeans. He should have undone the button and zipper to get a smoother fit, but he was on the chubbier side. It was probably tough enough on him that we'd walked in before he'd gotten dressed.

I'd been right about the idea of performance outfits. Onstage, they had a passing resemblance of a rock band. But here in Groffini's grubby office, back in their regular clothes, they just looked like two misfit Indians—one skinny and one chubby, a Rez Laurel and Hardy.

"So listen, guys," Groffini said, putting his feet on his desk. "As I said, terrific performance. The last band is still on. Once they're done, all the other bands'll be brought back out for the announcement. Winning band gets to play one last song. But, um, you don't get to go. Not even for the announcement. I'm sorry."

He dropped his feet, leaning forward. None of us said anything.

"Look. I don't make the rules. The band that went on was supposed to be the band that signed up. You would have been disqualified, even if you hadn't, um, chosen your particular unorthodox stage presence." Would Artie's team have been disqualified if Susan had stepped out? Could I make an issue because Tami went out onstage without being on his approved roster? I couldn't do that to my cousin, but I had to wonder.

"What's the real reason?" I asked. Groffini leaned back again, sighing. "They could *say* it's because I wasn't there, even though they blocked me from being there, or they could say it's because Lewis sang some unapproved 'fucks' in unapproved songs, but that's not the real reason." Groffini reached up under his cuff and scratched his impossibly hairy leg. Every single kid on the Rez knew this was his personal sign that he was going to lie to us.

"Hube?" he said. "The girls are being told the same thing right now. They should be out in the staging area. Maybe you could find them and tell them we'll be right along. I'll make sure you guys get out without any trouble."

"No," I said. "Whatever you have to say to us, you can say in front of Doobie. We're a band. We trust him with everything." Lewis nodded, slapping Doobie's back.

"I can't, boys," Groffini said, rocking forward again. "What I have to say to you concerns your academic record, and I can't share that with anyone but you, or your parents. Afterward, if you want to tell Hube? That's your business." And there was the Leg-Scratch Lie. Groffini spent most of his career bending school policies. That was kind of the nature of a Rez guidance counselor. He just wanted to ask me and Lewis something or tell us something, and he didn't want Doobie there for some reason. This should be interesting.

"It's okay," Doobie said. "I understand. See you guys out there." He stuffed his sweaty stage clothes into his bag and slumped out of the locker room. I could see in his shoulders the weight of every year he'd been stuck behind us since flunking kindergarten. This was just one more thing he was being left out of. I told myself to try never calling him Doobie again. After the door slammed shut, Groffini took the extra measure and shut the three of us inside his office.

"So, uh, I went looking for Mrs. Marchese tonight. I figured she might want to see if you tried to show up. Or not. She's awfully mad about her husband's Vendor Table situation."

"But—" Lewis started. Groffini raised his palm, and Lewis immediately shut up—guess his rule-following days weren't quite over yet. So much for rock and roll.

"I'm not saying anyone's right or anyone's wrong," Groffini said. "But I went looking, to see if *you* were going to get a deficiency if you'd figured out some way to get up on that stage." He looked directly at Lewis. "Sorry, Carson. There wasn't anything I could do to pull her back in from doing what she'd already done to you. But a little bird told me the others were planning something." Which little bird—Magpie? Is that what he was saying?

"Not all of us," Lewis said. "Just me and Hubie and Susan Critcher. I told them I was going to try, and gave them the option to join me if I made it onstage. I was surprised as anyone else when Maggi showed up out of nowhere." Lewis had no secret sign that he was lying. No leg scratch, no twitch. Or did he? I'd assumed he didn't lie much because he knew he was terrible at it. Maybe I'd been wrong all along.

"So Marchese can't do anything to her," Lewis added. Funny. He'd set it up so the person who'd done the most serious thing wouldn't be caught at all. I guess I had some things to learn about loyalty from my bandmates. My bandmates? Not my band? *Correct, Carson,* some other voice inside my head said. It sounded freakily like Lewis's damned Uncle Albert.

"See, now, that's the funny thing," Groffini said. "I did find Mrs. Marchese, but not until Lewis had already done his thing. It was during your last song." He rocked forward again. "Before I could even ask about the possibility of Lewis getting a deficiency, to argue against it, she took me out into the hall and said . . . she'd reconsidered her position."

"What does that mean?" Lewis asked. I knew what it meant.

"It means she pulled my deficiency. Right?" Groffini nodded. "What Lewis did actually worked? No shit. I'd have never guessed that."

"No, that's not it," he said, and sighed. Before I could ask, he continued, "She wouldn't tell me why she changed her mind. When I tried to ask—and I'm expecting you to be discrete about this, no awyock." We both silently decided not to correct him on his massacre of pronouncing Eee-ogg. "She got moody. Said something like isn't it enough I'm not failing that little bastard after what he did to my family. Not exact words, but you get the picture."

"I bet 'bastard' was an exact word," I said, laughing. Groffini gave a tiny grin. "Well, then how do you know she didn't cave *because* of Lewis and Maggi and Hubie and Susan?" I wanted their bravery, Lewis's finally growing a pair of balls on his own, to have meant something.

"That was the last thing she said. And this time I can quote. I wrote it down. 'It wasn't that stupid juvenile protest either. Don't those kids know the sixties are dead?'"

"Harsh," I said. "Guess she's kind of bitter that we had even a little effect."

"As someone who *did* grow up in the sixties," Groffini said, "I can say, it stung. And I don't think it had a *little* effect. You made a difference. I wouldn't be doing this job if I didn't believe *I* could make a difference." Lewis and I stood up. A weight was gone. We hadn't won, and our chances at New York City were gone gone gone, but we'd be free at the end of June. My New York City future would just have to rely on my own resourcefulness.

"Not so fast, men," Groffini said, and we both sat right back down, though we were itching to leave. "I'm only going to ask this once. And the answer will never leave this office. I promise you. Counselor-student confidentiality." That was a load of shit. He had to tell parents and teachers all kinds of things about any kid stuck in the system. But I was willing to let it slide. I believed him. "Let's assume she's telling the truth, that your protests didn't have any effect. Did one of you do something to make her back off? Extortion's serious. Do I have to start preparing some defense for you?" I was shocked Groffini was willing to do that, and to tell us.

"No idea," Lewis said. "None, whatsoever." Groffini looked at me, and I shook my head. He asked me to say aloud that I had no idea why, and I did. He let us go a few minutes later.

"You think Groffini was recording us?" I asked as we got to the staging area. "That that's why he made me say it?" He agreed it was possible.

Stepping into the staging area, I thought about what to say to Lewis next. It might have been a thank-you for sticking up for me tonight, but I still had the hardest time saying it, beyond a mumbled Nyah-wheh on the Rez. I found myself tensing up even now. I think maybe I inherited that trouble from my dad. He *never* said thank you. To *anyone*. He said it made you look weak if you were in someone's debt.

"Gotta do what's right when you have the chance," Lewis said. "Your Custard protest confirmed what I've believed all along, even if it didn't work out as you planned." I nodded, realizing I had trouble with generosity, period. My dad, with his screwed-up, random ways, had made me wary of even gifts. Whenever I got them, I wondered how long it was going to be before someone randomly snatched them out of my hands.

The moment passed and we joined the others, enjoyed ourselves as a group for a while. When Artie's band came back to staging after the announcements, we congratulated him on their win. He said it was the band's win, not his. I went to pass the praise around, but the rest of my band beat me to it. Marvin had made his way back too and was grinning at Maggi, impressed with what she'd pulled off at the last minute. Some others came up and talked with us, and after a few minutes, Susan said she was catching a ride with her brother, tagging along in their celebration. We told her we appreciated her going out onstage with Lewis, even though it meant she'd sacrificed the prize money and the trip. She said it was part of being a band.

"Hey, Marv?" Doobie asked, grabbing his bag. "You and Maggi need a ride? I'm heading out." We all looked around. Somehow, she'd vanished. Marvin frowned, then said he'd catch a ride with Marie. We all looked at him, knowing Marie didn't own a car, but he said she'd come with friends and then he peeled out quick, saying he'd better catch them before they left. Hubie tagged along with Marv, to make sure Marie hadn't left her brother behind.

"You ready?" I asked Lewis. We figured that Marie's ride was the skinny guy in the Old-Man Clothes that she'd brought to the protest, Ben something. Had Maggi gone with them? That was the only conclusion I could draw. The gym was clearing out, and brighter lights had been turned on. Lewis picked up his guitar. I wanted to walk out through the lunchroom atrium, to make sure Albert didn't need a ride. He'd probably left with my dad, but like Doobie, I wanted to be positive. I also wanted one last look at the vendor signs with no Custard's Last Stand sign.

"Listen, you kicked some ass tonight," I said, looking at him directly, in a way I never did unless I was talking him into something. He knew he'd kicked ass, but it was kind of like with Groffini making me speak out loud. I was still willing to say it.

It was the truth.

30

Air Talk
Magpie Bokoni

Marie showed a couple hours later. I'd already slipped the tags back on her things and put them away. Kind of gross, but I didn't want her knowing I'd borrowed without asking. "Nice show," she said after she'd crawled in. We had music playing low, the album Jim had given me, *Double Fantasy*. He'd been right. With every song, I remembered. Some was like I expected. To finally be held by someone, to know I was important and desirable to someone I loved, that I could cause an immediate reaction in him, that he couldn't bear to be an inch away, that all those things were even more charged than the way you imagined things, watching movies when the people on screen were passionate.

But no Sexy Movie Girl ever gets leg cramps from trying to sit in those gravity-defying magazine poses. She never winds up with the guy's arm accidentally pulling her hair because he's got all his weight on his forearms framing her head. She never worries that her socks are sweaty (because the Sexy Movie Girl is NEVER dumb enough to wear socks for an intimate encounter). How did Marie deal with these things?

"Lewis?" Marie said, shaking her head. "What a moron. Does he think Carson would do something like that for him? How'd they break into the school to swap out those stupid turkeys anyway? Do you know? Did your *bandmates* tell you?" she said, making fun of my loyalty.

"I did it, actually. The whole thing. Even the idea," I said.

"You lie! Goody Two-Shoes," she said, laughing. "So listen." She propped herself up. "Are you really gonna show those weird art projects you've been working on at the Bazaar?"

"Of course, unless Dark Deanna goes on a rampage. It's not going to put us in the black, but I think your trucker caps have us covered this year." The Bazaar was kind of like what the mall stores called "Black Friday": a Rez-wide combo Vendor Table roundup, craft demonstrations, food, with a Social at night. It was one of the few times of year people from the Rez stocked up for real on a fair amount of Traditional crafts. I think a lot of them bought stuff for their family members who'd moved away, to remind them of home. We maybe sold the last of the summer stock we had left, got our books balanced, and no one had to even leave the Rez to do that kind of shopping. It worked for everyone.

"Dark Deanna," my sister laughed. "You better watch out. You know that no one's buying that freaky thing, but it's weird enough that people are gonna notice it. They're gonna start calling you Morbid Maggi. Or Mortuary Maggi."

"Shut up," I said, and we both laughed.

"Listen. Pick your best work. I'll make sure Ma allows it. Even just this one time. Bee talked that reporter into doing a piece on my caps. Maybe he'll write something about both of us." Marie had started calling her man "Bee" because it drove her crazy that I made fun of him.

"I can't pick my *best*," I said. "It's all part of one big piece. I just finished sewing all the pieces together in the right sequence. Besides, it's not just mine. Marvin made half, and he helped me with a photo part too."

"I think he was looking to make some cash here," she said. She knew this wasn't the kind of thing you cranked out a tote full to sell, like the Boom Town she was having with her caps. Marie was always a little jealous that Marvin and I, as twins, had experiences she was left out of.

"He knows," I said. "He's made other things for sale. We both have, or Dark Deanna would come out for sure and slap us back to tradition." I dug the backdrop of my project out and showed her some Polaroids. Marie studied them on the table between us, like she was reading my tarot.

"So whose camera is this? I know it ain't yours. If it was yours, your big mouth would be yapping, 'I've got a camera and you don't have one, I've got a camera and you don't have one.'"

"Just a friend," I said. "A generous friend."

"I bet," Marie said. "This guy, right?" she asked, tapping one of the Polaroids. I'd had Marvin take pictures of me in various poses, and I'd carefully cut each one out and reshot the picture so Jim and I were in the same shot. He didn't move, of course, since I only had the one picture of him, but my movements gave the scenes some action. "People been seeing you with this guy. Everyone's always asking, 'Who's that paunchy one with the mustache and the scuzzy cap your sister's hanging around?' At least give him a new beaded cap to wear. Jeez."

I had thought it was a total cartoon cliché, but in fact, my jaw truly did drop at that moment. I only knew because Marie gave me a quick touch to it, clicking it shut. "You're catching flies," she said.

"But how did you—"

"You're living on the Rez, Maggi. Eee-ogg central. You know what Dad says. Out here, you can't take a whiz—"

"Without splashing on someone else's shoes," I finished. "A guy phrase, Dear Sister."

"Guy phrase or not, a fifteen-year-old girl hanging around with a middle-aged man? People notice. You work with him, isn't it?" That was when I knew Marvin had not only seen the passenger door of Jim's Bandit, but figured everything else out too.

"He your boss?" Again I didn't say anything. Marie pinched her lips together and then swept all the Polaroids together again, like they were a deck of cards. "First thing?" she said, handing them over. "Hide these. Don't go showing them to anyone. Especially Mom. You think you've seen Dark Deanna before, you ain't seen nothing."

"I can't!" I said. I had gone to great lengths to manipulate the images. "They're a major part of the work. If you leave it out, it's not the same story."

"First, there's no way you're affording a fancy camera when we're living in this Shack, so unless you want a way worse rumor going around about you, you gotta change some things. And second, you don't wanna give anyone photographic evidence of the two of you together. Which leads me to the third thing. You gotta quit that job."

"Says the girl sleeping with her old German teacher. Fräulein Marie."

"See? That's what I mean. I *did* something. First, Bee and I never did *anything* while I was in his *English* class, *not* German. *Anything*. We were just . . . *nice* to each other. Second, once I was out of his class, we just . . . stayed in touch. When it looked like our lives might go in a more complicated direction? I *did something* about it."

"We moved here so you could sleep with Ben-Yaw-Mean? Man, I hope it was worth it." I could really punch Marie right now. I mean, I was glad we came back, now, even if I wasn't at first. But to think that my sister was so driven by the needs of her jeet-nuh, that she'd just throw our whole lives into chaos to satisfy it, made me want to take that fancy red lacy bra of hers out of the drawer and strangle her with it.

"Jerk!" I said, thinking about all the parts of this that were still a drag. "Don't you miss being able to take a real shower? Use a real bathroom? Was it worth it to give up all those things just so you could be with him? Are you that serious?"

"Are *you* that serious? With this guy? What's his name? John?"

"Jim," I said.

"See, now that's the kind of mistake that can screw you up. If someone you'd prefer not to know gets something wrong, you let them get it wrong."

"So you were just testing me, right?" I said. My Fake-Out Know-It-All Sister.

"Jim Morgan. School District Buildings and Grounds. Started in 1968, which makes him either thirty-one or going on. Most proud that he was all-state football. Was I just testing you?" How long had she known? All this time, I was sure she was so preoccupied with Ben-Yaw-Mean and her new Beaded Caps Popularity that I could just slip out the side door. "Look, I get it. Obviously. Who knows? Maybe you got your taste from me."

Hardly, I thought. Ben-Yaw-Mean was tall and lanky and tried too hard to be cool. With his cords, clogs, button-up shirts with dick-ies, and elbow-patch tweed jacket, he was working too hard to look young *and* old at the same time. He didn't know who he wanted to be, even down to his stupid European exclusive car and the way he insisted on his name being unpronounceable.

"When did you and Ben . . . what do you want me to call him? That stupid name he insists on? I feel like an idiot saying it every time. Like I'm purposefully making fun of him."

"Ben's okay, I guess," she said, smiling a little embarrassed smile. "Sounds normal, isn't it? I'm hoping I'll get him to see how dumb it is at some point once we move in." *Move in???*

"Okay, when did you and him —"

"What?"

"You know . . . jig?" I asked. I'd felt like, if I used this Rez slang, I'd start laughing my head off. But no laugh came. This was serious.

"Have you slept with that guy, Jim?" she said, leaning forward, staring at me. I wondered if people could tell you were different by looking at you. Jim and I didn't get far in the break room, but we'd done some things that *had been* mysteries to me. The big things still were. I still had intact the fantasy of what my first full encounter was going to be like.

"Not yet. We're supposed to meet on Saturday. He's picking me up after Bazaar." No one had ever told me what would really happen the first time. Even from what I could feel through Jim's briefs, I was nervous about the physics. No one ever talked about that. Not even in the super-awkward health class. Those plumbing drawings had no connection to what Jim had asked me to gently squeeze as a *preview.*

"Are you crazy?" Marie jumped forward, her face inches away from mine, so close I could smell the wax in her lipstick. "You gotta call him and tell him no."

"I can't. He's going to his parents' place for Thanksgiving. He told me he wasn't going to be available, so I should just plan to be ready for Saturday. He left me a message with Lewis. Told me to bring a bag."

"Lewis knows?" she asked, alarmed. "Jeez. Why couldn't you just like *him*?"

"Right. Lewis is all about *you*, and *you* know it. You love that he's interested, and you can just shoo him away like a fly. Even if Ben-Yaw . . . Ben wasn't in your life, you still wouldn't give Lewis the time of day. You're still paying him back for calling you Stinkpot, and it wasn't even him."

I didn't want to go there, but I knew where she was going next. That was the one thing about fighting with your sister. When you've been doing it for over a dozen years, it was more a dance than a fight (but we'd each learned different steps over the last year and they were interesting—sort of like dancing in a minefield).

"I know you're gonna suggest Carson as a legit choice," I added. "Now before you do, remember I know that he *is* the person who named you Stinkpot. There's no denying that. You saw the exact same choices, and you made the exact same kinds of decisions. So just back off."

"I made those decisions *after* I turned seventeen. No matter what you're considering, it's illegal. Out here those laws don't apply, with that whole sovereignty thing. I mean, sort of? No cops, no enforcers. Besides, they'd have bigger worries than who's jigging who." We both laughed at this. "But seriously? This guy lives in New York. If you and *him* are jigging? His ass is going to jail if you're under seventeen. If not? If they can't prove anything? He'd still probably get fired. He's your boss."

"But what if we were married?"

"Pfft! This guy told you he's gonna marry you just to get in your pants?" I knew I was getting ahead of myself. Jim had suggested no such thing. Did he know how serious this was? It didn't seem likely that I'd go to jail, but still! In a weird way, it was exciting that Jim was willing to risk such a consequence just so we could be together.

"Is that what Ben-Yaw-Mean promised you? If Ma knew about the two of you, her Dark Deanna personality would possess her, permanent."

Marie dropped her head but kept her eyes on me. I knew that look. She was getting ready to tell me some truth that I really did not want to hear.

"Ma knows," Marie said so quietly, I almost didn't hear her. "She's met Ben. She didn't want to, but I told her we were probably moving in, soon's I graduate. I'll be eighteen. I'd need to wait until then to get married, or get her and Dad to sign the application, but I don't want to get married right now. Maybe someday. It'll *probably* be Ben, but who knows?"

"Ma *knows*? And you're still alive? And Ben-Yaw-Mean is still alive?"

"That's my point. I'm gonna be eighteen soon. And when I move out, you'll have your own room. I'm gonna share the Vendor Table with Ma. What else am I gonna do? I ain't going to college." Why couldn't she go to college? Who told her that? Was it the leftover bad vibe from being Stinkpot? Sometimes, I wanted to give Carson Mastick a chance, and sometimes I wanted to knock him out with the hardest punch I had. I wonder if things would have been different between him and me if he hadn't messed up my sister's life all those years ago.

"All I have to do is wait out the school year," Marie said. "And then, gradually, Bee can introduce me to his friends. We're only like six years apart. After a few years, it won't matter. He says it'll be weird, but we're tough." Now that I thought about it, Marie *had* been less careful in her coming and going in that stupid little Trabant. And our parents had seemed like they didn't care. I'd been so worried about my own situation, I hadn't even noticed that my sister had beaded herself an escape ladder, and was now almost ready to unravel it and climb neatly away.

31

Working Class Hero
Carson Mastick

Even from the start of the Bazaar, people stood in line to buy Marie's beaded caps. Their Table was divided up, caps on the right side, sweet-grass baskets, corn-husk dolls, and little carved figures in the middle, and Double-Heart Canoes on the left. Their signature piece. Behind their Table, they'd set up a tall rack to show off this super-freaky giant beadwork and craft thing that Maggi had made. I didn't know what you'd call it, maybe a kind of tapestry?

The thing wasn't a quilt. It was its own thing, the size of a single blanket. Weird, but cool. She'd taken things others thought were no good, and made something new. The foundation was a mass of purple velvet. I didn't think she had a Singer, but her stitches were professional.

Across the whole thing, nine individual scenes developed, three on top of three, on top of three. They had bead borders linking them with little sculptures inside, almost like a giant comic book page come to life. They reminded me of the way our Traditional stories used symbols. The foundation of each panel used a standard technique for beadwork picture-frame windows.

The photos looked like distorted Polaroids. There were people in them, but you couldn't quite make them out. Mostly, they looked like a sequence of photos starring a guy and a girl at different distances from each other. They looked melted or something, like you'd run a nail across the picture while it was still wet. They were mysteries, but I knew who she meant. The only other guy she really knew out here was Lewis, and he wasn't exactly the art-inspiring type. In the last one, the guy and the girl were next to each other, in front of a bright light, so all you saw was them in shadow. How would I let her know that I recognized us?

Below each photo, in a pocket pouch, was a messed-up version of the tourist thing her family made for sale: the Double-Heart Canoe. But they were busted, or in a couple looked like pieces wedged together with rawhide. Inside each, the hearts looked lumpy. Behind them were figures, some basswood, soapstone, and some corn husk. You could guess the people's relationships by size, placement, and way that Marvin had posed them. The pocket edges were scalloped in sweetgrass braids, twisted to look like stormy water, maybe even the rapids above the Falls. In the last panel, the girl basswood doll had left the four corn-husk people in a battered, overcrowded canoe, and had joined the soapstone man in a nicer canoe, with nicer-shaped stuffed beadwork hearts. The sweetgrass waves were calmer in that one. The whole thing was awesome and freaky at the same time. Right next to it was a sign in Maggi's neat handwriting.

" 'Sweet Birds of Paradox: A Heart Play.' What's that supposed to mean?" I asked Lewis.

"It's a reference to two different John and Yoko projects," he said.

"Oh jeez, you infected *her* too?" I said. Before he could offer me one of his long-winded Beatles explanations, I zapped him. "Never mind, I don't wanna know."

I was surprised their mom allowed the freaky piece to be displayed, but people were buying regular Double-Heart Canoes. They weren't moving like Marie's beaded caps, but they were doing okay. The ones moving the best were those with Marvin's little people sharing room with the hearts. Even with the caps Marie had given out at our Custard's Last Stand protest, they were still in serious demand. They didn't have enough stock to last to the Bazaar's end.

Where had Maggi gotten such a funky idea? Maybe she'd started working with our high school art teacher. He was crazy about Indians, and a lot of Rez kids signed up for his classes knowing they could be serious or blow it off. Depending on your mood, he'd just let you go, as long as you did some kind of Indian art before the school year was up. She definitely didn't get this idea from her mom and dad. Those Traditional art families didn't mess around. My mom did some beadwork, but she was more casual. If you were a part of those families, you had to learn to master their patterns. You didn't do new things. That was a violation.

I kind of wished now that I'd taken more than one section of that teacher's class, but I was trying to go forward and he was always pushing us to do "traditional media." Just like everyone else. Even for the Bazaar, I'd proposed that our band could play after the formal part was over, maybe generate some interest, but they already had Traditional singers in place to do a regular Social. They didn't think a rock concert was appropriate, unless you were Bob Dylan and Joan Baez, whose Rolling Thunder Revue blew through here a few years ago with a free show.

I helped my mom with our lacrosse and beadwork Table for most of the day, doing the circuit of other Tables during my breaks. Toward the end of the afternoon, I noticed Groffini nosing around near our Table and glancing over at us. Apparently we were going to have another talk, but I wasn't going to him. Eventually, he came over and small-talked my mom for a while so she wouldn't think I was in trouble, before asking to speak to me. He cocked his head in a *Follow Me* gesture, and we headed out.

"Cold out here," he said in the parking lot. "Wanna sit in my car?" He hit the heater as soon as he started it, and warm air came out immediately. He must have just gotten to the Bazaar.

Groffini really was the world's most dedicated guidance counselor. It was his job, but he made it a point to come to non-school-related community events, like this, even on weekends.

"Carson, you might be the world's luckiest guy," he said. "I'm going to give up on finding out what happened with Mrs. Marchese.

She's not the mind-changing sort, but it seems like I have to give my curiosity a rest. So, listen, what I want to say to you is . . ." He'd been rehearsing this. It was the kind of talk Groffini loved giving, and mostly, he only got to do it on the lacrosse field.

"Don't let these sacrifices go wasted, okay?" That was his big speech? "Do something. I don't know what. I'm your guidance counselor, but you've been pretty impervious to guidance, if you don't mind my saying." He laughed, and I did too. I had blown off his advice before.

"College? That's someone else's dream, not mine."

"Why *not* yours?" he asked, ludicrously gripping my shoulder, even though doing so made him grimace. "Arthritis in my shoulder," he added, seeming disappointed in his own body.

"I got other dreams," I said. "They don't involve going down the road to thirteenth grade."

"That community college works for a lot of people, even as a start. But isn't New York City your dream? Isn't that why you entered the Battle of the Bands? For the trip to the city?"

"I don't think I'm getting into New York City University," I said, dragging out the words, to confirm how ridiculous I knew that idea was. I had to give Groffini credit for knowing that much about my desires. That was nothing I'd ever told him.

"I think you mean NYU," he said. "And so what? No one said you had to shoot for something like that, but you *could*. It would get you to New York City. But let's say that's not for you. I don't know if it is or isn't. There's FIT too. Maybe a better fit, so to speak."

"What makes you think I want to go to Florida?"

"It's not Florida. The *F* is for Fashion. Fashion Institute of Technology. It's in Manhattan," he said, and slid a brochure off his dashboard. "I've seen what you can do. It's not easy to get in either, but you'll never know unless you try. You've done all these things, designing looks for your band and making those designs into actual outfits. You've got excellent fabric skills repairing those tricky uniform materials. If you got a full ride scholarship . . . you'd be living in New York City for four years. Assuming you could keep your grades up."

I had no idea such a place existed, and looking at the brochure, I was excited.

"I'm not going to lie," he said. "It's a long shot, but that's part of what I'm here for. I'll help however I can with the application process. I don't know what you did, how you got out of that failure with Mrs. Marchese, but don't squander it. You don't challenge the bear and come out on top very often." I shook his hand and headed back inside, promising I'd consider it.

The weird thing was that after all this planning my future away from here, the last couple of months had made the idea harder to consider. At first, when I saw Lewis onstage, I was pissed that he'd somehow led the others into becoming a band, even without me. But that had only happened because *I* had first led *him*. The biggest problem with being in a band is that you never get to evaluate your performance from the outside, unless you've got rich enough friends to shoot a show of yours. I was mad at first that they sounded good without me, but then I realized I'd been smart enough to recognize and put together the talent to make a real band.

Their performance showed me that my instincts were even more right to include Maggi. That hadn't been a sure shot, but I'd thought it would be a reason for us to spend more time together and maybe we could get more serious. But Maggi surprised me. She brought something to our sound you just didn't hear anywhere. She gave us that *It!* that every band that makes it has got—the thing that once you hear it, you say, oh that's *Such and Such*.

And now maybe she and I had a future together, here. Tonight would be perfect. I'd help them pack up and then see if she was ready to cash in on that date bet we'd made after yanking Albert from Sanborn Field Day. I was hoping she'd just maybe forgotten my promise to take her to John's Flaming Hearth because we'd been so busy. The other possibility, the one I hadn't wanted to think about, was that she was hoping I'd forgotten. But the tapestry and those little canoes said otherwise.

It was that lull between the Bazaar and the evening Social—time to ask her. I felt the smile come on as I reached the Old Gym's door. I didn't want to just take her to John's for something to eat. When we were there, in candlelight, I'd tell her how I really felt about her, how I'd felt since early summer and just couldn't tell her. I'd tell her that I'd been afraid that starting a relationship in a band had potential to screw things up, but now that we'd evolved into something different, something stronger, I was free to say what I'd wanted to, for so long.

"Too late," Marvin said when I stepped back in. He carefully swaddled a Double-Heart Canoe in Bubble Wrap. "Or are you back for the Social? Doesn't seem like your scene, but I got an extra horn rattle." Marvin didn't offer me a drum, politely noting that I didn't know the Traditional songs well enough to drum for others. The rattle was more intuitive, a starter instrument, since you had to learn in public. I hadn't been to a Traditional Social in years, and I felt embarrassed. It was tricky to avoid them when everyone knows you're a musician.

"I'm good," I said. "When did you start drumming for Socials?"

"While ago. We each find our own way, isn't it? You get help from some people, but others maybe need glasses. You can be right in front of them, and they don't even see you." He was telling me I'd been shitty to him by pretending he didn't exist. "They're a man short tonight, so I agreed. My first time with dancers. Hope I'm good, or at least good enough."

"How'd you guys do today?" I asked, pretending I didn't hear his jab.

"Sold out of every cap, at least half of the Double Hearts. You know, those are mostly for tourists." I nodded. "Maggi's weird thing didn't sell, but we knew that ahead. It *did* get noticed."

"Sometimes, that's all you can ask for," I said.

32

Growing Pain
Magpie Bokoni

Jim and I arrived at one of the few fancy hotels in Niagara Falls an hour after the Bazaar ended. There weren't many—it was mostly motels on the US side. Jim had a different kind of cap on, the kind you see old men wearing.

He must have seen the panic on my face, because he started laughing and took my hand.

"*Just* a dinner reservation," he said. I banged my head on the headrest and laughed. "Don't seem so relieved," he added. "I thought you wanted me to be your first."

"I do. I do. I just . . ."

"I know. Sorry. This *is* the place we're gonna go, but I planned for our first time for a different night. Didn't mean to scare you." He brought my hand up to his mouth, kissing my knuckles. "So I thought we'd take a stroll through the lobby, you'll know where to go, *next week*." We passed the registration desk, and he pointed to the elevators. "Pay attention to those," he said. We entered the restaurant, and he gave a different last name for the reservation.

"Look, Honeymoon Suite," Jim said, sliding a pamphlet to me. "It's not our honeymoon, but it'll sort of be like one, right?" I opened the brochure. My throat locked up.

"At first, I thought we might go to Canada," he continued, "but that could get tricky." Even with me using tribal ID to cross into Canada, they could ask him anything, and I'm sure he was hoping to avoid *And what's the relationship between you and this fifteen-year-old girl?* They'd probably ask me, figuring they could trip me up easier. They'd have no idea that I'd been crossing the border and sometimes answering their questions (depending on how militant my family was feeling) for my entire life. I could appreciate the suspicion we'd encounter at the border, though I thought it was almost as complicated to get a hotel room in Niagara Falls.

The brochure bed and bathtub were heart-shaped, and the bedspread looked like it was red satin. The towels were deep red too. I couldn't decide if that was awesome or creepy.

"I wanna tell you something," Jim said. "I know you think I haven't been good to *Lewis*." He wanted me to notice he hadn't said "loser." "But he really did mess up my nephew's life. I have a hard time getting over that." Carson had told me the whole story after the Battle of the Bands (a Carson version anyway). It helped explain a lot of things about Lewis.

"Oh, and another thing? I told Marchese *I* swapped the turkeys," Jim said, startling me. "That my mom had wanted one without the little pop-up thing and that I didn't think Marchese'd notice. I apologized. I got Vern to claim he saw me. You know, his ass would be in as much trouble."

"She believed you?"

"No, I don't think so, but this is a bigger mess than she wants, so I gave her an out. Teachers with high-maintenance classrooms? They know what happens when they piss us off."

"You did this for *Lewis*?"

"No, babe. I could give a shit about that little scumbag. I did it for *you*. I want you to know how much I"—he tapped the heart-shaped bed on the brochure—"you." We both smiled. When our dinners came, the salad arrived first. "Which fork you supposed to use first?" Jim whispered, and I laughed, shrugging. We each picked a different one.

"One thing about the room," he said. "Cheapest night's Monday. Sorry." He gave a sad smile. "I don't make that much. Gotta be creative. I figured this coming Monday was short notice, but with a week, you could maybe come up with an excuse to be away on a weeknight?"

"Monday?"

"Kind of tough for me too. That's my bowling night."

"You can't skip bowling in exchange for my virginity?" I said, laughing.

"Keep it down!" he hissed, looking around, but no one paid us attention. "It's semifinals. Normally, I could miss a week, but not then. I thought I'd pick you up like usual, and you could hang at the alley while I roll frames. There's a snack bar, video games. You like video games?"

"Never really played any."

"I'll get you some quarters before we go in. I usually stick around for Monday Night Football in the lounge with the rest of the league. We have a pool. I could win."

"How long is that?" My dad watched off and on. "Doesn't ever end when they say."

"Yeah, football's not exact. It ends when it does. But *everything* should look normal. You know that people won't understand if they found out."

We finished eating, and Jim took me back to the Rez. He wanted to park somewhere so we could make out before he had to drop me off, but I couldn't think of a single place. Any good spot would already have people partying—it was the Saturday night of a holiday weekend.

"What's all that about?" he said as we came up to the Old Gym, where the parking lot was still full. "Thought your thing was over at five."

"That's a Social. Different from the Bazaar," I said. "I can get a ride from someone here."

"We could find a spot somewhere near the back," he said, rubbing my thigh.

"Not in this car," I said. "Particularly not with my name on it."

"I can get rid of it," he said. "A friend of mine does pinstriping, and he gave me a good deal on it. I'd hate to do it, but . . ."

"Let's wait," I said. "It's a little complicating but I like it." I leaned over and gave him a quick kiss and hopped out before he got any more ideas. It was quite possible some people were in their cars in this lot, sneaking a little fun of their own, and I didn't want to risk being seen.

He pulled out, and I watched him disappear before heading to the back door of the Old Gym, near the kitchen and bathrooms and locker rooms for the basketball players. Right when I got near the door, Marvin stepped out of the building's shadows, crushing out a cigarette.

"When did you start smoking?" I asked.

"While ago," he said, offering me one, but I shook my head. I thought Jim's cigars were gross enough. I didn't need to contribute to that nasty cloud. "Suit yourself. Carson came looking for you then split. I invited him to stick around for the Social, but he flew out the door."

"I don't think Socials are his thing."

"No. Not his thing," Marvin said, taking a deep drag, lighting his face the way Jim did.

"Say," he added after a minute. "Wasn't that Bandit you just got out of the same that picked us up the other night? The one that *happened* to be coming through the Rez when we were walking to the school?"

"Yeah. Weird, huh?" I said. "He came to the Bazaar and then invited a few of us to go get something to eat." It is almost impossible to lie to your twin. Plus, given the Eee-ogg factor out here, it was quite possible others had noticed him, and Marvin was testing me.

"A few of you fit in that car?" Real Marvin was getting to be as nosy as Ghost Marvin.

"A couple cars."

"Marie and her man with you?" he asked. We'd silently agreed not to talk about that, but he was breaching the contract. I didn't say anything, and he took another drag. "I got eyes, Dear Sister. And they tell me way more things than you think."

"Like what?" I didn't want to hear it but figured I should.

"Like, for someone with no connections here," he said, "that guy in the Bandit spends a lot of time on the Rez, isn't it?"

"He knows me. He knows Lewis. Now he knows you. That's some connection," I said, but we could both hear how dumb it was.

"I got us a ride for when we're ready," he said. "They said I could come, but maybe we can strap you to the roof or something." He laughed then, like his old self. We went inside, but the Old Gym felt strangely smaller. Almost everyone in the room was doing a giant double-concentric-circle Round Dance. Because the inner ring of dancers had a smaller space to travel, their movements were always a little different, expanding, contracting, but caught by the same vibe and rhythm, like rows of corn waving in those conflicting breezes that arrive just before a storm. I wanted to join in but I couldn't find an opening, so I watched until it ended, and then Marvin and I got our ride home. I didn't have to be strapped to the roof, as it turned out, but I did have to sit on someone's lap, and they teased me for my bony hetch-eh. This was a pretty standard Rez joke, since we all had what Lewis called shovel butt. It made me feel like I was home. It had only taken six months.

PART FIVE
Unfinished Music No. 2. Life with the Lions

December 8, 1980
The Hunting Moon

INTERLUDE ONE

SOME TIME IN
NEW YORK CITY

December 8, 4:49 p.m.

One West Seventy-Second Street, Manhattan: A musician and an artist, husband and wife, are heading to a recording session that will also include a shoot with a well-known photographer, for a specific assignment. The musician and the artist have met with the photographer earlier, in their apartment. The photographer has been instructed only to photograph the musician. The artist and the musician have other plans. The photographer says for their plan to work, they must do something memorable. The musician strips naked in the session. This is not the first time he's lain himself so bare. Twelve years before, the musician and the artist posed nude on an album cover. They were not husband and wife at the time. The photo was taken on the occasion of the first time they made love. For this new photo, the artist, now the musician's wife, is fully clothed. The musician is testing the boldness of Rolling Stone *magazine. Its publisher has requested this session, to accompany an interview after a long period of silence. It is noteworthy. Will the magazine run so naked a photo on the cover?*

At an airport terminal miles away, a man lands in New York City. He is returning from the Netherlands, where he has sought international support to stop industrial dumping in Mohawk territory. He is a member of the Seneca Nation looking out for his people and their ongoing survival: cultural, political, physical. Nine years before, he had found allies in the musician and the artist, the husband and wife. With their high-profile support, New York State was unable to assert "Eminent domain," trying to take land at Onondaga Nation for a highway expansion. The man is a member of the Haudenosaunee, known by others as the Iroquois, also known as the Six Nations. The Six Nations are the Mohawk, the Cayuga, the Onondaga, the Oneida, the Seneca, and the Tuscarora. The man understands the power of using a united voice. The man understands the strength of speaking as a group of like-minded individuals, acting in concert.

A *third man has flown across the country. He waits outside the exclusive apartment building at Seventy-Second Street and Central Park West. He has lingered off and on for a couple of days. He holds an object. He talks with an amateur photographer who is also waiting. They wait for the musician living in the building. When the artist and the musician emerge from the building, the man thrusts the object in front of the musician. The object is an album, the musician's recently released collaboration with his wife, the artist. It's called* Double Fantasy. *The musician asks if the man wants it signed. The man nods, and the musician writes his name across the image of his own wife's neck, outstretched in a kiss with him. The amateur photographer captures this moment. The musician asks if that is all the man wants. The man takes the album back and nods. The musician talks with the photographer. They know each other casually. The musician and the artist are offered a ride by some radio professionals with whom they have spent the afternoon in a long-ranging interview. They plan to air it on Valentine's Day. The photographer has taken a photo that will be very important shortly. In this moment, it is just film, exposed to light for less than a second. The light leaves a permanent scar on the virgin film emulsion. The scar will become an image. The photographer sees the autograph on the record, messy but recognizable.*

John Lennon
1980

33

A Day in the Life
Carson Mastick

December 8, 5:59 p.m.

The Bokoni family was a lead Sunday Lifestyles feature in yesterday's *Niagara Cascade*. Maggi and Marie both got attention for their "installation," whatever Art-Fart talk that was. Bringing Maggi a copy would be a good excuse to stop by. We hadn't spoken since the Bazaar.

"Hey, Marvin," I said after he'd yelled for me to come in. He waved. "See yourself in the paper? Got it right here, if you want." I held it up. "Your whole family."

"I know what we look like already," he said, not looking away from the TV.

"Thought I'd bring it over for Maggi. Maybe she'll be excited your stuff's in the papers."

"She knows what we look like too." Stone cold. "We don't share your desire for fame."

"Just thought this could raise the profile of your work. Get you better going rates."

"Pfft!" he said, like his sisters. "Marie's man invited a whatchamacallit woman to the Bazaar. She picks art for shows in Buffalo. She gave Maggi a little card with her information. They don't need that rinky-dink paper to *raise their profile*."

"Did *you* get one of those little cards?" Marvin kept his eyes on the TV.

"Nah. Wasn't really my work," he said, pausing on a channel with sitcoms.

"Sure looked like your work to me."

"I was just following Maggi's ideas. I don't have those kinds of dreams."

"Still your work," I said. "You guys could get an art show if you wanted, I bet."

"That thing with art shows?" he said, switching channels. "They never pay nothing. When we lived in The Projects, I talked to artists showing their work at the Turtle. Said they only survived doing Traditional work. Stuff like Maggi wants to make? Nobody looking for Indian art buys that kind of thing. Museums might show it, but you know what they pay? Wall space."

"Don't know what you mean," I said, but I kind of did. The music industry magazines said most bands didn't get shit to make a record, only making money on tours and T-shirts.

"You don't get paid," he confirmed. "They think exposure on their walls is payment. Our ma has opinions about that. She ain't stopping Maggi's new stuff, but supplies gotta come out of Maggi's pocket, and she's gonna put up with it *only* if Maggi keeps doing stuff that sells too."

"The regular Double-Heart Canoes."

"Yup. The ones in that piece were rejects my mom wouldn't allow on the Table. Maggi stored up those busted canoes. Everyone in this shack has been kind of tense. You know, look at it. Not a lot of personal space. I made the weird little people to ride in those busted canoes to make Maggi and Marie laugh. I thought they might stick around longer if they were happier."

"Stick around?" I asked. I couldn't help but feel jealous. I'd had all these fantasies about running off to New York City, and I couldn't even keep my shit together enough to qualify for a stupid Battle of the Bands. "You and Maggi are, what, sixteen?"

"Fifteen. We'll be sixteen toward the end of next month."

"Okay. Still, not exactly a Peeling-Out-on-Your-Own kind of age. Look at you. *You're* not going anywhere." He shrugged. I felt like he wasn't telling me something, but Marvin owed me nothing. We hadn't grown close. Even as I hung out with his sisters, it was never at their house.

"No, I'm not going anywhere," he said. "But I don't have the opportunities others do."

"You pissed at me about not being in the band?" What else could it be? "Look, Maggi never told me you played an instrument."

"You are the vainest person I ever met," Marvin said, shaking his head. "Do you just sit around thinking about all the ways you think other people want to be near you?"

"I got a lot to offer," I said, but even as it came out of my mouth, it sounded like a lie.

"Not to Maggi, you don't. I mean, I don't even know what she wants anymore, but one thing's for sure, there's lots my sister never told you."

"Like what?"

"If you have to ask, then you must not understand how much." He cut a sharp sliver of mirror into my brain. "Ever since we moved back, she don't tell me stuff, and *we're* twins! Now it's just her and Marie, and Marie ain't even here half the time. If you think giving my sister that newspaper is gonna score you points, you don't understand anything about her. You think you gotta find something to pay her back for giving up her virginity for you. That's all you know, the Carson Universe."

Was that true? Weren't all relationships about what I give you and you give me?

"Wait, what?" I said. "If your sister was giving that to me, I think I'd know about it."

"She ain't giving it *to* you. It's not a piece of jewelry or a car! Damn, Carson, grow up! I'm fifteen, and I know more about the world than you. And my sister knows *way* more."

"Sorry, you lost me here."

"She's giving it *up*," he sighed, irritated. "*Because* of you. Partly. She must like the guy *some*, but I've seen him. He ain't nothing to look at." He shut off the TV. He offered me a pop, but drinking store-brand pop was a low-budj skizzler move, so I passed. "She was asking Marie for tips about . . . the first time. I'm not hip enough for that talk."

"Look," I said, urgent blood pushing from my heart, "I really don't know what you're talking about, but it sounds like I should. Truth? I really did come here to give her that paper, but as an excuse. I thought maybe me and her . . ."

"Some other fox has gotten to that henhouse, Carson," he said. A bizarre, old-fashioned statement, something my dad or Albert might say, but I understood. "Anyway, yeah, she thinks she's helping you and Lewis. Some old pervo named Jim who she works with, I think. I've been in his car — a sweet, sweet *Smokey and the Bandit* deal. He told her he lied for you three with a teacher over, um, a *turkey*? That sound right? Said he claimed *he* was the one who made the swap. And she was all, *Jim, my hero!* I don't know. Maybe? Maybe I misheard."

The pieces were starting to come together. Maybe there was a way to stop this. But who was the guy? Who had access to Marchese that could make her change her mind?

"You've seen the guy?" I asked. "You'd recognize him?"

"He's just a scummy guy. You seen them like that before." Marvin seemed weary. How long had he kept this inside? "When I saw what she was up to, and figured out she *wanted* to be tricked, I went back to *Lost in Space*, which I'm gonna do now." He turned the TV on. "Nope, *Land of the Giants*. If you dig, stick around."

"No thanks," I said. He had shit taste in shows.

"Old Dude's got her sold on how *deep* he is, how this is all for real with him. Even had her name pinstriped on the door. Girls are such suckers for that shit. They don't know they can be scraped off with a putty knife and buffed out with a little rubbing compound and Turtle Wax." He made scraping motions, and then blew debris from the invisible scraper he held.

"How do you know all this? Unless you got their room bugged, there's no way you'd catch that much. This is bullshit."

"When I wanted to surprise Maggi with new little people for her projects, I looked in this diary our mom forced on her, trying to shut her up at the Vendor Table." He stared at the TV for a while. "I knew she'd been using it to sketch out her new ideas. She'd shown me some."

"A diary," I said, thinking of all the ways I'd been able to keep my privacy at our house. This tiny shack didn't seem to offer any.

"Yup, you're smarter than you look, isn't it?" He reddened. "Turns out she wasn't just using it as a sketchbook. Turns out too, I'm kind of a shitty twin brother."

"Would you know this guy if you saw him?" I asked again. Marvin filled me in on what little more he was willing to reveal, saying he hadn't really seen the guy except by the Bandit's dome light. "Where is she now? How do you know it's tonight?"

"I don't know where she is. But your cousin Tami's covering, pretending she's staying over or some shit. Whyn't you ask *her*?" I didn't say anything to that. "Don't believe your cousin could lie to you?" Marvin said, laughing. "You know what they say about Karma."

"Yeah, it's instant and it'll knock you on your ass."

"I thought it was Instamatic," he said.

"That's a camera," I said, heading to their door. "If I find them, will you help me straighten this guy's ass out? Stop your sister from making a giant mistake?" The guy sounded big, by Marvin's description.

"I'm done trying to figure out my sisters," he said, sliding deep into the couch cushions for the long haul. "Besides, you only think it's a mistake 'cause this dude beat you to home base. She's serious about him. If you'd have looked at her art *for real*, you'd know that. She laid out their whole story, plain as day on that hanging, and the only ones who saw it were me, her, probably Marie, and maybe the guy himself. She thinks Old Dude's gonna take her away from our little shack."

I flipped to the newspaper article. Even in the fuzzy newsprint photos, the sequence told a story, like filmstrips from science class. The first strip shows a girl discovering her canoe was becoming fractured, splitting from too much pressure, too many others crowding her out. In the second sequence, she sees someone alone in a different canoe, and the third line traces the two of them reaching out to one another. All the Polaroids echoed those same ideas, the leaving of one canoe for another. When I'd seen her amazing piece at the Bazaar, I'd somehow imagined *I* was the man in the other rickety canoe, inviting her to leave hers and help stabilize my own.

Marvin turned the volume up, and we watched the *Land of the Giants* opening credits. A cartoon man ran from a spotlight across the screen. The owner of the spotlight was no regular man, though. The tiny man discovered too late that the spotlight was the least of his worries. It was actually a flashlight, belonging to a giant, who then scooped him up and carried him away.

"Find your buddy, Lewis," he added. "I got the sense that guy's been hassling him and now with Maggi involved, that don't happen so much. Lewis shoulda learned to stop getting his ass beat on his own, but you can't blame him for accepting the benefits of my sister's hooking-up life. Lewis is like the cartoon guy here. He knows what it's like to be squeezed in the giant's fist."

"Well, I have a pretty good guess where Lewis is. That's something. But if I need you?" I asked, getting up. "Will you . . . at least pick up the phone?" I had to find her, but what then? What could I possibly do by myself?

"I guess," he said, going back to his show. "One thing, Carson? Out here on the Rez, maybe you're special, but we've been living in the city. For every girl like Maggi, there's ten dudes like you lining up to try and impress them."

I left then, heading home. Marvin was impervious to my persuasion, so calling Tami was next, but I didn't want to. What if she confirmed she'd willingly lie to me? But I caught a lucky break. When I pulled into my driveway, I could hear music streaming from Derek's room.

"Hey, brother. I need your help," I said, taking the stairs two at a time. It felt strange to lean in his doorway the way he'd leaned in mine all those months ago. "It might get us in trouble. I'm pretty sure it's off the Rez. I wouldn't ask, all things considered, but I'm gonna need muscle."

"Where do I sign up?" he asked, grinning. "I owe you. But I'd do it even if I didn't."

I smiled back, mostly genuine but a little tough too. I hated seeking Derek, because he couldn't blend in like me off the Rez. And I hated that he was eager for trouble again, but I was running out of trustworthy options.

"Be back in an hour," I said. Normally, Derek ran on Indian Time, but other people were counting on us. *One* other person. And she didn't even know it. "If you're not ready, I'm gonna split. I gotta call Tami and get Lewis. I need you and him." He hobbled up. The Ass Toothache would be a part of his life for a long time, maybe forever. "When did Mom and Dad leave?"

"Hour ago? Dad wanted to warm up. Indian league's against the district this week."

"*Our* school district?" It was like a gift. I didn't need to call Tami after all. "Teachers?"

"Yeah, *our* district," he said. "Team's whoever signs up. Probably all maintenance guys and lunch ladies," he laughed. "Dad's always pissed because Darwin bowls for the school instead of the Indian league. That's why he wants to win so bad this week. It's personal for him."

I ran to my room and pulled out two tall cans of red spray paint I'd bought to make a Dog Street Devils backdrop for the band. The cans were full. I didn't know what I was going to find down at the bowling alley, but if this guy Jim felt about his car the way I felt about the Chevelle, I knew at least one way to maybe hit him hard, even without swinging a punch.

"An hour for real, a little less, maybe," I said to Derek when I passed by. "Not Indian Time." I pointed to the clock radio on his nightstand.

"Heard you the first time. You gonna tell me what you need me for?"

"Dress like you don't want to get noticed." He grinned at this and reached for the darkest pair of jeans on his dresser, untying his boots to swap out of the faded jeans he had on.

December 8, 6:59 p.m.

"Lewis!" I yelled, stepping in. He was upstairs, trying to play along with the new David Bowie. Someone was with him. They were picking out a new tab. My job! "It's Carson! Can I use your phone?" I asked, already dialing. Marvin answered on the second ring. I asked him if he thought they might have gone to the bowling alley. He said he'd told me everything he knew and again suggested, more irritated, that I talk to Tami. I could hear isolation in his voice. Maybe he wanted me to confirm that I was almost as isolated, that my own cousin had worked against me.

Lewis's bike was leaning in the corner, his giant chain wrapped around the seat shaft. Perfect. I quietly twisted the chain off, 'round and 'round. Heavy-duty and hard-core, exactly what I needed. Maybe I'd be okay with just Lewis after all, if Derek flaked on us.

This beautiful heavy chain would be almost invisible once inside my bulky winter coat. I was going to use it either on that guy Jim's car or on his ass, depending on how I found him. I thought of Marvin's Instamatic karma comment and grinned to myself. He'd given me all the keys I needed. And now I was prepared. "You sure you don't want to come? Last chance."

"Don't call me again," Marvin said. "Whatever my sisters find, they find." He hung up.

"So what's up?" Lewis said, coming down from his room.

"Your phone get cut off for lack of payment?" Doobie added, following behind him.

"Funny," I said. "Where's your truck?" Lewis was easier to sway when he was alone.

"Lewis's mom borrowed it to run to the store." I couldn't imagine lending the Chevelle.

"She's not a big Bowie fan," Lewis said. "She was getting sick of hearing 'Scary Monsters (and Super Creeps)' over and over." He *always* insisted on using full titles whenever he talked about songs, like I'd confuse it with a different "Scary Monsters." "We need Susan's keyboard to sound decent. My acoustic isn't getting me anywhere. Chords are easy, but everything's processed." It also needed a lead player, since it continued, even when Bowie sang.

"Listen, I went to Maggi's, I was gonna drop off a copy of the paper."

"I don't think she cares that much," Lewis said, frowning at his bike in the corner.

"That's more your thing," Doobie added as he wiped down his bass and cased it.

"Like you're not trying to get your picture taken with every ambulance in the county," I said to him. He shrugged, letting me know that was a pathetic jab. "Anyway, she wasn't home. Marvin says she's with a guy, and that she's gonna . . ."

I couldn't even say it. It was supposed to be *me*! I'd done *everything* right! I was from the right place! Coming back was hard enough. Coming back and getting involved with someone who wasn't from the Rez? You might as well have stayed in the city. It never occurred to me to watch out for guys from the outside.

In September, I'd welcomed her to join us at the little back hallway where all the Indians hung out between classes. Marie was easy to have back because we knew her. But we weren't the Welcome-Wagon types, by nature. I felt a little bad now we hadn't helped Marvin more. Could we have made an effort instead of looking at him like he was a new kind of insect anytime he'd cracked a joke? Yeah, but then Maggi would have thought I did that for just anyone. She wouldn't know that I thought she was special.

"Look! They're gonna . . ." Was there a non-ridiculous way to say this? "Gonna do it."

"How would Marvin know that?" Doobie said. Like Lewis, he was always interested in Eee-ogg sources.

"I'm supposed to be interested in this story?" Lewis added. "I mean, you're hot for her, but if you're too lame to ask her out, that's not my problem, or even all that interesting." He turned to go back to his room, but stopped. "Hubie's right. It isn't Marvin's business, *or ours.*"

"It might not be Doobie's, but it *is* yours. Will you just come with me? I need your help."

"My help?" Lewis said, giving out the laugh that was really more like, *You are insane!* I wanted him to rise up and help Maggi. To help me, because it was the right thing. "Am I supposed to be your cheerleader?" he added, switching on a ludicrous pom-pom girl voice: "Come on, Maggs! Carson's better than Jim! You should go! Instead with him!"

What??? *Carson's better than* Jim???

"You already *knew*!" I yelled, forcing myself not to punch him. I'd hoped he might recognize the guy when we got there, because it seemed like the guy was someone Lewis worked with. But Lewis already *knew* which guy it was *and* knew they were doing something and he *never* said anything to me? I could picture that Bandit, the one Marvin said had Maggi's name pinstriped on the door. It had been parked with those other hot cars at the garage. Lewis saw it every day. "How long?"

"How long what?" he mumbled, pretending he hadn't just mentioned the guy's name.

"Have you known this old guy *you work with* has been trying to get into Maggi's pants."

"A while, I guess?" He seemed a little awkward, but not nearly enough. "Look, man, he's not the only one checking her out. She's a hot sixteen-year-old girl who goes out of her way to *look* like a hot sixteen-year-old girl."

"Fifteen."

"Whatever, fifteen. She's wearing clothes that shout *LOOK AT ME!* Just like you. Except she's working around a bunch of horny middle-aged men who enjoy her choices. These guys have *Hustler* centerfolds up in their *break room* lockers. The place they eat lunch! The one woman on that crew warned those guys about getting too close to her."

"How come this guy's ignored that advice?" Time was running out.

"Works at the school. Just punches in and out and grabs his work truck at the garage. When he's not being an asshole."

"Wait," I said. Something Marvin said just clicked. This was a guy he said had been hassling Lewis. "It's *that* guy! The one who used to pants you. The one who pisses on the floor instead of in the urinal so you gotta clean it up? The one who headlocked you and *dragged your face* inches away from his piss puddle. Right?"

I'd been hearing about this guy for years, almost since Lewis got that job. The pieces were coming together, like a camera focusing.

"Didn't he punch you in the balls once? Like a real Wham-O! Punch? No wonder you don't want to help me. You're *afraid* of him."

"He's not like that anymore," Lewis whispered. "Since Maggi's been, um, friendly with him, he's kind of left me alone." His cheeks got redder. "He even pisses in the urinal now."

"So you weren't telling me, even though you knew I've been trying to get her to notice me. All because *your* life has gotten easier, since she's been all nicey-nice with him."

"An easier life is no small thing," he said, then screwed his face into a frown. "Has anyone ever pantsed you in a room full of people when you were carrying a bunch of stuff you couldn't just drop? Nooo! That kind of shit doesn't *ever* happen to the Great Carson Mastick."

"You ain't got nothing worth checking out anyway. I've seen you in the locker room."

"Exactly what Jim says. And between the two of you? Lately *he's* been the nicer one."

" 'Cause Maggi *made* him stop."

"So what's it going to take to make *you* stop this?" Lewis said. Doobie fidgeted. "Jim *never* claimed to be my friend, but you? We've been through a lot together. Why are you *always* such a dick? Even after we went out on the line for you, *twice*, you couldn't bother to say thanks." Doobie nodded. There was truth in what Lewis was saying. I had complimented him on his playing at the Battle of the Bands, but I hadn't said thank you.

"There's your ma," Doobie said when headlights flashed. "I'm heading out."

"You just . . . I don't know," Lewis said as Doobie headed upstairs. "Do you just *expect* that people owe you something?"

INTERLUDE TWO
IMAGINE

December 8, 6:59 p.m.

The Seneca man worried about the contamination starts to travel across Manhattan. He intends to seek out the musician and the artist, though he does not know their schedules. He wishes to enlist their help again, hoping they will lend their voices. He is exhausted from traveling and decides he will head home, to the Onondaga Nation Territories, the place where they had become allies. Though his cause is urgent, he is not worried, believing there will be another day.

The man who traveled across the continent waits. He has purchased a book during the day that he feels represents him. He writes in the book that this is his "statement." The man talks more with the amateur photographer, who eventually departs. The man talks with a young woman who also waits. This is a common activity for local fans of the musician. The man asks her out, but she declines and leaves. He has several plans, but one overall goal. If his plan is altered by any interaction this evening, he is not worried, believing there will be another day.

The musician and the artist are at the Record Plant, mixing a new song. It is called "Walking on Thin Ice." The wife sings lead, and the husband declares this will be her first number one. He says they should do all their future projects together, supporting each other. The photographer plans to show them "proofs" and take more photos at the studio. Things do not go according to plan, and she doesn't get there. She is not worried, believing there will be another day.

34

Give Me Something

Magpie Bokoni

December 8, 6:59 p.m.

"All right, now," Jim said, leaning over, inches from me. His cologne hadn't started to mingle with him yet. "Make these last." He dropped two rolls of quarters into my hand.

"Why can't you skip out on this?" I said. "I mean, it's friggin' bowling." I kissed his sideburn. "Isn't what we're gonna do more important?"

"Told you. Semifinals. This'll decide our ranking, and . . ." he said, grinning with a weird pride, "we're in the running to win the tourney." He held my chin, his calluses, hard and tough. "If I missed, they'd know something was up."

I went into the bowling alley, giving Jim time to come in alone. I called Tami to remind her that I was supposedly staying at her place. I couldn't even anticipate a time when Jim would be done with bowling and his stupid Monday Night Football. When our dad watched, it pissed Marvin off because they never ended when they said they were going to and he liked *M*A*S*H* reruns at 11:30, on a different channel. Our dad would say, "Wanna watch your own shows? Buy your own TV." (As if we could just do that.)

Some people were open-bowling. The front-desk guy (who rented out hideous shoes to people who didn't have their own) reminded them over the PA that leagues started at 7:30, and they had to be cleared out by 7:15. I found a snack bar, lounge, and two sets of restrooms (near the lounge and snack bar). A bunch of photos on the walls featured past leagues. I was supposed to be in the arcade section before the league players started wandering in. The quarter rolls Jim had given me felt impossibly heavy and like nothing at all, two strips of silver minutes I'd have to spend until we were together again.

December 8, 7:59 p.m.

The arcade, such as it was, had three pinball machines, a pool table, and two boxy machines the guys in my school loved: *Space Invaders* and *Pac-Man*. I wasn't any good and felt guilty spending Jim's quarters. I wanted to save them, but the big NO LOITERING IN ARCADE sign was a direct signal that I needed to drop quarters if I wanted to go unnoticed.

It felt weird to be the only person playing video games. I pictured other kids my age doing homework or watching TV or whatever regular high school sophomores did on a school night. I could have thrown my history book into my bag to study for Friday's unit test, but I didn't want even the smallest reminder of that part of my life.

A couple of guys wandered in and took turns on *Space Invaders*. We didn't recognize each other, so we didn't talk (our school's stupid sports rivalry bled over into all aspects of school life, like I even cared). One eventually snapped a quarter on *Pac-Man*, laying claim to the machine as soon as I lost. It didn't take long.

I wandered down the lanes where Jim wasn't playing (he'd told me not to hang around, since his league was made up of district workers we'd both know). This side must have made up a Rez league. The bowlers were mostly what Carson called ChameleIndians, like him. The kind of people he'd asked to be involved in his Custard's

Last Stand protest. They might not know me, since I'd only moved back so recently. I thought I was safe until I got near the snack bar.

There, near the far lanes, I saw Carson's parents. I peeled back and ducked into the front ladies' room. It wasn't even nine o'clock yet. I couldn't stay there all night. I'd brought a cap (one of Marie's bead-work jobs, so no disguise whatsoever). I did have an enormous pair of gradient sunglasses Jim had given me, calling them my Yoko Ono glasses. He joked that he'd buy me hot-pants outfits like hers if I let him take them off me.

I tied my hair with a little purple elastic into an explosion on top, to go with the glasses. Not flattering, but no one from the Rez would expect an Indian girl making this hair statement. I headed to the snack bar on Jim's side, studying the plaques and photos so I didn't face the bowlers. All along, laughter burst from every lane. I just didn't see how bowling could be that fun. Maybe it was something that happened to you when you got older.

December 8, 8:59 p.m.

If anyone paid attention to me, wandering, they'd notice I was LOITERING. Those boys had the two arcade room video games monopolized with their marathon games, and eventually I got sick of all this dodging. I placed a snack bar order for fries in Jim's name, asking them to page him over the PA, and went to the back ladies' until his name was called. He stomped in a little later, slightly drunk and irri-tated, ready to insist he hadn't ordered any damn fries. "I had to get your attention," I said, stopping him. "I know you didn't want me going where you're playing. But the other side must be a Rez league. I can't stay there either."

"What do you want me to do?" he grumbled. "I can't leave. No one can think anything weird."

Jim had told me the few times we'd been out in public locally that if we were recognized, he'd flee the scene and leave me hanging wher-ever I was, then circle around later to meet up again. Tonight didn't feel like that. No matter what, he wasn't going to ditch me and come back acting vaguely guilty. That was when I knew for sure this was going to be it. No teasing. No maybe. We weren't just going to see where the night took us. He had definite ideas. We were planning something trickier than a secret between two people.

"Then just give me your keys," I said. "I'll stay in your car until you're ready to leave. I'll listen to the radio, but I won't start it up except to run the heat when it gets too cold."

"They're in my jacket!" he said. "Go hang in the shelter. It's gonna take a few minutes to meet you. Gotta change my shoes." He had on those weird multicolored shoes bowlers wore. (Worse, his name was embroidered onto them—he *owned* them!) Like Carson's parents.

I went out. In the reflected glass of those framed photos, I could see Liz, the garage woman who'd taken a dislike to me. Her eyes followed me. I had to fight the urge to speed up. I couldn't let her think I was *me*, running away from *her*.

The bowling alley had been built into a hill and stuck out, held up by pillars. This area was the "shelter" (which wasn't much of one as far as I was concerned). The wind whipped me, and I stood against a pillar near Jim's Bandit. He finally showed and unlocked the car, starting it up. "Get in," he said. "Brought you these," he said, handing me the little boat of fries I'd ordered.

"Sorry, sorry, sorry," he continued with a murmur as we got in. After glancing around the shelter, he reached over and kissed me hard. He slid his left hand up under my top and stroked my boob through the bra. "Oh, yeah, that silk one again. Just a little while longer. I'm gonna take that off with my teeth."

For the first time, Jim didn't taste like Binaca. It was a combination of beer and cigar with a little bit of french fry grease and ketchup on top. He pulled away, doing that weird lip-puckering thing.

"Man, I want you so bad I could take you right here and right now." He kept rubbing on me and then took my hand and placed it on the crotch of his jeans. It was firmer than I expected. "I gotta get back in there, or I'm gonna pop," he said, grinning. "What you do to me!"

He rammed his head into the driver's side headrest and exhaled jaggedly. Then he looked over and smiled. "I filled the Bandit this morning. Run it as long as you want. Just watch the temperature gauge. Don't let that get too hot." He pointed to a dashboard dial with a cartoon thermometer on it.

"Oh, here's something for you to do, while you're waiting," he added, reaching under his seat with a grin. He held out a flimsy brown bag. "I picked it up today. Brand-new interview with your *friends* John and Yoko." He pulled out a shiny, brand-new issue of *Playboy*, and handed it to me, flicking his eyebrows up and down. "Ignore the nudie pics. *I* do. I buy it for the *articles*," he laughed.

"Right," I said. "The articles."

"They do great interviews. You'll get to catch up with your idols. All right, see you soon." He ran in, and I switched to the driver's seat. The fries were cold and rubbery, but I ate them. It was nearing ten o'clock. At least another hour, maybe longer, to go. The car heater was drying my eyes out but was luxurious, so I closed them to doze a little, slinking down to enjoy the dark and warm heater fan. If I had imagined correctly, I was going to have a later night than usual, and I wanted to be fully alert, for when my whole life changed.

Even drowsy, though, my curiosity started nagging at me. I sat up and grabbed the *Playboy*, looking at its cover. Their names were there, with a promise that they were going to talk about love, fame, money, and sex. It stressed the Beatles were going to be a major topic too. That other magazine Jim had given me, that *Avant Garde* art magazine, had also featured them on the cover. I wondered what life was like when you were so famous, every little thing you did became the cover story. I guess that's what Carson was shooting for, while I had to slink around, trying not to be noticed by anyone. It was a good thing I didn't want that fame life.

I wasn't so big a fool that I could pretend this relationship wasn't going to be tricky. If Jim and I stayed together, we were going to have to do it in private, at least for a few years. He was white and in his thirties. He could blend in almost anywhere he wanted, but if you put an underage Indian girl next to him, people were going to notice, and it wasn't going to be in a good way. We would have to be strong enough to face that together. We were.

The cover also mentioned Stephen King, the guy who wrote *The Shining*, and some other science-fiction people. Maybe I should take it home so Marvin could have some thrills. He'd be mortified if I gave him a naked-lady magazine (mostly because we both knew he'd check it out when he was alone). The model on the cover was Barbara Bach, who I thought was dating Ringo Starr. It really *was* a Beatles issue. I opened the *Playboy* and found the interview. It was long.

Flipping through, I tried ignoring the "pictorials." (They weren't as outright in your face as John's drawings of Yoko had been, but these were real people! Real women who'd known they'd had a camera pointed at them and they took off their clothes anyway!)

Yeah, imagine some pervy old guy, standing there, staring at you while you took your clothes off in front of him, Ghost Marvin contributed.

I found myself studying the women's faces, and then looking in the rearview mirror. It still wasn't easy for me to make those expressions. Definitely not natural. Mostly I looked like a dork (or more accurately, a constipated duck). Maybe you could only make that face turn into something sexy after you were a woman. I'd have to look in the mirror at the end of the night to discover if I'd learned a new expression.

INTERLUDE THREE
REVOLVER

December 8, 10:49 p.m.

One West Seventy-Second Street, Manhattan, New York City: The musicians, husband and wife, skip dinner plans. They return to see their five-year-old son before he goes to bed. The weather is warm for early December. They decide to be let out of their hired car at the sidewalk instead of behind the gates, inside the secured courtyard. The musician walks to the building's entrance. Maybe he sees someone who seems vaguely familiar, but he moves on.

The man who had held out an album hours ago now holds a different object. It is an object whose name is linked to the musician, from a different marriage, a different life. The musician and his group of three other musicians had, during their ten-year marriage, once named an album for this object. They said they named the album because albums spin on a turntable. Albums are revolvers. Billboard *hits are "Number 1 with a Bullet!" Bam! The man who traveled across the country did not make this trip to meet the musician with an album in hand. He planned all along to meet the musician with a different Revolver. A .38. The man fires at the musician's back five times, at close range. Four of his hollow point bullets, used for maximum damage, find their target. The musician falls and says he's shot. The doorman calls the police. When they arrive, the doorman points at the man with the Revolver. He tells them the man shot John Lennon.*

The Seneca man gets home. He discovers that the world keeps revolving, but not for everyone.

35

Scared
Carson Mastick

December 8, 10:59 p.m.

"Thank you, Lewis," I said. "Thank you for *everything* you've done. There! Better?"

"No, it's not better," he said, and I frowned, impatient. "You don't mean it."

"Okay. I wasn't really hoping you'd be good backup in a fight," I said, still struck by the lies people can tell themselves. Doobie had left, and Lewis, alone, thought he had the edge here.

"That isn't something a friend would say, but it *does* sound like you," he said. I had to turn over my last card and hope it worked. If I had to reveal a secret weapon, I was glad I had one. I thought about everything I'd overheard that guy say in the garage that afternoon, the way he'd treated Lewis at the Labor Day party.

"But it *is* something a friend's telling you," I said, picturing those *Land of the Giants* opening credits, a cartoon Lewis in a spotlight he didn't want, captured by a massive man. "This friend. For your own good. Ever wonder why that Jim messes with you? Why, out of all the scrawny work kids, he dumps on you?" Lewis knew I was going to tell him the truth.

"Cowards go for easy targets," he said. He *couldn't* think his luck was that shitty, could he? "I've been small my whole life. I never get to control things." He thought, forming ahead whatever he wanted to say. "*You* surround yourself with people you think you can control. But you really just deliver a good enough time that I choose to stick around. There's one small thing I can control. *I* put up with *you*, even though you're a dick. It's never occurred to you, but I can walk away at any time. You don't put up with me. I put up with you." Did *I* want the truth? Was *I* ready?

"Please? Just come! I'll give you the details on the way, but we got to go!" I said.

"Look, Maggi's choices are her business, not mine. You're mad she didn't pick you. That's in *her* control. You feeling like you've been blocked isn't reason enough for me to act."

"You think it's as messed up as I do but you *like* being left alone. You think that guy's done with you? She's probably gonna sleep with him partly to keep him off *your* back, and because he did us a big favor."

Lewis gave me his patented *Yeah, Right!* Look.

"Remember Groffini didn't know why Marchese pulled the deficiency mark? That guy Jim told Marchese he swapped out the turkeys, and he apologized." I still hadn't been clear enough for this to sink in. "Lewis! Guys who buy *Hustler*? Even their favorite centerfolds, they eventually get rid of them when the right new one comes along."

"What? Look, drop this. She . . ." He hated when I used his own info against him.

"Lewis," I said, locking eyes. "Grow up! That guy Jim can't take Maggi's virginity twice. Once he's got that itch scratched, he'll need some other kind of fun, then it's straight back to yanking old Lewis's drawers down and nut-punching him. Don't kid yourself. Maggi's just a little pause in this guy's life."

"What do you think that has to do with me?" I'd wanted Lewis to do this for my reasons, but I had to go with the nuclear option, the one thing guaranteed to get a reaction out of him.

"That guy is Evan Reiniger's uncle, Lewis. Evan's uncle. Maybe as close as you and your uncle. I overheard him talking about you once, but I didn't put everything together until just tonight. Evan's *still* hassling your ass even though he hasn't been in school for what? Four years? Did you think he was going to forget about you? He still found you, and it ain't gonna end because that Jim finally got the piece of ass he's been fantasizing about." I handed him his jacket, the jacket his own uncle had given him.

"You are *so* lying," Lewis said. But Evan Reiniger, I could see, still lived inside Lewis's brain. The guy who stole Lewis's Brainiac title. The boogeyman who had never left.

"Decide when we get there whether you're gonna help or not, but you might get some satisfaction giving this Jim some of the shit he's been dishing you. You can stay in the car if you're too chicken, but please!" Lewis's breath rushed through his nostrils, more fear than anger. He'd stood up for Derek, and for me, and now I wanted him to stand up for himself. "Use that new pair of balls you grew," I said.

It was too easy to get him that way, but it worked, and I didn't have time to fart around. A few minutes later, with Lewis riding shotgun and Derek in back after we picked him up, I headed to the bowling alley.

"Sorry, guys." Derek said when we pulled into the shelter. "I was up for a rumble, but *that* would send me to jail." He pointed at a van. Its side was covered with the Custard's Last Stand logo, including a cartoon of Marchese's husband, guns blazing. Teachers *did* bowl?

"How about this?" I said, pulling the two cans of red spray paint.

"That I can do," Derek said, grinning. I watched as he rattled spray paint cans.

"So, any ideas?" I asked Lewis as Derek started a red cloud around the van.

"I'm going to wander around, see if I can find Jim's car," he said.

"Well, you *do* know what it looks like. Marvin says it's got Maggi's name pinstriped on the passenger door." Lewis dropped his eyes. He'd already seen that, maybe even some time ago, and he'd kept silent. Inside my coat pocket, I wrapped Lewis's chain around my wrist, leaving a few feet hanging before the lock. I wanted the power of swinging the chain. If I found that Bandit first, I could bust windows or dent doors, or tear side mirrors off for starters.

Derek was a natural vandal. He'd have better ideas.

"What the hell are you doing?" I asked, walking over to where he was working.

"I don't want to go to jail, Little Brother. You can't change the world from a jailbird cell. But he'll see this message." In the gravel, he'd sprayed a crime-scene body outline in the stones, the ass all saturated. "Custard's gotta know what he's doing is messed up, right?"

I wanted to be honest, but I just looked at him. I still didn't really get why he'd walked into Custard's that night to rob the place, why he had chosen to strike fear, why he avoided a peaceful protest. Didn't he remember how the Onondagas had made it work? Had Derek maybe chosen to forget, thinking that alone, he'd never bring enough people together?

"I don't mean *just* about shooting my ass," Derek said, holding my eye. "What I did was stupid, no argument. So maybe my First Aid Scar will remind me there's all kinds of bad ideas floating around out there. Don't make the same mistake I did, okay? I coulda come out much worse. But the rest? The name of the place, his stupid costume, that sign? He's gotta know that's screwed up, right?" He didn't wait for me to share an opinion and handed me the second spray can, still full. "Soon as I'm done, I'm taking the back way to Red Man's Drop and following it to the Rez. Don't forget to pick me up when you're done."

36

Walking on Thin Ice
Magpie Bokoni

December 8, 11:09 p.m.

The last section of the *Playboy* interview was about writing songs, both the Beatles' and John's solo work. Jim had teased me, saying "your friends John and Yoko" when he handed me this magazine, but he was kind of right. Even without my being aware, they'd somehow become a part of me, a part of my life and the ways I thought about the world. And their world wasn't so far away from mine.

Yoko was having an art show in Syracuse, her first solo show in America, and they'd heard the Onondagas were refusing to let the state build a thruway through their Rez. The state kept raising the stakes, thinking the Onondagas were holding out. They couldn't understand our connection to our land, the thing that brought my mom back to my dad. She claimed it was for us, but I think I understood now, months after, that she'd been waiting for the day she could return.

I could imagine John and Yoko coming here, and standing up for the Porter Agreement, so my family could keep our Table without worry. We had treaty rights but still were forced to apply for our permit every year, as if we'd stopped being Indians sometime in the previous 364 days. John and Yoko were living, breathing examples that you could take preexisting ideas and forms and make them your own, that you could be true to your traditions, yourself, and your art (and to one another, which brought me back to a new truth creeping into my horizon).

I hated that this love of my life had to be secret. I thought I was going to be okay with it, but the longer I sat in this car, the more I realized I wasn't. Girls in school always said *my boyfriend did this and that*, but what was I going to say?

My boyfriend lent me his porno mag while he went bowling on the night we made love for the first time, was Ghost Marvin's suggestion.

In the interview, John had no issue saying which songs were his and which were Paul's. Even when it wasn't a fifty-fifty partnership, they worked together, and all those Beatles songs wouldn't be the same if they hadn't shared responsibility. This new album was different. You knew John's songs *and* Yoko's. I couldn't decide which was better.

I loved playing in the band, adding my own signatures, and being able to make those additions with confidence. With Jim, I felt less like I was that bold. You didn't have to love your music partner, but you should be able to have a say in how your romance develops without worrying about upsetting that person's desires. The way this whole night had been planned out came from Jim's mind and Jim's alone—I would never have come up with the idea of sitting in a car, waiting for hours because someone didn't want to be seen with me. I don't know how I would change things, but I hadn't had the opportunity. Which was better, collaboration, or clear, single decisions made by two separate people toward the same goal?

I dug around the cassettes inside Jim's console to find some music. Bingo! *Beatlesie Love Songs for My Girl.* The tape began with "And Your Bird Can Sing." The lame joke I'd heard my whole life, but Jim had somehow made it seem okay to hear my name as MaggiPie. The second song was "Woman," the one Jim played for me the night we almost finished taking each other's clothes off. I could picture him in the break room in only his briefs. Without him really standing that way in front of me right now, my memory made it seem sexy instead of goofy.

Suddenly, I couldn't wait until later, when I'd finish undressing him for real. Until this moment, I'd thought that I'd take his clothes off because he liked that idea, but I admitted to myself that, in the right place, I did want to do this. When was this going to end? I listened to the whole tape, trying to make time pass faster.

Partway through a second listen, I ejected it. Weirdly, John Lennon was on the radio too. How random! And it wasn't even a hit. It was "Remember," from *Plastic Ono Band*. Lewis always noted how *raw* it was, but it just sounded like John Lennon to me. Maybe stripped down (Jim in his briefs popped into my head again, and I laughed what Carson called my Scandalous Rez Girl Laugh, and that blue flash sparked through me again).

I could hear individual instruments as the song went on. Piano, bass, and drums. Yeah, stripped down. (Again, Jim. Again, laugh.) Its drum pattern was so weird. I wasn't sure I'd be able to master it if we ever decided to do it. I liked that it ended with a sound effects explosion too. Just neat and sudden. A shock you couldn't anticipate.

"And that was 'Remember,' by John Lennon," the DJ said when it ended. "Off the classic, raw *Plastic Ono Band*." (Did Lewis get all his ideas from DJs?) "And that is what we're doing tonight. Remembering John Lennon." (What?) "For those of you just tuning in, tragic news from New York City. As we get more details, we'll pass them along. A little before eleven o'clock tonight, John Lennon was shot and killed outside his apartment building. Just forty years old. For the rest of the night, we'll be bringing you—"

I switched it off. It had to be wrong.

I looked around the parking lot. No movement. Nothing different. Shouldn't the world look changed? It felt changed. Like it would never be the same. I pulled the keys and ran into the building. Everything at the lanes looked the same, people sitting around, adding scores, drinking beers. The DJ *had* to have been wrong.

Then I looked at the man at the counter, setting a big, clumsy microphone on the desk, and he looked like he was going to be sick. He made a brief phone call, and a few seconds later, "Imagine" came over the speakers mounted in the ceiling, and I knew it was true. I ran to the lounge. Even if they tried to kick me out, I had to find Jim.

Inside the murky room, my eyes adjusted. The far corner was dominated by a projection TV straight out of Marvin's space shows, cheaply futuristic. Three light cannons, blue, red, and green, were mounted below a curved screen, pointing at a low unit that reflected onto a big screen. The picture was like TV through a dirty fish tank.

The packed room buzzed. Some talked quietly while others raged. No one paid me any attention. On TV, *Nightline* began, Ted Koppel saying they had a suspect in custody. He cut to footage of the Beatles. The woman reporting got basic Beatles facts wrong, stuff even *I* knew!

Some people in the lounge held each other, crying, but a lot studied the TV, like maybe there was some way they could change the facts of the past hour, to alter the way this fell apart. I worked my way to the front, to catch people's faces. Finally, I spotted Jim at a table, his eyes on me.

As I moved, he shook his head slowly and held his hand up in a small "stop" gesture.

Anyone else would think he was telling himself this news couldn't be, but I knew what he was saying. I understood, suddenly, that this was what he'd be saying to me for at least another year. Probably longer. We'd never hold hands window-shopping at the mall, or go for ice cream, trying each other's cones. We'd never kiss at the edge of the Falls, with a giant rainbow spraying out of mist, like all the other couples in love visiting our city. We would never shop for just the right tourist souvenir to commemorate our vacation. I had known we wouldn't, but now I *knew* we wouldn't, and I knew I wanted it. I wanted it and I deserved it.

I wasn't ever going to be MaggiPie, not really. I might be Motel Room Maggi, but that was it. I hadn't even seen Jim's apartment yet.

Liz, the garage bitchlette, came up and hugged him, crying. I had a hard time feeling bad for her. At first, she'd insisted on using Magpie, the full name I hated, but even that wasn't humiliating enough. Lately, she'd settled on SkagPie—calling me what she'd thought of me all along.

Emphasis on the "Skag," Ghost Marvin jabbed, my predictably charming twin.

Liz shared one of Carson's talents. Like all crappy nicknames, like Stinkpot, Liz knew how to arrive at those that would stick. If Jim and I started seeing each other in public, I'd be SkagPie forever.

37

Happiness Is a Warm Gun
Carson Mastick

December 8, 11:29 p.m.

"I found Jim's car," Lewis said, and I stood up to follow him.

"You should spray paint a big cherry on the Bandit's back deck," Derek said, a phrase I'd never use. Vulgar for something special. Okay, I would for someone else, but not someone I cared about. "I'm outta here," he called. "Don't get caught." Dressed in black, he disappeared. He'd learned how to be a Vanishing Indian, even without the help of Edward Curtis's camera.

The Bandit's hood was still warm when we got to it, engine ticking. "Maggi's bag," Lewis said, pointing to the passenger's seat. "And *Playboy*?" Weird. What the hell was going on? The word *MaggiPie* and a tiny pinstripe bird were still on the door. Naturally, this asshole would have a giant predator on his hood for himself and a vulnerable bird for her. Like Marvin said—easily scraped and sanded off, buffed out and polished into nothing.

"Listen," Lewis said. "I'm going inside. Maybe I can talk her into leaving with us." He walked toward the bowling alley and disappeared. I stared at the Bandit for a while, thinking Lewis would be right back. I knew what it was to love a car. Eventually, I pulled out

Lewis's bike chain and swung the lock for momentum. Aiming, I neatly busted the taillight.

Maybe I could spray that hood decal too. How would that look with a big gash across it? Not Derek's suggestion, but something else. What? Something he'd have to see every time he drove. I really wanted to swing this lock and whack that guy's nuts as hard as I could. Put him out of commission. But Lewis should get to see that. Where was he?

Just then, a PA system clicked on. Did this rinky-dink bowling alley have security cameras too? I had a trucker cap and hooded sweatshirt on under my coat, but cameras would have caught the Chevelle's arrival. I was so stupid! Instead of a Rent-A-Cop yelling at me to freeze, though, John Lennon's "Imagine" started playing. What the hell? Was he *everywhere*? His new album was decent, but it wasn't *that* good.

The music faded out, and I heard someone take a breath.

"Attention, Frontier players and patrons." The guy's voice sounded thick, like he had a cold. "If you're still at your lanes, you haven't heard. The news just reported that John Lennon's been shot outside his home in New York City. He was rushed to Roosevelt Hospital, which I guess is nearby? . . . But he was pronounced dead on arrival. We'll extend lounge hours. Monday Night Football's just ended. *Nightline*'s beginning full coverage, if you're interested. Up here, we'll keep piping his music, from us at Frontier, to you, as we report this terrible news."

"Imagine" came back, followed by "Strawberry Fields Forever," as I walked to the entrance. Was this some prank of Lewis's because he'd chickened out? Typical, but getting a bowling alley clerk to use the PA? Impressive. I had to check it out, admit he'd gotten me. He was usually a crappy prankster, but this was amazing. Maybe the best ever, for him.

Before I got to the door, a guy charged at it. Not the one I'd come here for, but maybe better. Even without his Cavalry costume, I recognized Custard and his ridiculous mustache and pageboy. He was alone. I slid my hand in my coat pocket and felt Lewis's bike chain. When Custard stepped out, I ducked behind a pillar, eventually following. I knew where he'd parked.

The parking shelter PA piped in audio from *Nightline*. Ted Koppel said they were cutting to a reporter outside the New York City hospital. It was real? You could hear people surrounding the reporter, hundreds it sounded like, and you knew the kind of goons they were without even seeing them. They were the kind just trying to get on TV, even as the cameraman would attempt to zoom on the reporter, and for the rest of their lives, they'd say in their gooniest voices: "I was on TV the night John Lennon got shot."

The ER doctors did a press conference. They confirmed the victim was Lennon and that the damage was so bad, he'd probably been dead when the first bullet hit. Seemed like a convenient lie to me, a way to say there'd been nothing they could do. But you could understand the impulse to lie, to save face. And to most of those directly in front of them, what they said didn't even matter. I could picture the goons, not even listening, trying to get their ass faces on TV. Like Custard, parading around on local news after he'd shot Derek in the butt. That's what so many ass faces thought *FAME* was: being at the right place at the right time.

Here, there were only two of us. Me and Custard. No witnesses. No one to say, "I was there when Custard *really* made his last stand." No one except me. And I wasn't gonna talk.

"What the hell?" he muttered, looking at the red body outline. He unlocked his van, threw his bowling bag in it, and started kicking gravel, spreading the stones. Truth? I was relieved. He'd seen it. He'd remember it. And there was no evidence it had ever existed.

"Feeling guilty, General Custard?" I asked, stepping out.

"What?" he said, looking up, puzzled. Tears on his cheek shone in the shelter lights. "What do I got to feel guilty about?"

"You don't remember shooting someone recently?" I asked, stepping closer.

"I shot someone in self-defense. Said he had a gun!"

"Did you see a gun?"

"Said he had one. Said it was in his sweatshirt pocket. Looked enough like a gun to me."

"Does this look like a gun?" I said, pushing my pocketed hand forward. "It's not. Just so you know. In case you're still strapping handguns around your waist."

"Don't get cocky, son. You do this? The spray paint? I know you. You're the kid who screwed up my business this fall. I kept that article. I got your face blown up on the wall."

"Like a Wild West poster? Wanted Dead or Alive?"

"My workers have orders to refuse you service and call the cops on your trespassing ass."

"Don't you even get that you *shot someone*, you redneck piece of shit?" I said, stepping closer. Custard did not back down. Maybe he *was* still carrying a gun. "That you decided to pull a loaded gun out of a holster, and point it at another person, and then fire."

"Like I said," he mumbled, shrugging. Then, suddenly cocky, he grinned. "Self-defense. Wasn't me stepping into a place of business, planning to rob someone. Live by the sword—"

"You're crying about the news and you say *that*? Did Lennon live by the sword? Or did some asshole with a loaded gun just decide that shooting someone was okay, the best thing to do?"

"You can't compare what I did to this! This was one of the Beatles! Someone who changed the world! That little shit at my place was just another drunk Indian! Maybe I shouldn't have aimed so generous. I'm a good shot, and I was in the right." He looked with worry at the way my hands were bunched inside my jacket pockets.

The PA said the person in custody was being called a local screwball. Who had been the local screwball here? The burger joint owner strapped with revolvers, naming himself for a western Indian Killer, or my stupid brother, trying to make a political point by stealing burgers and cash?

"If you were in the right, how come you lied? That revolver wasn't loaded with blanks."

"How would you know? You involved?"

"*You* know those were live rounds," I observed.

"I was involved."

"But you lied on record. You get rid of bullets and casing? Tampering with evidence."

"No one come forward to complain about what kind of bullet was in his ass. Just my word out there." We stared at each other. The news in the air listed ways things should have been better—Lennon lived blocks from the hospital, the cops arrived immediately—but it didn't work out. "Kid. Take your hand out of your pocket. Please. There's been enough violence for one night."

Even here, Custard was on guard, and I only noticed in that moment that his hands were in his coat pockets too. The PA faded the news out and put music back on. Must be a greatest hits. I imagine they'd release something else now, including a couple songs off the new album. Now that there wouldn't be any other new ones.

"Kid, please," he moaned. I slowly pulled my hand out. The chain was wrapped around it several times. Eventually, the Master Lock end dropped, dangling in the breeze. I started twisting my wrist, and the lock swung, its arc getting wider and stronger.

"General Custard? Take *your* hands out of your pockets," I said, stepping forward.

38

I'm Moving On
Magpie Bokoni

December 8, 11:39 p.m.

"Maggi!" someone whispered in my ear. Damn! I'd been noticed. "I've come for you."

"Lewis?" He put his arms around me, and we cried together. I could feel his body hitch.

"I feel like I've been heart-punched," he said, hugging me harder. "Like I've lost someone in my family." It felt good, but not like the way Jim hugged me. Lewis wasn't pressing his pelvis into mine. This felt like someone who cared for *me*.

Not for my body, my own internal voice suddenly said. It had been waiting to spring and leapt as soon as I'd seen Jim hold up his hand to stop me. That was not the action of a man who loved me. It was the action of someone who, even in a moment like this, was worried about being caught in some compromising position. And once that idea landed in my skull, others joined it.

Sometimes they sounded like my mom, sometimes Marie, and sometimes, of course, Ghost Marvin. The harshest ones, though, I recognized as my own, the observations I'd been unwilling to acknowledge. Naturally, *I* wanted to be seen as an equal to Jim, but the flip side was more questionable.

Right, the new voice said. *An adult has a world of experience to offer a young person, but* why *does a thirty-year-old man* want *that kind of relationship with a fifteen-year-old?* None of the answers were great.

But there could be a reasonable answer. Maybe you're more fun when you're young. You don't know what kind of life you'll have when you're thirty, I tried to tell the New Voice.

Exactly! it said back. Every time I tried to convince myself we'd come this far because I was so mature, all I could picture were the times he'd rubbed up against me because it made him feel so good, and the sexy things he'd said when no one else was around, the things he asked me to do for him, and the ways he asked me, always, to take things further than I was ready for. I could only come up with one answer.

What he wanted was sex with a fifteen-year-old.

Jim had made it clear we weren't going to be together in any regular sense, because others wouldn't understand, and somehow, I'd told myself that it was worth it, to be considered mature enough.

"Carson's here too," Lewis said as he pulled away. He looked directly into my eyes, seeing me, a person with my own choices. "Marvin told us what you're planning."

You're welcome, sister, Ghost Marvin said, but I did not dignify it with a response.

"We had some lame idea to . . ." Lewis said, pausing. He knew he was about to say something stupid, something wrong he couldn't take back. "I don't know, rescue you? I don't want you doing something you're going to regret, just to help me, or to help Carson. You should love the person you . . . you know. Shouldn't you?"

"What I do is my business," I said, my teeth gritted between my lips. "I *have* feelings for Jim." With that harsh voice inside my head, I suddenly couldn't bring myself to say I loved Jim. Not to Lewis. Maybe not even to myself. But still. "I was going ahead because *I* wanted to. No one decides what I do but me!" (But someone *had* been trying to decide, hadn't he?)

"You don't want to anymore?" he asked. Lewis, always the grammarian, heard me use the past tense.

"You and Carson can't decide who I'm interested in, or who Marie's interested in, or anyone." He nodded. "Look up there. Yoko Ono didn't break up the Beatles. She just fell in love with someone who loved her back. And he just *happened* to be a Beatle. Look at the shit they went through together." I kept picturing Jim holding his hand up, that little shake of his head.

"And now she's probably in some stupid emergency room, all alone," I added, appreciating the feeling, a small tear in my heart, bleeding out, with no one to tell.

"I don't know what Carson's doing out in the parking shelter, but I pointed out Jim's car," Lewis said. "We might wanna get out of here. I'm sure this is all over the radio."

"Lewis! Jeez, you guys!" I punched his chest, tight, with the butt of my hand, as we held each other. "Grow up," I said. "I have stuff in there. And *I've* got the keys!"

"Damn!" he said, and looked down for a second, then tried studying the room, but his eyes were always drawn back to the TV. "Okay," he said, finally, trying on a face like the one he wore before the wrestling match months ago. "We're going to sit down with Jim, as if we just happened to be here. If Carson wanders in, I'll distract him." He started, and I had the choice to walk away or join him, which wasn't really a choice at all.

We walked deeper into the lounge and over to Jim's table, where he pretended not to see us. Eventually, without any other option, he looked up, eyes wide in fake surprise as we sat down. All three of us simmered in silence.

"I'm leaving with Lewis," I said to Jim after a minute. Some of his initial alarm was gone, and he listened, clenching his jaws. "I gotta get my bag from your car and I'll leave the keys in that magnet box." He'd shown it to me, hidden in a wheel well, saying he was going to put a set there for me one day. "I understand that you can't walk me out. We'll pretend we bumped into you." He tried to keep neutral, but a few tears slid down his cheek. He didn't wipe them away. Maybe they were for John Lennon.

"How can you even be crying?" Lewis said to Jim. "You and your fucked-up family have been casually ruining people's lives for years. That's what makes this possible. This asshole who just killed John Lennon? He just wants to advertise how powerful he is. What a big, strong man. Sound familiar?"

Jim leaned forward, his knuckles on the table. "Only a few more months, you little turd," he said, grimacing. "You won't be going to school anymore, and you'll be an adult. Better hope I don't find you somewhere alone."

"But you don't like adults, Jim," Lewis said, and he gave him the same kind of face pat Jim used to give to him at the garage. "In fact, you prefer people who aren't. A lot of people know that?" Jim's cheek muscles jumped. A look passed between them.

"I'm not afraid of you, anymore," Lewis said. "Or your asshole nephew who has to send grown men to fight boys. You're both just a couple of pathetic losers. You're so sad you can't even find a woman your own age who wants to spend time with you, let alone sleep with your sad, pathetic loser ass."

I grabbed Lewis's hand away before he could use Jim's old trick back on him, finishing that pat in a real slap. He didn't know Jim like I did.

Or maybe he knows him better, the New Voice said.

"See you around, Jim," Lewis said, more confident than I'd ever seen him. We stood up and left the lounge.

39

Give Peace a Chance
Carson Mastick

December 8, 11:49 p.m.

"No!" a stranger's voice shouted from behind me. I turned, and in that second, I knew I shouldn't have. Custard jumped from the front and the stranger crashed into me from behind. I guessed it was Jim, whose face I now recognized. We all whaled on each other, landing random punches. For all my badass talk, I'd never been in a real brawl.

A real punch to the face is not like what you see in movies. You feel the knuckles. I don't know whose, but I got clocked a few times, mostly wild swings popping my cheeks. I was going to have a black eye, maybe two. Suddenly, one of those guys was off. Jim. Lewis must have slammed him in the gut and now they were tangling together to the side.

I scrambled up, and when Custard tried to do so next to me, I rested a boot heel on his right hand. He struggled, attempting to get his hand free. Was he going for his jacket pocket?

"Don't move if you wanna keep your trigger finger," I growled. He moaned and started to move, and I loosened my foot suddenly as I saw the bloodied crushed stone underneath him.

Then I realized it wasn't blood. It was the stones Derek had sprayed red. I flashed to Lennon, probably surrounded by a similar pool, only real, as he took his last breaths on that sidewalk in New York City. How had that happened? Didn't he have security? Had he gotten too confident? I pictured Derek, staggering to my car, driving it the twenty minutes from Lockport hoping he'd reach home and not pass out, rather than call me for help. I thought of all the ways terrible things could and did happen, every day. And the way I could make this scumbag understand what it meant when you really chose to inflict harm on another person.

I lifted my boot fully and gave Custard a hard kick in the ass. He fell back on his belly and crawled away. He got up finally by his van and turned around to glare at me.

"You're gonna know real violence, someday," Custard snarled. He reached into his jacket pocket, but came out only with a set of keys. "Your kind always do—just you wait and see."

"Your kind too," I said, but he was already peeling away, red dust kicking up in his wake.

I turned away to investigate the noise coming from behind me. Lewis was now straddling Jim's back and squeezing his thighs together, digging into his sides. He raised both fists above his head, about to box Jim's ears. I just watched. The guy deserved a little pain from Lewis.

Jim arched his back, trying to stand, to throw him like a bronco, and Lewis grabbed at the guy's collar to hang on. I had this weird burst of Albert at the Sanborn Field Day, and then flashed on Jim's face. He was the guy who helped me get Albert out of that Beer Tent. I could kick his ass, literally, or poke the insides of his elbows, and he'd go down with Lewis on top of him. He'd never see me coming.

"Stop it! You jerks!"

That scream, Maggi, reverberated across the shelter and froze us all. Impossibly loud, her voice blasted out of her tiny rib cage and echoed off the corrugated tin shelter ceiling, like a high-powered guitar effects pedal. "Didn't any of you learn *anything* tonight! Grow up!" I looked at her for a second, then whipped my head back to the action.

Lewis and Jim slowly circled each other, both locked in, a little bloody and resigned. Lewis looked ready to go ahead, knowing it was going to cost him, but Jim looked wary at me over Lewis's shoulder. Lewis had already landed a few shots too. Jim understood that he'd be fighting us both and that he could come out bad. Unbelievably, though, before they could start anything, the PA started piping in "Give Peace a Chance." But it wasn't John Lennon—it was like a thousand terrible voices. The TV reporter said it was a crowd gathering outside the Dakota, singing, a sudden memorial.

We all looked up at the corrugated metal ceiling as Maggi joined us, Lewis and Jim pulling slightly away from each other. I couldn't read her expression—was she mad?—so I put my arm around Lewis. The places where his leather jacket had been mended were torn again, the newer threads broken.

"We're done here, buddy," I said, lifting a flap of leather. "C'mon, I'll fix this for you." The old me would have tried to convince him to leave it, because it would be badass. But Lewis liked things to at least seem neat on the outside, even if they were batshit crazy on the inside. "Better this time. I promise. For you. Let's go home."

"You remember what I told you," Jim said, scowling at Lewis as he joined me. "Better hope I don't find you alone."

"*You* better hope you don't," Lewis said back, and Jim suddenly got that vaguely fearful look again. I had no idea what they were talking about—there was some part of that story I was missing—but it didn't seem to matter. Lewis wasn't the stronger fighter, and he'd taken the worst of their scuffle physically, but he'd gotten this guy somehow. He had won.

"You coming, Maggi?" I said as we walked to the Chevelle. We didn't even bother keeping an eye on Jim.

40

There's No Goodbye
Magpie Bokoni

December 8, 11:59 a.m.

"You guys *go*," I said, with the strongest steel voice, one I almost never used. Well, no more. "Just *go*! I've got a ride here." I looked at Jim, deciding to be clear. "To the Rez." He pursed his puffy, split lip. I snapped my eyes, and he understood, nodding and lowering his head.

"Hey," Carson said, staring at me, standing in some gravel that I swore seemed to have blood on it. He tried coming closer, but I stepped back. "We came all this way to—"

"I make my decisions *on my own*, Carson! Not because you came down here, doing whatever dumb-ass thing you were planning." That was what I'd wanted to say, but by itself, it sounded too . . . something, given what had happened tonight. "Thank you, though, for thinking you were doing the right thing." I looked again at the gravel, and I saw the shattered red plastic behind Jim's Bandit.

"Paint," Carson said. "Not . . . something else." I pointed to the plastic. "Yeah, taillight too."

"Even wrongheaded, thank you too, Lewis." I turned to him. "For everything."

"You sure about this?" Lewis asked, giving me his no-bullshit eyes. "Want us to follow?"

"If you're really my friend, you won't," I said, which wouldn't sit well with him. "I can call your house when I get home. Let it ring once." I said that as much for Jim as for them, to let him know I wasn't changing my mind. If he didn't want to take me home, he should say so now, but I'd prefer that we get a chance to talk. The boys got in Carson's car and slowly pulled away.

"We're not going to the hotel," Jim said once their taillights had disappeared. He tried to say it firm, like he wanted it to be a decision and a question. Still thinking he was going to sleep with me tonight. Unbelievable! I wondered if he was even starting to get aroused as easily as he usually did, and this time, as I thought it, I got a different shiver. It was no longer excitement.

"We're not. Lewis expects my call. He knows how long it takes to get there from here."

"Fuck Lewis," he said, his voice like broken glass. "I want to take you to bed tonight and treat you right because I love you. Nothing's changed that." Others filtered out of the building, and Jim noticed. "Let's get in the car," he said, confirming everything I thought again. He was trying to hide resentment, but I knew the sound of that tone as well as I knew the sound of any song I'd committed to memory. Still, I got in, and we took the back exit.

"Jim, I *like* you," I said, and it hurt me to say it. "But I can't live my life waiting for the day *you* think it's okay for us to be a real couple. If all I am is some sex fantasy of yours, that's not a relationship. I know it sounds stupid and, I guess, young, but I want my first time to be with someone I love and who loves me the same."

"But I do, really," he said, and I could see a sad, horny hope in his face. Some juvenile part of him still thought he could argue his way into that Honeymoon Suite tonight.

"I'm at the beginning of high school, and *you've* probably got a decent chunk of retirement savings." He started to interrupt, again, thinking he still might find a yes tonight. "No," I said. "It's my time to talk. We can maybe figure something out, for the future. Or maybe in a little over a year, you'll still think this is worth looking into." I thought of all the things he was willing to just not let me experience, like regular dates, getting to know someone who's learning the world at the same time, even the senior-year craziness Marie was locking herself out of (there was no way Ben-Yaw-Mean was taking her to the prom, or that kind of thing).

What I didn't say too, and what my damned inner voice wouldn't let me unhear now, was that a thirty-year-old guy *shouldn't* find a fifteen-year-old that interesting, no matter how mature she was. I was a nice person, a nice girl. It felt funny saying that to myself, and to mean it, when I'd been fighting to be seen as a woman for so long. But it was true. There would be someone who loved me for me, someday, but it wasn't now, and it wasn't this. That one major thing making me attractive to him—that would be gone, I guess, by the end of an hour, if we went to the hotel. Surely that wouldn't keep us together. And even if there was more than just that detail, I was going to grow up. I decided not to say those things, but I added what I'd come to understand.

"Maybe *I'll* think it's worth looking into too. But there aren't any guarantees. We'll see then."

Even as I said it, I thought about that album Jim had given me. I wondered if I'd ever be able to play it without thinking about him, and if he would too. Our lives would be what happened to us, while we were busy making other plans.

"Reach into the console," he said as we drove down Dog Street, his voice ragged. He wanted to pretend he wasn't crying, in the same way I pretended I wasn't.

"I made a mixtape for you," he said. "Maybe you'd call it a Mixed-Up Tape, now. The label says BEATLESIE LOVE SONGS FOR MY GIRL. Corny, but that's what you do to me. You make me feel like a kid again, instead of the old man I'm becoming." I pretended to search, but I knew which one it was. "Play it and maybe think of me. I'm gonna put in a work transfer for you to go to the garage. Be too hard to see you, if we . . . if we're not . . ."

"No," I said, my new voice easier to access. I was tired of other people deciding my future. "Christmas break's coming. Wait 'til January. If it's too hard then, I'll put in a transfer request for the Rez school, and you can sign off. And if that doesn't work, I wanna stay where I am. You know, we can work it out," I said, making a lame Beatles joke. He laughed, but it sounded thick and choked.

Jim headed to my home and pulled in to the driveway. It was nice to be dropped off at my house instead of down the road. I could get used to that. "Thank you for the ride," I said, and leaned over, kissing his cheek. This time, he didn't turn, and I was glad.

Inside, Marvin was watching one of his shows. It didn't sound like *Lost in Space* or *Land of the Giants*. "Hey," he said. "Thought you were gone for the night for your big giveaway."

"Our tribe doesn't do that and you know it," I said.

"Yeah, there's no Indian giving there," he said. "Once that's gone, it's gone for good."

"I didn't do what you think."

"Your red knights came to your rescue, then? They figured out where you were, isn't it?" He didn't know Lewis had ratted him out. "Smart little Indian boys." Or maybe he did.

"Smart Indian young men," I said, and I meant it.

"I'll have to take your word, but that wasn't Carson's car dropping you off."

"No, it wasn't." The commercials stated that *Lost in Space* was next. "How many times a day do they show that nonsense? I swear, it's like you've found the *Lost in Space* Channel."

"Three, different episodes each slot. I guess it's cheap. And it's an hour, so it takes up time they can sell commercial slots for." Marvin knew too much about independent TV stations.

"Did they ever make an episode where they found their way home?" I asked. Usually, any question about his shows was enough to get Marvin to engage.

"Nope. Probably one of the other benefits for syndication. Anyone watching, hoping for an ending, is never gonna find it. They'll just keep staring at the glowing box." He seemed disconnected from this world he usually loved so much. "Waiting and waiting."

"You ever wish they got the cast back together to film one? Where they came home?"

"Nah." He looked directly at me, instead of the sideways glance he usually gave. "Even if they made their way back, it'd be a different place. Not home. They'd be just as lost here."

"Maybe I'll watch with you, if you don't mind."

"So you can check out Major Tight Pants?"

"No, just . . . we haven't spent a lot of time together lately." I picked up the phone.

"Starts in ten minutes," Marvin said. "By the way, check out that soapstone head for the *Imagine* piece. Why'd you want to go with the back cover? Looks cool, but I could have done the standing-up front cover." On the table sat an amazing soapstone carving of John Lennon's head, all polished and smooth, lying prone. It would slide onto my velvet and beadwork backdrop. Lying with his face up, staring into a cracked dome of the Sky World, soapstone John Lennon looked like a premonition. Marvin probably hadn't heard yet. On his TV station, it was always 1967, and right after Thanksgiving, the Beatles had just released *Magical Mystery Tour*.

Lewis answered during the first ring, not giving me time to hang up. "I'm home," I said.

"Carson wants you to look out in your driveway," he said. I did, and Carson's Chevelle was there, with the lights off. I hadn't heard it rumble over the obnoxious *Lost in Space* theme music. "He told me he'd wait ten minutes after you got home. If you don't go out, he said he'll leave. Do what you want. What he did, what *we* did, was stupid. But it's because he cared. And it was the most generous thing he's ever done. That is the absolute truth, for what it's worth."

"Thanks," I said. "I've got something for you," I said. "Tomorrow." I hung up and headed outside. A cloud of exhaust vapor swirled around the car, making it seem like one of those bizarre space vehicles on Marvin's shows. Carson leaned over and rolled down the passenger's side window. More John Lennon streamed from inside the car. I imagine most radio stations were sending out that signal tonight.

"It's cold out there," he said. "Can we talk?" I hesitated, trying to decide what kind of signal I wanted to send. "Just talk. That's all. Right here, even. If you want."

"Too cold to go to your rooftop penthouse?" I asked, getting in.

"I took it apart. I couldn't stand up for my brother in public and run away from his problem at home. Ladder's in my trunk if you don't believe me."

"I believe you," I said. "Brothers. They're a funny thing."

"Yours is watching out for you right now," he said, pointing to our living room window. The curtains were closed, as they always were, but a sliver of TV light cut through the heavy fabric. Marvin was watching out, through the gap.

"I don't need him to do that," I said. "I'm good on my own."

"On your own?"

"I'm good making decisions for myself." I wasn't justifying myself to Carson. I liked being in a band with him, the way I was able to find my own voice in it. And from now on, I'd have time to discover the range of that voice. "What you did tonight?" I said, and I could see him perk up. "No. It was wrong." He deflated again instantly, like the *Lost in Space* robot's heart. What had Marvin called it? The diode timer? The timer diode? Some nonsense name, trying to hide the way our hearts were all fragile. Even robot hearts. "You don't get to choose who I like."

"I didn't do it *just* because you liked that guy," he said, looking at me, with the softest vulnerable look I'd ever seen. I didn't think Carson Mastick's face came equipped with that look. "I mean that's guy's a . . . nevermind. I did it because . . . it killed me not to be that guy for you. I'd gotten so used to being able to make anyone notice me, I didn't know what to do when you just didn't."

"It's not always about you," I said. He shook his head, bitter, but for the first time maybe ever he didn't have a sharp cutback.

"Does that mean it can't be?" I didn't know what to say. Could he stop being a jerk? I wasn't interested in fixing him. Jim had tried to make me into some fantasy girl he'd invented. I wasn't going to push Carson into being someone else. But he could maybe become someone more interesting on his own. "I brought you this," he said, sliding over his dad's pamphlet he'd shown me from Yoko Ono's art show: *This Is Not Here.*

Well, It Is Now, and I'm Here with It, I thought, in my own new Ghost Voice, which I guess was going to stick around.

"Nyah-wheh. I'll be careful and get it back to you quick."

"No, it's for you. If my dad asks, I'll just say I haven't seen it. He loses shit all the time. Even things that are important to him." I had a guess at what he meant.

"Well, for sure, Nyah-wheh," I repeated. "Hey, listen. You got a tape deck?" I still had Jim's "Mixed-Up Tape." Earlier, I'd ejected it after one and a half times through—I knew it'd be too painful to keep. Knowing what the next song was going to be, I slid it in. A repetitive drone, like drums and seagulls, began.

"What is this?" he said. It was weird and cool, and sounded edgy, like what they might play in those New York City clubs he always talked about, like Mudd Club or CBGB. The stuff they were calling New Wave.

"'Tomorrow Never Knows,'" I said. "Your friends the Beatles." John Lennon sang, inviting us to turn off our minds, to relax and then float downstream. He wanted us to surrender ourselves to the void. It was the final cut on *Revolver,* the last album before everything changed for them, when they quit playing live onstage together and transformed into something else. It was like a window into their future.

Maybe I *could* keep the cassette. Tomorrow, I'd ask Marie if Bee could make a copy for Lewis and one for Carson. I'd scrape the label off this one. I needed new memories, and Lewis and Carson could develop their own. We could each come up with new titles for ourselves. Maybe we'd call it The Way We Honor John's Memory, or The Night John and Yoko Made Us Come Together, or better yet, The Night Someone Gave Us Some Truth.

PLAYLIST & DISCOGRAPHY

As with my previous young adult novel about this community, *If I Ever Get Out of Here*, each part title is borrowed from album titles, in this case by the Beatles and John Lennon. In the previous novel, each chapter was named, in alternating order, for a Beatles song and a Paul McCartney post-Beatles song. When I knew *Give Me Some Truth* was going to be shaped thematically around John Lennon, I felt it needed, more accurately, to be shaped around John Lennon *and* Yoko Ono, since their lives, personal and artistic, were so enmeshed. So the order here is: Beatles; Yoko Ono; John Lennon; Yoko Ono; repeat.

I also chose to use (almost exclusively) music officially released before December 8, 1980, with a couple of exceptions for songs inextricably tied to the events of that day. Following, I have listed the album most commonly associated with the song's release, in our time. Some were singles that were never released onto an album (the culture at the time), so a few of these albums are later compilations. I have also identified other songs that are referenced in each chapter, with occasional repetitions, as bands do tend to have "crowd-pleasers," songs they know people are expecting, or which they know they play exceptionally well live.

Links to online versions of these songs are available on my website at www.ericgansworth.com/GiveMeSomeMusic.html.

Part One
Unfinished Music No. 1. Two Virgins, John Lennon and Yoko Ono: *Unfinished Music No. 1. Two Virgins* — album title

Chapter 1
"Nowhere Man," The Beatles: *Rubber Soul* (or *Yesterday and Today*, from *The U.S. Albums*)
"Julia," The Beatles: *The Beatles* (commonly called "The White Album")
"Golden Slumbers," "Carry That Weight," "The End," The Beatles: *Abbey Road*

Chapter 2
"Sisters, O Sisters," Yoko Ono and John Lennon: *Some Time in New York City*
"Bohemian Rhapsody," Queen: *A Night at the Opera*

Chapter 3
"You Are Here," John Lennon: *Mind Games*
"Julia," The Beatles: *The Beatles* (commonly called "The White Album")
"Working Class Hero," John Lennon: *John Lennon/Plastic Ono Band*

Chapter 4
"Mind Holes," Yoko Ono: *Fly*

Chapter 5
"Strawberry Fields Forever," The Beatles: *Magical Mystery Tour*
"Fame," David Bowie: *Young Americans*
"Fame," Irene Cara: *Fame Original Soundtrack*
"Jambalaya," Hank Williams: *The Ultimate Collection*
"Cold, Cold Heart," Hank Williams: *The Ultimate Collection*
"Kaw-Liga," Hank Williams: *The Ultimate Collection*
"Your Cheating Heart," Hank Williams: *The Ultimate Collection*

Chapter 6
"Men, Men, Men," Yoko Ono: *Feeling the Space*

Chapter 7
"Cleanup Time," John Lennon and Yoko Ono: *Double Fantasy*

Chapter 8
"Sleepless Night," Yoko Ono: *Onobox Disc 4: Kiss Kiss Kiss*
"One After 909," The Beatles: *Let It Be*

Chapter 9
"In My Life," The Beatles: *Rubber Soul*

Chapter 10
"This Is Not Here," Yoko Ono: *This Is Not Here* (art exhibit title, Everson
  Museum, Syracuse, NY)
"Old Moccasin Dance," "Stick Dance," "Standing Quiver Dance" (listed
  as "Stomp Dance"), Allegheny River Singers: *Social Dances of the
  Iroquois* ("Rabbit Dance" absent from this release)

Part Two
"Mind Games," John Lennon: title song from *Mind Games*

Chapter 11
"Instant Karma (We All Shine On)," John Lennon: *Lennon Legend*

Chapter 12
"Midsummer New York," Yoko Ono: *Fly*
"Stars and Stripes Forever," (you're kidding, right?????)

Chapter 13
"This Bird Has Flown," The Beatles: *Rubber Soul*
"Norwegian Wood (This Bird Has Flown)," The Beatles: *Rubber Soul*
"All Together Now," The Beatles: *Yellow Submarine*
"We Can Work It Out," The Beatles: *Past Masters, Volume 1*
"Day Tripper," The Beatles: *Past Masters, Volume 1*
"Ten Little Indians," (horrifying) anonymous "traditional" American
  children's rhyme, set to the tune of Irish folk song, "Michael Finnegan"
"Jugband Blues," Pink Floyd: *A Saucerful of Secrets*

Chapter 14
"Straight Talk," Yoko Ono: *Feeling the Space*

Chapter 15
"One Day (at a Time)," John Lennon: *Mind Games*
"Jambalaya," Hank Williams: *The Ultimate Collection*

"Cold, Cold Heart," Hank Williams: *The Ultimate Collection*
"Kaw-Liga," Hank Williams: *The Ultimate Collection*
"Lovesick Blues," Hank Williams: *The Ultimate Collection*
"Your Cheating Heart," Hank Williams: *The Ultimate Collection*
"We Can Work It Out," The Beatles: *Past Masters, Volume 1*

Chapter 16
"Paper Shoes," Yoko Ono: *Plastic Ono Band*

Part Three
"Rock 'N' Roll," John Lennon, *Rock 'N' Roll*—album title

Chapter 17
"Hey Bulldog," The Beatles: *Yellow Submarine*
"Sympathy for the Devil," The Rolling Stones: *Beggars Banquet*

Chapter 18
"I Felt Like Smashing My Face in a Clear Glass Window," Yoko Ono:
    Approximately Infinite Universe
Love Songs, 1977 collection by The Beatles
"All You Need Is Love," The Beatles: *Magical Mystery Tour*

Part Four
"Help!" The Beatles: title song from *Help!*

Chapter 19
"Cold Turkey," John Lennon: *Lennon Legend*

Chapter 20
"Nobody Sees Me Like You Do," Yoko Ono: *Season of Glass*

Chapter 21
"All You Need Is Love," The Beatles: *Magical Mystery Tour*
The Beatles (commonly called "The White Album") 1968 release by The
    Beatles
"(Just Like) Starting Over," John Lennon and Yoko Ono: *Double Fantasy*
"Standing Quiver Dance" (listed as "Stomp Dance"), Allegheny River
    Singers: *Social Dances of the Iroquois*

Chapter 22
"What a Mess," Yoko Ono: *Approximately Infinite Universe*

Chapter 23
"(Just Like) Starting Over," John Lennon and Yoko Ono: *Double Fantasy*
"Radar Love," Golden Earring: *Moontan*
"Amazing Grace," John Newton, trad., Tuscarora translation: Marjorie
   Printup
"Come Sail Away," Styx: *The Grand Illusion*
"Silly Love Songs," Paul McCartney and Wings: *Wings at the Speed of Sound*

Chapter 24
"I Have a Woman Inside My Soul," Yoko Ono: *Approximately Infinite
   Universe*
Mind Games, 1973 release by John Lennon
Imagine, 1971 release by John Lennon
Double Fantasy, 1980 release by John Lennon and Yoko Ono
Rubber Soul, 1965 release by The Beatles
Revolver, 1966 release by The Beatles
"Watching the Wheels," John Lennon and Yoko Ono: *Double Fantasy*
"Yes, I'm Your Angel," Yoko Ono and John Lennon: *Double Fantasy*
"Woman," John Lennon and Yoko Ono: *Double Fantasy*
"Working Class Hero," John Lennon: *John Lennon/Plastic Ono Band*

Chapter 25
"You've Got to Hide Your Love Away," The Beatles: *Help!*
"Working Class Hero," John Lennon: *John Lennon/Plastic Ono Band*

Chapter 26
"Now or Never," Yoko Ono: *Approximately Infinite Universe*
"You've Got to Hide Your Love Away," The Beatles: *Help!*

Chapter 27
"Give Me Some Truth," John Lennon: *Imagine*
"Imagine," John Lennon: title song from *Imagine*

Chapter 28
"Don't Count the Waves," Yoko Ono: *Fly*
"Give Me Some Truth," John Lennon: *Imagine*
"(Just Like) Starting Over," John Lennon and Yoko Ono: *Double Fantasy*

Chapter 29
"I'm a Loser," The Beatles: *Beatles for Sale*
"We Will Rock You," Queen: *News of the World*
"Ballroom Blitz," Sweet: *Desolation Boulevard*

Chapter 30
"Air Talk," Yoko Ono: *Approximately Infinite Universe*
Double Fantasy, 1980 release by John Lennon and Yoko Ono

Chapter 31
"Working Class Hero," John Lennon: *John Lennon/Plastic Ono Band*
"Surprise, Surprise (Sweet Bird of Paradox)" John Lennon: *Walls and Bridges*

Chapter 32
"Growing Pain," Yoko Ono: *Feeling the Space*
"Round Dance," Allegheny River Singers: *Social Dances of the Iroquois*

Part Five
"Unfinished Music No. 2. Life with the Lions," John Lennon and Yoko Ono, *Unfinished Music No. 2. Life with the Lions*—album title

Interlude One
"Some Time in New York City," John Lennon and Yoko Ono, title song from *Some Time in New York City*
Double Fantasy, 1980 release by John Lennon and Yoko Ono

Chapter 33
"A Day in the Life," The Beatles: *Sgt. Pepper's Lonely Hearts Club Band*
"Instant Karma," John Lennon: *Lennon Legend*
"Scary Monsters (and Super Creeps)," David Bowie: *Scary Monsters (and Super Creeps)*

Interlude Two
"Imagine," John Lennon, title song from *Imagine*
"Walking on Thin Ice," Yoko Ono: *Season of Glass*

Chapter 34
"Give Me Something," Yoko Ono: *Double Fantasy*

Interlude Three
Revolver, The Beatles, *Revolver*—album title

Chapter 35
"Scared," John Lennon: *Walls and Bridges*

Chapter 36
"Walking on Thin Ice," Yoko Ono: *Season of Glass*
"And Your Bird Can Sing," The Beatles: *Revolver*
"Woman," John Lennon and Yoko Ono: *Double Fantasy*
"Remember," John Lennon, *Plastic Ono Band*
"Imagine," John Lennon: title song from *Imagine*

Chapter 37
"Happiness Is a Warm Gun," The Beatles: *The Beatles*
"Imagine," John Lennon: title song from *Imagine*
"Strawberry Fields Forever," The Beatles: *Magical Mystery Tour*

Chapter 38
"I'm Moving On," Yoko Ono: *Double Fantasy*

Chapter 39
"Give Peace a Chance," Plastic Ono Band: *Lennon Legend*

Chapter 40
"There's No Goodbye," Yoko Ono: *Onobox, Disc 4: Kiss Kiss Kiss*
Imagine, 1971 release by John Lennon
Magical Mystery Tour, 1967 release by The Beatles
"Tomorrow Never Knows," The Beatles: *Revolver*

A WORD ABOUT THE ART

I have been fortunate to have found editors who trust that the kind of specialization that prevails in the broader culture of the United States is not really applicable in indigenous communities. I've been a professional visual artist for exactly as long as I've been a professional writer. The two are inextricably linked. In most indigenous communities, this is largely a matter of course. In addition to the kind of bridge I've navigated my whole life, I've known many ironworker/leatherworkers, roofer/painters, social worker/beadworkers in endless variation. That my professional fields are solely in various arts is perhaps more uncommon.

That said, my talents in any of the Traditional arts are woefully inadequate. I know just enough to understand how much I do not know. One thing I've always found fascinating in that world is the adventurous sense of reinvention present within those artists. Popular culture subjects often wind up reflected in Traditional art media. For example, I've been given two separate Beadwork Batman emblems. When I knew this novel would be about that bridge indigenous artists build daily, I felt like the paintings should reflect that sensibility.

In *If I Ever Get Out of Here*, the characters had a fondness for *Wacky Packages* Trading Cards, satirical reimaginings of real products, so those paintings were done in the style of *Wacky Packages*. That did not seem like the right take for this novel, and as I played with ideas, I remembered that, as a child, my nephew had a corn-husk doll of Superman that his grandmother had made for him. It wasn't solidly in either world, and yet, entirely of both. It was so very clearly both a corn-husk doll and a Superman action figure. I decided to imagine what a Traditional Haudenosaunee artist would do in rendering these iconic album covers, so I limited the re-creations I painted to imagining them in Traditional media. The figures have been recast as if created in beadwork, beadwork and silk and velvet, cornhusk dolls, ribbon work, soapstone and basswood carving, sweetgrass weaving, and images from wampum belts. Haudenosaunee's primary colors are purple and white, the colors of shell beads that make up wampum belts: our culture's defining documents. Even though I knew the images in the book would be reproduced in black and white, any time an original image appeared in black and white, I painted it in purple and white. The images here are details from larger, more expansive paintings. You can view the paintings, in both detail and full, at www.ericgansworth.com, under the Give Me Some Truth visual art gallery.

ACKNOWLEDGMENTS

If you're a teacher using this book in class, first, thank you for your commitment to diverse voices, and second, please do not use this passage for quizzes . . . not even for bonus points (you know who you are). If you're a young person taking such a quiz, I apologize in advance. This book has been five years in coming, and could not have been written without these contributions, so this list is a little long. I'm hoping not to get "played off the stage," but if you must, let it be to "Imagine."

As always, thank you first and foremost to Larry Plant, first reader, endless reader, co-Imaginer in all things. Thank you to E.R. Baxter III for continuing to read drafts after all these years. Thanks to Jeffery Richardson who diligently tracked down key media I was unaware of—like the film *Lennon NYC*—that boosted my memory and clarified key information. Thanks (and admitted tremendous jealousy) to Cliff and Sharon Greathouse, for detailed and repeated shared memories of their experiences at The Toronto Rock 'n' Roll Revival, where they witnessed the first public performance of the Plastic Ono Band.

Thanks to the following friends who were willing to have complex, nuanced, occasionally tough conversations, and some of whom read key passages, so that the book would benefit from insights that *definitely* would have eluded me: Susan Bernardin, Jen Desiderio, Heid E. Erdrich (Turtle Mountain Chippewa), Allison Hauck, Kathleen Steele, Amy Wolf.

Nyah-wheh, eternal, to Debbie Reese (Nambe Pueblo) for her essential work at American Indians in Children's Literature (http://americanindiansinchildrensliterature.blogspot.com/) for her courage, kindness, activism, fierceness, and generosity, and for sparking this flame in my voice that was waiting for the right person to wake it and then know where to point it. And Nyah-wheh to Cynthia Leitich Smith (Muscogee Creek) for her enthusiastic commitment to community.

A bittersweet thank-you to Cheryl Klein, my editor who took this book on the first leg of its journey, for her sound advice and sharp eye and for making me a better editor of my own work. A *relieved* thank-you to Nick Thomas who saw this novel through to the end, intuiting the final missing pieces and knowing how to help me find them and serve them with fava beans and a nice Chianti. Thanks also to the broader supportive community at Scholastic: Arthur A. Levine, Lizette Serrano, Tracy van Straaten, Emily Heddleson, Chris Stengel, and to Ellie Berger, for guiding that ship with warmth.

Thanks to Jim McCarthy for making that leap of faith, taking so much mystery out of the process, for his unfathomably quick responses, and for his overall commitment to diverse voices.

Thank you to Canisius College for its support, specifically the Joseph S. Lowery Estate for Funding Faculty Fellowship in Creative Writing. Thank you also to colleagues and students who always keep me on my toes, and a special shout-out to Deanna Pavone and Victor Mandarino for some immense last minute help. Thank you to Carol Ann Lorenz and Chris Vecsey for facilitating an NEH-sponsored Visiting Professorship at Colgate University during the period I worked on this book.

Nyah-wheh forever, to my family, ever complex, ever fascinating and inspiring, even when they don't know it. Nyah-wheh to the women who taught me how to do beadwork when I was young, quietly showing me what it meant to add one more bead, like a seed, to take the story one layer forward. And as a last time, finally, thank you to the Beatles, the family of my soul, and to John Lennon and Yoko Ono, specifically, for knowing it ain't easy, how hard it can be, but who kept going anyway, imagining a world of possibilities other than the one in front of your face.

ABOUT THE AUTHOR

Eric Gansworth (S·ha-weñ na-sae?) is Lowery Writer-in-Residence and professor of English at Canisius College in Buffalo, NY, and was recently NEH Distinguished Visiting Professor at Colgate University. An enrolled member of the Onondaga Nation, Eric grew up on the Tuscarora Indian Nation, just outside Niagara Falls, NY. His debut novel for young readers, *If I Ever Get Out of Here*, was a YALSA Best Fiction for Young Adults pick and an American Indian Library Association Young Adult Honor selection, and he is the author of numerous acclaimed books for adults. Eric is also a visual artist, generally incorporating paintings as integral elements into his written work. His work has been widely shown and anthologized and has appeared in *Iroquois Art: Power and History*, *The Kenyon Review*, and *Shenandoah*, among other places, and he was recently selected for inclusion in *Lit City*, a Just Buffalo Literary Center public arts project celebrating Buffalo's literary legacy. Please visit his website at www.ericgansworth.com.

ABOUT THE AUTHOR

Eric Gansworth (S·ha-weñ na-sae?) is Lowery Writer-in-Residence and professor of English at Canisius College in Buffalo, NY, and was recently NEH Distinguished Visiting Professor at Colgate University. An enrolled member of the Onondaga Nation, Eric grew up on the Tuscarora Indian Nation, just outside Niagara Falls, NY. His debut novel for young readers, *If I Ever Get Out of Here*, was a YALSA Best Fiction for Young Adults pick and an American Indian Library Association Young Adult Honor selection, and he is the author of numerous acclaimed books for adults. Eric is also a visual artist, generally incorporating paintings as integral elements into his written work. His work has been widely shown and anthologized and has appeared in *Iroquois Art: Power and History*, *The Kenyon Review*, and *Shenandoah*, among other places, and he was recently selected for inclusion in *Lit City*, a Just Buffalo Literary Center public arts project celebrating Buffalo's literary legacy. Please visit his website at www.ericgansworth.com.

This book was edited by
Cheryl Klein and Nick Thomas
and designed by Christopher Stengel.
The production was supervised by Rachel
Gluckstern. The text was set in Sabon MT Std,
with display type set in Oz Handicraft BT.
This book was printed and bound by at LSC
Communications in Crawfordsville,
Indiana. The manufacturing was
supervised by Angelique
Browne.